"WE CANNA DO THIS
NOW, MARY."

ALEX PULLED BACK FROM ME AND STARED INTO MY eyes. "We'll wait until yer neither injured nor tipsy. Nor feeling indebted. What yer feeling is the joy of finding yerself alive when ye weren't sure ye would be."

"No, Alex," I said, pulling him down to kiss him heartily. "What I'm feeling is the joy of touching you. Kiss me again." He kissed me, then gently broke my grip as he sat on the edge of the berth. He took a deep breath as he shook his head.

"Lass, I don't want ye ever to say ye dinna understand what was happening—or that ye were just doing this to thank me for saving ye. It's the shock of them attacking ye, combined with the brandy that's affecting ye. When we . . . when we . . . go further I'd have it be a little more special than in a ship's berth in the winter on the way to Cornwall."

I rose to lean on one elbow. "Yes," I said deliberately, for when I moved I could feel the brandy hit my head again. "But, Alex, what I'm feeling just now is not gratitude. . . ."

KiLGANNON

Kathleen Givens

A Dell Book

Published by
Dell Publishing
a division of
Random House, Inc.
1540 Broadway
New York, New York 10036

This novel is a work of fiction. Names, characters, places, and incidents either are the product of the author's imagination or are used fictitiously. Any resemblance to actual persons, living or dead, events, or locales is entirely coincidental.

Dell® is a registered trademark of Random House, Inc., and the colophon is a trademark of Random House, Inc.

ISBN: 0-440-23567-7

Printed in the United States of America

Published simultaneously in Canada

October 1999

10 9 8 7 6 5 4

OPM

For my husband, Russ,
who taught me how to live and love;

For my daughters, Kerry and Patty,
who taught me the joys of motherhood
and who keep me young;

For my mother, Violet Rose,
who taught me to know and love
our heritage;

And for the memory of my father,
who taught me to plan my work
and work my plan.

Acknowledgments

No NOVEL IS PUBLISHED WITHOUT ASSISTANCE AND this one had considerable. I would like to thank Maureen Walters and Maria Angelico of Curtis Brown, Ltd., for their unfailing enthusiasm, kindness, and encouragement; Maggie Crawford of Dell, who shared a vision and helped shape it; Russ, for being the kind of man a woman wants to write about and for his insight into the male mind; Kerry and Patty, for reading every word, for laughing and crying in the right places, and for never complaining when their mother was in the eighteenth century; my mother, Violet, for all the family stories and for her unwavering belief; Peggy Gregerson, for gently reading every draft and keeping me writing; my brother Rich and the whole family for their optimism; my sister, Nicole, for her speed-editing; Georgene Fairbanks, Mary Lewis, and Rick Capaldi, the Lunch Bunch, and the Go Ask Alice Writing Group for their encouragement and support; the staff of the Westminster Abbey Library for their patience; and the countless historians, librarians, and museum staff members who guided me back to Mary and Alex's world. Any inaccuracies are mine alone.

PART ONE

O my Luve's like a red, red rose,
  That's newly sprung in June;
O my Luve's like the melodie
  That's sweetly played in tune.

As fair art thou, my bonnie lass,
  So deep in luve am I;
And I will luve thee still, my dear,
  Till a' the seas gang dry.

Till a' the seas gang dry, my dear,
  And the rocks melt wi' the sun:
O I will love thee still, my dear,
  While the sands o' life shall run.

And fare thee weel, my only luve,
  And fare thee weel awhile!
And I will come again, my luve,
  Though it were ten thousand mile.

A RED, RED ROSE: ROBERT BURNS

ONE

June, 1712

I YAWNED FOR THE FOURTH TIME, DRAWING A GLARE FROM the seamstress. "Miss Lowell," she said with asperity. "You must stand straight and please pay attention. Your aunt wishes this dress to be ready for the Duchess's party tomorrow night, and I cannot finish it if you fall asleep." She rose from the hem she had been working on and watched me with narrowed eyes and stiff posture, her hands clasped before her.

"I am sorry, Miss Benton," I answered, "truly I am, but you have made me closets full of beautiful dresses and I cannot help but think that one more will make no difference." Her expression did not vary, and I sighed. "I will stand straight, I promise, and we shall finish this afternoon."

Mollified somewhat, she nodded. "This particular shade of deep blue looks marvelous on you, Miss Lowell. It compliments your eyes very well, and the rose we'll work on next brings out the blush in your cheeks."

"You said this was the last one, Miss Benton." I tried to keep the note of despair out of my tone as I looked out the window at a beautiful summer day. The only fair day we'd had in weeks and I was in my sitting room trying on yet another dress.

"You do have many dresses, Miss Lowell," Miss Benton

agreed, concentrating on her work once again, "but your fashionable gowns are all black and you are no longer in mourning for your mother. Your aunt has asked me to help get you ready for these last parties. The Season is almost over."

I nodded. *And high time,* I thought. When I'd first come to London I'd loved the Season, enjoying the parties and the flirtations and the endless rounds of socializing. I'd grown proficient at discussing affairs of both the state and the heart. But when my mother grew ill and I retired with her to our home in Warkwickshire, I'd had a great deal of time to reflect on the shallow nature of London society. I'd found I didn't miss it greatly. Since her death I'd been traveling with Aunt Louisa in Europe, avoiding France, of course, with which England was currently at war. We had returned for Christmas, in time for the liveliest part of the Season.

It was early June now and most of London would be leaving town soon, heading for country estates and the summer visits of friends and family. I turned as Miss Benton gestured, and sighed again. My aunt was paying for these dresses in the hope of a brilliant marriage for me, and since I had no means of my own beyond the small share of the rents on the lands my brother now owned, I could not dictate to the woman Louisa had hired. But it was so boring. Still, I reflected, the days when I was mistress of my time were over. My mother's illness and death had postponed the inevitable. I was to be married. Oh, the groom had not yet been selected and my personal wishes had not been considered, but Robert Campbell was the current front-runner. The freedoms I'd had in my upbringing were long gone now. Even at home at Mountgarden I could no longer do those things I had taken for granted. I smiled to think of the reaction if I were to take my shoes off and help with the haying as I had done as a girl. How I missed my parents. My father, unlike so many men, had considered education important for a girl. "Educate a woman and you educate a family" was a favorite saying of his, and he'd lived it as well, but I'd not had any

KiLÇANNON 5

need lately of my Latin and French nor of my ability to do sums. My brother had recently married Betty Southall and handled the accounts at Mountgarden himself now, badly, but the estate was his and so was the responsibility. I visited less frequently, although when I did I still straightened the accounts out with Will's blessing, taking great joy in their order.

Miss Benton asked me to stand straight again and I did, wondering if I dared send a runner to the library for a book. Perhaps if I could read while she worked I might survive the afternoon. I lifted my head as she requested and stared at my reflection. And frowned. Properly dressed I might pass for fashionable, but I would never be the beauty my Aunt Louisa and my sister-in-law Betty were, both small and dainty women, Louisa with dark curls and Betty with the fair hair of the true Saxon. I was neither small nor dainty, nor beautiful, despite Louisa's kind comments. I knew I needed this dress finished, for without the requisite wardrobe I might never land a husband. But I detested the process. "Do you know what I've done today, Miss Benton?"

"No, Miss Lowell," she murmured, her mouth full of pins.

"I dressed for breakfast, then changed my clothes to accompany Aunt Louisa to the Duchess's to discuss the party. Then I returned home and changed my clothes for luncheon with my brother, Will, and his wife, Betty. Now I am changing my clothes so that you may finish these dresses. And then I will change my clothes to go to the Mayfair Bartletts for dinner."

"A lovely day, Miss Lowell."

"You do not think I should accomplish something more than changing my clothes?" The seamstress did not answer, and I turned as she'd gestured. A woman who made her living dressing people would not be sympathetic to someone who did not want to change her clothes all day long, I told myself, and looked out the window again, resolving to be compliant and let her complete her task. My mind wandered while I tried to keep my back straight. Robert would be home soon and that would start the gossips buzzing again. All of London society assumed that an announcement of our engagement was imminent. *Perhaps he'll be delayed,* I thought, wincing at my disloyalty. It wasn't that I did not want to see him again, for I was genuinely fond of Robert Campbell, but I was in no hurry to marry him, or anyone for that matter, and he seemed to be of the same opinion. In the last two years Robert and I had grown accustomed to each other's company and London had grown accustomed to seeing us together. Louisa, my mother's sister, had been pleased, sure that a marriage with the Campbell family would be a good alliance for me. She thought I was at a marriageable age, that Robert was a prime catch, and that I was not trying hard enough to catch him, but despite our constant companionship there had been no commitment or declaration of love on either side. Robert was in France with his cousin John, the Duke of Argyll. While I wasn't sure what it was he'd been doing, I knew it concerned the war, though he'd not been in the field lately. When I'd asked Robert what his duties were, I'd been told not to bother about it, as though my understanding what he did would confuse or distress me. Louisa's husband, my uncle Randolph, in France with so many of the other men, had given no direction on the matter and I was content to float along in this limbo, knowing that when the war was over we would have to come to a decision. Until then, Louisa and her friend the Duchess would continue to try to find me a suitable husband and I would resist. I knew Robert was a good man, but I wanted . . . well, more. I looked out the window and tried not to mope.

I was rewarded for my good behavior by the announcement of Rebecca Washburton's arrival and her appearance in the doorway a few moments later. Becca, my dearest friend, and I had known each other since we were babies. Our mothers had been friends as girls, my aunt Louisa with them, and I could not remember a time when Becca and I had not been as sisters. We even looked alike, with dark hair and blue eyes, and although I was much taller we were often confused by strangers. But that would be changing soon. In November she would be marrying Lawrence Pearson, a cousin of the Mayfair Bartletts, and moving with him to his home in the Carolinas. I would miss her terribly.

"Miss Benton." Rebecca nodded to the seamstress. "And Mary, dear." Miss Benton stood stiffly to one side as we embraced. Becca stood back with a smile. "Please continue, Miss Benton. I'll sit out of the way and talk while you finish." Miss Benton returned to her work while I met Becca's merry eyes over the seamstress's bent head. "That dress suits you, Mary," Becca said. "You're tall enough to wear hoops and not have them look silly."

Miss Benton answered. "I'm glad you like it, Miss Washburton."

I must be invisible, I thought, and Rebecca smiled. She knew how I detested these fittings and teased me by telling of her long ride with Lawrence. I made a face at her.

"My dear Mary," she said breezily as she settled herself into a chair by the window, "you must be properly dressed so that the Duchess can find you a husband." With a glance at Miss Benton she continued in the same tone. "Lord Campbell should be home any day." I glared at my friend, knowing that she knew I could not respond freely in front of Miss Benton, for everything I said would be repeated to all who would listen, and in London many were willing to listen. And she knew that Robert was not my favorite topic. "It's a shame," Becca continued, smiling wildly now, "that Lord Campbell won't be home for the Duchess's party, but he may be here for your aunt's evening next week or Lady Wilmington's the following week."

"Yes." I glared at her over Miss Benton's head.

Becca refused to be intimidated. "Actually," she said, glancing out the window, "I've come with my mother to give our apologies to Louisa. We are going with Lawrence's family to Bath on Tuesday, and we'll miss her party."

"Becca!" I cried. "Can you not postpone your trip? Just a

day or so? How will I get through the evening without you?"

Miss Benton raised her head before Becca could answer. "Your mother is here with Countess Randolph, Miss Washburton?" She rose, firmly pushing pins into the cushion she wore on her wrist.

"They are in the parlor, Miss Benton," Rebecca said. "Do you wish to speak with her?"

Miss Benton nodded. "I must discuss the fittings for your wedding gown with her, and if you will be away next week we need to schedule them for some other time." She gave me a cursory glance, already moving toward the door. "If you'll excuse me, Miss Lowell, I will return in just a few moments." I nodded, with what Rebecca called my "regal" look, but Miss Benton was already gone and I turned to my friend.

"How horrid you are!" I said, lifting the dress high so that I could stalk over to her. "Why did you mention Robert? Did you see her reaction? She stopped working to hear what we would say. She'll repeat every word!"

Rebecca laughed. "Mary, you act as though she isn't always listening to everything. Give them something to talk about."

"Why not you instead of me?" I flounced into a chair.

"I'm old news," she said, arching her eyebrows, "already engaged and the wedding day set. The only thing of interest about me before my marriage would be if Lawrence was found in some dreadful woman's company or if I suddenly started gaining weight."

"Easy for you to say," I answered. "The vigilance has been relaxed. I'm still watched every minute. Really, Becca, I do envy you. Once you are married you will enjoy much more freedom than we do now." It was true. My every moment was observed for signs of appropriateness and propriety. If Robert and I were together we must be under the watchful gaze of a relative or my maid, and the door of the room we were in must be left ajar. I often wondered just what exactly my maid could prevent if Robert chose to misbehave. But, I reflected, Robert would never misbehave.

"Poor Mary," Rebecca teased. "Life is so very difficult."

"You don't have to dine with the Mayfair Bartletts tonight."

"We did last night and survived."

"Let me guess. You discussed politics."

Rebecca nodded. "Queen Anne, King Louis, and the war with France, King Philip and whether Spain will side with us or France next time. Lawrence was spellbound."

I shook my head. "I get so bored with it. Endless discussions of the same things. And don't forget the gossip. Lord Someone spoke to Lady Someone at a party and Miss Someone accepted a sip of punch from Mister Someone. Hours' worth of discussion."

Becca laughed. "You'll survive, and tomorrow is the Duchess's party."

"For which we will prepare all day. And then we'll spend the next week preparing for Louisa's party." I grimaced. "At least Will and Betty are still in London."

"How much longer will they stay?"

"Two weeks, then they're off to Mountgarden. Perhaps I'll go with them," I said, feeling a sudden longing for my childhood home. "But it's not the same with my parents gone. I don't know what I'll do."

"You'll go with them. You know Will enjoys your company."

I nodded. "And I his. But, Becca, it's their home now. I have no home of my own. I live with Louisa or Will and Betty. There is nowhere that is mine, truly mine."

Rebecca patted my hand. "I know," she said, suddenly serious.

I shrugged and smiled at my friend. "What will I do without you to listen to my complaining? What a spoiled child I am, thinking of such things when Will has offered me a home for forever, and Louisa as well. I should be more grateful." But just now I didn't feel grateful. Outside, a cloud passed before the sun. Tomorrow, no doubt, it would rain. And I would change my clothes four times before dinner.

I did survive dinner with the Bartletts, although I amused myself only by counting the number of scandalous stories waspish Edmund Bartlett told. Twelve, I decided at the end of the evening, unless I'd forgotten one. I smiled genuinely as I climbed into the coach with my aunt and Will and Betty. The evening was over.

The Duchess's party the next night was a great success, crowded and happy, and I enjoyed myself much more than I had thought I would. My aunt's dear friends, John and Eloise Barrington, the Duke and Duchess of Fenster, had warmly welcomed me, lavishing compliments on the new blue dress, and I had laughed and bantered with them. Lawrence was very accommodating, and Becca and I had time to talk with our friends Janice and Meg. Even my sister-in-law, Betty, was in great spirits after having been complimented by several men, which meant that Will had a good time as well. The party was over before I'd expected. If I had found the handsome man Becca said had watched me for hours my evening would have been complete, but despite our roaming through all the rooms he was nowhere to be found, and I teased Rebecca about inventing a mystery man for me. The only cloud in the evening was the chilly manner of the few Whigs invited. The Barringtons were influential Tories—the party that currently dominated the Parliament and vied for Queen Anne's attention—and were considered quite tolerant to invite the opposition to their home, although many Tories were doing that lately. Both political parties were in their infancy, but the Tories generally favored the Anglican church and were considered insular by the Whigs, who favored the dissenters and military involvement in Europe. While the Whigs were polite to me and my aunt, we were both aware that we were mere women and therefore of little consequence. For the most part they ignored us, which suited me. Their behavior and its political ramifications would be discussed endlessly, I knew, in the week before the next event, and I would hear hours of it. There was no need to dwell on it tonight.

The next week flew by, a kaleidoscope of preparations for Louisa's party. I trailed behind her in awe as always of her effortless abilities. She managed household and servants with the ease of a born commander, and I watched and learned. Serene at all times, Louisa dispensed orders to her staff and instructions to me in one breath, and we hurried to do her bidding. By early afternoon the day of the party, all was in place. Louisa was resting and I was in my bedroom with my maid, debating which new dress to wear. Louisa had strongly suggested the rose gown, and in the end that was what I wore, with my mother's simple jewelry and a white rose from Louisa's garden tucked in my sash. Becca had left for Bath with Lawrence, the Pearsons, and her parents. Janice and Meg were both already gone from London, and Robert had not returned from France. I expected a lonely evening.

I noticed him the moment he stepped into view in the doorway of Louisa's ballroom. He was waiting to be announced, but I knew who he was immediately. I did not know his name, but surely this was the man Becca had talked about. He certainly fit the description she'd given and was as memorable as she'd hinted. He wore traditional Scottish Highland clothing while everyone else was dressed in the latest London style. Taller than most of the men in the room, he was simply groomed with no wig, his blond hair pulled into a queue at the nape of his neck. He wore a very white shirt under a muted green jacket that topped a plaided kilt. Over his shoulder was the rest of the plaid, fastened with a simple gold brooch. He was lean and graceful, his shoulders wide, his legs long, the muscles visible under dark socks below the kilt. The other men in the room suddenly seemed overdressed.

My interest heightened as the Earl of Kilgannon was announced and walked down the stairs. I watched as my aunt approached him with a welcoming smile, and I admired her easy grace. Louisa, the Countess Randolph, married to the Earl Randolph, was accustomed to greeting nobility, for she moved in titled circles. The Duchess, at her side as usual, also greeted the newcomer warmly. Behind me I could hear the murmuring of two men who were not pleased that a "damned Scot" was among us. I recognized the voices and turned to find my suspicions confirmed: the men were the Whigs who had ignored me at the Duchess's party. I turned back to watch the Scotsman.

"Not only a Scot, but a Highlander," growled one of the Whigs. "He'll likely stab someone before the night is out. They have the manners of pigs. Barbarians. What is the matter with the Countess Randolph that she has him here? Damned inconsiderate."

His friend laughed. "I believe he's some sort of relative. She was married to a Scot, remember. She says he makes her laugh."

"So does my dog, but I don't invite him to dinner."

They continued, but I was only half-listening now, my attention focused on the blond man as he bowed over my aunt's hand and said something that had her laughing and playfully smacking his arm with her fan. Why had Louisa not mentioned him before? He was certainly more interesting than any man I'd seen in London. Well, at least more handsome. I lost sight of them as people moved between us, then I saw the Scot standing alone, scanning the room as though looking for someone. Our eyes met and he smiled. Without thinking, I smiled in return. He began to walk toward me, but Lady Wilmington stopped him, tilting her head and laying one fleshy hand on his arm. He looked at her hand, then at me, and then smiled at her. Will said something to me then and I gave him my attention. When he and Betty left me a few moments later to dance, I turned to look again for the stranger. And found him standing in front of me.

My eye level was at his collarbone, and I looked at his silver buttons and lace collar before I met his gaze, aware of the curious stares directed our way. I tried in vain to control the flush that stole into my cheeks and wondered if I was now the same color as my gown. His hair was a golden blond, thick and shining. Prominent cheekbones and jawline and a straight nose complemented a well-defined mouth. His eyes, surrounded by dark lashes, were a midsummer's sky blue, his expression pleasant as he spoke.

"Miss Lowell? I am Alexander MacGannon of Kilgannon. Yer aunt suggested I make yer acquaintance." His accent was noticeable, his tone light. He did not sound like a madman. I offered my hand and he bowed over it. As he straightened, a lock of his hair slipped out of the band that held it and framed his face, and I had the ridiculous urge to brush it away from his cheek. I pulled back from him more strongly than I had intended. He brushed his hair back while he looked at me intently, but something had flickered in his eyes and I knew he had seen me flinch.

"It is customary, Kilgannon, to have a third person introduce you," laughed the Duchess, suddenly at his side. The small plump woman looked up at him affectionately.

"It is also less direct than I wish to be, Your Grace," he answered, bowing to her. "But I bow to yer wishes in all things."

"In all things, sir, or just those you wish to?"

I was astonished. The Duchess was flirting with a Scotsman? I studied him as they bantered, pretending as I waited for them to finish that I was not noticing every detail about him. At last the Duchess turned to me. "My dear Mary, may I present Alexander MacGannon, the tenth Earl of Kilgannon. Kilgannon, Miss Mary Lowell. Two years ago in France, Mary, the Duke made the Earl's acquaintance. My husband reports that the Earl was charming and

deadly." She placed a small jeweled hand on his arm and
smiled up into his face. "Such an interesting combination."

The Earl laughed. "Aye, madam, we Scots are always
charming and deadly. When we're not acting like savages."

"Oh, Kilgannon," she twittered, "take Miss Lowell for a
walk." She smiled at me. "He's currently unmarried, dear."
I felt my cheeks flame again as she waddled away, but before
either of us could speak, one of the Whigs was at my elbow,
staring aggressively at Lord Kilgannon. The man spoke
abruptly.

"Kirkgannon, is it? What do you think of the Union?"

"Kilgannon, sir." Kilgannon bowed stiffly and spoke
coldly. "I think it's the law now. Has been for several years,
I believe."

"So you Scots will obey the law this time?"

"As always, sir. If ye will excuse us now, Miss Lowell has
expressed her wishes for a bit of fresh air." I made no protest
as Kilgannon took my hand and pulled it through his arm.
He led me silently to the opposite side of the ballroom and
out onto the porch, ignoring all the eyes watching us. Outside, he released my hand with a sigh and leaned against the
stone railing. The night was gentle, the moon a crescent in
the black sky. A slight breeze ruffled our hair and brought
the scent of roses as I watched him by the light of the lamps
beside the door. He glanced over his shoulder at the dark-
ness before turning to look at me.

"I'm sorry, lass. I dinna mean to drag ye off. I was afraid
I'd say something unforgivable and yer aunt would ban me
from her house. And . . ." He turned and looked out over
the gardens, his cheeks coloring slightly. "I'm sorry if I was
too direct. I just thought it was the simplest way to meet
ye." I looked at his profile and tried to think of an answer.
When I did not respond, he shot me a sharp glance. "Are ye
angry? Shall I leave?"

I looked at him for a long moment before answering,
then smiled. Anger was not what I was feeling. "Am I angry
that you wanted to meet me, sir?" I asked. "Or am I an-

gry that you refused to be drawn into an argument with a boor? Or am I angry that you flirted outrageously with my aunt and the Duchess? Or am I angry that a Scotsman would attend a party like this when we all know you're likely to burn London down at any moment?"

He turned to me, surprised at first, and then, reading my expression, he started chuckling. "Yer a one. All right, which is it?" His smile played around the corners of his mouth.

"I'm deciding. Hmmm. I'm not angry you wanted to meet me."

"And?"

"And I'm not angry that you wouldn't argue politics. And I'm not angry that you would attend this party, assuming, of course, that you were invited."

"I was. And?"

"And I am outraged that you flirted with my aunt Louisa and the Duchess."

He laughed out loud and turned back to the garden. "Yer aunt said ye were bright as well as beautiful."

"My aunt always says I'm bright and beautiful, sir," I said. "In truth, I am neither."

"I disagree, Miss Lowell. She dinna say the half of it." He stole a look at me again, his expression softening. "Thank ye for being kind to a stranger."

"My lord, it was easy to be kind to you."

"Not my lord, lass. Just Alex."

"Not the Earl of . . ." I couldn't remember.

"Kilgannon. No. Alex. Alex MacGannon. Will ye remember it?"

"Alex," I said, meeting his eyes.

"Here you are! We wondered where you'd wandered to." We turned to see the Duchess standing in the doorway with Will and Betty. She introduced everyone and turned to smile at me. "The Earl saw you at my party last week, Mary," she said, "and asked to meet you, but he left before I could arrange it, so I am delighted that he has joined us tonight."

I watched Kilgannon watch me and Will assess him. "I see," I said. "The Earl was most direct."

The Duchess laughed. "And successful, it would appear."

Will raised his eyebrows and I said something about the weather, forestalling his protective reaction. We talked for a few moments, Will and Kilgannon polite, Betty pouting in the background. The Duchess interrupted when the topic shifted to politics. "No, no, not tonight, gentlemen," she said with a wave of her hand. "Come inside, the dancing is about to begin again." She led the way and we followed.

In the ballroom Betty was at Kilgannon's side at once. "Do you dance, sir?" she asked in her affected high little voice.

He nodded. "Aye, mistress, but not the minuet."

"Oh," she said, and a moment later was swept off onto the dance floor by Will. I stood with Kilgannon and watched the dancers, very aware of him at my side, trying to think of something to say that wouldn't sound idiotic. Jonathan Wumple stopped before us, bowing, and I groaned silently. Jonathan, whom I had known forever, always asked me to dance. Tonight, however, he asked Kilgannon if I could dance. The Scot glanced at me.

"It's the lady's decision, sir. Just dinna flirt with her. She despises flirting," he said with an impassive expression and then laughed at the face I made at him behind Jonathan's back.

I danced with Jonathan, but I watched Kilgannon where he stood alone at the side of the room. In a very short time he was surrounded by women, and he laughed and leaned over to hear them speak but resisted all attempts to dance. Nor did he move from the spot, even when joined by a beautiful redhead in a daring dress. Lady Rowena de Burghesse, the wife of the Marquess of Badwell, looked into his eyes with a knowing look, and I felt my face flush. How I detested Rowena. I had always disliked her but never more than at this moment. I wondered what she said to him as

Kilgannon's expression grew remote and his eyes flickered toward me.

When the dance ended we were at the opposite side of the room, and I chatted with Jonathan and his sister Priscilla for a moment before Priscilla whispered behind her fan. "Kilgannon's very handsome. Where did your aunt meet him?"

"At the Duchess's party, I believe," I said, turning as I spoke to look for him. But he was gone. The wave of disappointment I felt surprised me, and I searched the room as she whispered again.

"It's said he has a wonderful castle on the side of a lake. And two little boys. His wife died when the second was a baby. Perhaps he's looking for a new wife."

"If so he'll no doubt find one," I said, glancing around again. "The women are very fond of him already."

"I wouldn't say no," she said, her eyes dreamy. "But you, of course, have decided on Lord Robert Campbell."

I shook my head. "There is no agreement between us."

She smiled archly. "I have heard differently."

"Miss Wumple," I said briskly. "I would be aware of an engagement that concerned me. There is not one." Priscilla smiled a meaningful smile, her lead paint cracking at the edges of her mouth. *I have to get out of here,* I thought, hastily giving my excuses. As I left the ballroom I stopped to greet many that I knew in the brilliantly dressed crowd but saw no Scotsman.

In the hall I took a deep breath and turned to see Louisa returning from the dining room. My aunt smiled as she approached.

"You might have said something, Louisa," I said. My tone reminded me uncomfortably of Jonathan's sister.

"About?"

"The Earl of Kilgannon."

Her eyebrows raised. "I believe I did. But goodness, child, you look as though you've seen a vision."

"I have."

My aunt's eyes narrowed. "He is a man, Mary, not a vision. Do guard your expression more next time, my dear." She smiled to soften her words. "And apparently it's quite mutual. He seems quite smitten. He has asked everyone in London about you."

"What did you tell him?"

"That you are as brilliant as you are beautiful, that you deserve a husband who will treasure you, that Scotland is too far away and too dangerous for my niece, and that you are accustomed to the company of Lord Campbell." She looked at me with bright eyes. "I thought Alex's appearance here tonight and his interest in you might bring Robert to heel. It's more than time that he proposed. How unfortunate that he has not yet returned from France."

"I see," I said tartly. "How charming to have been discussed by the two of you so thoroughly. I feel like a prize mare."

She laughed. "Goodness, Mary, give the man a chance to talk to you, if only because he is my cousin. Well, by marriage at least. I think you will like him, and it will be good for Robert to discover he is not the only man in the world to have noticed you."

"All this on one night's conversation?"

"My dear, I have known Alex since he was a child. His mother was a Keith and your uncle Duncan was a Keith, remember? Or have you forgotten that I was married to a Scot for twelve years? I met Alex many times when he was young."

"You might have told me about him." I sounded all of ten.

She patted my arm. "I was surprised at the man he's become. He will turn many heads in London. Yours was not the first and certainly won't be the last. Enjoy his company for the moment. Robert will be home soon. It's only dinner, Mary. I ask that you be polite for one evening. You'll probably never see him again." She glided into the ballroom, leaving me alone.

TWO

WHILE I WAITED FOR DINNER TO BE ANNOUNCED I searched the ballroom for Kilgannon. I chatted with my aunt's friends and our acquaintances and at last with the Duchess, who glowed with smug satisfaction as she guided me away from the others and to the outside doors. "Why don't you wander out to the porch, dear?" she asked, flicking her fan over her smile. "The air will do you good."

I smiled in return and walked outside. There he was, leaning against the railing and staring into the gardens, the soft light illuminating the long lines of his frame. He glanced over his shoulder and nodded at me when I halted in the doorway.

"Will ye join me, Miss Lowell? 'Tis a glorious night."

"It is, Lord Kilgannon."

He shook his head. "Not Lord Kilgannon, lass. Just Alex." He turned to me and watched my reaction, his expression unreadable.

"Mary," I said in the same tone, coming to stand next to him.

He smiled slowly and nodded. "Then Mary and Alex it is."

Mary and Alex, I thought, Alex and Mary. "We are breaking all the rules, sir," I said. "We should be using titles."

He nodded. "Aye, we'll have to behave in front of them."

"But not with each other?"

He watched me for a moment, then smiled. "Not with each other."

I hoped the light was too dim for him to notice my blush and blurted out the first thing that came to mind. "You do not like to dance, sir?" I flinched at the similarity to Betty's words.

He nodded again. "I do. But I dinna know the minuet nor do I have the desire to learn such a mincing little dance. It looks like everaone is tiptoeing." I laughed and leaned against the railing, the stone cool under my hand. I could think of nothing else to say. His finger traced the stonework pattern, but he was watching me. "Mary, are ye engaged to Robert Campbell?"

I looked at him, startled. "You are very direct, sir."

He nodded. "Aye, it saves much time. Are ye?"

"No."

"Ah." He stared into the gardens and I watched his profile.

"Why do you ask me that?"

He turned to me without expression. "The women said ye were."

"And if I were?"

"I would take my attentions elsewhere."

"I see." It was my turn to glance into the gardens.

He frowned to himself. "That's not true."

"What's not true?"

"I wouldna turn my attentions elsewhere. I'd have to have ye change yer mind." He was grinning now.

"I see." I stared at him for a moment, then returned his smile. "Have I any say in this?"

"Aye." He was suddenly serious. "It will be as ye wish."

I shook my head. "I don't know what you mean," I whispered.

"It will be as ye wish, Mary Lowell. If ye wish me to leave ye alone, I will. If ye wish my company, I'm here."

"You're not going back to Scotland?"

"Oh, aye, I must go back to Kilgannon. I have two sons and other responsibilities. But I will return if ye wish it."

"How can you do that?"

"Ride verra quickly." He was grinning again and I laughed. "We wouldna be bored in each other's company, I can tell, Mary."

We stood in awkward silence for a moment and then, mercifully, dinner was announced. Exchanging a look as we moved back into the ballroom, we stood watching couples move together into the hall. Couples. The thought of him sitting next to someone else during the meal was intolerable. I stole a glance at him.

"Alex." I sounded like a child, and when he looked at me I could not finish. I stood there gazing up at him like an idiot.

He smiled. "Aye, Mary?"

"Will you escort me into the dining room?"

He gave me his arm. "I will indeed, thank ye, lass. It's verra nice of ye to be so welcoming to a stranger." I put my arm through his, feeling the strength of him under the soft velvet, and smiled.

Louisa's elegant dining room was lavishly appointed, and so that no one forgot she was a married woman, the chair at the head of the table was these days left empty when she entertained, as though my uncle Randolph would return from France for the evening. Alex and I were seated together, mid-table, Rowena on his right. I wondered how she had managed that or if it were a ploy of Louisa's. Rowena acted as though she'd never met me. Of course, I told myself, it was quite possible she had not noticed me the other times. I'd not been in a man's company.

"You are Countess Randolph's niece," Rowena said to me, leaning onto Alex's shoulder as she spoke across him. I said I was, but it wasn't enough. She asked about my parents in great detail, determining exactly where I fit in the London hierarchy. I was tempted to say something sharp about her questioning but swallowed it and looked across Alex's profile to her again. "And your family? Have you any in London besides your aunt?" she persisted.

"My brother, Will, and his wife, Betty, are here tonight. They, with Aunt Louisa, are the only family I have in London."

"You are also the niece of Sir Harry Lowell, the Duke of Grafton?"

I nodded. Rowena glanced at her husband, seated down the table, and I followed her gaze. The Marquess looked to be nearly seventy. No wonder she looked at Alex as if he were a tempting dish. *And my uncle the duke outranks your husband the marquess,* I said to myself, but found little comfort in it. My uncle Harry, the Duke of Grafton, was an unsociable man, very different from my father. As far as I knew, Harry had not been to London in years. He said the crowds bothered him too greatly and so he stayed on his lands. He had never married nor to my knowledge produced an heir. I had seen him twice since my mother's death.

"Is he in London as well?" Rowena asked.

"No. My uncle lives on his estate at Grafton."

"How interesting," she said, dismissing me as she turned to Alex with a smile and dimples, her head tilted. Alex chuckled.

"And where, Miss Lowell," he said, imitating Rowena perfectly, "does yer uncle keep his money? At Grafton or in London?" Both Rowena and I looked at him in surprise. "And Miss Lowell, what will ye have for breakfast?" He leaned toward me, his eyes merry. "It's verra important that we know." He winked at me, and I laughed.

Rowena narrowed her eyes but forced a smile as he turned to her. "Tell me of the war in France, sir," she said, watching his lips. "Was it terrible? I have been told you were wounded."

Alex's expression was bland now. "It wasna terrible, madam. I wasna there long enough to suffer."

"Is that why you returned before the war is over?"

"I wasna with the army. I returned home when my wife died."

"Oh! How dreadful for you."

"Aye," he said, and gestured for more wine. He watched the footman pour it as if it were very important.

"You poor man! What happened to her?"

"She sickened and died of a fever." Alex gave Rowena a polite smile. "Do you and the Marques have many children?"

"None, to my regret."

"Well, good luck to ye," he said, and leaned toward me. Rowena's eyes flashed, but her anger was quickly suppressed and I tried not to laugh. "Have ye been to Scotland, Miss Lowell?"

"To Lothian when I was very little, sir, to visit Louisa's first husband's lands, but I don't remember much of it."

"Then ye've never really seen Scotland." His eyes were dancing. "The Highlands are as like Lothian as the sun is to the moon. Ye must come for a visit. Ye might enjoy yerself hugely."

I was laughing again. "I might at that."

"Ye would. I'll speak to yer aunt about arranging it soon."

"I've never been to Scotland either, sir," said Rowena. "Where do you recommend visiting?"

I was addressed then by the man on my left and reluctantly answered him. I could not hear Alex's answer nor what he and Rowena continued discussing. For the next course I glanced at them when she laughed, which was often, and seethed when she put her hand on his arm while gazing into his eyes. I wanted to say something devastating to her but could think of nothing that would be appropriate at Louisa's table. I consoled myself with shooting her looks of disdain, which she never noticed. By the third course I felt much better, for Alex and I were engaged in an interesting discussion with people across the table about the future of the colonies, while Rowena talked with the very young man on her right.

I watched Alex listening intently and nodding or arguing a point with our companions. His conduct was impeccable and his manner winning. He soon had them laughing and agreeing to some silly suggestion of his, and I sat quietly, entranced with his performance. He was at ease in the company, not at all the uncouth Scotsman he was supposed to be. Of course, I reminded myself, he was an earl, the tenth of his line, and no doubt had had some polish applied along the way that the ordinary Scot might not have. He answered my questions in a straightforward manner but with little elaboration, and I tried not to imitate Rowena. The man across the table asked if it were true that Alex traded with the Continent. Glances were exchanged as he said it was, and I watched it noted that the Earl of Kilgannon was in trade. There were few worse social sins than to be industrious.

With the end of dinner my aunt's guests moved back to the ballroom, some men withdrawing to smoke. Alex, glancing at me, politely declined their invitation to join them. As she escorted her guests out of the dining room, Louisa paused behind my chair. "Why not go into the ballroom?" she asked, putting a hand on my shoulder. "The music is about to begin again."

I nodded to Louisa, but when she was gone I did not move, reluctant to lose Alex in a roomful of people. Rowena rose, however, and Alex stood and made the necessary polite remarks, bowing over her hand. She flounced away in a swish of silk, looking for more cooperative game elsewhere, leaving us alone in the dining room with the footmen. Alex sat down next to me again with a grin, leaning his chin on his hand. "What were we saying, Mary?" he asked, and I laughed. I had no idea.

We talked while everyone else went to the ballroom and

while the staff began clearing, and when they needed us to move we sat at a part of the table already cleared, still talking. Louisa floated in and out of view in the hallway but never approached us. No one approached us, and dimly I became aware that the servants were yawning and putting out tapers. When Louisa and Will and Betty appeared at the dining-room door, I realized that everyone else had gone and the evening was over. Alex looked up at Louisa with a start and stood abruptly, reaching for my hand as I rose next to him. His hand felt warm and strong in mine and I did not want to let go of it, but he released me and we waited at the foot of the table as Louisa approached, my good sense returning with her. I knew we had behaved outrageously and would be the talk of London tomorrow. Before either of us could speak, Louisa stretched out her hand to him. "Good night, Alex," she said graciously. "You have monopolized my niece enough for your first meeting."

"I am sorry," Alex began, but she waved his words away.

"Hush, I am too exhausted to hear anything. You may call on me soon to apologize. Good night, Alex." He bowed over her hand and with a smile to me excused himself. Will shook his hand. Betty yawned. And then Alex was gone. I waited for Louisa and Will's comments, but neither said a thing except good night. I went to my room in a daze, still feeling the touch of his hand in mine.

In the morning I felt the same, and I thought of Alex with an excitement that was almost intoxicating. Whatever London thought of us, I had enjoyed our conversations and revisited them now. He was the tenth Earl of Kilgannon, but he had dismissed it with a shrug, saying that he'd been raised to it and that it was more important to him that he was the chief of the MacGannon clan. "It's a vast responsibility, being the laird at home," he'd said, "not like in England, where ye just wear nice clothes and collect yer rents and remember yer title. In the Highlands, to be a laird means ye have many tasks that only ye can see to and ye have the responsibility to see that all yer kin are well fed and prosperous. If ye fail they starve." He had been so serious that I did not have the heart to laugh at his description of peerage in England nor to correct his perception.

How different our lives had been, I had thought as I listened to him talk. He was the oldest of the four children of Ian and Margaret, but two of the children had died in childhood, leaving Alex and his brother Malcolm. Alex's father had died when Alex was nineteen, and he had assumed the leadership of the clan. Two years later he had married Sorcha MacDonald, as his parents had pledged when he was a boy, and they had had two sons, Ian and Jamie. Alex's mother had died the year after Jamie's birth, and soon after that Alex had been asked to go to France as a show of unity to Queen Anne. While he was there Sorcha had died. Ian was four now and Jamie two and Alex the leader of five hundred.

In contrast my life had been uneventful. Raised at Mountgarden in Warwickshire, on the lands my father had inherited, with Will as my companion and ally, I had been pampered and protected. It was only in the last few years, when my father had died and my mother became ill, that any unpleasantness had touched my life, and even now I was cared for and comforted by my aunt and friends. My greatest accomplishment thus far had been to resist marrying the men paraded before me, but even that had been simple since until recently I had been in mourning.

I stretched and remembered Alex sitting next to me, his hair a golden frame around his face. I'd wondered what it would be like to touch that hair or the lean cheek it caressed, and then he'd asked me something and I realized I'd not heard anything he said. I began to pay attention. Alex would be returning to Scotland soon, but he'd come back to London to see members of Parliament. He did not say when. I'd asked if he were a member of Parliament and had been met with an icy look. "There're 154 peers in Scotland. I'm one of 75 earls, but we are allowed only 16 peers in the House of Lords. Ye English have 190. We have 45 in the

House of Commons, and ye have 513. How much representation do ye think we have? We must buy our votes from the
English peers. It's why I'm in London and why I go to these
evenings. 'Tis not my choice. I've had a bellyful of English
politics." His expression had been grim.

"I see," I'd said, and he brought his gaze back to me, his
expression lightening.

"Well, lass, that's not completely true." He'd smiled. "I
came tonight because ye'd be here."

I couldn't think of an answer and at last stammered.
"Why?"

"Why?" He'd paused again, looked at the ceiling and
back at me. "Have ye no' seen what ye look like, Mary? I'm
sure ye've been told that enough times." I felt my cheeks go
scarlet. He straightened his back and looked at his hands as
he brushed imaginary lint off his kilt. "I surprised myself. I
thought I was here on business, but when I saw ye at the
Duchess's party I thought ye were very beautiful and I could
not stop looking at ye. I dinna do that sort of thing. I'm a
bit old for it, don't ye think?" He shot a glance at me and
then looked across the room, the lace of his cuffs falling
on the back of his hands, white against the tan skin. Long,
slim fingers, one crested ring. "I left, thinking I'd forget ye
straightaway. But I dinna forget ye, and I came here tonight
to see ye, to see that ye were not as beautiful as I'd remembered." He'd raked a hand through his hair and disarrayed
it. "But ye are, and I dinna think ye would be so pleasing
to be with. And everaone tells me yer spoken for." His
eyes met mine. "But ye dinna behave like a woman who is
promised elsewhere."

"I'm not."

"Good." He'd nodded and then laughed. "Dinna look
so afraid, Mary. I'll not steal ye off, though it's no' such a
bad idea. How would ye like Scotland, lass?" He leaned on
one elbow and smiled. I wasn't sure if he was joking. I
wasn't sure of anything except that I wanted to keep him
talking to me.

"But you do not even know me, sir!"

"And we must change that. I do know a bit about ye, though."

"Such as . . ."

"Such as ye like to dance and ye dance verra well, but ye dinna like that Jonathan man. Yer fairly new to London again since yer mother's death and yer travels, and all the lads think yer verra beautiful, but Lord Campbell says yer his, and all of London seems to think ye are. Yer brother inherited lands through his wife's family in addition to Mountgarden and will probably inherit your uncle's Grafton title and estate as well. Yer currently living here with yer aunt Louisa, but when her husband comes back from France ye'll probably leave. Ye have no lands of yer own, and yer verra fond of chocolate. Shall I go on?"

"No. That's certainly a bit more than I thought."

"Aye, and there's more."

"I see." I'd watched him, wondering what was next.

"Aye." He'd looked at the carpet for a moment. "Mary," he said, raising blue eyes to me. "May I see ye again, or shall I leave? Tell me now, lass, before I make a fool of myself."

I wasn't sure if I was wise to keep talking to him, but the thought of never seeing this man again was unacceptable. I should tell him to go away, that any romance between us was unlikely and ill-suited. We were too different, our worlds incompatible. I'd watched him watch me, his eyes clear and honest, and I took a deep breath.

"Yes, Alex, you may see me again."

He'd let his breath out in a huff and smiled. "Good, then I will. And if we both like what we see, then we'll talk further."

I'd felt my eyebrows lift in surprise. "Then I will see you again before you return to Scotland?"

"Aye, lass, and often if I have a say." We'd shared a smile.

I stretched now and pulled the cover farther over my shoulder. I knew that Alex was not as uncomplicated as he appeared at first, but he fascinated me as no other man did. Certainly not Robert. Robert was also Scottish, but I had never thought of him as that, perhaps because he had lived most of his life in England and he and his Campbell cousins owned as many properties here as in Scotland.

I smiled as I admitted to myself that it was delightful to have a man like Alex so vigorous in his pursuit of me. I could not say I was not intrigued. I had been unduly aware of how his lean legs stretched out, his shoulder touching mine occasionally, the way those blue eyes disarmed me. There was no doubt that physically he was immensely attractive and that his directness and humor were wonderfully refreshing. I had a sudden vision of me brushing that errant strand of hair back and leaning in to kiss him. Oh, no, I was not immune to Alex MacGannon. Nor, apparently, was he to me. I smiled at the thought.

Louisa did not leave her room until late afternoon, and I wandered the house with Will and Betty. When Betty excused herself after luncheon for a nap, Will and I at last had a chance to talk alone, and I looked at my brother with affection. Often the buffoon, sometimes dictatorial and difficult, he was always a loving brother, and now he smiled at me. I was grateful he was here. "Your Highlander has written a note asking my permission to see you," he said, his expression curious as he fished a note from his waistcoat and handed it to me. "Louisa has received one as well, so it seems he's asking us both. What shall I tell him?"

"He's not my Highlander, Will," I said crisply, as I read Alex's very proper note asking Will's permission to *become better acquainted with your sister*. He wrote with correct English spelling, but I could somehow hear the Scot's burr. "Tell him yes."

"And what about Robert?"

I looked up at my brother. "What about Robert?"

"Do not be trying. Everyone assumes you are marrying."

"If so, perhaps Robert should declare himself."

His eyebrows rose. "You do not have an understanding?"

"He has not asked me to marry him, if that's what you mean."

"But I thought—"

"Apparently, so does all of London. But a woman does not assume she's marrying unless something a little more formal happens."

"Then Robert's a fool."

"Perhaps. Or perhaps he is not as interested as you presume."

"If he does not watch his back, Kilgannon will steal you away."

"For heaven's sake, Will, do I not have some say in this? Robert has not asked me to marry him, nor, dear brother, has Lord Kilgannon. But if Kilgannon wishes to be in my company and I wish it also, he shall be. And at this moment I wish it."

After a moment Will threw his head back and laughed. "Do you? I liked him too, which surprises me. I'd heard very different things of him than the man he appears to be. Louisa admits he's a bit of a surprise to her as well. Of course, she hasn't seen him in years. I daresay we've changed since childhood ourselves."

"You haven't," I said, laughing.

"Well, perhaps you're right." He laughed with me. "But, Mary"—he leaned forward—"shall I really tell Kilgannon yes?"

"I'm not thinking of marrying him on the basis of one evening. Good heavens, Will, I just met him last night." I sighed. "But he is a fascinating man."

"You spent the night with him in the dining room."

"Not exactly," I said dryly.

"Everyone was talking."

"Of course." I shrugged, pretending to be unaffected. "But tomorrow they'll be talking about someone else."

"Probably." He nodded, yawning, and then stood as Louisa swept into the room. She flitted around the table and at last faced Will, her hands clasped at her waist, her manner brisk.

"Mary and I are going to walk in the garden," she said.

Will laughed. "I believe I have been dismissed," he said and, bowing, left the room. Louisa gestured to me to follow her.

But in the garden she was silent. I walked with her through the roses, then sat with her on a bench. Still she said nothing, and I grew worried. When at last she did speak, it was in a bemused manner. "I hardly know what to say to you, Mary."

"I am certain that you are angry with me, Louisa. . . ."

"No, dear, I am not angry." She looked at me, her beautiful eyes serious and her tone quiet. "I am afraid for you. When I sat you together, I thought Alex MacGannon would be an interesting diversion for you for the evening, a change from the men of London. I thought you would find him good company for a few hours while Robert was gone. I did not expect to see you gazing deeply into his eyes after a few moments of acquaintance. I have underestimated his charms, it would appear." She frowned as she looked across the gardens. "And yours. I should know better."

I flushed at her description of our behavior. I did not remember gazing deeply into his eyes. Or perhaps I did, I thought, as a sudden vision of Alex's face appeared in my mind, his eyes brilliantly blue. I sighed. "He is fascinating."

"So it would appear." She glanced at me. "'But he's Scottish."

"Louisa, you married a Scotsman and were very happy."

Her gaze grew distant. "I was very happy," she said, nodding. "But, my dear, Scotland is not England, and Alex is not your uncle Duncan. I was not joking when I told Alex that Scotland was too dangerous and too far away." She sighed. "I have known Alex since he was a boy, and he does not appear to have changed a bit. He was as straightforward at ten as now, but he told me only last week that he was not planning to remarry yet and I believed him."

"Perhaps he's not, Louisa. All we did was talk. He's not proposing, nor am I accepting."

She sighed again. "When I received his note today, I

realized that he is considering courting you. I hardly know what to do."

"There is nothing to do."

"You mean there is nothing to be done."

"Louisa, you are worrying too much. I've only met him once."

"Why isn't Robert here, the fool? I should not have listened to the Duchess. I'm afraid I'll lose you to Scotland."

I shook my head. "I intend to marry no one at the moment. And besides, if I married Robert I might live in Scotland."

"No, dear, if you married Robert you would live in London or at his estate, and you'd visit Scotland once a year as I did, and no matter what happened in that strange country you would be safe in England. If you marry Alex you will live in the back of beyond, and I might never see you again. It is well-known he is devoted to his sons. He comes with a ready-made family and many responsibilities. And apparently—whether he knows it or not—he is seeking a wife." Her shoulders slumped. "I have been very foolish." She drummed her fingers on her lips and straightened. "I shall tell him he may not see you. Then he will go home and marry some Scotswoman with rough ways who will suit him infinitely better, and you and Robert may continue your eternal courtship. That will solve the problem."

My first reaction was anger, then I paused. The fact that I was reacting so strongly meant she was right to worry. Perhaps my interest in Alex was a sudden infatuation that would fade upon further acquaintance. Perhaps I had simply been dazzled by a handsome newcomer in foreign dress. But never to see him again? I could not bear it. I would not. "Louisa—" I began.

She put up her hand. "I knew you would object. Very well. We'll tell him he may come. But you will not be left alone, and I will speak to him. Mary, you do not know what his life is like at Kilgannon. Being an earl in Scotland is hardly the same as here."

"How can you say that? Duncan was a Scot, and you were happy."

"Duncan was not a Highlander. He was very civilized." She leaned toward me, her eyes bright. "My dear, I thought of Alex as a companion for the evening, not for life."

I straightened my back. "Don't you think this has gone extremely far for one evening's conversation? We've talked once. Perhaps I will think differently of him when I see him again. But, Louisa, I will see him again." Our eyes met, and she sighed.

"I was afraid you would say that. Oh, dear, how I wish your uncle Randolph were here. I have been very foolish."

"No." I shook my head. "I am responsible for my own behavior, Louisa, and Alex for his. We have done nothing but talk. I may never see him again." But in my head I heard him saying that we'd talk further if we both liked what we saw. And I liked what I saw.

She nodded with a frown.

As the day drew to a close, I tried to pretend that it did not bother me that neither Louisa nor Will had mentioned if they'd sent a return note to Alex. We dined simply, the four of us, and were about to leave the table when a maid brought a note for me. Louisa's eyebrows rose, but she said nothing as I reached for it. I did not recognize the writing or the crest that sealed the letter. It was, of course, from Alex.

"Another apology, do you suppose?" Will asked.

"What do you mean?" I said as I broke the seal.

Will laughed. "Your Highlander apologized profusely to Louisa for monopolizing you last night. I believe it's the only reason he still breathes." Louisa protested, but I ignored them as I read Alex's letter.

Dear Miss Lowell, Alex had written. *Your aunt and brother have been good enough to allow me to see you again. I would like to call upon you in the morning and introduce my cousins. If this is not acceptable, please send a reply. Yours,*

Alexander MacGannon. He'd enclosed his address. I read the letter aloud.

"He certainly is persistent," said Louisa sharply. "We shall receive him, I assume?"

"I shall," I said, turning to my brother. "Will?"

Will nodded at me. "Of course. When will Robert return?"

"Tomorrow, I believe," I said, keeping my tone as light as his. "Perhaps we'll see him."

"Perhaps." He smiled, his eyes merry.

I excused myself and wrote the note quickly, giving it to the tall young man who had waited so patiently. He was very fair and very handsome and looked so much like Alex that I knew he must be a relation. I asked him when I brought my note to him, scandalizing Louisa's butler, Bronson, who believed that young ladies should never speak directly to strangers and certainly not to strangers' messengers. Bronson thought me much too bold. I ignored him as much as possible, and he me.

"Aye, miss," said the young man when I asked him. "I'm Matthew MacGannon, Kilgannon's cousin. Alex is outside waiting for yer answer." He was younger than he had first appeared and very earnest, and I smiled at him, fighting the impulse to fling open the door and see Alex for myself. Ellen, one of the maids lingering in the hall, laughed behind her hands as she met my eyes.

"Tell him good evening and that I will see him in the morning," I told Matthew, trying to ignore Ellen's laughter.

"Aye, miss. Good evening to ye," Matthew said, bowing awkwardly, and turned on his heel. I stood for moment looking after him and then exchanged a smile with Ellen.

THREE

THE SUMMER MORNING DAWNED BRIGHT AND WARM,
and I changed my clothes four times before breakfast. The
white dress I'd first put on was not right, so I changed to
the lavender. When I saw myself in the mirror in the parlor I
knew the lavender was all wrong and changed to the green
but soon scrambled back to my room. In the dining room I
decided the rose dress was too similar to the color I'd worn
the night I'd met Alex. My maid sighed as I pulled gown
after gown out of my wardrobe and pondered them. Why
had I ever fought Miss Benton's efforts? I could use ten
more choices just now. I was deciding between the light
blue and the floral pattern when Ellen knocked on my door.
My maid answered and Ellen rushed in, flying past me to the
window.

"Miss Mary," she said breathlessly. "They're here." I
moved to her side and together we peered through the lace.
Matthew stood next to his horse, and Alex watched the
upper windows as his horse danced in a circle. A third man
was dismounting. I drew back before Alex could see me and
met Ellen's merry eyes.

"The floral," she said. "It's perfect for walking in the gardens, Miss Mary." We smiled at each other.

I'd never dressed so quickly. My maid hurried me into
the bodice and skirt, while Ellen put a few touches on my

hair before declaring me perfect. Even my dour maid agreed.

"But you should wear shoes," Ellen said, laughing as I crossed the room in my stockings.

I threw myself down the two flights to the ground floor and then paused in the hallway to catch my breath. Bronson stood in the hallway opposite me, and I realized that someone was in the foyer between us. Several someones. I flushed with annoyance as I realized that Bronson had kept Alex and his cousins waiting in the hall and was now standing around the corner listening to them. No doubt the dreadful man thought he was being loyal to the absent Randolph by delaying the visit. Perhaps he thought that if he kept them waiting long enough they would leave. And that is just what, apparently, Alex's cousin thought they should do. I stood rooted to the spot, staring with hostility at Bronson.

"Alex," an unfamiliar voice growled, "how much longer are we going to wait? If her blessed Miss Lowell wanted to see ye, we'd be with her now." Boots tapped on the marble floor. "I dinna understand why we're here. We have enough elsewhere to busy us."

Alex's tone was calm. "We're here, Angus, because I want ye to meet Mary Lowell. And that's what we'll do."

"What can come of this?"

"What needs come of it? I like her company."

"Ye'll only be rejected, ye ken. Even if she likes ye, her family willna let ye court her. Why do this? If ye wish a woman's company, go home and see Morag. She'd marry ye in a minute."

"Aye, and break Murdoch's heart," Alex said without heat. "If ye wish to leave, then do so. And, Angus, if I thought I'd be rejected, we wouldna be here."

Angus grunted. "And how much longer will we wait?"

"Until I see Mary Lowell." There was silence then, and Bronson and I moved forward at the same moment, but I turned the corner before he did. Alex greeted me with a smile, and Matthew, in the center of the hall with an older man, was visibly relieved.

"Lord Kilgannon," I said cheerfully, "here you are. I have no idea why you're still in the hall. How rude of you, Bronson, to make our guests wait here. Where is my aunt Louisa?"

Bronson bowed stiffly, his eyes registering my attack. "I do apologize, gentlemen," he said smoothly. "The Countess Randolph awaits you in the gardens. She bids you to join her."

"And I do as well," I said, extending my hand to Alex, who bowed over it. He wore a kilt and shirt this morning, a plaid over his shoulder, a hat with feathers, and a badge under his arm. I thought he looked splendid and smiled at him again.

"Miss Lowell," he said clearly, and then in a voice only I could hear, "Mary, ye look lovely. How are ye this fine morning?"

"Wonderful," I said. And it was true. I was wonderful now.

Alex gestured to the other men and introduced his cousin Angus. "Ye've met Angus's son Matthew a'ready," he said. Both men bowed to me, Angus's expression polite, Matthew's smile genuine. Angus MacGannon was older and taller than Alex, a giant of a man with silky golden hair that looked out of place on his big body. This man was sturdy, his chest a barrel. Dressed in Highland fashion, he looked huge and intimidating, his blue eyes missing no detail as he bent over my hand. He greeted me courteously but with reserve. There were traces of him in his son, but Matthew was young—fifteen, I guessed—and time would tell whether he would grow to the size of his father. Matthew's greeting was warm, and I felt my smile widen in response. At least he was glad to see me.

Bronson led us to the terrace, where Louisa and Will waited. Alex bowed over Louisa's hand, and his cousins followed suit as Alex introduced them, Matthew awkward but

earnest, Angus silent and watchful. Louisa nodded stiffly as
Angus and Matthew bowed over her hand, and Alex turned
to me with dancing eyes, grinning as though we had accom-
plished something remarkable.

"Well, we've that done," he laughed, and turned to Will,
asking where his beautiful wife was. Will explained that
Betty had complained of a headache, and Alex extended his
wishes for her recovery. Will smiled and said Betty would
improve soon. I doubted Betty would ever improve, but I
kept that to myself. When Bronson reappeared with a tray,
we seated ourselves and chatted about trivialities. Louisa
thawed enough to smile occasionally, and to my surprise
Angus and Will grew engrossed in a discussion of hunting,
which continued even when Louisa suggested we walk in
the garden.

Louisa's gardens were large by London standards, but
still small, divided into the formal garden that surrounded
the house and the informal one through which she led us
now. If it were a walk of any duration we'd cover the same
ground several times. At the foot of the stairs she linked
her arm in Alex's, drawing him ahead of the rest of us.
Within moments they were out of earshot, talking earnestly.
In front of us Will and Angus were deep in conversation,
and Matthew and I fell into step. We walked beneath a row
of trees in full bloom, slowing our steps to enjoy the cool
shadows.

"Do you like London, Mr. MacGannon?" I asked.

Matthew smiled at me. "Oh, yes, Miss Lowell. I've been
to many other places, but London seems more comfortable." He puffed his chest out and tried unsuccessfully to
sound sophisticated. "Trading, ye ken. We travel often."

"I see." I tried to hide my smile. "And where do
you go?"

"Paris. Alex and my da go to the Low Countries and Ireland. I've been to Ireland, of course, many times."

"Of course," I said. "Does your father go on all the
trips?"

"Aye, and Malcolm—that's Alex's brother—often goes too."

"Your mother must miss you terribly when you both travel."

He glanced at me. "My mother's dead these three years."

"Oh, I'm so sorry." I felt like an idiot as I looked at the boy next to me. "I've lost my mother as well. It's very difficult."

The blue eyes so like Alex's clouded. "Aye, it is. My da misses her terrible." He glanced at his father and then met my gaze without guile. "I'm sorry about yer mother too."

I thanked him, touched by his sincerity, and we walked for a moment in silence. Alex and Louisa had drawn even farther ahead, and I assumed that Louisa was explaining in great detail how unsuitable any relationship between us would be. I wondered if Alex was agreeing. They walked out from the shade of the trees and Alex's hair caught the sunlight, gold against the scarlet of the hat he now wore. As though he felt my gaze he turned, found me, and grinned. I felt immensely cheered. No, I thought, Alex MacGannon would not be sent away, Louisa or not. I smiled back at him, my heart much lighter. "Matthew," I said, my eyes still on Alex. "Tell me about your family. Tell me everything."

Matthew was happy to talk. Alex was his father's first cousin, and the two had grown up together. Matthew's mother had been Mairi MacDonald from Skye, and his parents' marriage had been very happy. Since Mairi's death, Matthew had been traveling with his father and Alex on their trading journeys and he enjoyed it, but he was always happy to go home. "Do you all live in Kilgannon?" I asked.

"It's the home of the MacGannons. Where else would I live?"

"Of course." I laughed. "Where else?"

Matthew said that Alex's sons were lively and a lot of fun, but that they didn't travel with their father. I asked about Alex's brother, hoping I didn't sound like Rowena. Matthew, unperturbed, said that Alex's brother James and his sister Katrine were dead and that Malcolm lived at Kilgannon as well.

"Is he here in London with you?" I asked, but never got an answer, for Alex approached us then, his smile wide.

"Yer aunt would have a word with ye, Mary," Alex said as he drew to my side. I gave Louisa a nervous glance, and Alex laughed. "I've assured her I have only the most honorable intentions. We are dining here in two days, Angus and I, with ye and yer Robert Campbell." He nodded at my startled expression. "We ken each other. I must deal with Argyll, and Robert is often there as well." Alex grinned at me and gestured to Louisa. "Now, go and talk to yer aunt, lass, and then come back to me if ye would. I wish to be with ye today, not all yer kinsmen, and we've not had a moment."

I nodded and went to Louisa, who met me with a smile and a wave of her hand. "I will not fight the tide, Mary. You may see the man if you will. Did you know that Robert has returned?"

"No, I've not heard from him," I said, glancing back at Alex.

"Nor I, but he arrived last night. I sent him a note this morning. I'm not sure how pleased he'll be with you."

"I am not bound to him, Louisa. If I were engaged to Robert, Alex would not be here this morning."

"I understand, but Robert may not approve." She looked at the men, who were laughing about something. "Alex MacGannon is a man who knows what he wants, and right now that seems to be you. Be careful, my Mary. We know who Robert is, but in many ways Alex is an unknown. Don't be taken in by his looks and charm."

"I'm not a fool, Louisa," I said. "And Alex is not an unknown. He is your cousin by marriage."

"You will find, my dear, that in Scotland everyone is related." She sighed. "Go talk with him, Mary. I can see you wish to. But for heaven's sake use your head."

Will and Angus joined Louisa as she walked away, and

Matthew trailed along behind them. For just a moment I stood and watched Alex. The green canopy of the trees framed him against the white of the house. His gaze was somewhere in the distance and I savored the chance to study him unnoticed. Was I just swept away by the magnificence of the man? To be sure, few women would not be. He was a man who would cause many feminine hearts to race, but what of the man underneath? Somehow he didn't seem a stranger, and yet Louisa was right—that's what he was. I decided to be more considering, but then he looked at me, smiling a smile that lit his face, and I walked to meet him without any further thought.

We strolled in the gardens for the better part of an hour, and at Louisa's insistence they stayed for luncheon on the terrace. Betty joined us for the meal, all traces of her headache gone. It was cool and fragrant in the shade and we chatted easily, even Louisa laughing often. I was seated between Alex and Matthew, and somehow it seemed natural to look across the table and share a smile with my aunt as we shared a meal with the MacGannons. Angus had effortlessly drawn her into a protracted discussion of the Lowlands versus the Highlands. Alex's cousin had the manners of a gentleman as he courteously assured Louisa that the Lowlands were no match for his home. But most of my attention was on Alex. He had been relaxed and lively, but now he watched the others talk, then leaned toward me, his voice quiet.

"Seems as though we've done this before, does it not, Mary? Seems strange to think a week ago I'd never seen ye."

"Three days ago I'd never seen you."

"Oh, aye, that's true. I was invisible at the Duchess's party."

"I truly did not see you, Alex. I would have remembered."

"Aye?"

"Yes. You are quite noticeable."

"Aye, well, so are ye, lass. I was watching all the pretty girls and there ye were, on the other side of the group." Our eyes met and he smiled. "The most beautiful woman I'd ever seen. Ye were laughing and hugging the others, and I thought it was verra nice to see a beautiful woman who liked people, so I watched ye." I felt my cheeks flame. "And then a man came over, and ye and yer friend Rebecca left with him to go to another room."

"That must have been Lawrence."

"So I discovered. The Duchess was most informative."

"She's very fond of you. I think you've made a conquest."

"I hope so," he said, laughing. "Oh, do ye mean the Duchess? She's a verra nice person, but I dinna pay much attention to other men's wives." He smiled again, and I laughed.

Long before I was ready, Alex and his cousins were leaving and Louisa and I stood in the foyer wishing them farewell. When the bell rang we all turned to watch Bronson answer it. Robert stood in the doorway, his hat in one hand, flowers in the other. Next to me Alex stiffened, and Angus gave him a glance. I looked from Alex to Robert as he stepped into the foyer. He answered Louisa's greeting calmly, but his brown eyes kept flickering to the MacGannons.

"Welcome home, Lord Campbell," I said, echoing Louisa.

Robert handed me the flowers. "For you, Miss Lowell." He nodded at my thanks. Louisa began to introduce Robert to the MacGannons, but Alex stepped forward, extending his hand.

"We've met before, Louisa," Alex said, his tone cheerful. "How are ye, Lord Campbell? Just arrived from France?"

"Yes." Robert shook Alex's hand. "And you, Kilgannon? What brings you here?" They both glanced at me and then at each other.

Alex laughed. "To London? My ship. Have ye met my cousins Angus and Matthew?" Angus stepped forward, offering Robert his hand; Robert shook it, then nodded to Matthew.

"We're just leaving, Campbell," Alex said, "so the field is yers for the now. But I'll return." He turned to my aunt. "Louisa, I thank ye again for yer hospitality and yer forbearance."

Louisa laughed at him. "Alex MacGannon, you do test me."

"Aye, Countess, and ye always pass." Alex grinned at her, his blue eyes sparkling, then turned to me. "Miss Lowell, farewell for a bit."

"Lord Kilgannon," I said, watching him bow over my hand.

"I'll see ye in two nights," he said for all to hear and then in a lower tone added, "I count the hours, Mary. Dinna let the Campbell carry ye off in my absence. Guard yer heart, lass."

He gave me a crooked smile and walked through the door Bronson held open. Angus and Matthew made their farewells and followed. I looked after them until Bronson closed the door, then turned to meet Robert's dark eyes, full of questions. I smiled.

Louisa led us to the drawing room, where we discussed Robert's trip. The war with France, it appeared, was truly almost over and treaty discussions were under way. Robert was pleased about that but concerned about the situation in Spain, and I watched him as he and Louisa talked. Tall and fit, he was a handsome man, his even features now, as usual, set in a pleasant expression. Many women would seek his company—and had. His hair was tied back simply and his clothes, fashionable without any affected ostentation, were impeccably tailored, chosen to complement his dark hair and deep-set brown eyes. He stretched a leg, clad in buff, before him, and I admired the lines of his body. And realized again how fond of him I was. *Fond.* Not struck breathless. With a meaningful glance at me, Louisa left us. For the first time in our relationship I was reluctant to be alone with Robert. We walked in the formal gardens together in awkward silence.

"How have you been, Mary?"

I turned to him with a fixed smile. "Fine, Robert. And you? It's lovely to have you back in London. Tell me of your trip. What was it you were doing in France if you were not in the field?"

"It would not interest you, Mary," he said dismissively.

I lifted my chin, thinking of Alex discussing Scottish politics the night we'd met. "I'll tell you if it bores me, Robert," I said lightly. "What did you do?"

He smiled. "Truly it would bore you." He spoke mildly, but his scrutiny belied his tone. "I am pleased to have returned but quite surprised to see you in the company of a man like Lord Kilgannon."

"I met Kilgannon at Louisa's party." I paused, watching his reaction. "I've never heard you mention him."

Robert shrugged. "There never seemed to be cause to before. We seldom travel in the same circles. He's rarely in London."

"Do you see him in Scotland?"

He laughed. "The MacGannons are an insignificant clan, but they are allied with the MacDonalds. I'm a Campbell. We are polite here in London when we must be, but in Scotland we are enemies."

Startled, I stared at him. "Surely it is not that strong."

"Scotland is not England, Mary. The hatreds have been there for centuries. They will not fade because Scotland is now part of Britain. The enmity lives on, especially in the Highlands, and in the papist Highlands most of all. And that brings us to the matter of religion. I can only assume that MacGannon is papist." He paused. "He's not what he appears in London."

"I see."

"No, you don't, Mary. The man may seem interesting to you, for he's unlike the men you are accustomed to meeting.

I'm certain he's behaving properly here, but at home he's very different. You have no idea what the Western Highlands are like. Illiterate heathens who can't even speak English. They make war on anyone who doesn't have the same name. It's barbaric. And Kilgannon is their leader. He lives a life you cannot imagine, full of violence and ancient ways. He's not an Englishman and not your sort."

I resisted the angry defense of Alex that sprang to mind as I realized with a sudden insight what this first strong emotion I'd ever seen from Robert meant. *He's jealous*, I thought. *Of Alex. Well. So he does have feelings for me he hasn't admitted.* "Robert," I said mildly, "you are Scottish. And a Highlander."

"I am," he said, raising his chin. "But I am a Campbell."

"Which makes you superior."

To his credit he laughed. "Of course." I laughed with him.

"Enough, Robert. Tell me about your trip." I tried to listen to Robert tell me of French fashions as we walked, but I couldn't help but think of Alex. *I must ask him about his home,* I thought. It was impossible to believe that Alex Mac-Gannon allowed his people to live in ignorance and poverty. Or was it? I had seen the man only twice. Perhaps Louisa was correct after all.

Robert stayed for two hours and might have stayed even longer if Louisa had not found us and reminded me that we were dining at the Duchess's. She extended her hand as she ended his visit and I bid Robert farewell, my thoughts in a muddle. After his one outburst Robert had retreated into the pleasant behavior I'd come to expect and we'd not discussed Alex again, nor Robert's activities. Nor anything of any substance. As usual.

I trailed behind Louisa as she climbed the stairs to prepare for the evening. "It is lovely to have Robert home," she said, with a sharp glance at me. "And I'm pleased that he'll be joining us for dinner with the MacGannons." I agreed and she sighed. "Despite my best judgment, I like the MacGannons. God only knows what will come of this, but it's impossible not to like them."

"Louisa," I said, as though it had just occurred to me, "what did you and Alex talk about when you walked in the garden?"

Louisa laughed, not fooled for a moment. "You. He apologized again, and I chastised him for telling me he was not seeking a wife and then pursuing you for all London to chatter about. He quite disarmed me. Either he's an honest man or he's the most convincing liar I've ever seen. Time will tell." She waved my protest aside as we approached my room. "Wear the lavender tonight, dear," she said, and disappeared around the corner.

The talk that night was politics and gossip. The Duchess drew me aside, however, after the meal and told me how delighted she was that I'd met Alex. "He was here this afternoon, my dear," she beamed at me, "and with a little prodding admitted he'd seen you this morning. He's a special man and I am very fond of him. And indebted. If not for the Earl, my dear Duke would be dead. Lord Kilgannon saved his life, and I will be eternally grateful."

I blinked at her stupidly. "What do you mean, Your Grace?"

"You don't know this story?" The Duchess settled in to tell the tale. "Well. The Duke was in Paris and one day, after negotiations with the French, on his way back to his lodgings, three men attacked him. His footmen immediately disappeared and my dear Duke thought he was lost. But from nowhere, Kilgannon arrived and fought the men off with him. The Earl saved the Duke's life, my dear. The Duke will always be in the Earl's debt, and I as well, which is why I am so fond of him. I cannot imagine life without my Duke." She smiled at her husband as he approached us, and I considered. I had heard the story many times but had never marked the rescuer's name. *Alex,* I thought now with a private smile. *Alex.*

"What's this, my dear?" asked Duke John. She extended her cheek for his kiss and he obliged her.

"I am telling Mary about Kilgannon rescuing you in Paris and how grateful we are to him," the Duchess said to her husband.

"We are indeed, Mary," Duke John said. "But don't play matchmaker, Eloise. You know how that always ends up." He turned his merry eyes to me. "Edmund Bartlett will not speak to us just now because of my wife's attempts to marry him to Lady Wilmington."

"She would have been perfect for him," said the Duchess. "All that land . . ." She sighed. "It would have been ideal. They could discuss everyone! Who else would marry him?" I laughed with her.

The next day was quiet, spent at home with Will and Betty, all of us watching Louisa plan her dinner. I thought we would be a small group but now learned there would be eighteen in all. Louisa had invited the Duke and Duchess, of course, and Alex, Angus, and Robert, two of our Fairhaven cousins, and Becca's parents, just returned to London. Three other friends and, of all people, the Marquess and Rowena would also be included. *If only Becca and Lawrence had not stayed in Bath with his parents,* I thought. I needed her here with me now. I suspected Louisa was inviting Rowena just to make it interesting and told her as much. She laughed.

"Mary, if Alex's head is so easily turned you need to know that at once. And Robert will be there to keep you company."

Betty fluffed her hair and frowned. "I think it's foolish to have Lord Campbell and Lord Kilgannon here together."

"If they cannot behave like gentlemen in my home, they will be asked to leave," said Louisa crisply. "My dinners have never been anything but a success, and this one will be no different. Robert is always well behaved, and I cannot imagine Alex being anything less. Remember that he is my cousin, by marriage, at least."

I swallowed a smile, thinking that Alex had bewitched Louisa as well. But I agreed with Betty. I had no doubt that Robert would behave properly and I assumed that Alex would do the same, but I would rather not have them at the same table and rather not have Rowena in the same country. I hoped Alex's remark that he did not pay attention to other men's wives was accurate and wondered if I could be well behaved if Rowena flirted with him as she had done last time. And then I caught myself. *His. Him.* As if there were no other man on earth. I was farther down this road than I'd thought.

The day dragged by with no word from Alex. That evening I could not sleep and sat alone in the library after everyone else had retired, searching for every bit of information on Scotland that I could find. I found several treatises that claimed dismay over the barbarity of the Scots and their horrific land. I had almost given up hope when I found an atlas and pored over the maps, finding Lothian, where I had visited Duncan and Louisa. The general outline of Scotland I knew, of course, and that there were highlands and lowlands, borderlands and the north, the many lochs and Glen Mohr. I found Robert's Argyllshire and Alex's western Highlands. They were not as far apart as I had remembered, at least on the map. How very far apart were they in reality? I stared at the page. How could such a small country be so difficult to manage? For centuries now, one group or another had been trying to dominate this bit of earth and its people. I found Skye and the Hebrides off the shore of the western Highlands, but Kilgannon was not marked. Almost nothing was noted in that region, and I wondered where in that remote, rugged terrain lay Alex's home.

The following evening I found myself dressed in blue silk, pacing in the dining room, more anxious than I'd been in months. I'd tried to pretend to myself that it would simply be another of Louisa's elegant dinners, but I knew it would not be. What if Robert and Alex were rude to each other? *In Scotland we are enemies* rang in my mind. And Rowena. Next to her I felt much too tall, ugly, and clumsy, the country cousin who never quite measured up. It was in this state that Louisa found me and laughed kindly.

"You're beautiful, Mary," she said, embracing me. "Just be yourself. If either Robert or Alex is disconcerted by the other, then so be it. Robert should have asked you to marry him months ago. Perhaps Alex being here tonight will spur him on. As for Alex, I suspect that a man who looks like that is used to easy conquests. Let him see he is not without a rival." She smiled. "Mary, one of these men might be your husband one day. Watch them closely. How a man behaves in polite society under duress gives you a glimpse into his soul. If either misbehaves you'll see it and you'll be armed with that knowledge. Picking a husband is a complicated undertaking, my dear, but you must live with the consequences. Get the most for what you're bargaining."

Ellen ran in to announce that the first guests were here. Alex, Angus, and Robert had arrived together.

FOUR

ᘺE HEARD LAUGHTER AS WE APPROACHED THE PAR-
lor, and at the door Louisa and I exchanged looks of surprise. Alex was pointing at Robert, saying something while
the others laughed, and I quickly realized what had caused
all the commotion. Alex was in English clothing, a frock
coat and breeches, and Robert wore Highlander dress, his
plaid blue, a beautiful garnet brooch at his shoulder. Alex
walked toward me, both hands extended, his grin wide.

"I'll never argue with yer effect on men, Miss Lowell," he
announced. "Ye have both of us playing the fool. But ye
must agree that I do look better than the Campbell, no?"

"Not so, Kilgannon," laughed Robert, approaching as
well. "I wear this much better than you do."

I stood still, amazed to see them joking together, and
then smiled as I took Alex's hands. "You both look wonderful," I said with a laugh, noticing how warm and strong
his hands felt in mine. He smiled into my eyes and released
me with a gentle squeeze of my fingers. Before any of us
could speak, the Duke and Duchess arrived and new greetings were exchanged amid more laughter. This was not how
I'd envisioned the evening, but it continued in the same
fashion. Alex and Robert tried to outdo each other in their
jests, both becoming increasingly outrageous, to the delight
of all. Will joined in eagerly, and even Angus was silly. The
hours flew by and we were saying good-byes before I real-

ized the evening was over. Robert left first, still in a jovial mood, and Alex, at my side, called after him, "Yer knees are lovely, Campbell."

Robert bowed, laughing, and waved. Alex and Angus left us moments later, thanking Louisa for the evening. Alex gave my hand a squeeze as he said good night. Angus smiled broadly and thanked us, and then they were gone. Rowena, all but ignored throughout the evening despite her placement at the table between Alex and Robert, now embraced me, whispering, "I'd marry Robert and see Alex on the side." Her laughter followed her out the door. I shook my head and turned my thoughts elsewhere.

I would never understand men, I decided. One would think Alex and Robert had been the best of friends for years. I smiled to myself, thinking of their lightheartedness. It had been a wonderful evening. How silly I had been to worry.

The next morning I woke to rain but refused to let it dampen my spirits. Louisa and I left after breakfast, returning well past midday. Ellen met us with the news that the Earl of Kilgannon was in the library. "He's been here for ever so long, Miss Mary, but he said he was happy to wait," she said. "And he brought you flowers, madam," she added to Louisa, gesturing to the bouquet I had not even noticed.

Louisa nodded and asked if Alex had been invited to luncheon. When Ellen said Alex had eaten with Will and Betty, Louisa said then he could wait a little longer and sailed off in the direction of the dining room without looking back. Will and Betty were upstairs, Ellen said, her eyes twinkling. I went to the library.

Alex was stretched out on one of the sofas, his long legs well past the arm, his nose in a book, and one of Louisa's cats on his chest. I closed the door behind me, knowing full well I should leave it open. Alex looked over his shoulder and sprang upright, the book and cat flying. I laughed to see him try to catch the cat, succeed, and then let it go as it twisted out of his grip. It landed on the sofa and after a disdainful look at both of us began cleaning itself. Alex looked up with a smile as I approached.

"Alex, what a surprise!" I said. "How long have you been here?"

"Not verra long. Good day to you, Mary." He bowed, his discomposure short-lived. He wore his Highland clothing again, the dark blue of his vest making his eyes even more extraordinary.

I moved to the sofa and picked up the volume he'd been reading. *"Le Misanthrope,"* I read aloud. "Molière? In French?" I raised an eyebrow. "You surprise me."

"I dinna think ye'd mind if I read while I waited."

"I don't," I said, and put the book down. "You read French?" He shrugged and nodded. "What other surprises do you have for me?"

"Ah, let me think." He paused, rubbing his chin as though deep in thought. "Well, I can quote verse to you."

"In French?"

"Or Gaelic. Or English, if ye dinna mind my accent."

"Your accent is lovely," I protested.

"That's kind of ye. Some say I speak like a barbarian."

"I do not," I said, and moved across the room.

"Good." He grinned as he watched me.

"Did you enjoy last evening?" I asked.

He nodded. "Aye, Mary, I enjoyed myself hugely. Did ye?"

"I did." I moved to the fireplace and toyed with a candlestick. "Why did you wear English clothes?"

"To show ye that I could. I find that if I wear yer clothes I'm treated differently."

"If you wore my clothes you would be treated differently."

We both laughed. "Ye ken what I mean, Mary."

"Robert wore Highland clothing. I wonder where he found it."

Alex shrugged, moving closer. "In his clothes chest, no

doubt. He is a Campbell, ye ken. Even though we dinna like to admit it, Argyll is in the Highlands. Not the proper Highlands, to be sure."

"But his kilt was different than yours. Yours today is different than the others you've worn." I gestured to his clothing. He glanced down at his kilt and then up at me. I wondered if anyone else had ever had eyes so blue or legs so long.

"Well, each breacan is different," he said. "That's the weave. Each clan or sept has its own mix of colors, but the breacan depends on the weaver. All of mine come from Kilgannon weavers. They use the same patterns over and over. That's called a sett, when the pattern is always the same. Campbell setts are different, and that's what Robert was wearing. There are many who can tell a man's name by the pattern he's wearing. And each clan wears a different badge on their bonnets as well."

"I saw your badge on your hat yesterday. And feathers."

"Aye, each clan has its badge and a plant that marks the clan, but only the chief or the chief's family wears the eagle feathers."

"It's very different than in England," I said, thinking how foreign his world seemed to me. He shook his head and picked up the cat that was rubbing around his legs. He petted her absently.

"No, it's verra much the same. A farmer from Kent doesna dress like a sailor from Portsmouth. Each wears the badge of his territory and rank. It's the same in Scotland."

"Were you comfortable wearing English clothes?" I watched his hand stroke the cat. He frowned thoughtfully.

"Was I comfortable? Do ye mean did I feel strange, like I was wearing a costume?" I nodded. "No, lass, I wear English clothes often when I travel. I'm just more comfortable in my own clothes, and sometimes I dinna think it makes any difference what I wear. The very look of me marks me as a stranger."

"You look like a Scot."

"I look like a Gael," he corrected me. "Like a Highlander. Lowlanders are not so tall as a rule."

"Are all Highlanders tall?"

"No, but many are. More so than Lowlanders, who are descended from the Picts and Britons and Normans. We're taller. It's our Celtic and Norse bloodlines. That's where we get the fair coloring as well." The cat stretched to his touch. "Is this yer cat?"

"No, it's one of Louisa's. My cat is in Warwickshire."

"Oh, aye, Warwickshire." He nodded at me. "That's where Kenilworth and Warwick are? Yer home is called Mountgarden?"

"Yes. My home is not far from Kenilworth."

"Norman country, but verra bonnie. And verra flat."

"Not really," I said, ready to defend my home. "There are many hills. Mountgarden is on a hill."

"Hmmm. When ye come to Scotland ye'll see mountains. England doesna have any that I've seen." He looked at the cat.

"Alex," I said after a moment. "Did you come today to discuss kilts and cats and mountains?" He held the cat with one hand and brushed back the strands of hair that had fallen around his face with the other. I could hear the cat purring as he stroked her.

"I came to see ye, Mary. I'll talk about whatever ye wish."

I felt my face redden. "You're very direct, sir," I said, trying to keep my tone light.

"Aye," he said slowly, almost smiling. "As ye were. I told ye, lass. It saves time." He put the cat on the sofa and brushed his hands on his thighs. "Mary, I dinna have any chance to talk with ye alone last night, so I thought I'd like to see ye today. Am I interrupting something ye have planned?"

"I had nothing planned."

"Good. And I thought if I came today I'd have a fair chance of beating yer Robert Campbell to yer door."

"He's not my Robert Campbell, Alex."

"Oh, aye, lass, he is. I dinna ken why the man hesitates, but it's fine with me. Now, what do ye want to talk about, if not kilts and cats and mountains?" I moved to the sofa and sat down. Alex joined me, and the cat jumped on his lap at once.

"You've made a conquest," I said, petting the cat on his lap.

"Again? First the Duchess and now ye? Or d'ye mean the cat?"

"The cat. I suspect you make a lot of conquests."

He nodded. "Aye. Cats like me. Dogs too."

"That's not what I meant."

He grinned. "Duchesses are mad about me."

"Yes, and she told me why. You saved the Duke's life. You were very brave to help him, very heroic. Tell me what happened?"

He shrugged. "It was years ago, lass, and it doesna merit the telling. I came upon three men attacking one and I lent a hand. It was no' an act of heroism. It was an act of courtesy."

"I think you're wonderful. And so do the Duke and Duchess."

He laughed. "I am. But, Mary, what I did was the only thing a decent man could do. Who would walk away from an outnumbered man?"

"Lots of men would."

"Then I dinna want them walking by when I need helping. Remind me of that, will ye, at the appropriate time?"

"I will. I'm sure the Duchess will continue to adore you."

"Aye, but I don't pay attention to other men's wives."

"Not even the ones like Rowena? She is very beautiful."

"Aye." He grinned and suddenly I felt hideously ugly, thinking of the lovely Rowena looking up into his eyes. I tried to smile. His grin faded and he watched me for a moment, then leaned toward me, one arm stretched along the back of the sofa. "Mary," he said, his tone quiet. "Rowena isna a tenth as beautiful as ye. Ye looked verra beautiful last night. Ye looked like a goddess. Ye look like one today." I stared at him. He leaned back against the cushions and then smiled broadly. "But a woman must have more than beauty to recommend her. What are yer talents?"

"Talents?" I looked at him blankly.

He nodded. "Aye. Can ye cook?"

"No."

"Can ye fish?"

"No." I laughed when he shook his head as though that were a serious deficiency.

"Can ye tend cattle?"

"No," I said, laughing harder.

"Can ye sew?"

"Yes. And embroider. And all the needlecrafts."

"Aye, well, I canna picture Rowena with a needle in her hand. So ye see, yer ahead of her there too."

"And what are your talents?" I said, feeling much better. "Besides reading French and having duchesses and cats adore you?"

"I can skip a stone on the loch seven times."

"That's very important."

"It is when yer ten and yer cousin's fifteen and he canna."

"Angus?"

"Aye. It bothers him still, no doubt. Dinna shame him by asking." He shook his head as though it were a sad thing, but his eyes were laughing. "I canna think of any other talents."

"Can you cook?"

"Aye." He was watching my lips.

"You can? What can you cook?"

"Whatever I can catch. If I'm hungry I find a way to cook it."

"Don't they feed you at home?"

"I'm not talking about when I'm home."

"Oh. Well, can you sew?"

"No, but with a plaid ye don't need to. Ye just need to know how to fold cloth. I can do that."

"Can you fish?"

"Aye. Ye dinna grow up on the water and not know how to fish."

"Can you tend cattle?"

He laughed ruefully. "I have done it, but I'm not good at it. I get bored."

"Then you do have some talents to recommend you as a woman."

"Oh, those were womanly virtues?"

"They were when you were asking me."

"No, actually," he said, his voice growing husky, "I was wondering if I might hire ye for Kilgannon. Ye have the look of a fisherman about ye." He put the cat on the floor.

"I'm not for hire," I said primly, smoothing my skirts.

"Aye." He leaned toward me again, his eyes dark. "I think I'd have to marry ye." His face had almost reached mine when the door flew open and Ellen entered with a tray. Alex sprang up, standing a foot from the sofa.

"I brought you some tea. Madam said to interrupt you," Ellen said cheerfully, her eyes missing nothing. She set the tray on the table before the sofa while Alex withdrew to the window.

"It's stopped raining," he said.

"Oh, yes, sir, ages ago," answered Ellen, and giggled as she crossed the room. "You were probably not looking out the window." She closed the door behind her. Alex turned from the window with a smile, and I returned it as I watched him approach. If he'd asked me to fly away with him at that moment I would have said yes.

"There are three cups," he said, pointing to the tray. "That means Louisa will be here soon. We'd best be well behaved." He sat in a chair at the end of the sofa, but a moment later sprang up and came back to me, sitting where he had been before. He put one hand behind my back, wrapped the other in my hair, and pulled me to him. "Before we're interrupted again, lass," he said, and kissed me, gently, and then again, more insistently. I had been kissed before, but not like this. His lips were soft and I yielded to him as I had never done with another. What was it about this man that affected me so? My head was spinning, but somewhere in the back of my mind a little voice was shouting a victory song. He paused and smiled, and I looked into his eyes and willed him to kiss me again.

"I've wanted to do that since the first time I saw ye," he said quietly as he pulled a strand of my hair over my shoulder and rubbed it between his fingers. "Yer hair is like silk. I knew it would be." He kissed me again. I put my arms around his shoulders to hold him to me, but he was already drawing away, and I watched him go to stand again at the window while I wondered what had gone wrong. At last he turned to me with a wry smile. "Mary, forgive me. I have overstepped myself."

I paused, then shook my head. "No, Alex, you have not."

He looked at me for a long moment. "Yer a one, Mary Lowell," he whispered. "What will I do with ye?"

"You'll think of something," I said, and his smile in return was radiant. *Dear God,* I thought, *he lights the room.*

The door opened then and Louisa entered, looking from one of us to the other. We spent the next half hour discussing English and Scottish politics over tea. Mostly I listened, thinking of his kisses and the feel of his shoulders under my hands, the way his eyes had closed as he leaned in to me. I wanted to pull him to me and kiss him again. I watched his lips as he spoke and tried to focus my attention on the discussion. Soon Will and Betty joined us, and the conversation became general. Betty pouted quietly except when addressed. Alex was subdued but behaved like a gentleman. I acted like a ninny. I could not concentrate and answered all the wrong questions. Alex watched me and wrestled with a smile. At last he pleaded business concerns and excused himself. Will walked him out and a moment later returned, saying he was going with Alex to the wharves to see Alex's brig. He ran out to join Alex like a small boy.

I sat listlessly while Louisa and Betty talked about clothes, and at last I excused myself to walk in the gardens. The fresh air did not help. I could not focus my thoughts, or rather, I could not unfocus my thoughts. I felt like a fifteen-year-old. I told myself I was being an idiot, but I kept remembering his kisses.

The day dragged toward evening and at last Will returned, fired with enthusiasm about Alex's ship. Apparently the brig was one of several, and these were Alex's trading vessels.

"He's leaving in two days for the Low Countries," my brother said, beaming. "He says he'll bring back chocolate for you."

I did not hear what else Will said. Alex would be gone in two days. I could not believe he had not told me. Robert, Louisa was saying, had written and invited us to dine with him and his mother in two days. In two days, I thought, Alex would be gone. A week ago I hadn't known him, and now his departure left me lonely. I told myself I was ridiculous and tried to listen to the others.

The next day dragged endlessly. Louisa, Betty, and I had a full schedule, calling on friends in the morning and visiting the landscaper Louisa had employed for her new garden in the afternoon. I thought the gardens lovely as they were, but Louisa wanted them renovated for Randolph's return. Randolph probably would not even notice. I truly tried to pay attention to the conversations around me, but everywhere I turned I saw a tall blond man with a radiant smile. Could he really be leaving without a farewell? I must be the greatest fool ever born or, perhaps even worse, just one more in his list of conquests. I would forget him, I decided, and if I ever met him again I'd pretend I couldn't remember his name.

Tired of the endless floral discussions, I waited on the steps outside the landscaper's office for Louisa's carriage. Louisa and Betty were still inside, and I knew I'd have several moments before they joined me. I looked idly up the street. And saw Alex. At first I thought I'd imagined him but soon realized he was actually there as he walked toward the office, his shoulders swaying with his long steps. He wore the hat with feathers today, and his hair, loose under the hat, shone like a flame against the gray wall behind him. He did not look like an Englishman. He moved easily through the crowd of people in the street. Many gave a second glance at the tall man in strange clothes, but he seemed unaware of their interest. And then, as if he felt my gaze, he saw me and grinned. He stopped on the step below, sweeping his hat off and bowing. "Good day to ye, Mary. How are ye this afternoon?" He seemed very pleased.

Be composed, I told myself. *It's only a chance meeting.* "I'm fine, thank you, sir. And you?"

"Delighted to see ye waiting on the step for me."

"I am not waiting for you, Alex," I said crisply. "What are you doing here?"

"Coming to find ye, lass." He grinned up at me.

"How did you know where we were?"

"Yer brother. He's a great source of information." Alex stepped up to the stair I was on. The green of my dress was the same as his kilt, and he smelled like soap. I took a deep breath. So much for my nonchalance. Before I could gather my thoughts he opened the door and spoke to someone for a moment, then returned and, catching hold of my elbow, began to guide me down the stairs.

"What are you doing?" I asked, although it was obvious.

"Borrowing ye for an hour or two. I just left word with the girl to tell Louisa. Yer waiting on the stair made it vastly easier to spirit ye away, and I'm grateful for yer cooperation."

I stopped. "Alex, I can't. Louisa will be furious. She'll say you've compromised my reputation. You will have."

"Nonsense," he protested. "There's nothing wrong with a walk in the middle of the day in a crowded city. How can I possibly do anything to ye in a crowd? Forget yer reputation. Yer own view of yerself is more important than others' view of ye, lass." I shook my head. "Mary," he said, his tone earnest now. "Listen to me. I leave tomorrow for the Continent. I couldna leave without talking to ye one more time. That's all I ask, just a walk in the middle of the day. I'm not going to cosh ye on the head and drag ye off to my lodgings."

"Louisa—"

"Louisa kens me better. Come, lass, I just wanted an hour with ye." He looked at me and then grinned. "Here are yer choices: my lodgings, willing or no, or a quiet walk through the streets of London with witnesses." He was laughing now, and after a moment so was I. *Damn the consequences,* I thought, and I took his arm.

FIVE

As WE WALKED, ALEX ASKED ABOUT MY DAY AND LIS-
tened attentively, though I knew he couldn't possibly be
interested. Still, his courtesy was charming. When we passed
a park he led me into it and stopped under a tree, gesturing
up at it with a smile. "How do ye like my lodgings?" he
asked with a grin.

I laughed at him. "You're living in a tree?"

"No, but I thought if I took ye somewhere without walls
ye might be less suspicious of me." His expression changed
from merry to unreadable, and when he spoke again his tone
was quiet. "I'll not harm ye, Mary Lowell, nor would I ever
force ye. Ye can trust me." He sighed and crossed his arms
over his chest. "Of course, that's just what I would say if I
had evil intentions, is it not? How do I let ye know I'm
trustworthy?" I looked at his worried expression, at the way
the vest emphasized the lines of his body and the way his
hair lay against the soft wool of the plaid.

"If I did not think you were trustworthy, Alex Mac-
Gannon," I said softly, "I would not be here with you now,
compromising my reputation."

Alex smiled. "Aye, well, there is that." He let his arms fall
from his chest and straightened his shoulders. "Well, now
that yer reputation is irrevocably compromised, what else
d'ye suppose I can get ye to do, Miss Lowell?" he asked, his
tone lively again.

"I think that's sufficient, Lord Kilgannon."

"Aye, probably," he said, nodding. "Just as well, since I'd have to admit I have no lodgings."

"Where do you live?" I gestured to the tree. He shook his head. "Then where are you staying?"

"On my brig."

"On your ship?"

"Aye," he said, his eyes lighting up. "Do ye want to see it?"

"Won't that compromise me further?"

"Not if I don't take ye belowdecks. Besides, Angus and Matthew are there. They can be yer chaperons."

I laughed and waved a finger at him. "Oh, yes, Alex, that would be grand. I'll explain to Louisa that since I did not think it proper to be alone with one man, I was alone with three. I'm sure she'd agree I acted most wisely."

"There's a lot more than three men. The whole crew should be coming back by now."

"Even better. What more fitting place to ensure my reputation than a shipload of men?"

He frowned, his disappointment obvious. "Yer right. I canna take ye there." He glanced around. "Well, I'm hungry. Surely there's a place we can eat without me having to marry ye first."

"We wouldn't want that."

"Not before I eat."

"Let's go toward Westminster," I suggested. "At the worst you can get something from one of the street vendors."

He grinned as we walked away. "Aye, that should impress ye fully, no? We could stand on the side of the street and eat with our hands. Yer fine Robert Campbell would do the same, no doubt."

"Alex, he's not my Robert Campbell, and I don't need to be further impressed. You are quite impressive as is."

"Oh, aye? Well . . ." For once he was speechless, and I laughed as we threaded our way through the crowded streets.

"I did it to you," I said.

"What? What did ye do?"

"Made you speechless. You do it to me all the time."

He grinned. "It's fun, no? I like to see yer eyes widen and ye start to speak and then get all red."

"Makes me sound lovely."

"Ye are, Mary. With yer dark hair and pale skin it is quite lovely to watch ye change color. I could watch ye all day." He fought his smile. "Or all night." I felt my cheeks redden, and he roared. I shook my head at him with a smile.

We wandered through the streets without direction. I could not think of another man with whom I had been so relaxed. Will, of course, but he was my brother. At one point a carriage came closer than it should have, and Alex grabbed my arm and pulled me into a doorway next to him. Except for that moment he did not touch me at all, but we were comfortable together. We bypassed the chocolate houses where someone might know me and found a small inn that looked respectable. Alex had his food at last and I had tea. I watched the girl pour and looked through the steam at him.

"How exactly am I to explain this to Louisa?"

"Well," he said, tearing a piece of bread off the loaf between us. "Given a wee bit of luck, ye'll have little explaining to do."

"What does that mean?"

"It means that supposedly Will took ye off and the two of ye will return home together. He'll have more explaining to Betty than ye'll have to Louisa."

"And Will agreed to this?"

"Obviously." He looked at me over his cup as he drank. "Of course, he did threaten to kill me if I touched ye, so ye'll please tell him I dinna overstep myself." I tried not to smile. And failed. "Aye. Ye laugh, but I respect that. I'd do the same to any man coming after my sister."

"I see." I laughed at him.

"I doubt that ye do, but never mind that now. I've got yer company for an hour or two and I'm content."

"And I yours."

He leaned back in his chair and watched me. "Is that good?"

"Alex, I've sacrificed my reputation for two hours with you."

"I'm worth the sacrifice." He grinned and I laughed again.

"So you say. Now, tell me, when you stuck your head in the landscaper's door, did you say you were my brother?"

"No, I said ye were leaving with yer brother and to please tell the Countess." He took another piece of bread.

"You were masquerading as Will?"

"No." He shook his head. "I doubt that anyone would take me for yer brother. I was masquerading as yer brother's messenger."

"And when Louisa discovers the messenger was a man wearing a hat with eagle feathers, she'll have no idea who it could be."

"The girl dinna even notice me."

"Oh, no. Tall blond Scotsmen wearing Highland clothes are an everyday occurrence at a London landscaper's office."

He frowned. "Details. And it's not a hat. It's a bonnet."

"It's a hat." I picked it up from the chair between us.

"Bonnet," he said, and took another bite of bread.

"It matches your plaid."

"This is a *feileadh beag*," he said.

"Same thing."

"No, nine feet different." At my expression he laughed. "A *feileadh moh* is a plaid. Eighteen feet long. Ye pleat it about yer waist and throw the rest over yer shoulder. And when it's cold or it rains ye put it over yer head or wrap it about yerself."

"And what are you wearing?"

"A *feileadh beag*. A kilt. The top is separate. It's easier to wear. I can take the top off and still be decent."

"Well," I said, sipping the last of my tea. "I like it on you. Ye have lovely knees," I teased, mocking his accent. He laughed and stretched out a leg beside the table.

"Always thought it one of my finer points." He nodded toward the door. "It's raining. We'll have to perfect yer story."

I turned to look at the rain. "How will I meet Will?"

"Matthew will bring him to meet us. With the rain we'll have to revise how yer getting home. We have," he said, fishing a pocket watch from the pouch at his waist, "an hour left."

I sat back in my chair. One hour. "How long will you be gone?"

"About ten days, then back for two, then I leave again."

"I see."

His eyes met mine. "I'm not pleased about it, lass," he said quietly, "but it was decided upon long ago."

We were silent for a while as he ate. Much as I wanted to beg him to stay, I couldn't, and I searched for another topic for conversation. "Alex," I said at last, "how did you learn English?"

He shrugged. "I was raised speaking Gaelic and English. Some—well, most—of the people in the Highlands speak only Gaelic, but English is the language of power. We spoke English at home."

"And French? How did you learn that?"

"A tutor. And travel. Necessity as well. I spent a year in Paris when I was sixteen. And I trade with France."

"We're at war with France."

He paused, then spoke. "England is at war with France."

"But our countries are united now. It's been five years."

"United, aye, but we're no' the same." He paused, looking at his food, then back at me, his expression guarded. "The Union doesna sit well in most of Scotland, lass. There's many that think Scotland was sold to the English for the money, and I'm one of them. When the Union began we were told that there would be no tariffs on malt and linens and salt, but there are now, and taxes on my land and everything I sell. I have to pay taxes to keep what I already own. It's been a rough few years, with tariffs restricting what I can sell and taxes taking all the profit. Add that to no representation and it's no' a pretty situation. When ye take away a people's livelihood and their say in government and ye rub their noses in it, it's no' verra wise." He took a drink from his cup.

"So what will happen?"

He leaned back against the chair and looked at me evenly. "In the short run, I don't know. In the long run, England will win."

"Why?"

"Well, study yer history. Look at the Romans. Look at what happened in Ireland. What the English are geniuses at is colonizing. Like the Romans. What do ye do when ye want the land and the people to work for ye, but the land's leaders are against ye? Ye buy what leaders ye can. Those ye canna buy ye remove. When more leaders spring up, ye remove them as well, and this time yer harsher in yer reprisals and ye make communication between factions difficult with yer army in the middle. Then ye take away what means they have of supporting themselves. Now, at the same time, ye prevent them educating their bairns, so they are poor and ignorant. Eventually ye win. If not in that generation, then the next. Ye have to have a large military presence, of course, to make it work. If yer lucky, the leaders will fight amongst themselves. That's what happened in Ireland. If the Irish had united, it might have been a different ending. It's the same in Scotland. If the clans do not unite, eventually we'll be defeated."

"But the Romans never took Scotland," I said, trying to remember my history.

"They never took the Highlands," he growled. "They were all over the Lowlands. But yer right, the Scots pushed them back and did the same to the English under Wallace and Robert the Bruce four hundred years ago. But I dinna think we'll see that again."

"What will you do?"

"Survive. That's why I'm in London, trying to find a way to survive. England is too powerful not to deal with. I dinna

ken what will happen. The way we've dealt with England
before hasna always been successful for Scotland. But that
may change. Who kens, maybe some miracle will occur." I
felt my eyes widen.

"You think James Stewart will return," I said.

He stared at me, his fork halfway to his mouth. "I've not
mentioned the man."

"But you do think he will return."

His tone was cautious. "Until he's dead, that will be a
possibility."

"Will you join him?"

He frowned and shook his head. "I dinna like the man.
To tell the truth, Mary, I dinna like anyone in the government, any government." He called for the girl. "Enough
seriousness. I've a mind to see Westminster Abbey, and it's
near to where we're to meet Will. Does that meet with yer
agreement?" When I hesitated he leaned forward. "I'll keep
ye safe, Mary," he said solemnly. "Are ye willing to go or
shall we stay here until our hour is gone?"

I met his eyes and then smiled. "Since my reputation is in
tatters, why not? All we need to do now is meet someone I
know."

"Dinna say that. I'd have to marry ye at once."

"We wouldn't want that," I said, shaking my head.

"Oh, no." He laughed and leaned forward, whispering.
"I'd have to see yer beautiful face every day. It would be the
first thing I'd see when I opened my eyes." He watched me
redden and he laughed. "I told ye, it's fun to make ye
speechless."

"Alex . . ." I began, quite flustered.

"Do ye find it a repulsive thought?"

I was saved from answering by the arrival of the girl. Alex
pulled his watch out again and consulted it. "That's beautiful," I said, and he handed it to me with a pleased smile.

"I bought it this morning." The watch was a brilliant
gold, the case filigreed with an oak pattern, the face white

with Roman numerals. Today's date was engraved inside the cover.

"Trenchant and Son," I read, glancing at him. The watchmakers were well known for their quality workmanship. I handed it back to him. "It's lovely, Alex," I said. "You have exquisite taste."

He nodded. "Aye, I do. And in watches as well." He took the watch and put it away in the bag at his waist, his color rising. "I felt like celebrating," he said, glancing up at me.

"So do I," I said softly, and felt my own flush.

"Good," he said, standing and wrapping his half plaid around me with a smile. "Then it's as it should be."

Westminster Abbey was quiet, few people present. I showed Alex around and he was an avid student, asking questions and looking everywhere. He was subdued as we walked through the Lady Chapel where queens Elizabeth and Mary Tudor were entombed and where Mary Stuart rested. When we got to the poets' alcove we stopped and I pointed out different poets. I said one of my favorites was John Donne, who was buried at St. Paul's.

"Oh, aye," Alex said. "*No man is an island, unto himself . . .* Good words to live by." He looked down at the stones as we walked. "My favorite poet isna buried here either. Andrew Marvell. Do ye ken his work?" I shook my head. "I'll give ye part of a stanza, lass." He circled me slowly with a half smile, his eyes dark, his voice caressing me. I stared into space as the words poured over me and felt his gaze on each part of me as he spoke. I'd never felt so aware of my own body, nor had my body ever responded so forcefully. I closed my eyes and savored it.

Had we but world enough, and time,
This coyness, lady, were no crime.
We would sit down, and think which way
To walk, and pass our long love's day. . . .

An hundred years should go to praise
Thine eyes, and on thy forehead gaze;
Two hundred to adore each breast,
But thirty thousand to the rest;
An age at least to every part,
And the last age should show your heart.
For, lady, you deserve this state,
Nor would I love at lower rate.
  But at my back I always hear
Time's wingéd chariot hurrying near . . .

"That's the beginning," he said huskily, and was silent so long that I opened my eyes, looking across the dark stones to where he stood in shadow. "I always thought that poem a grand thing to say to a lass, if seduction were yer object."

"Is it your object?" I whispered.

"Well, I wouldna say no." He moved into the light slowly, coming to stand before me with an intent expression. Over his head the arches of the alcove seemed to sway, and he caught my arm as I wavered. I closed my eyes when he pulled me against him. *"An hundred years should go to praise thine eyes,"* he said, and kissed my eyelids softly in turn. *"And on thy forehead gaze."* He kissed my temples, letting his lips rest on my skin for an instant at each. *"Two hundred to adore each breast . . ."* He ran his hands along my shoulders and down my arms, then pulled me closer and kissed my hair. I could feel his body's unmistakable reaction to mine and felt my own tremble in answer. *"For, lady, you deserve this state,"* he whispered. "Och, Mary, I canna . . . but make no mistake, I do want ye." He kissed me with a passion I'd never known, and the world faded. For a few moments we explored each other, then turned as one at a discreet cough behind us. We saw no one there but reluctantly stepped apart, facing each other.

Alex smiled slowly. "I kent it, Mary. We'd not be bored."

I shook my head, unable to answer. No man had ever

spoken to me like this or kissed me like that and I wasn't sure of my reaction. I gestured to the side door, and he followed me without a word through the cloisters and into the street. My mind was in a tumble, and I pressed my swollen lips together. I knew I should have stopped him from touching me so boldly. I had chosen not to.

Outside, the rain had stopped, and I watched steam rise in wavy plumes from the street while he consulted his watch. "We'll have to hurry," he said, leading the way. "Yer brother will be only so tolerant, I'm thinking. I really was well behaved, ye must agree."

"You were outrageous," I said quietly.

"Ye dinna ken my thoughts, lass. I was very well behaved."

I ignored my flush but touched my fingers to my lips and remembered. Alex watched me with a serious expression, and I searched for something to chase the thoughts away from both of us. "You'll be back for only two days? And then leave again?"

"Aye, that's the plan, but I'm going to see what I can do about that. I've already sent Malcolm on ahead to"—he frowned to himself—"to Holland instead of going myself; that's why ye've not met him. Ye will soon enough. I must go myself now."

"You're going to France."

He raised his eyebrows. "Am I?"

I nodded. "Yes. You say you're going to Holland, which you may be, but you're also going to France."

He glowered at me. "Are ye always so damned clever, lass?"

"Sometimes I am very stupid." *And sometimes very foolish,* I thought, then laughed. I felt reckless. And very happy.

"I canna believe that. Yer a clever woman, Mary, and ye make me laugh more than any woman I've met. I enjoy that verra much."

"Don't change the subject. You're going to France. Why?"

He laughed wryly. "Yer also the stubbornest woman I've met."

"Yes, Alex, and you're evasive," I said.

He paused, his eyes a dangerous dark blue. "If we were not in public, Mary Lowell . . ." he said, and started walking again.

"Why are you going to France?" I trotted along behind him.

"Wine."

"Wine?"

"Aye. The English love their claret, even if they're not supposed to buy it because of the war. I bring them their claret. And chocolate from the Low Countries. I'll bring ye chocolate, lass."

"So I will see you again?"

He stopped and turned to me. "That's for ye to decide, Mary. If ye say the word I'll be at yer side the minute I land. If ye say no, I'll not bother ye again. Ye've been most kind."

"I've not been kind at all, Alex. I've enjoyed every minute," I said, and then shook my head. "Well, perhaps not every minute."

He looked worried. "What did ye not enjoy?"

"If you remember, sir, I don't like flirting, and that includes Rowena."

He smiled slowly. "I'll remember that."

"Do you know what she told me?" He shook his head. "She said I should marry Robert and see you on the side."

His eyebrows arched. "What is yer feeling on this suggestion?"

"I'd never be unfaithful to my husband."

"Yer Campbell will be most pleased to hear that."

"Perhaps not." I held his gaze. "But perhaps my husband would be."

He blinked. We walked for another minute in silence.

"Alex?"

"Aye?" He sounded distracted.

"You're right. It is fun." When he looked confused, I smiled up at him. "Speechless."

He shook his head slowly. "Yer a one, Mary Lowell."

"Alex, you did not answer my question. Will I see you again?"

He stopped again. "I told ye, lass. It's yer decision. Do ye wish to see me again, or shall I go away and no' come back?" His hair blew around his shoulders, and the weak sunlight glinted off the tiny golden whiskers on his cheeks. I watched his chest move with his breathing and a vein beat in his neck. How could his eyes be so blue? I wanted to stroke his cheek, to kiss those lips, to hold him against me. Had there ever been a man like this?

"The minute you land, Alex, I'll expect you at my door."

"Mary, ye . . ." I'd not seen Alex flustered, but that's what he appeared to be. "I . . ." He looked at the buildings around us and took a deep breath. "The minute I land, Mary."

I smiled and then jumped as a shrill voice sounded behind me.

"Miss Lowell, how lovely to see you! Who is your friend?"

I turned to see Madeline Shearson, a fearsome gossip, and her daughter, Katherine. When I introduced Alex as the Earl of Kilgannon, Madeline took a closer look. Katherine needed no prompting, simpering as she offered her hand. He bowed over it very properly. The gods were with us that day, for just as I would have had to explain what I was doing alone with a Scottish earl on the streets of London, Will appeared at my side.

"I'm back, Mary," he said cheerfully. "How nice to see you again, Madam Shearson, and the beautiful Miss Shearson. Have you met my friend Kilgannon, who is visiting me from Scotland?"

I gave Will a bright smile and watched as he managed them effectively. Within a moment he had bundled me into a carriage that had appeared at the curb and herded Alex in with us. We waved good-bye to the Shearsons, and Will quickly explained that we were dropping Alex off at the next corner and returning home at once. "We will talk later, Mary," he said, trying to glower at me. I laughed and he looked at Alex. "Kilgannon?"

Alex held up his hands. "I was an angel, Lowell. Ask yer sister. Until the last we had amazing luck. I'm in yer debt, sir."

As the carriage drew to the curb again and stopped, Alex jumped out. "The minute I land, Mary," he said, and closed the door on his smile.

Will raised an eyebrow at me. "I hope I don't regret this."

"I don't, Will," I said with a contented sigh. "Thank you."

My brother frowned.

SIX

THE GODS WERE INDEED WITH US THAT DAY. LOUISA
and Betty hardly mentioned that we'd been gone. Randolph
was coming home, and the house was in an uproar. I swore
to myself that I'd do ten good deeds for this day. It wasn't
until I was alone in my room that I realized I still had the
half plaid. Any other day Louisa would have noticed it
immediately, I thought as I wrapped it around me. The
cloth smelled like Alex, a masculine scent that reminded me
of soap and the sea. My imagination, no doubt, but I liked
the idea. And I liked that Alex talked to me as though I had
a brain. I was weary of being told not to worry about the
things men discussed. No other man I knew included me in
his thoughts the way Alex did. No one.

To my surprise the next few days flew by. Randolph
arrived safely, and Louisa was with him constantly. He was
devoted to her, as usual, which had always surprised me, for
Randolph was often brusque with the rest of the world.
Although he and Louisa had been married for over eight
years, I did not know him well. At first I'd been too young
and then I'd been at Mountgarden while my mother was ill.
In those first years I had resisted Randolph mightily. He was
not my uncle Duncan, and I resented that. I realized now
that my affection for Duncan probably played no small part
in my willingness to consider a Scotsman as a suitor.

But I was not unnoticed. Someone had been telling tales,

and Randolph took his duties as chaperon most seriously. We had a long discussion, during which I argued that I had done nothing untoward at Louisa's party. *All this for some conversation in the dining room,* I thought. What would he say if he discovered I'd seen Alex again and roamed the streets with him? Randolph stumbled through what he thought he needed to tell me, softening it at the end with an apologetic smile. My resentment faded as I watched his faltering attempts at being my uncle. The man meant well, I knew, but he did not need to know what was in my heart. It was enough that I did.

Alone later, I told myself to be sensible and heed Randolph's warnings. I really did not know Alex. I knew how very blue his eyes were, how golden his hair, and how contagious his laughter. He was the most charming companion. *But be realistic,* I scolded myself. *He may never appear at your door again. And that might be for the best.*

Dinner with Robert and his mother was enjoyable, but I kept hearing the echoes of Alex's laughter, and even Robert seemed to notice the difference. He did his best to be engaging and witty, which was unlike Robert, but he had no counterpart. Under other circumstances, I suspected, he and Alex might have been great friends.

At last Rebecca returned from Bath, and I dined twice with her family and Lawrence's. Louisa had, of course, discussed Alex with Becca's mother, Sarah, her closest friend, a strong-willed woman who was no stranger to London's prejudices. Sarah's father-in-law had seriously opposed his son's marriage to "an outsider," as he had called Sarah, but Rebecca's father had married Sarah despite the opposition and the marriage had been happy. She had been kind to me through the years and tonight greeted me warmly. As I knew she would when the men withdrew, she asked me about Alex. I was only too happy to discuss him, and we talked at length. And I talked of him again with Becca when we were at last alone.

She laughed at me. "I told you he was memorable, Mary,

but honestly! I should never have left you here without me. You should see your expression when you talk about him. You silly goose! What will you do?"

"Wait."

Becca's expression grew worried. "Mary, you're from very different worlds. He's a Scot. If he does come back, are you prepared for what that will mean?"

"What will it mean?" I laughed, but she was serious.

"You know what it will mean. Louisa will not be pleased. Everyone expects you to marry Robert. Are you prepared to marry a stranger and go to Scotland and live there the rest of your life?"

"Becca, I hardly know him! Alex has not asked me to marry him. We have talked a few times, that's all. Besides, I'd not be leaving everything I know as you are. It's not the same at all. Your decision was much larger. Do you not worry about it?"

Rebecca shook her head. "I cannot live without Lawrence, and I will go to where his home is." She sighed. "I'm happy to marry, but I'm not happy to be leaving everything and everyone I know. Mary, who would have expected this? Me going across the Atlantic? I would have thought we'd be in London together the rest of our lives. I thought we'd be like your aunt and my mother, great friends and neighbors, living three houses apart for years. Will we ever see each other again after I leave? Will we still be friends when we are their age? Promise me we will be."

"Becca," I said, embracing her. "Of course we will. We'll always be friends," I said, but I wondered how we could be with thousands of miles between us.

In the next few days we visited with other friends, and they all asked about Alex. When I said he was the handsomest man I'd ever seen, Janice sniffed with distaste, declaring that he was too big and his chin too pointed. "It's uncivilized that he won't wear a wig. He wears those ridiculous clothes and has children. And," she paused for emphasis, "he trades with other countries."

"Indeed he does," I had laughed. "That alone has stopped me from marrying him already." But Janice had not been amused. I sighed and sat quietly, dreaming of Westminster Abbey while she explained yet another reason that Alex was unsuitable.

Nine days went by faster than I could have imagined. Will and Betty went home to Warwickshire as planned. I had been scheduled to go with them but begged to stay in London for another week. On the tenth day I refused all invitations and stayed at home the entire day, pretending to read. No one came to the house, no one brought a message, and I told myself that ten days was how long Alex would be gone. I really couldn't expect to hear anything until the eleventh. On the eleventh day I told myself that I'd hear any moment. On the twelfth I was bursting into tears unexpectedly all day, making speeches in my head and calling myself the world's greatest fool. I was grateful that Will was gone to Mountgarden, for he'd have something to say to me about this. Late that afternoon, with both Louisa and Randolph gone, I walked aimlessly in the gardens and turned at the sound of shoes on gravel to see Bronson approaching me. He wordlessly handed me a letter, his disapproval obvious. I did not recognize the writing, but the note carried the MacGannon crest, and as Bronson left I ripped it open.

It was not from Alex. Angus had written to me instead, giving his apologies. Alex, he wrote, was ill and not able to visit me. He would call on me when he returned to London. I read the note four times before I started crying, and then it took me an hour to decide what to do. I reasoned that the situation was one of two. Either Alex was indeed ill or he was avoiding me. Whichever it was, I decided, I would see him and find out.

I ran the three houses to Becca's and pounded on the door. If I'd been entirely rational I would have been more circumspect, I'm sure, but that was beyond me at that moment. Her parents were with Louisa and Randolph, and Lawrence was somewhere with his family, so she was alone. When I explained what had happened and what I proposed to do, she argued with me. I burst into tears. Within minutes we were heading for the docks. I'd insisted that she stay behind, but she'd refused, stating firmly that either she came along or I had no carriage. I knew my reputation would indeed be in tatters if we were discovered and was willing to take the risk myself, but I did not want Becca to suffer in any way for my indiscretion. We argued as we drove.

After some reluctant searching, Rebecca's man discovered the *Gannon's Lady*, which I knew must be the ship. I ran down the dock, heedless of the curious looks from the sailors, and was about to run up the gangplank when I was stopped by an imperious voice asking us what we were doing. Becca, close behind me, bumped into me, and by the time we had sorted ourselves out a familiar laugh rang out above us. I froze: Alex was laughing at us. Dear God, he was well and I was indeed the world's greatest fool. I looked up and into blue eyes, but they were not his, and I said a quick prayer of thanks as I watched the man. He was like Alex, but different. Alex was tall and lean, with wide shoulders and a trim waist, and this man was tall and square. His chest was wide, his face very like Alex's, but fuller. It was an interesting mix of features. If I had not known Alex so well I might have taken this man for him.

"You must be Malcolm," I said, my voice sounding much calmer than I felt. His surprise was evident.

"And ye can only be the Miss Lowell my brother talks about every minute." He smirked. I disliked him at once. Something in the way he'd said that—so contemptuous of Alex—and the way he looked at Rebecca and me made me distrust him immediately.

I drew myself upright and in my most patrician voice said, "I am. Please take me to Kilgannon. At once." I put my foot on the gangplank and he called out to someone behind him.

As I climbed, my progress hampered by my skirts and the swaying of the gangplank, Angus's face appeared over the rail of the ship. He said something in Gaelic, which I assumed was a curse and was grateful that I did not understand. He moved to the top of the gangplank and glowered down at me. "Mary Lowell, what are ye doing here? Have ye lost yer mind, lass?"

"Not yet, Angus," I said as I reached the deck. Becca stopped by my side. Angus glared from under his eyebrows while Malcolm stood next to him, examining us. Behind them I could see the sailors, some looking worried, some laughing. They looked like very ordinary men, most dressed in Highland fashion. They did not seem threatening. The two in front of us, however, were another story.

Angus frowned. "Did ye no' get my note, Mary?"

"Yes, Angus, of course," I said. "How else did I know to come here?" I looked behind him. "Now, please let me see Alex."

"Ye canna see him, lass. Go home. At once."

"I will not. I came to see Alex and I will see him."

Angus turned to Becca, who met his glance with an anxious expression, her enthusiasm for this adventure obviously ebbing. "Miss, can ye not take yer friend home where she belongs? It's a foolish thing for ye to be doing. Go home."

I answered before Rebecca could. My heart was pounding and I was as unsure of our situation as she, but I would not let them see that. "I will not go home, Angus. If Alex is ill I will see him."

Angus shook his head. "He is too ill to see ye, lass." He turned to Becca again. "She has no sense. Take her home."

"I will not go," I said. "And if you do not show me which is Alex's cabin, I will wander around until I find it." I moved toward the stairs that led belowdeck, but Angus placed himself squarely in front of me. Behind me, Malcolm laughed.

"Can ye do nothing?" Angus asked Rebecca.

"You might have noticed, sir," said Becca, sounding

much calmer than she looked, "that Miss Lowell is quite headstrong."

I shot her a look of displeasure. "Determined," I said.

"Foolish," Angus said, annoyed. "Mary, do ye no' ken that this is no' a place for a woman like ye?"

"Angus." I lowered my voice so that only he could hear. "If Alex is ill, I will see him. If he is not ill and does not want to see me, I would know that too. I need to know."

His eyes widened in surprise, but he answered me in a quieted voice. "How could ye think that, lass? Alex would never lie to ye, nor would I. I wrote ye the truth of it. He is ill, lass."

"Then all the more reason for me to be here. I will see him. Please."

He nodded. "So be it, lass. But it's ye who will answer to him, not I. Alex will no' be pleased by this."

I did not answer as I followed him belowdecks, though my heart was hammering, and I exchanged a look with wide-eyed Becca. She trailed behind us without a word, but I imagined she'd have much to say to me later. The boat swayed with the movement of the water as we descended, and I gripped the rope railing. Belowdecks the light was dim, but the brig seemed clean and tidy, the smell of cooking wafting through the deck. Angus led the way along a short passage and stopped to knock on a door. Malcolm joined us, standing behind Rebecca. There was no answer to Angus's knock and he opened the door, placing his hand in front of me to prevent me from entering.

"Wait a moment, lass. He's probably sleeping." He disappeared into the dark cabin and closed the door behind him. We waited in silence until he reappeared, a lit lamp in his hand. "He's asleep. Ye may come in to assure yerself he is ill, and then ye must leave."

I followed him into the cabin. It was a small space with three berths lining the walls. Angus hung the lamp on a hook where it lit the room with a warm glow. In the middle of the cabin was a desk and a chair, charts rolled on the desk.

On the far side of the cabin, in the middle of the berth, Alex was asleep, on his back, his chest and shoulders naked, the bedcovers at mid-chest. Behind me Rebecca gasped, but I looked only at Alex. He was indeed ill. His skin was gray and the smell of sickness permeated the cabin. I knelt beside him and felt his forehead. It was much too warm. I felt slightly dizzy as I smoothed the hair back from his face. The beginnings of a beard were on his sunken cheeks, his breathing was shallow and his skin clammy. "How long has he been like this?" I asked Angus as he came to my side.

"Three days," he said. "Most of the time he sleeps, but when he wakes he vomits. Lass, ye must go now."

"Have you called a doctor?"

"No. He'll be a'right in a day or so."

I pulled the cover to Alex's shoulders and he stirred under my touch, opening his eyes one at a time. He looked at me and closed his eyes again, then reopened them. "Mary?" he asked, his voice weak. He struggled to sit up, the bedclothes sliding to his waist, exposing a golden-haired chest and a taut stomach. I rose and stood next to the berth, my knees suddenly weak. Even as ill as he was, he was extraordinary. Alex looked behind me. "What the devil? . . ." He sounded very tired.

"I couldna stop her, Alex," said Angus over my shoulder. "She's a headstrong lass with no common sense at all." He added something in Gaelic. Alex looked from Angus to me, frowning.

"I came to see if I could help," I said.

Alex sighed. "I'll live, lass, but ye should not be here."

"You need a doctor."

He shook his head slowly. "No, no. I'll be fine as soon as I can stop quoting Latin." He pulled the bedclothes tighter around his waist and looked at all of us. "A very strange group to waken to, I'm thinking," he said, rubbing his hand across his forehead. "Angus, will ye find my shirt, please?" Angus moved to my right and handed Alex the shirt off the shelf next to me. Alex struggled into it as we all watched him.

"Alex," I said, "you're feverish. You've been sick for days and now you're making no sense."

"Mary," he said, with a ghost of his normal tone, "I just awoke and we're having a party. I think I'm making fine sense."

"Quoting Latin?"

His mouth twitched and he waved at Angus and Malcolm. "Well, lass, ye ken what Julius Caesar said when he dinna like a place?"

"I have no idea," I said briskly. "Alex—"

The three men chanted in one voice. *"Vene vici vomiti."*

Malcolm and Angus laughed and Alex smiled while Becca and I exchanged looks of wonder. I shook my head at them and leaned over Alex, opening the window above the berth. "Very clever. We're getting a doctor. Perhaps for all of you. Becca," I said, turning, "send your man for Dr. Sutter. He's the only one I can think of who will come here." I looked at Alex's brother. "Malcolm, go with him to bring the doctor back."

"Aye, Yer Majesty," Malcolm said, but followed as Rebecca scurried out of the cabin.

Alex watched me through narrowed eyes, then rubbed his forehead again with a slow movement. "Mary, ye smell like roses. But what are ye doing here? Angus, what is she doing here?"

I spoke first. "I came to see if you were ill."

"Do I look ill to ye?"

"Yes, you do. What happened?"

"I have no idea," he said. "Ate something bad or . . ." He shrugged. Behind me Angus had made a sharp movement as Alex spoke. Alex, visibly weary, closed his eyes again. I glanced at Angus, his expression grim. Something was not right here. I wasn't being told everything and was very glad we had a doctor coming. Becca returned after a few moments, saying that Malcolm had gone for Dr. Sutter. I thanked her and smiled, then moved Alex's clothes and sat on the shelf next to the bed while Angus hovered behind me, clearly unhappy. Alex opened his eyes and looked at me. "Mary, lass, ye must go. Yer reputation will truly be compromised if this is discovered."

"Hush, Alex," I said. "I'll go when I know you're getting good care. And not before." He nodded and drifted into sleep. I turned to see Angus watching me gravely, and I raised my chin. We waited in silence. I looked at Alex as he dozed, seeing how shallow his breathing was. He must be very weakened to sleep so easily, I thought, and he was much too ill for having had one bad meal. He stirred again, opened his eyes, and rubbed his forehead.

"Does your head hurt?" I asked him, brushing his hair back.

"Aye, a bit. I'm just verra tired, Mary."

"When did you eat last?"

He looked at me through half-closed eyes. "I canna eat. I canna keep anything down. I'll just sleep until it's better. Mary, lass, dinna talk about food just now."

"Oh! I'm sorry," I said, abashed. "I didn't think."

He shook his head. "No, I'm the sorry one. I dinna mean to worry ye. I was going to see ye the minute I landed. Did ye remember us saying that?"

"Yes." That was understating it nicely.

"My stomach had other plans. France dinna agree with me."

"See, you should not have left London." I tried to keep my tone light. A rumble of laughter came from him.

"Aye, that must be it," Alex said, and the next moment was asleep. I watched his gray face, his eyelashes dark on his pale cheeks, and prayed for his recovery, but I was interrupted when Angus took my arm and led Becca and me into the passage.

"Well, Miss Mary Lowell," Angus said, closing the cabin door, "are ye satisfied? Is he indeed ill?"

"You should have gotten a doctor two days ago."

"Alex would have none of it." He gestured to the stairs. "Wait above 'til the doctor comes. I'll not argue with ye again, lass."

We waited on deck, Rebecca and I silent as we huddled together, ignoring the curious glances of the crew. No one spoke to us. At last Dr. Sutter arrived with Malcolm, who looked irritated. We sat where we were while Angus and Malcolm went below with the doctor, and after what seemed like an eternity Dr. Sutter returned to us, Angus behind him. "How is he?" I asked.

"He'll live," Dr. Sutter said. "I've given him some medication that will quiet his stomach, but I'd like to know what really—" He glanced at Angus. "Watch him closely, Mac-Gannon. If he is not better tomorrow, call for me. And if anyone else becomes ill, then I'll admit I'm mistaken."

"Yer not," said Angus grimly, and the two men exchanged a look.

Before I could ask what they meant, Dr. Sutter turned to Rebecca and me. "What are you two young ladies doing here?"

"I was concerned about Lord Kilgannon," I said.

The doctor spoke very quietly. "Are you staying on this boat?"

"No," roared Angus.

"Oh, no," Rebecca cried. "Dr. Sutter, we arrived shortly before you did. There has been no improper behavior."

The doctor nodded. "That's what the gentleman below assured me as well, and I assured him I would have you leave with me. Now."

We did. He lectured us all the way home.

It was too much to ask to have gotten away with that. I spent hours closeted with Louisa and Randolph and still more with them and Rebecca's parents. Even Dr. Sutter was brought in to bear witness. The Inquisition must have been more fun. Louisa cried and I felt dreadful for having caused all the commotion, although I steadfastly maintained my innocence. And Becca's. I established immediately that all blame was mine, that she had been an unwilling companion, and that we had done nothing wrong. But I knew I had shocked them. Proper young women did not behave as I had, and I had no reasonable explanation. How could I tell them that I had felt that I must see Alex again, that I was so attracted to this man that I would risk my reputation and my future just for one more hour with him, that I had to know if he were deceiving me? My own feelings made little sense to me, and I knew that knowledge of them would only further damage me in their eyes. When I was with Alex it seemed so right to be with him, and although he had not been pleased, Angus had not treated me like a fool. The Scots had treated me with courtesy, and I admitted to myself with chagrin that I had relied on that courtesy. If they had not been the gentlemen I believed them to be, this might have had a very different ending. But I'd had to know how Alex was. I had to know.

It was concluded by the men after an interesting discussion that I had not lost my virtue. I tried to keep my temper. *This would have been a lot quicker,* I thought, *if they had asked me.* They determined that I was simply a misguided young woman. Becca's mother, Sarah, watched me, saying little, and I wondered how much of my true motives she suspected. She never said anything about the incident to me after that day, but something in her manner made me realize that she knew far more about my state of mind than I said.

By morning, judgment had been delivered. I was being packed off to Will and Betty at Mountgarden immediately. That suited me. Alex would be leaving soon, so what was the point of staying in London? I had no chance to speak to Becca in person, but I wrote to her to thank her and to apologize for causing all of this furor. Lawrence visited me the day we left with news of her, his manner distant. He made me well aware that he thought I was foolish and headstrong. Of course, I did not learn until months later that he, with Randolph and Becca's father, had gone that night to the brig and insisted upon meeting with Alex and Angus. Apparently, Alex's condition and their explanations assuaged his feelings of outrage.

Warwickshire was beautiful in the summer, abloom and fragrant. Mountgarden had been our father's and it was Will's now, but he swore that it would be my home as long as I lived. How I loved this house, I thought, as we arrived. Its elegant lines were graceful and without extensive decoration. Symmetrical and rectangular, it was situated on a small mount from which it drew its name and from which it dominated the woods and pasturelands around it. Built with comfort in mind, it embraced me as I entered its halls. I sighed. Home. Not mine, but still home. Not a bad place to be in exile.

Will had been very angry at my actions, and we sat in our father's office and argued heatedly. He was furious with me for risking myself in such a manner and lectured me fiercely. I might be quiet with my aunt and uncle, but I roared back at Will. I told him that I had done nothing to embarrass either myself or him, but that I had to see Alex again, whether it made sense or not. I told him that I'd truly been worried about Alex and of my fears that Alex had not wanted to see me again. He became surprisingly understanding then, as if he'd played his role of protector well enough and now could simply be my brother. He was not happy with my judgment, but he understood my motives. At last he sighed and smiled, the Will I'd grown up with once again.

"Mary," he said, "since I met Betty, there has never been another woman in the world for me. Both you and I know that she's silly and vain and sometimes incredibly witless, but most of the time she makes me feel very important and loved. I don't want any other woman on earth, so I understand why you went to see him. But you were still wrong." He nodded as though he were sixty years older than me instead of two. "You were very foolish."

I nodded and he beamed at me. *Dear Will*, I thought, *dear, sweet, underestimated Will*. Everyone else was worried about money or position, but Will wanted a silly woman to make him feel good, and he had her. Who's to say who was the wiser?

In the next few weeks I had plenty of leisure in which to think. I conceded to myself that I had been both fortunate and foolish. It might have not been my brightest idea to visit a man I did not know well on board his boat and put my well-being and that of my best friend completely in his hands. Still, I was very glad I had gone, if for no other reason than that I was convinced that Dr. Sutter had saved Alex's life, and without my visit Dr. Sutter would not have been called. Even if I never saw Alex again, I had the memories, although I did blush every time I recalled them. I determined that I must have some coarse blood in what was supposed to be a very patrician lineage. I had kissed him without shame, and when I had seen Alex lying naked in that berth I'd wanted to climb into it with him. Surely a gentlewoman would not have such thoughts. Was this how women of low repute began their careers? I would have to guard my virtue from myself.

At least my foolish trip had taught me that Alex was not leading me on. What would happen now I could only guess.

But nothing happened.

SEVEN

FOUR WEEKS PASSED AND MOUNTGARDEN LULLED ME INTO its sleepy life. Will and Betty were in their own world, spending most of the day together and often disappearing in the evenings. While envious, I was also glad that Will was enjoying his marriage. I spent days sorting out the accounts, glad of the diversion and enjoying the work. Will and I shared the secret that I kept the accounts and he took the credit. We were both content with our agreement.

Louisa and Randolph came to visit often and I was pleased to see them, even when Louisa explained that if the story of my unseemly behavior were to seep out, no man would marry me and I would be shunned as a fallen woman forever. I pointed out to her that bundling me off to the country would only cause more talk. Louisa explained that it was still summer. Few people were in London and no one noted that I was gone. She said I had been extremely foolish and would stay in the country until I fully understood what I had done.

Rebecca and her family, with Lawrence in tow, came to visit as well. At first Lawrence watched me as though I would lead Becca astray under his nose, but he eventually thawed when I told him I knew I'd been imprudent but that I had been worried about Alex. He willingly believed that I was foolish and naive but would not feel comfortable with the idea that I had been aware of the rules of society as I was breaking them. So I didn't tell him. Becca was wonderful and I realized again how very much I would miss her. Her marriage was fast-approaching, and Louisa had at last told me that I could return to London for the wedding. To my amusement, it had been Randolph who had been my champion. After lecturing me thoroughly on the evils of men and the dangers likely to befall young women who were foolish enough to be alone with them, Randolph told me that I was a lively girl. He called Alex "that Scotsman." When I explained that Robert was Scottish as well, Randolph amazed me by saying that he thought Robert too cautious. I threw my arms around him and surprised a grin out of him. Things were much better between us after that evening, and I began to know my uncle.

Robert arrived and was charming, but formal again. I never knew whether he had been told of my visit to Alex's ship, and I did not tell him now, but I found myself wondering disloyally if he would ever do something impulsive. I thought not. I missed Alex so much. How could a stranger find his way into my mind so often? I haunted the gardens and grounds, hearing his laughter echo in my head, feeling the empty space beside me. I revisited our every moment together over and over. I slept with the half plaid thrown over my bed and dreamed of a blond man leaning to kiss me.

As the sixth week began I reluctantly faced the fact that I would never see Alex again. No doubt my brash behavior had repulsed him. I told myself that I was the greatest fool ever born. I threw myself into working on the accounts and my mother's roses and kept busy with neighbors and the village. The weather, which had been fine for weeks, now turned cooler each day, the last of the summer dying and with it part of me. I spent much time alone in the garden, and that's where I was when Alex's letter came.

It was addressed to Louisa's London house, and who knew how long it had taken to reach me. Louisa and Randolph were in Berkshire with Randolph's sister, so someone else in the London house had forwarded it to me. Surely not that odious Bronson. It must have been Ellen. I held the letter with trembling hands before opening it. Alex would no doubt be telling me that it had been lovely to meet me, but had he mentioned that he was marrying next week? I unfolded the letter. It was dated two weeks after I had seen him, and I took a deep breath. *My dear Mary,* he had written. Of course, I told myself, a proper salutation. I must not read more into it. He was not actually saying that I was dear to him.

I am writing from Kilgannon. I have recovered from my illness, except for a very strange dream I keep having in which a beautiful woman is leaning over my berth, telling me to eat and summoning doctors. Mary, what were you thinking to come to the brig? I fear for your reputation and I fear I am indeed the barbarian, for I am grateful you came. Thank you for your concern and thank your Dr. Sutter for his help. How have you been? Have you had any consequences of your visit? I wish I could have accompanied you and explained to your aunt and uncle. I'm sorry I was not with you and you had to face them alone.

We left London the day after your visit for Ireland and then home. It is good to see Kilgannon again and my sons, who seem to have grown considerably in my absence. All is well here and the last of the summer is very beautiful, but I miss you very much. Do you ever think of me? If so, please write to me and tell me of your life. If you do not, please forgive me for once again overstepping myself. I remain yours, Alexander MacGannon.

I hugged the letter to my breast and did a whirl. I wrote to him that night, trying to duplicate his tone, keeping my comments about the inquisition light, and explaining that I was now at Mountgarden. I sang as I sealed the letter.

We wrote to each other for three months. It seemed that he wrote to me immediately each time, for the time between letters grew shorter and shorter. As did the days. By November I was back in London with Louisa and Randolph, and I was in everyone's good graces again. Rebecca's wedding had been wonderful. As Becca and Lawrence drove away to begin their wedding journey, I stood with her mother in the cold air, both of us in tears, and wondered how I could live in London without Becca and her laughter. I would miss her terribly, but even were she to stay, I knew we'd reached a milestone at which our relationship would never be the same. She was Lawrence's wife now, and while I was happy for her, I felt the loss of my dear friend grievously.

Alex's letters helped fill the gap. He sent sketches of his sons, who seemed miniature versions of their father, and he sent drawings of Kilgannon. It looked lovely, the castle surrounded by blue water and indigo mountains, but it was difficult to imagine what it would look like in person. His letters were full of his life there, and I learned much about the people. Alex lived with his two sons, Ian and Jamie, and with Angus and Matthew and Angus's mother Deirdre, Malcolm, and assorted cousins of indeterminate degree. As for the rest of the clan, some of them were staff in the household, some tenant farmers, some herders, some fishermen, some sailors. Add to that the necessary mix of smiths, masons, and the other trades, and it was a varied mix of people.

For my part I wrote of my childhood with my parents and Will at Mountgarden, of my parents' deaths, of traveling with Louisa, my life in London before he'd met me, and about my friends and politics. I never mentioned Robert.

Alex told me in every letter how much he missed me and that he thought of me constantly, but he never mentioned love. He wrote that he had no plans to return to London in the near future, although he was doing much traveling. I took a deep breath when I read that. He alluded to some business problems, and I translated them as a shortage of coin. I was a faithful correspondent, but the weeks and then months dragged on, and I asked myself why we were writing if I was never to see him again. He wrote also to Louisa and Randolph, and although I was not privy to the contents, whatever he had written softened their attitudes toward him considerably.

At the same time Robert was becoming much more insistent. He seemed to be confident that Alex was no longer a rival, and although I did tell him that Alex and I were writing, he seemed unperturbed. He astonished me by arranging evenings that were filled with laughter and surprises, and more than once I found myself truly relaxed in his presence. Perhaps Louisa was right that all Robert had needed was the hint of a rival. All of this would have been fine if I had not become so fascinated by Alex. I was afraid that I was unintentionally deceiving Robert and tried to have serious discussions with him about Alex, but he always changed the subject and eventually I got the hint.

And then, without warning, one rainy evening in late November, a case of claret was delivered to Louisa's door, and I knew immediately who it was from. A very proper note accompanied it, which said Alex had returned to London and asked permission to see me. Louisa and Randolph exchanged significant looks and withdrew to discuss it, but whatever their decision, I was determined to see him.

The next morning I sat alone over my breakfast and looked out the dining-room window at the third day of rain, enjoying one more cup of tea and the fact that Alex was in London and I'd see him soon. This morning a note from Robert had arrived and I held it in my hand, but I had little interest in his invitation for us—Will and Betty as well—to visit his estate for his annual Yule parties. Robert's family would be gathering for Christmas in Kent, and they always entertained beforehand. Last year we had attended before retiring to Mountgarden for Christmas. *I'll think about this later,* I thought, and put the note on the table.

"Mary," said a voice I remembered, and I whirled around. Alex filled the doorway, his bonnet in his hand. He wore a Kilgannon kilt and a wide smile, and my heart leapt. "Mary," he said again, and I was out of my chair. He met me halfway across the room and enveloped me in his arms.

"Mary, Mary," he whispered into my hair, then kissed me. I had forgotten how soft his lips were and how hard and lean the rest of his body was. I stroked my hands from his shoulders to his waist, feeling the solidity and strength of him, and when I leaned even closer I felt his body respond to mine as before. His kisses intensified when I arched my neck to receive more, and he laughed deep in his throat as he bent to his task. "I forgot how good it feels to touch ye," he said, and stepped back from me. "How I have missed ye, lass."

"And I you, Alex," I said, and reached for him again. Several moments later, breathless and disarrayed, I withdrew. "A warm welcome, sir. You have quite recovered."

"No, lass, I have the same illness I've have for months now."

"Alex," I began, suddenly worried, "is it your stomach?" I searched his face while he grinned at me.

"Oh, no, my stomach's fine. It's other parts have been aching." I felt my cheeks redden and he laughed, then sobered and watched me. "I've missed ye every moment since I saw ye, lass. I canna bear to be away from ye that long again." He brushed the hair back from my cheek. "Yer even more beautiful than I'd remembered, Miss Lowell. Did ye miss me?" he asked in a husky voice. I kissed him as an answer. "Is that a yes?"

"Yes," I said, and threw my arms around his neck.

He kissed my forehead and unwound my arms from him. "Lass, we'd best stop now or I'll not answer for my actions. Talk to me and perhaps I'll listen."

"Thank you very much," I said primly, and he laughed. "Alex, why are you here? Why did you not tell me you were coming? How long can you stay? How are Angus and Matthew? And your sons?"

He grinned down at me. "Did you speak?"

"Tell me," I said, leading him to the table. He was properly seated at it when Louisa and Randolph entered. Thank God she had not arrived five minutes before, I thought. I'd be back at Mountgarden before luncheon. They greeted each other cordially. We talked for some time and I watched them, remembering the inquisition of three months before. What a difference. Louisa had an appointment that morning and soon left us, and shortly after that Randolph's agent arrived and he withdrew to discuss business. At last Alex and I were alone. We roamed the lower floor, stopping in the ballroom where I'd first seen him. He opened one of the doors to the balcony and looked at the rain.

"Five months ago, Mary, I stood there and thought ye'd send me away for being too direct."

"Five months ago, Alex, I enjoyed your company."

"And I yers." His eyes met mine. "Lass, how have ye been? I'm sorry I was not here to protect ye from the inquisition."

I laughed. "I did not need protection, Alex. I needed common sense. I've been fine. Truly. Just lonely."

"As I have been, Mary." He closed the door and faced me. "I still canna believe ye came to the brig. Why did ye do that?"

I searched his face. "Did Angus not tell you?"

"Tell me what?"

I took a deep breath and wondered if I would be wise to tell him. *But, Mary,* I asked myself, *when have you ever been wise?* "When I got Angus's note I thought it was one of two things. Either you were indeed ill and perhaps I could help, or you were trying to avoid seeing me again. I wanted to know which it was."

He looked at me, eyebrows raised. "No, Angus dinna tell me that. How could ye think that I would not want to see ye again? I told ye I'd see ye when we landed."

"Men often say things . . . that they do not mean later."

"I do not."

"I know that now. I wanted to see if you were . . ." I had an all-too-vivid image of him naked in that berth, and I lost my train of thought. Those shoulders and that chest were under that shirt.

His eyes were very dark blue. "And was I?"

"Very," I said breathlessly.

His tone was tender. "If ye choose next time to go to a man's bed, Mary Lowell, try to pick a time when he's not quoting Latin."

"I did not go to your bed, Alex."

"Actually, lass, ye did. So remember."

My cheeks flushed, but I met his gaze. "I will."

He shook his head. "Yer a one," he said, then wandered around the room while I watched him, admiring his grace and the lines of his body. He turned midway across the room. "How could I not want to see ye again?"

"Alex, there must be many women in your life."

"There are not."

"There must be."

"Wait, let me think on it." He appeared to ponder as he walked back to me, stopping halfway. "Oh, aye, Mary, yer correct, hundreds. But I dinna think on them. There is one, though, that I think on often, with dark hair and dark eyes that show me what she's thinking and a body waiting for teaching in other areas." He raised an eyebrow and grinned.

"There must be others, Alex."

"Areas?"

"Women," I said. He shook his head. "You were married. Do you miss your wife?"

"Sorcha?" His expression sobered. "Lass, ye dinna understand. I dinna choose Sorcha and she dinna choose me. It was an agreement made when we were children. I was six when she was born, and we were promised then and both raised with the idea."

"Did you love her?"

"I was fond of her. Sometimes. Sometimes I quite disliked her, and sometimes she disliked me verra much."

"Did you love her?"

His eyes met mine. "No." The one word was said quietly, without emotion. We stared at each other before he continued. "I was faithful. So was she. In time perhaps we would have come to terms with each other. But I never loved her." He shook his head. "She said I was rough and unrefined." Of all the descriptions I could think of for Alex, rough and unrefined would not be among them. He was big and he was direct but graceful and courteous.

"What happened to you two?" I asked.

He wandered to the side of the room and fingered the draperies on the windows. "After Jamie was born she told me that she had given me two sons and that I would not come to her bed again. Angus's Mairi had just died in childbirth, and I thought Sorcha was afraid. I could understand that, so I stayed away. My mother told me to give her time and we'd be a'right again. But we never were, and after a while I stopped even noticing how distant we were." He moved farther from me, stopping at the next door to look out.

"After my mother died I traveled more, and when I was home I kept myself verra busy. Sometimes I forgot Sorcha was there. And then half the crew came home ill from a trip, and the fever spread throughout Kilgannon." His voice grew quieter and I had to strain to hear him. "The crew got well quickly and so did most everyone else, but Sorcha did not. She was not terribly ill, ye ken, just not completely well. When the invitation came to go to France I dinna think I should go, because of her health, but she told me to go. She said I'd done enough damage to her life and I should leave. So I went. And while I was gone she died." He looked at me then, his face expressionless, and then back at the window as he continued. "My aunt Deirdre—that's Angus's mother—told me there was nothing I could have done even had I been there. There was nothing she could do. That helped, but I always wondered." He straightened his shoulders, lifted his chin, and looked at me again. "We were not suited. She loved another, Ian MacDonald, and he loved her, but they could not marry because our parents had promised us to each other. She said she'd begged her father to release her from marrying me. She was a faithful wife and a good woman, but she never loved me." He shook his head. "It's a system that enlarges fortunes, but no one seems to think about the ones living the arrangement. My sons will have none of it. And that's why, Mary Lowell, I am here. This time I will choose my own woman, and she me. No woman will ever be forced to be with me again."

I moved to him then and he took me into his arms. "She was a foolish woman, Alex," I said to his chest. "You're worth ten Ian MacDonalds."

He kissed my hair. "Thank ye for that, lass, but ye dinna ken the man." He shrugged and his tone lightened. "Nor do I, for that matter. I've seen him. He isna much like me."

"I don't need to know him." I looked into his face. "You're not unrefined. But you are direct, sir."

He stroked my cheek. "Aye, lass, I'm working on it."

"Don't."

"Don't?" His chest rumbled with his laughter. "First ye say yea and then ye say nay?"

"Direct is simple to deal with."

"So I'm a simple man?"

"No, Alex, you're a darlin' man."

"I am that." He kissed my hair again and released me. "And now, lass, this darlin' man must go. I have my own agent to see. One of the brigs is overdue, and I must find what information there is about her." We crossed the room, pausing at the door. "Can I assume ye'll appear at my lodgings later?" He grinned at me, clutching his chest. "I've been verra ill."

I laughed. "No, Alex, I will not appear at your lodgings."

"I'm devastated, Mary." He grinned and was gone.

A short note came from him the next day, saying that he had some business matters to attend to and would contact me soon. Two days passed, but Louisa and I were busy with Christmas preparations and the hours flew by. We dined at our Fairhaven cousins', where we discussed politics and gossip, and with the Duke and Duchess, where we discussed the same. And more. At each event someone had pointedly told me that Alex had been seen gambling and carousing with a string of beautiful women, including Rowena. None of the gossips had actually seen him themselves, but they'd each heard of him from a very good source.

"And I've heard he's considered marrying again," my Fairhaven cousin Matilda said without malice. "He's been linked to some Scottish woman with a strange name, Morgan or Morna—"

"Morag," I said, remembering Angus pacing in Louisa's foyer, telling Alex to seek Morag's company. Matilda nodded.

The third morning came and went, beautiful and cold, brilliant with brittle sunshine. I wandered the house alone, wondering why I had heard nothing from him. We would be leaving to spend Christmas in Warwickshire soon. Where was he? I knew he sought my company, but he had never said he loved me. If he did not care, then why had he returned? Why had he written for months? He might not feel the same about me as I did about him, but what he'd said in the ballroom made me think he did. What if I'd misinterpreted his words? Was he fond of me, as I was of Robert, but no more? Were his feelings mixed with pity for this girl so obviously smitten? And where was Morag in all this? It was a long day, and I spend it pondering my future.

I prepared slowly for dinner with the Mayfair Bartletts, my spirits on the floor. I had investigated and found Alex's poet Andrew Marvell and his "To His Coy Mistress," which was indeed a poem of seduction. I considered whether Alex was telling me something indirectly. Or, in this case, quite directly. Well, I decided, I would have none of it. I had been foolish long enough. Alex MacGannon would have to look elsewhere for his mistress. I would play the fool no more. But of course I did.

eight

T HE DINNER WAS WORSE THAN I COULD HAVE IMAG-
ined. I felt quite incapable tonight of dealing with the gossip
and political discussions and sat woodenly as the lively
guests chattered around me. Rowena was here, just to make
the evening complete, and Janice as well, but she did not
help. It was a disaster. Before dinner Edmund Bartlett approached me with his usual oily manner.

"Ah, Miss Lowell," he said, bowing over my hand and
studying my clothing. "I am so surprised to see you here
unaccompanied."

"I am with my aunt and uncle, sir," I said, taking my
hand from his and resisting the urge to wipe it on my skirt.

"But of course I meant your Scotsman, or I should say,
one of your Scotsmen. You seem to have a strong affinity for
our northern neighbors." I forced myself to smile. Of all
topics, this was the one I least wished to discuss. "I hear that
Lord Campbell has been quite displeased," Edmund continued, tilting his head.

"Has he?" I smiled, no doubt looking like a gargoyle.

"So I hear. But, of course, you would know that."

"What would she know?" asked a voice from behind me.
It was Rowena, looking more beautiful than ever.

Edmund smiled and stepped back to allow Rowena to
join us. "She would know that Lord Campbell is displeased

that the Earl of Kilgannon pays so much attention to Miss Lowell."

"Or"—Rowena smiled like a cat—"is it that Miss Lowell pays so much attention to Kilgannon? No wonder Campbell is annoyed."

"Yes," Edmund said, sharing a smile with her. *The evening cannot last forever,* I told myself. *It will just feel like it does.*

"Of course," Rowena laughed as she watched me through half-closed eyes, "many women pay him undue attention. You should have seen them today in the shops." She waved her hands airily. "They were peeking out of windows to see him. They look so small next to him. It was charming to see him among them." *Charming,* I thought, wondering if they had practiced this conversation beforehand. "And he enjoys the attention so."

"Do you think so?" Edmund asked, watching my reaction.

"Of course he does," Rowena said, turning to glance over her shoulder, then lowering her voice as if what she was about to say was confidential. "He gives the shopkeepers that smile of his, and they fall all over themselves trying to help him. Today he was looking at a white silk nightdress and robe." She paused for effect. "So thin you could see the light through it. Very beautiful. I assisted him in his search. It was very pleasant." She smiled archly and fanned herself as if overwhelmed. Edmund laughed, and they exchanged a confederate smirk. I hated them both.

Dinner was announced and I breathed again, but my comfort was short-lived. I could not concentrate on my meal or on the conversations around me. I spilled my wine and dropped a fork on the floor. By dessert I was exhausted and sat silently with the women when we withdrew. It was all lies, I told myself over and over. But I wondered. I did not sleep well, wondering how I could be so wrong about Alex. He was obviously nothing more than a handsome philanderer, and I his willing fool.

* * *

I was still in that frame of mind the next morning, alone in the library with my foul mood, when Ellen popped in, giving me a conspiratorial look as she announced that the Earl of Kilgannon was here. A moment later Alex stood in the doorway with two packages in his hands and Randolph, already talking about horses, just behind him.

"Alex," I said, offering my hand and trying to keep my annoyance under control.

"Mary." Alex grinned as he bowed over my hand, his eyes merry. Obviously he saw nothing wrong with his behavior. "I realized I'd not given ye the chocolate I promised. I've been carrying it with me all this time." He handed me the smaller package. "And I had something made for ye," he said, adding the larger one. "I canna wait to see ye in it." Before I could respond, Ellen leaned into the room and told Alex that someone was asking for him at the door. Eyebrows raised in surprise, he went to see who it was. I looked at the packages in my lap while Randolph moved around the room and chatted to me. The smaller one held the familiar shape of a chocolate box, and I put it on the table next to me while I examined the larger of the two. I was certain that it contained a white silk nightdress and robe. Apparently seduction was in fact on his mind. *Had we but world enough, and time* indeed. His arrogance knew no bounds.

I was sitting stiffly on my chair, staring into the fire and paying little attention to my uncle, when Alex returned. He moved to stand in front of me, his manner much subdued, his face pale. "I must leave immediately, Mary," he said hoarsely.

"Indeed you must, Lord Kilgannon. Perhaps we do not know each other as well as you had thought." I gestured with the package. "Or as well as intended. How could you possibly give me such a thing? Do you really think a silk nightdress is appropriate?"

He looked bewildered. "Mary, it's not—"

"Oh, it's not? And why not? Is it the wrong gift for me, or is it just the wrong time to give it to me?" I stood, angrier by the moment. "Were you waiting until you had successfully seduced me, Alex? Or is the nightgown a gift for another woman?"

"Neither, Mary. Please listen—"

I thrust the package at him and stormed across the room, turning at the door. Alex held the package in his hands, his eyes wide. Randolph's mouth hung open in shock. "I will not be seduced, Alex MacGannon, so if that's what you had in mind, you'd better think again. And if it's for another woman then . . . then damn you." I burst into tears and turned blindly out of the room. In the hall I bumped into Bronson, who sniffed and stepped back. "You hideous man," I snarled. "Go listen at another door!" I ran upstairs.

Eventually I cried myself to sleep. When I woke it was early afternoon. I had no tears left, but I was still angry. I went downstairs to find Louisa, but both she and Randolph were gone. As I stood in the foyer trying to decide what to do next, I saw the packages on a table by the door, a folded note sticking out from beneath them.

Miss Lowell, Alex had written. *I am leaving these packages for you as I have no use for them. One is the chocolate that I've mentioned and the other I had made for you. Keep it or not, as you will. Alex'r MacGannon.*

"Bronson," I called without turning around. He was there at once, and I knew he'd been watching me. I thrust the packages at him. "Have these delivered at once to Kilgannon's ship. It's called the *Gannon's Lady.*"

"Is there a message, miss?" he asked.

"None."

Two hours later, curled up with a book in the library, I was startled to hear a banging on the front door and the sound of loud voices. Ellen burst into the room, followed by Bronson. And Alex. All three spoke at once, Ellen trying to warn me that Alex was here, Bronson telling me he tried to

stop him, and Alex, his anger obvious, saying that he wished
a word with me. I rose to my feet and slowly put the book
down before turning to them. I put a hand on Ellen's arm
to reassure her and told her and Bronson that I understood
but that all was well. I would, I said, speak with Lord Kilgannon alone, and I thanked them for their concern. They
nodded, moving to the door, but at the threshold Bronson
turned.

"Miss Lowell?" he asked quietly. "I will stay with you if
you wish it." I met his eyes across the room and for once
saw no derision or disapproval, only concern. Ellen peered
over his shoulder, her face pale.

"That is most kind of you, Bronson," I said. "But I have
no doubt that Lord Kilgannon will behave as a gentleman."
I turned to Alex and met his eyes. "Won't you, sir?" I asked
frostily.

He stared at me for a moment, then turned to Bronson.
"Leave us. This is not yer concern. Miss Lowell will call ye if
she needs ye." At my nod Bronson left us and I turned to
Alex. He watched me with a stony face, crossing his arms
over his chest. He looked very large. And very angry. And
very handsome. The silence stretched unbearably and at last,
weary of the tension between us, I moved to stand before
the fireplace, my back to him. It was difficult to remember
to hate him when he looked like that. I sighed and tried to
stay cold and disciplined.

"Mary," he said, his voice tight with control. I didn't
turn, and he didn't speak again. At last I glanced over my
shoulder to see him looking down at his watch with a frown.

"If you need to go, sir, please, don't let me delay you," I
said, turning fully. He looked up at me with an unreadable
expression, his hands falling to his sides.

"I do need to go, Mary, to see my shipping agent. He
says he may have more news and I'm to meet with him in
half an hour. I dinna realize it was so late."

"Then, by all means, go, Alex. A meeting with your shipping agent is much more important than talking to me."

"No, but it's close." He took a deep breath and I did the same. "Lass, the message I received earlier was from him as well. Do ye ken the brig I've been worried about, the one that's been missing?" I nodded, thawing despite myself. He looked exhausted. "Well, it's gone down off Cornwall and is lost with all its crew and cargo. They were not Kilgannon men, but I must discover what happened. And that means I must leave as soon as possible. I have to meet with the agent and then I go to Cornwall." I nodded, and he frowned again. "But I couldna leave without discovering what made ye so angry. I dinna understand what happened here this morning, Mary. Why are ye so angry with me?"

I wondered if any man had ever been more impossible. "Why am I so angry? Only a saint would not be. You're marrying Morag, Alexander MacGannon, and you've been seen all over London with women, including Rowena, and you have the gall to shop with her and buy a nightdress that you give to me and you tell me you cannot wait to see me in it. Why would I not be angry?" I crossed my arms over my chest and glared at him. "Tell me why I should not be angry."

He blinked, then laughed. I watched some of his tiredness melt away as he shook his head and laughed again. "If any of that were true, lass, I'd agree with ye and be angry at myself along with ye. But it's no' true. None of it."

"You're not marrying Morag?"

"No. Nor do I wish to."

"Who is she?"

"Morag MacLeod. From Skye. My friend Murdoch Maclean is in love with her. Has been since we were lads."

"And you're not? And haven't been?"

He paused. "I was. But it was a long time ago."

"You were in love with her?" My voice was shrill, and I winced.

He nodded, shifting his weight. "When I was sixteen I convinced myself that I loved her and that I wouldna marry Sorcha."

"And what did Morag say?"

He looked uneasy. "She was in agreement."

"I see," I said, and sat down on the couch heavily. This was all wrong. He was supposed to hotly deny it and reassure me. I didn't want to hear more. "So it's true."

He shook his head. "No. I was shipped off to France for a year, and Morag was shut up in Skye. Neither my father nor hers would have any of it. And when I saw her again, she dinna seem so wonderful. And then I discovered that Murdoch felt the way he felt, and I had to marry Sorcha, so . . ." He shrugged. "It was just a youthful fancy, is all, Mary, nothing more. I haven't seen her in a while. She's nothing to me."

"But I heard—"

He made a sharp gesture. "Ye heard wrong. Morag MacLeod means nothing to me, lass. Nothing. Whoever's been talking to ye has filled yer head with nonsense. I willna marry Morag, not now nor ever, and I havena been out in London with women. I saw Rowena when I was shopping, aye, and she was there when I was looking at the nightdress. I am the world's greatest fool not to have realized that she would tell ye and make the most of something that was a chance meeting. I dinna spend any time with her, lass. It's not her company I desire."

"I see," I said.

"No, ye don't." He took a deep breath. "Mary, ye canna always believe what ye hear. I have done nothing improper nor have I spent any time with Rowena. Do ye not ken that she's jealous?"

I looked at him in surprise. "Jealous?"

"Aye, because yer beautiful and much younger."

"I'm younger, Alex, but I'm not more beautiful."

"Aye, Mary, ye are. Ye win the contest, believe me. I've seen many Rowenas. If I wanted a woman like her I'd have one. I don't." I felt my cheeks flush and saw him note it. His expression softened. "Mary, is that what was bothering ye?

That ye thought I was courting ye and betraying ye at once?"

"Are you courting me?"

"Lass, how could ye not ken I am? Did ye think I was always seeking yer company because I couldna abide ye? What did ye think I was doing if not courting ye?"

"Seducing me."

"Seducing ye." He looked at me for a long moment.

"I knew you liked me, but I thought I'd frightened you away after I went to your brig or that I'd led you to believe by my behavior that seduction would be acceptable to me. And there was the poem. And the nightdress."

His eyes widened and he paced the room, shaking his head. "I'll never understand a woman's mind. Do ye think me such a fool or such a cad that I'd try and seduce ye in front of yer aunt and uncle and with the blessing of the Duchess of Fenster?" He stopped and faced me. "Mary Lowell, ye credit me with much more intrigue than I am capable of. I told ye, lass. I'm direct. It's ye I'm courting, and ye I'm here with." He pulled out his watch again and frowned. "But not for long." He watched me for a moment, then extended his hand. "Mary, will ye come along with me to the agent's? I must go, lass, and we'd have a chance to talk in the coach. Please."

I nodded and I threw convention to the wind once more.

Alex's agent was not at his office near the docks but at his house, not far from Louisa's. Bronson and Ellen had watched us with worried eyes as we left, Ellen handing me a cloak without a word, and Bronson nodding at my explanation that I would soon return. I shuddered to think what Louisa and Randolph would say, but I could not refuse Alex.

We talked more in the coach he'd hired, and I was soon completely convinced that Alex had been maligned by Rowena, who had access to all those who had helped spread the tales about him. It seemed that despite my notion that I knew London society, I still had more to learn about the wars of love.

At the agent's house I told Alex to go inside without me. It was enough that I was with him again without a chaperon. If the agent recognized me or knew my name, the word would soon be out. I waited patiently for a while, hugging myself as I reviewed our conversations. Alex was courting me. He'd still not spoken of love or marriage, but I was content for now. What a difference a few hours made, I thought, and ignored the coachman's movements. He seemed to be moving a lot and making strange noises. *This is why Louisa insists on having her own coaches,* I thought. *One never knows what one will get with a hired one.*

When the door of the coach flew open I was surprised that Alex was so hurried. But it wasn't Alex. Two men faced me in the gathering gloom, silhouetted against the outside light. They wore kilts and plaids, and I relaxed, thinking they were Alex's men.

"He's got a woman in here," said the man with his hand still on the door handle. "Kilgannon's got a woman for us." He laughed, and my blood froze as I cringed back into the cushion. Surely Alex's man would not say such a thing nor leer at me so. Behind him the second man craned to see me, and a third dropped from the roof of the coach, dragging the bloodied body of the coachman behind him and showing his companions. He threw the coachman onto the road. The three men laughed and kicked the lifeless form to the gutter. And then turned to me. I screamed.

The first man lunged at me as I screamed again and turned my head out the window to scream a third time. A rough hand clamped over my mouth and I bit it. Cursing me, he yanked me in from the window, smashing my head against the frame as he pulled me backward. I thrashed about and he cursed again. Behind me I heard a second man climb into the coach and the door slam shut. And then the coach began to move. No one would ever find me if they drove away, I thought. *Alex, oh, please.* Or had they already dealt with Alex? Was he now in the agent's house injured or worse? They'd known his name, so this couldn't be a random attack. I screamed and struck the man in front of me.

It took only a minute for the men to subdue me. A swift slap across the face left me stunned and bleeding, and I soon stopped struggling. I lay on the floor of the coach, the first man lying heavy atop me, panting, the second sitting on the seat above us. I looked up at the open window and realized we were no longer moving. We could not have gone far, I thought. Maybe I could still escape.

The thought was no sooner formed than the man on top of me laughed and lifted himself off me. "Might as well have some fun, eh?" he said to his companion, who laughed. With one hand pressing against my throat, he put the other at the neck of my bodice. And tore it in half. As the air hit my skin I started fighting again. I still had my corset and shift but knew they would not last long. I screamed, and he hit me on the side of the head. And then I felt the second man grab my left leg at the ankle and laugh as he pulled it up on the seat. The first man fumbled at my skirts as I writhed against him, twisting away. There was no doubt what he planned and I probably could not prevent it, but I wasn't going to submit.

"No, no, no!" I screamed, and beat at him with my arms. He pressed against my throat again. I couldn't breathe. I saw a bright light over his head and felt as though I were falling. I thought I heard Alex's voice, but that seemed impossible. Still, it was comforting to think that his voice would be the last thing I'd ever hear. A man's hand was on the skin of my leg and moving upward, but I could no longer fight it. I closed my eyes.

NINE

I WAS ALIVE. I SWALLOWED PAINFULLY AND GROANED, RAISing my hand to my throat as I opened my eyes. The man atop me was turning to his companion, his hand at last off my neck. Behind him, in the coach's open doorway, was a tall man lit from behind by a lantern. The second man on the seat cursed and raised a knife to attack the newcomer. It was Alex. I tried to scream and warn him, but no sound would come out, and I struggled to sit up as my attacker was distracted. With a lunge Alex impaled the second man against the coach wall, his sword vibrating in the air. And in the next instant pulled the man from atop me, dragging him out of the coach.

Alex gave me a sharp look. "Mary, are ye a'right?" he asked in a harsh voice. I nodded, and he turned from me and dealt with the first man, who was struggling to get away. For a long moment there was silence in the coach, and then the man on the seat gurgled and thrashed before slumping over Alex's sword. I stared at him in horror and then turned my eyes away. But what I saw was no better. The man who had attacked me lay on the ground dying, bleeding from a wound in his neck. Alex, breathing hard, stood over him, his cheek and arm bloodied. I must have made some movement, for Alex turned sharply, the knife in his hand raised. When he saw it was me he lowered his arm. But what I had seen in his face shocked me, and I recoiled.

Behind Alex there was a sudden flurry of activity as the lantern moved closer and I saw several men there, more arriving. Windows were being thrown up and neighbors called down. Now that the danger was over, people were everywhere. Alex extended his arm to me and ignored the questions being thrown at him. His expression softened as he leaned in to me.

"Thank God, Mary, yer alive. Did he . . . did he . . ." I shook my head. "Are ye truly a'right, lass? I thought I wouldna be in time. Three to deal with was more than I thought, and the driver was most difficult." *The driver,* I thought. Alex had killed three men. I glanced at the man on the seat, and Alex followed my gaze. He said something in Gaelic, sneering at the man. "Scum," he said, reaching up for his sword, then changing his mind as I cringed. "Come, lass, come out of there."

I did slowly, my muscles trembling, and emerged from the coach to gasps from the onlookers. Lanterns were everywhere, and voices were asking me things I couldn't understand. I felt the cold air against my naked shoulders and hugged my arms across my chest. Alex reached behind me and pulled my cloak from the coach, wrapping it around me hastily and then pulling me gently to him. "Tell me, lass, are ye a'right? Did they hurt ye anywhere I canna see?"

"You killed them," I croaked.

Alex nodded. "Aye," he said, "and I'd do it again if they attacked ye."

I did not answer but leaned against him, my trembling increasing. His heart was beating furiously, but he seemed undisturbed now. He held me lightly and kissed my hair. *How can a man kill another and talk so calmly?* I wondered. "Thank God ye screamed and kept screaming, Mary. That's how I found ye. They'd not gotten far." He turned as a well-dressed man touched his arm.

"Kilgannon," said the man. "The Guard is coming. Before they get here we need to look at these men. Do you know who they are?"

Alex loosened his grip on me, leaning over my attacker's body with the gentleman. A servant moved a lantern closer, and two others dragged the third dead man before them. All three assailants were dressed in kilts and plaids, and Alex let me go altogether as he leaned to touch one of the kilts with a grunt. He rose and stood before me, wiping his hand on his thigh.

"Are they your men?" asked the gentleman.

Alex shook his head tightly and looked at me as he spoke. "No. That's a Campbell plaid." He leaned over the dead men again and cut away a large piece of the plaid that one of the men had worn thrown over his shoulder. Folding the material and tucking it into his belt, he turned to the coach, his face grim. I didn't watch as he leaned in to retrieve his sword but heard the body slump to the seat, then to the floor. Alex wiped his sword on the man's clothes.

"I am William Burton, miss," the gentleman said to me, "Kilgannon's agent. Won't you come into the house and wait while we deal with the Guard? I'm sure you don't want to stand here while we talk."

"Aye," Alex said, and guided me through the crowd. He gazed deeply into my eyes and tenderly ran his knuckles down my cheek before leaving me.

The next hour was a blur. Clutching my cloak tightly around me, I sat silently in the agent's parlor with his wide-eyed wife while Alex was outside with her husband and the Guard, then inside with them. Mrs. Burton handed me a warm cloth to wipe my face and hands, and I did so without speaking. And then the Guard wanted to ask me questions. I glanced up at Alex and nodded that I would talk to them. He knelt next to my chair and held my hand.

"I dinna want any mention of this lady's name in yer report," he said to the two guardsmen, who exchanged a glance. "It's no' her fault she was attacked, and I don't want her name bandied about London. Do ye agree?" The guardsmen nodded and one politely asked me what had happened.

My voice came out in a hoarse whisper and it hurt to speak. I swallowed again and my voice cracked. "Lord Kilgannon saved my life," I said, and told them briefly that I had been waiting for Alex when the three men attacked. I was not asked nor did I say that the men knew whose coach it was and that this was not a random assault. I did say that although their clothes were Scottish, their voices were English. Londoners. Alex started at that, and his eyes narrowed. The Guard mercifully breezed over the details of the attack and then were gone.

As the door shut behind them, Alex reached to help me to my feet. I wobbled but was able to stand. "Mr. Burton, Mrs. Burton, I thank ye for yer kindness and rely on yer discretion. I trust that Miss—this lady will not have to fear that ye will reveal her identity."

The agent gave his assurances and offered the services of his coach. Alex accepted, thanked him, and we left at once.

We rode in silence. I watched Alex's profile and realized that what I had said earlier was true. He had saved my honor and probably my life, and he didn't seem to think that an amazing thing. It was to me. The men who attacked me had been brutal and their intentions obvious. I had little doubt that they would have disposed of me as easily as they had the coachman.

"Alex," I said. "You saved my life. Thank you."

He turned to me then. "I thank God I got there in time. How are ye feeling?"

"My head hurts and my throat, and I think my cheek is swelling. But it's nothing compared to what could have been," I said. He studied my face in the dim light and nodded.

"Aye, ye'll have bruises there. They struck ye?"

"Yes. I was . . . uncooperative."

He smiled grimly. "I could hear ye, lass. I heard ye from inside the house. When we looked out the window they saw us and started away. And outside it was yer screams and the kicking against the door that helped me find ye. If ye'd been quiet they would have whisked ye away and I'd never have found ye. It was the matter of a moment."

"They knew that the coach was yours," I said. "I think they meant to get into the coach and surprise you when you entered. But I was there instead. You were the target of the attack, Alex."

He turned to me with an unreadable expression. "Perhaps."

"They used your name," I said, and told him what they'd said.

He was silent for several minutes, then spoke evenly. "They all ken who ye are, Mary. All of them—the Burtons, the Guard, the neighbors. I dinna tell them, but they all kent it, and now all of London will hear of this. Whoever set up this Campbell attack may be listening."

"It can't be Robert," I said. "It can't be. You cannot believe that of him. Why would he attack you?"

Alex started to speak, then stopped. When he continued his voice was quiet. "I can think of reasons that Robert Campbell would want me gone."

"The men were English."

"They wore Campbell plaids."

"But they were from London."

"Where Campbell has property and employs people."

"You cannot believe Robert would do this!"

Alex met my eyes. "It's interesting that ye defend him so strongly, lass. What I ken is that the men who attacked ye wore Campbell plaids and that the man who has courted ye for two years is a Campbell. Need I say more?"

"I don't believe Robert would authorize an attack on you!"

Alex grunted. "Aye, ye'd think it a stupid thing for him to do, and the one thing I do ken about Robert Campbell is that he's no' stupid. I dinna ken him as well as ye do, though, Mary."

I turned quickly to make a sharp remark but stopped when the pain shot through me. My throat and neck protested my rapid movement, and my eyes filled with tears. At once I lost whatever composure I'd had and sat back and closed my eyes. When Alex leaned over me and gently asked if I was all right, I began to sob.

I didn't pay any attention when the coach stopped, nor when the door was thrown open, and in my confused state I didn't think it odd that Matthew was there and not Louisa. I clung to Alex as he lifted me from the coach and sobbed against his shoulder as he carried me on board his ship and down the stairs into his cabin, fielding questions from his crew. Angus looked up from the table in the center of the cabin and rose to stand before the charts he'd been studying. Alex spoke in Gaelic, and Angus answered in the same as Alex put me on his berth and wrapped a blanket around me. I wiped my eyes and nose on my handkerchief and sipped the brandy that Matthew handed me, then drank the refill as well. And closed my eyes, listening to the men's voices. I'd go home in a bit, I thought, but just now it felt good to be safe.

I woke when Alex tried to straighten me out from the pile I'd slumped in, and I looked up to see his smile. His cheek had been attended to and he'd changed his shirt. He smelled like soap and whisky. "Ye need a rest, lass, so dinna fight it. Just let yer body heal. And yer mind." The cabin behind him was dim, no Angus or Matthew. Alex kissed my forehead and I reached up for him. He stretched out next to me on the berth and stroked my hair. "Ye need to rest, Mary," he said as I held him to me.

"Thank you, Alex," I said, dangerously close to tears again. "You saved my life. I'll never forget looking up and seeing you in the doorway and realizing you were rescuing me."

"And I will never forget the sight of seeing that pig on top of ye, Mary." He fingered my torn bodice. "Ye'll need a new dress, I'm thinking, and yer cloak is covered with blood."

"Yes," I said, and sighed. We lay quietly until he kissed

my forehead again. "My lips aren't bruised," I said. He gave a deep laugh as he bent to kiss me on the mouth. And then again, this time longer. I ignored the complaints of my neck and laughed when he gently kissed my bruised cheek and said he'd try to make it all better. And I concentrated when he kissed my neck and my shoulders and strayed lower to the tops of my breasts. I opened my eyes when he pulled the shreds of my corset aside and bent to caress the space between my breasts with his lips and shuddered when his hand cupped my breast next to his head. His touch was light but sure, and I felt, even through the overlay of spent emotion and brandy, my body respond and his answer. I pressed myself against him and stroked my hand through his hair, pulling it loose from its binding so that we were lost in a curtain of blond silk. My own hair, long ago dropped from its prim pinnings, slipped across my shoulder as he turned with a groan and rubbed his hand along my hip. Our hair, black entwined with gold, rubbed against my bare shoulder and fell across my breasts.

Alex pulled back from me and stared into my eyes. "We canna do this now, Mary. We'll wait until yer neither injured nor tipsy. Nor feeling indebted. What yer feeling is the joy of finding yerself alive when ye weren't sure ye would be."

"No, Alex," I said, pulling him down to kiss him heartily. "What I'm feeling is the joy of touching you. Kiss me again." He kissed me, then gently broke my grip as he sat on the edge of the berth. He took a deep breath as he shook his head.

"Lass, I don't want ye ever to say ye dinna understand what was happening. It's the shock of them attacking ye, combined with the brandy, that's affecting ye."

I rose to lean on one elbow. "Yes," I said deliberately, for when I moved I could feel the brandy hit my head again. "But, Alex, what I'm feeling just now is not gratitude."

"Ye've had a scare," he said, straightening his kilt and belt.

"I have. And now I need comforting," I laughed, and after a moment he joined me, although ruefully.

"Yer a one. No, lass, when we . . . when we . . . go further I'd have it be a little more special than in a ship's berth in the winter on the way to Cornwall."

"What do you mean?" I asked, sitting up now.

"In a proper bed—"

"No, Alex, what do you mean, 'on the way to Cornwall'?" I turned to the window and pulled aside the curtain. He was right. We were moving. "Alex! We're sailing!" The lights of the shore passed by to my right. We must still be in the Thames, I thought, but these lights were much too sparse to be London's. "We're leaving London? We're going to Cornwall?"

He nodded. "I told ye I must go as soon as I saw the agent, lass. The attack dinna change that, only made it more critical. I'm thinking someone dinna want me to make this trip perhaps."

"Where are we?"

"Almost at the mouth of the Thames. It'll get rougher soon, when we get into the open ocean, so I thought I'd make sure ye were comfortable. I dinna mean to wake ye."

I stared at him in horror. "You cannot be serious," I said. "You cannot mean to take me with you to Cornwall?"

"I couldna leave ye behind."

"You most certainly could have."

"Mary," he said as though to a child, "as I told ye in the coach, whoever planned the attack now kens ye were involved. I couldna leave ye in London without protection while I go to Cornwall. I had to take ye with me."

"No, Alex, you didn't," I said crisply. "You could have taken me to my aunt's house. I have plenty of protection there. What were you thinking, bringing me to your brig?"

His tone was cold. "I was thinking of yer safety."

"And what of my reputation?"

"Ye dinna complain when I brought ye aboard, Mary."

"I was in no shape to think clearly."

"And ye dinna complain when ye heard all the commotion of us leaving the dock."

"I'd had two glasses of brandy by then. I thought that was just normal noise aboard your ship. I wasn't paying attention to what the others were doing. Alex, how could you just . . . just abduct me? How could you? What were you thinking?"

"That I was protecting ye, Mary."

"Alex, you know what people will think. How could you do this to me?" I felt my tears threatening again. "How dare you?"

His expression grew remote. "I was thinking of yer life, Mary, not yer damned reputation. Why is yer own good opinion not enough for ye? Why do ye have to do what society thinks is proper instead of what yer heart tells ye? I've already proven I don't mean to take advantage of ye. I could have taken yer body just now and used ye for my own satisfaction. And yours, I might add. Ye were willing enough." I turned my face away, feeling the flush steal over me. "But I dinna do it, so don't preach to me."

We had an awkward moment of silence while I reviewed my thoughts. The brandy haze seemed far away now. He was correct that I had not protested about being brought on board. And it had been me who had escalated our lovemaking. He, not I, had stopped it. But how could he not realize that removing me from London for days or weeks would be the death of any reputation I had left? Like it or not, London was the world in which I lived, and what he had done, if it were discovered, would mark me forever.

I looked at him again. "Alex, you have to take me back. Louisa will be frantic. She'll think I'm dead."

He shook his head and spoke brusquely. "I sent word to her before we left that ye were with me. They'll ken yer safe. By now the word of the attack will have gotten everywhere. I dinna have time to take ye back. I've lost enough time as it is. Ye'll come with us and return when we return."

"You have no right to abduct me, Alex. Take me home!"

"Abduct ye, Mary! I dinna abduct ye. I saved ye!"

"And now you are removing me against my will. Is that not an abduction? If not, pray, sir, tell me what is."

"I dinna hear any protests a bit ago."

"Don't change the subject, Alex. You have to take me home."

"No, Mary, I do not. Ye have no say in this!"

"No say! If anyone should have some say, it is I! Take me home, Lord Kilgannon. At once. And that, sir, is not a request."

Before he could answer, there was a knock on the cabin door and Angus stuck his head in, then entered and closed the door behind him. "Ye can both be heard clearly in the hallway," he said, crossing his arms over his chest and looking grimly at us. I pulled the blanket to my chin and glared at Alex, who paced across the room, then grabbed his hair back with jerky movements, wrapping it tightly before speaking. Alex gestured to me.

"Mary is angry with me for having brought her with us."

"I told ye," Angus said, and Alex glared at him. "Ye should have brought her home. Her family will care for her."

"Not like we would," snapped Alex.

Angus shrugged. "Perhaps; perhaps even better. They can spirit her away to Mountgarden or Grafton, and no one could harm her there. I told ye this earlier."

"You must take me home at once, Alex," I said.

Alex looked from Angus to me, and when Angus nodded, Alex stormed out the door. I could hear him calling Calum, the captain, to turn around and go back to London.

Angus watched me without expression. "He's verra angry now, lass. Are ye sure this is what ye want?"

"I must go home, Angus. There will be enough to-do about my absence as it is. My aunt will be frantic."

"We sent word to yer aunt."

"That I am here with you all. Do you have any idea what troubles I had after my visit here to see if Alex was sick?

Imagine what will happen if I go with you now to Cornwall and then return to London. I'll be ruined."

"What does that matter? Ye ken Alex would care properly for ye. Ye've insulted him and hurt his feelings, lass. Ye seem to care more for people's opinion than for yer own safety."

"It wasn't me they were after, Angus. It was Alex."

He nodded. "I think so too."

"And Alex should have asked me."

Angus shrugged. "Alex is used to making decisions, Mary."

"And I am used to being consulted about my movements."

"As ye wish, lass. I hope ye'll be happy with yer choice."

He left me then and I started to cry, hearing the echo of his words. As I wished. Isn't that what Alex had said when we'd met, that it would be as I wished? I wiped my eyes and lifted my chin.

I was on deck when we sailed into London in the early hours of the morning after having fought the morning tide the whole trip west. The lights of London glowed quietly as we passed, looking like landlocked stars, and I concentrated on them rather than on the tall man standing so silently behind me. When we landed, Alex went ahead, and it was Angus who handed me down the gangplank. At the foot of the dock Matthew held a horse, and Alex stood before him.

"Sorry, Mary," Matthew said. "I couldna get a coach at this hour. I could only get a horse." I wondered if I were expected to find my way alone across London on a strange horse.

"It'll do," Alex growled, and turned to give me a hand up. I climbed to the horse's back and gasped as Alex vaulted himself in front of me. "Hold on tightly, Miss Lowell," he said as he wheeled the horse around and we leapt away.

I threw my arms around his waist and turned to see Matthew and Angus standing with open mouths and the men of *Gannon's Lady* lining the rails to watch us. And then

I had to concentrate on staying on the horse as Alex galloped him through the streets, the wind blowing Alex's kilt far up his thigh. When we went around a corner much too fast, I leaned my head on his back and closed my eyes. I'd never see Alex again after this, I realized, and tightened my arms around him. And maybe, I thought, maybe it was for the best. I opened my eyes as he took a deep shuddery breath. No, not for the best. But maybe it had been inevitable. Our worlds were too different.

London was just awakening when we rode through, and Alex had to slow as the carts and vendors filled the roads. I tried to avoid the curious glances we were thrown and tried not to wonder what I must look like. My hair, never repinned, bounced on my back, and the blanket I still wore slipped at moments from my shoulder, revealing the torn bodice and naked arm. By the time we got to Louisa's, the horse was walking and still we'd not said a word to each other.

The front door was open and Bronson stood on the front steps. As we approached, Randolph's coach came from the stables and paused by the step. And Robert and Randolph and Louisa came out from the house. They watched us with shocked expressions and glad cries as we drew near. When we stopped, it was Robert who helped me down as Alex dismounted, and Robert who stood with me facing Alex. Alex raised his chin, nodded at Louisa and Randolph, and gestured to me.

"Here she is," he said to them all in a brittle voice. "She's unharmed except for bruises and bumps. She'll tell ye the story of what happened. I took her to my ship afterward to be sure she was a'right and she wanted to be returned, so here she is." He bowed to me. "Miss Lowell, I'll take my leave."

I felt my eyes fill with tears. "Alex, thank you. Thank you."

"For saving yer life or yer reputation, Miss Lowell?" He looked at Robert. "She'll make ye a fine wife, Campbell. I've only kissed her, not more. She's not lost her virtue." Alex pulled the square of Campbell plaid from his belt and handed it to Robert, who took it with a puzzled look. "Yer men botched the attack. They dinna get me, but they almost cost ye a bride." His voice softened as he glanced at me, then back to Robert. "Care for her well, man. She's worth yer effort." He reached out and gently stroked my un-bruised cheek. "It's probably for the best, Mary," he said, and walked back to the horse.

"MacGannon," Robert said. "I didn't send men to attack you."

Alex looked at Robert over the horse's back. "But ye ken of it, I can see," Alex said, his voice harsh again.

Robert nodded. "All of London knows of it, Alex. They weren't my men. I wouldn't have done that." The two men stared at each other, and at last Alex nodded as well.

"Damned if I ken why, but I believe ye, Robert," he said, and vaulted onto the horse's back. I ran to him.

"Alex," I said. "Don't leave like this."

"It's too far to walk, Mary," he said in a harsh tone, but when I came next to the horse he almost smiled. "I told ye, lass," he whispered bleakly, "that it would be as ye wished. And this"—he gestured at the group behind me—"is what ye wished. I hope it's what ye wanted."

"Alex, will you come to see me?"

He did smile then. "I think not, Miss Lowell. I've told ye, I don't pay attention to other men's wives."

I stepped back as though slapped, then raised my chin. Two could play this game. "Thank you for bringing me home, Lord Kilgannon," I said clearly. "I appreciate your efforts. And I'm sure you're correct that it's probably for the best."

Alex nodded. "Aye. I can see ye have not the stomach for life with a man such as me."

"And I can see that you could not handle life with a woman such as me. You should find yourself a woman who enjoys having no say in her life. I'm sure you'll find one."

"And what do ye mean by that?"

"I thought you were different, Alex, but when it came to it you're just like all the other men. You tell me that it will be as I wish, but you decide what's best for me. That was most illuminating. And in your arrogance you cannot even see why I might be angry."

He looked at me for a long moment, then leaned closer. "I'll just take my arrogance and leave ye be, then, Mary," he said, but I could see the hurt and I paused, unable to continue that way.

"Oh, Alex," I said softly. "What a way for us to part."

He nodded slowly. "Aye," he said.

"Safe journey," I whispered. "Safe journey, Alex MacGannon."

"And to ye, Mary Lowell," he said. And left me. We all stared after him as he rode away. And then I gathered my skirts and turned to face my family and Robert.

TEN

$\mathcal{M}$UCH LATER, AT THE END OF THAT VERY LONG DAY, Ellen knocked timidly on my bedroom door and peeked her head around the corner. "Miss Mary," she said. "I thought you'd want these. Your aunt said to call if you were going to open them." She handed me the packages Alex had brought yesterday. It seemed a lifetime ago. I held them in my lap and tried not cry. I'd explained what had happened to Louisa and Randolph and Robert and then again to the Duchess and Duke when they arrived, and later still to Becca's parents. I'd found myself realizing that Alex had acted in what he thought was not only a proper but a necessary way. To my surprise Robert agreed, saying he would have done the same thing. I left them to discuss it and retired to my room. Now, Ellen said, all the guests had left and Randolph had fallen asleep in his chair.

"Please go and get Louisa, Ellen," I said quietly. "I'll open them." I turned them in my hands while I waited, wondering if the larger one contained anything as offensive as I had imagined.

When Louisa arrived she watched as I opened the smaller package and found the chocolate that had been promised. The larger one I'd imagined was a silk nightdress and robe, held instead a velvet cloak, a muted green, the color of the jacket Alex had worn the night I had met him, lined with a

Kilgannon tartan. The red background caught the eye; the green was the same as the velvet. It was very beautiful, finely sewn, and I remembered him saying, *I had something made for ye. I canna wait to see ye in it.* Obviously, I would not have taken offense at this gift. I felt tears spring to my eyes again, and I sniffed.

"It's beautiful," Louisa sighed. I nodded blearily, holding the soft wool to my cheek. "What does his note say?" she asked, gesturing to the note that had fallen from the folds of the cloak.

"Dear Mary," I read aloud. *"I had this made for you at home. The sett is a Kilgannon breacan and is one of my favorites. I hope that you will enjoy it and that you'll think of me when you wear it. Yours, Alexander MacGannon."*

I glanced at my aunt and then read the letter to myself again. Alex had written this note before our arguments, before the attack, I thought. Before I had angered him so. I would, I knew, think of him each time I wore the cloak. And every day, whether I wore it or not. The future stretched bleakly before me. I started crying again. "I should have gone to Cornwall with him. I wasn't brave enough or free enough; I cared more about my reputation than his feelings. And I was so angry that he made the decision for me without even asking me, without even thinking of what it would mean. Now I'll never see him again! Oh, Louisa, I don't understand! I know he loves me. He's not said so, but I know he does. He saved my life; he killed those men for me. Why hasn't he asked me to marry him?"

Louisa bit her lip. "He all but has," she said. "Both Randolph and I told him it was too soon when he asked to marry you months ago. He probably assumed you understood his intentions or that we told you we had all discussed it."

"Why didn't he ask me? Why didn't he tell me?"

"We told him it was too soon, but that was his plan. And he wrote to us later that he planned for you two to wed when you'd known him long enough. That's what he told Randolph when they went to his ship after you went to see him, when he was ill."

And so that story came out. Alex had told them back then that he planned to marry me, and the men had told Louisa and Sarah when they returned. I smiled. *Alex wants to marry me,* I thought, and then corrected myself, my smile fading. Alex *wanted* to marry me. I looked at the note in my hand. Perhaps I had truly lost him now. It would be no more than I deserved. "Louisa," I said. "I've been a fool." My aunt shook her head.

"You're not a fool, Mary. Alex is. If a man has not asked you to marry him, you have no assurance of his intentions. I don't know why he didn't tell you. And you were right to refuse to go to Cornwall. You do have the right to determine the course of your own life. He was very high-handed, no matter how well meaning his motives." She sighed. "You need to talk to him."

"Yes," I said. "But how? He's gone."

"Then write to him," she said patiently.

"Oh, yes, I will!" I hugged her. I would simply write to him.

It proved not so simple. Every time I put pen to paper I ended up crumpling the note. At last I wrote a short letter, thanking him for the cloak, then apologizing and saying that I would like to see him again. I sent it to Kilgannon. There was no reply.

London buzzed, as I'd known it would, with false versions of the attack and Alex's part in it, but with my family and Robert at my side, none dared to press the issue. I felt very protected. And lonely. I missed Alex at every moment. I would hear a voice of the same timbre and turn to be disappointed, or see a man of his height with blond hair and strain to see his face, only to be looking into the eyes of a stranger.

We decided we would go to Robert's estate as planned

and after the Yule parties would retire to Mountgarden. Louisa said that by the time we returned after the new year, London would have other topics to discuss. It did not matter greatly to me what the gossips said. The irony was that in saving my good reputation I'd lost the desire to have it. How I wished I could return to that moment on Alex's ship when I'd asked him to take me home. My decision would be different now. But I couldn't turn time back and reluctantly faced the immediate future.

Robert. As kind as he had been, he was still Robert. I was grateful to him that he trusted both Alex and me to have told the truth, and I told him so, but I didn't feel what I had felt when Alex was near. I was comfortable with Robert, but then, I was comfortable with Will. It wasn't enough. And he must have sensed the same, for as polite as he was, he'd not asked me to marry him. I suspected I might go to my grave a much-maligned virgin.

We were among the first to arrive at Robert's Kent estate and were soon helping Robert and his mother greet the newcomers. *I must stop thinking about Alex,* I told myself. *He surely has gotten my letter by now.* I sighed. If he had wanted to marry me, why had this man, usually so direct, not just asked me? I thought of the distance to Kilgannon and consoled myself with the thought that perhaps my letter had not reached him yet. I tried to put my worries aside as I wandered, looking around Robert's grand rooms, wondering if one day I would be mistress here. Perhaps I would, if Alex never came back. And he might not. And if Robert asked me to marry him. And he might not.

The weather was cold but clear and we kept very active, which helped the days to pass. Robert was never far from my side and had me seated to his right at the huge table in the dining hall at every meal. Each night, sometime during the second course, he reached for my hand under the table. I felt I had no right to refuse him this simple gesture, but my heart was torn. I esteemed him, I respected him, yes. But I didn't love him.

The last night of our visit, when all the guests were gathered in the red parlor before dinner, Robert left my side and called for everyone's attention, his smile wide and his face flushed. This was so unlike Robert that several of his friends teased him about his big "surprise." I smiled as well, but a terrible fear began to grow while I watched the guests gather around and finally grow quiet.

"I have a surprise tonight for the lady I love dearly," Robert said with a large gesture to the door. Two footmen opened the double doors to the foyer and stood awaiting Robert's signal. To his left Robert's mother smiled and gave me a nod, her eyes sparkling. Louisa moved to stand on my left and gave me a sharp look. "This lady," Robert continued, "has brightened my days for many years, and now she will soon brighten this house as well."

Eyes turned toward me, and Robert gave me a smile. I took a shuddery breath. *Dear God,* I thought, *he means to ask me to marry him in front of all these people. This cannot be happening.* Robert gestured to the footmen, and we all turned to look.

Four footmen staggered under their burden as they entered, carrying a large rectangular object covered with gold velvet forward to Robert's feet. It was obviously a painting of some sort, and Robert smiled as he waited for the group to quiet again. Taking his mother's hand, he gestured to the footmen to remove the shroud, and the painting was revealed. Robert's guests clapped their approval. The painting was of Robert's mother and showed her seated in her favorite chair in this very room, posed in front of the same fireplace over which the painting would now hang. Robert's mother beamed and kissed her son's cheek, and we applauded, none louder than I.

"I thought you were going to ask Miss Lowell to marry you," shouted Jonathan Wumple, and the guests turned to look at me. Robert smiled and moved through them to stand in front of me, then bowed and took my hand. *Dear God, no,* I thought desperately.

Robert kissed my hand and kept it in his grasp as he turned to face the others. "Tonight we are celebrating my mother," he said, and the moment passed. I heard Randolph's sigh of relief.

If I had needed any clarification of my feelings, that night showed me where my heart was. I could no longer pretend. I could not even entertain the idea of marrying Robert. And that meant I could no longer give him the impression that I would. How ungrateful I felt. Robert, in the face of London's condemnation of me, had championed me. In his own way he was courageous and cared as little for convention as Alex. I could not belittle his generosity and steadfastness. But I could not lie to this good man and pretend that I loved him. It served me right to have had such arrogance to think that I was that important to Robert.

We left the next morning with the other guests. I had been careful not to be alone with Robert, but he seemed not to notice. As he handed me into our coach he smiled and kissed my hand, then said he'd be at Mountgarden within the week and turned to hand Louisa in behind me before I could answer.

Christmas came and went, and the following day Louisa and Randolph left to visit his sister. Will and Betty and I had three quiet days, then Robert arrived. I greeted him with trepidation, but my worries were for naught. Robert, holding my hand in front of the fire in my father's office, looked deeply into my eyes and told me he'd promised his mother not to ask me to marry him for six months. I stared at him open-mouthed while Robert blushed and stumbled through an explanation that made it very clear. His mother, while fond of me and vaguely approving of our marriage, wanted to be sure that any possibility of my carrying Alex's child was visibly demonstrated to the world. By June, Robert hinted, we would all know, and then he and I would talk about the future.

I flushed with anger, and Robert took it as shame. "I have never doubted your story, Mary," he said earnestly. "But this way there will never be any talk of whether . . ."

"Of whether any child I might bear is yours?" I said coldly. Robert nodded, clearly unhappy. "As I thought. Thank you, Robert," I said, extending my hand, "for your honesty. It is very welcome. But I must tell you, for your own knowledge, that there is no possibility of my bearing any man's child. No man has been with me, not my attacker, the man in the Campbell plaid"—he flinched, both at my tone and my words—"nor," I went on, "Alex MacGannon. He never touched me."

"Alex said he kissed you," Robert said with a spark of anger.

"Yes," I said, and took my hand back. "He did." I left the room. Robert left Mountgarden soon after that. Will was furious.

January passed slowly. I stayed in Mountgarden despite everyone's attempts to lure me back to London. Randolph even came to argue that I should go and beard the lions of chatter in their own dens. Staying in the country, he said, made it appear that I had something to hide. I smiled and thanked him but stayed where I was. And the Duchess came, full of kindness and news of other people. And of Alex. He'd been in London again, it seemed, and had visited her. When she'd mentioned me he said he had nothing to say about Mary Lowell. I resisted her invitation to return to London and thanked her for the news. She sighed and patted my hand. That night I folded Alex's half plaid away in the bottom of a trunk.

Robert did not come to see me. He sent flowers from his greenhouse and occasional tidbits from his estate. I sent his mother my thank-you letter for the Yule parties and received a polite, but distant, note in return.

I stayed in the country through February and into March, wrestling with my anger and my hurt and at last coming to terms with the fact that I'd never see Alex again.

No doubt Alex had married Morag by now. I considered joining a convent and determined to never care for another man. I would never marry Robert. I'd be a doting aunt to Will and Betty's children. It would have to be enough.

Louisa, the Duchess, and Becca's mother visited mid-March, saying as Randolph had, that I needed to be seen in society again to reclaim my position there. "Show them you have nothing to hide," the Duchess said. "And we'll be with you." I agreed. So back to London I went, back to the endless dinner parties and balls and theater and talk of politics and gossip. Randolph patted my shoulder and said I was brave. I didn't feel very brave, but I was back. I was received at first with curiosity and open appraisals of my waistline, and then, much sooner than I had imagined possible, was simply one more of the crowd. The gossips had moved on. And so had time.

An early spring was upon us, mild and wet, and I filled my days so full that I fell asleep as soon as I climbed into bed each night. But I could not control my dreams. In them I walked through the streets of London with Alex, laughing outside Westminster Abbey, or danced with him in my aunt's ballroom while her guests smiled at us. Far more disturbing, I dreamed that I rolled on a bed with a blond man, caught in his arms, feeling my hair slip across my naked shoulders as I leaned down to caress his thigh. And my nightmares, which had started after the attack and slowly left me, came back with a vengeance. In them, I was on the floor of a coach and the two men were attacking me. And Alex never came.

As March continued I faced my future. I'd braved London and survived, but it meant nothing to me. I'd seen Robert at several parties and had been, to his relief, cheerful and welcoming. But I'd refused to see him otherwise, and Louisa had not invited him to her house. The Duchess, as considerate as ever, arranged evenings one after the other for me, always consulting me on the guest list. Meg married a man thirty years her senior and I danced with Robert at her wedding, setting tongues wagging again. And Janice was now engaged to a minor lord in Hampshire. Everyone's life was changing except mine.

On the first day of April Robert arrived at Louisa's house with a bouquet of flowers and an invitation to his house in Kent for Easter week. And a note from his mother, sweetly written, asking us all to please join them. I had, it seemed, been deemed still acceptable. I held Robert's flowers before me, pretending to smell them, and considered. What were my choices? No other man had approached me, and Robert was attentive again. I'd be a fool to send him away. I could stay single and grow old alone, dependent on the charity of my family, or I could have a polite, if passionless, marriage. I didn't love Robert and I suspected I never would, but perhaps we could find a way to make some sort of life together. Certainly his wealth would help. I smiled at Robert and extended my hand. And watched his eyes light up.

Louisa and Randolph, and Will and Betty, had accompanied me to Robert's estate. Neither Randolph nor Louisa was especially pleased that Robert was courting me again. Both still harbored resentment for him and for his mother, but no one would have suspected it when they greeted Robert and his mother at her door like old friends. Which, I reflected, they were. Will was the one who was icy, thawing only when I reminded him that Robert, for all his faults, was a good man. Just not the man I wanted. Will pressed his lips together and nodded. There was more, I knew, that he wanted to say, but he said nothing now.

We stayed the week, keeping busy with riding and games and huge dinners every night. On the third day I wandered through Robert's garden with the other guests and paused beside an unexpected display. Bursting with pink blossoms, one lone rosebush demanded attention and I leaned over it, breathing in its fragrance with delight. As though he were behind me I heard Alex's voice say, *Mary, ye smell like roses.* I turned, but no tall blond man greeted me, and I shook my head to clear the memory. Alex was of the past, I told myself, and asked Robert's guest to repeat what she'd just said.

On the last day of our visit Will and I, with several other guests, were returning from riding when we saw two familiar figures on horseback outside Robert's main door, a horse with an empty saddle next to them. Angus and Matthew, visibly angry, watched us.

"It's Kilgannon's cousins," Will said.

"Where is Alex?" I asked, as though he might know. Will shrugged and we rode forward to meet them. The Scots were tight-lipped and pale. Angus responded when I greeted them. "Angus, where's Alex?" I asked, my horse dancing away from his. "Why are you here?"

Angus's tone was cool. "Yer Campbell willna admit us. He says ye dinna wish to speak to Alex."

"That's absurd! I did not even know he was here!"

"We sent a message to ye yesterday that we were arriving today. Matthew brought it."

I looked from Angus to Matthew. "Who did you give it to?"

"The butler, Mary," said Matthew, obviously unhappy.

"I never received it. I will discover what happened." I looked from one to the other of them. "But where is Alex?"

Angus gave me a tight smile. "Alex climbed the garden wall."

"He climbed the wall? He's in the garden?"

"Or somewhere. He said he'd look until he found you." I didn't wait for more. I threw myself from the horse and ran for the door. "Mary," Angus called after me, and I turned. "Be careful, lass, Alex is verra angry." I stopped and faced Angus. The rest of our riding party were reaching the Scots and watching us. Will was dismounting.

"With me, Angus?" I asked. "Is Alex angry with me?"

Angus gave a rueful shake of his head. "Alex canna stay angry with ye for more than a minute, Mary Lowell. No, lass, it's Robert Campbell that has Alex so irate. And no doubt Robert is as displeased with Alex. I dinna ken what ye'll find. Be careful."

I nodded at Angus and ran up the stairs two at a time, pushing the huge door open, to the consternation of the staff just within. Ignoring them, I ran through the house to the garden, hearing Will pounding behind me. I did not see Alex, but several of Robert's guests surrounded me, eager to explain that a mad Scotsman, equipped with several swords, had jumped into the garden and demanded to speak with me. He'd asked where I was, but they had run from him, screaming. Robert had ordered Alex to leave, but Alex ignored him and roamed the house, asking everyone where Miss Lowell was, while Robert followed him, shouting. At last someone had told Alex I was out riding with a group, and still glaring at each other, Alex and Robert had withdrawn upstairs. I ran back into the house and found a page who said he knew where they were and would lead me to them.

Will clasped my arm. "Mary, let me go with you," he said.

"There's no need, Will. Truly." I patted his hand. "Neither of them will harm me." I patted the hand on my arm again to cushion my remark. "Will, I must go alone. Please." He nodded reluctantly.

Robert's house had been built in the late 1500s, with deep walls and doorways that were actually short passages, a door at each end of this enclosure. I nodded my thanks to the page and entered the first door. The second was partially ajar and I stopped before I reached it, for I could hear Robert and Alex arguing. Alex's voice changed in volume as if he were moving around the room, but Robert's angry voice was clear and close to me. I took a step forward and listened. Robert was speaking.

". . . in a fashion that cannot continue, Alex. You are a dying breed. The Highlands cannot continue as they are. The world will come to you and that will destroy you. My cousin Argyll sees that, but you refuse to. You cannot seriously mean to take Mary there. She does not belong with you."

Alex's voice was cold. "That's not for ye to say."

"Someone has to get you to see clearly. You are not suitable for her. Mary has been raised in luxury among her peers. Kilgannon is not a place for someone like her. I cannot imagine you'd put Mary in a crofthouse, but you cannot give her the luxury she deserves. You have no money."

"Ye dinna ken my home," said Alex, his voice angry. "Kilgannon is not a crofthouse." There was a silence, then Alex's voice continued, quiet now and controlled. "I find ye disloyal to yer own people, Robert. Yer cousin Argyll sold our country to the English. That's why ye have money."

Robert's tone was icy. "Scotland was not sold, MacGannon."

"Aye, Campbell, it was. By yer family among others, and now yer prospering while the rest of us starve."

"Then wake up and understand what is happening. The English have the power. That's why we backed the Union. Join the English and you will have the power too."

Alex snorted. "Ye mean sell myself."

"No," said Robert. "But the old ways are dying. Join us."

"Never. It's what makes me a Scot instead of a lackey for the English." There was another long silence and then Robert spoke.

"You're papists," he said. "She'll never accept your faith."

"She doesna have to," Alex answered.

"What of children? What religion would you raise them in?"

"This is none of yer concern. It is between Mary and me."

"You are only thinking of your own desires!" Robert cried.

"As ye are! Dinna pretend yer trying to protect her."

There was a pause and then Robert spoke again in a

calmer voice. "Think, Alex. All your wealth is in your land or your ships, and you now have one less of them. If you need ready coin you have none. But I do. I can offer her safety. She can stay among her own people in England. I can give her everything she will ever need. I will keep her safe. If you care for her, you will withdraw your suit. Leave now and she'll never know you were here."

Alex's voice was weary, each word weighty. "I'll not discuss this with ye further, Robert. Mary will decide what her wishes are, not ye, not I. If she chooses me, ye will have to accept it."

"And if she chooses me?"

"Then I will accept it. But I'll hear it from Mary, not from ye—and not from yer damned butler—that she doesna wish to see me. I willna talk further on it with ye. I'll go and find her now."

I pushed the inner door open. "That won't be necessary," I said. Both men turned to me. The room was large and handsome, high-ceilinged and paneled in dark walnut, with rugs scattered on the floor. Robert leaned on a long table that ran the length of the room, while Alex stood in front of the fireplace opposite him, flanked by tall windows. With the light from the window behind him, I could not see Alex's face clearly. Robert's had paled as I entered.

"Mary," Robert said, moving toward me. Alex stood motionless.

"Robert," I asked, "did you tell the MacGannons I would not see Alex?"

Robert raised his chin but did not flinch. "Yes."

"And," I continued, "was there a note delivered yesterday for me saying that Alex would arrive today?"

"I did not think it wise that you see him."

"I see," I said. "And you did not think I might have some part of this decision?"

Robert gestured to Alex. "He's leaving, returning to Kilgannon. What difference does it make if you see him now?"

I turned to Alex but could not see his expression. "Is this true?" I asked him.

"Aye," Alex said. "I must go home."

"I see." I waited a moment. "Why are you here?"

Alex glanced at Robert, then looked at me. "To talk with ye."

Robert looked as miserable as Alex sounded. "Robert," I said. "I'd like to speak to Alex alone." With a nod Robert walked stiffly past me, shutting the door behind him. I could hear the second door close as well, but I opened the inner door to look. The passage was empty. When I turned, Alex was before me.

ELEVEN

THIS WAS AN ALEX I'D NEVER SEEN, PALE AND WEARY, A bleak expression in his eyes. He looked as though he hadn't slept in days. "Mary," he said, "how much did ye hear?"

"Enough." I moved to the fireplace, then glanced at him. "I want to thank you for the cloak, Alex. It's one of the most beautiful things I've ever seen."

"Yer welcome." He looked out the window, then back to me. "Mary, I . . . It's good to see ye."

I felt my cheeks flush. "And you, Alex. How have you been?"

"Fine." He shook his head. "No, lass, that's not true." He met my eyes, then turned abruptly away. *We can't make this work,* I thought. *We both want to, but we can't.*

"How was your Christmas?" I asked quietly.

He went to the window and stood looking out. "Lonely."

"Mine too," I said, and took a deep breath. "Alex, I'm very sorry for the way I behaved the last time I saw you." He turned to me in surprise. "I hope you will forgive me." I watched as his expression grew warmer.

"Forgive ye, lass? It's ye who should forgive me."

"You've done nothing that needs forgiving. The fault is mine. You saved my life, Alex, and you thought I still needed protection. I understand that now."

He nodded. "Mary," he said, taking a step toward me and then stopping. "I'm sorry for the things I said to ye, lass. It's true, I wasna thinking of the spot I'd put ye in by taking ye with me. I dinna mean to make ye the sport of London. Ye must ken that, Mary. I would not have had ye face that alone."

"Who told you that I did?"

"Yer brother wrote to me often. He's kept me abreast of . . . of what's been happening with ye."

"I see," I said, remembering Will's behavior of late. His anger with Robert had not dissipated as I had thought. "I wrote to you as well," I said. "Months ago. Did you get my letter?"

"Aye." He started to say something, then pressed his lips together. There seemed nothing else for me to say then. He'd gotten my letter and chosen to ignore it. I nodded. "Lass," he said, his voice gentle. "I thought I was doing the best thing by not responding to ye. I thought ye wanted me out of yer life and that it was for the best."

"So I wrote to you because I wanted you out of my life?"

He made a futile gesture. "It made sense at the time."

"You were still hurt."

He met my eyes, then nodded. "Aye, and fair angry as well."

"And now?"

He looked over my head. His cheekbone stood out in sharp relief against the dark shutter behind him. "I've not been angry for some time, Mary."

"Alex, why are you here?" I almost whispered the question.

"Why am I here?" Blue eyes met mine. "Will wrote that ye've starting seeing Robert again and that yer considering marrying him. And he wrote me about Robert's mother asking him to wait until June." He paused as his cheeks colored. "To be sure that ye were not carrying my child. I canna tell ye how angry I was then and . . . and it was then that I stopped lying to myself. So I thought I'd come and see ye and discover where we stand. We dinna part on the best of terms, lass, if ye remember. But I've been to London and Grafton and Mountgarden looking for ye and used up all my time. I must go home now." My eyes filled with tears and I could not speak. He moved closer and his tone was tender. "Mary, why do ye cry? Have I made ye angry again? I dinna mean to make ye cry."

"No." I shook my head. "No, I'm not angry. Oh, Alex, I missed you so." I could not say more, and his arms flew around me. I clung to him, my face buried in his shoulder.

"Mary, Mary," he said into my hair. "I had to see ye once more. We must talk. I couldna believe it when Robert's man said ye wouldna see me." He leaned back to look into my face and brushed the hair back from my cheek.

"I would never refuse to see you," I said. "I did not know you were coming. I saw Angus and Matthew in front of the house and I came to find you."

He kissed my forehead gently. "Come, lass, come sit with me." He led the way to the chairs pulled in front of the empty fireplace. "I kent you were here for several more days and by the time ye returned to London I would be gone, so, Campbell or no, I came to talk to ye." He glanced at the door. "Ye heard Robert and me arguing?" I nodded. He leaned back, the lost expression on his face again. "Despite what I said to him, he's correct about much of it. I dinna ken what to do now," he said softly. He stared at the floor, deep in thought, and I watched him for several minutes.

"Alex?" I said at last. "Do you care for me at all?"

His head lifted. "Do I care for ye? Mary, have I not been proposing since the night we met? Have I not had the devil of a time keeping my hands off ye? Have I not told ye how I love ye?" I shook my head, not trusting myself to speak. "No? I havena? No? Truly? Well, I do." He knelt in front of my chair and took my hands in his. "Mary Lowell, I love ye, lass, and I suspect I always will. How is it ye dinna ken this? Have I not told ye in every way? Curse me for a fool if ye dinna ken it."

"And I love you, Alex. I have from the first, but I didn't know what you intended. You never said you loved me. You never proposed."

"I mentioned it fifty times. Ye never said yes, and I was beginning to bore myself. I told ye I was courting ye. I thought ye kent my mind. What did ye think I meant by that if not marriage?"

"You mentioned marriage, yes. Proposed, no."

"How could ye not know how I feel? I've been miserable these last months thinking of ye with Robert, thinking that's what ye wanted for yer life. I couldna get ye out of my mind."

"Nor I you." I pressed my hand to my mouth and tried to force back the tears. "Alex, I missed you so—"

His arms were around me then, and he lifted me against him as he stood. "Mary," he said into my neck, "I couldna stop thinking about ye, about yer beautiful body and . . ." He raised his head to watch me. "And about how ye responded to me." I felt my cheeks go scarlet. "No, lass," he said, shaking his head. "Dinna think badly of yerself. It's a good thing. I'm thinking it bodes well for us. But, Mary, I dreamed of ye, of having ye in bed and of finishing what we began on the brig." He kissed me then, deeply and completely, and I met him in kind. "Mary," he said, almost savagely, and lifted me against him, then shook his head and stepped back. "I canna do this, lass." He moved away from me, straightening his clothing and taking deep breaths.

"You cannot kiss me, Alex?"

"I canna stop, Mary. If we go on I willna. It's best we stop here." He ran his hands through his hair and looked at the fireplace. I brushed my own hair into some order, then smoothed my dress, still feeling the warm, exciting sensations Alex's intimate caresses had evoked. I pressed my hands to my cheeks and found them flaming. My whole body was hot, and I threw open the window. Behind me, Alex laughed wryly.

"There's only one solution for this, Mary lass, and this is neither the time nor the place." He moved closer. "But at least we ken ye'll be an apt student."

"I beg your pardon," I said primly, and he laughed again. I watched the weight of his cares lift for just a moment and thought, *This man loves me. He has killed for me, and right now I'd kill for him.* It was a sobering thought. There were parts of me I'd not known. "Alex," I said, "must you leave?"

He nodded. "I have no choice, lass. I must get home. But I will return if ye'd have me. Ye ken that."

"I know no such thing," I said, taking his hands in mine.

"Mary, have I not told ye from the first day? It will be as ye wish. If ye wish me to return, I will. If not, I won't."

"How can you say you love me if you'd leave me so easily?"

He shook his head. "Yer a one. I dinna say it would be easy to leave ye. I said I'd do it if that's what ye wished. I'll no' beg ye to love me if ye don't, Mary. I dinna beg. But I'll love ye 'til I die. It's that simple. Now why are ye crying?"

"I'm happy." I tried to smile.

He shook his head in wonder. "Yer happy."

I nodded. "Oh, Alex, why do you have to go? Why can you not stay here, at least for a few days?"

"With Robert Campbell? I dinna think he'd invite me."

"No," I said. "In London. No, not in London," I corrected myself, and met his eyes. "Someone in London does not wish you well. Stay with us at Mountgarden."

He shook his head. "I canna, lass, much as I'd like to. If I had my way I'd steal ye off with me, but I canna do that either. Ye dinna like it much last time I tried that." He gave me a crooked smile. "I must go home. I've some sorting out to do." He frowned at himself. "Ye ken that things have been difficult for us lately. Strange things have been happening."

"What things?"

"Well, do ye not think it strange that the first time I charter a ship to another captain it goes down without a trace? We spent weeks in Cornwall trying to discover what happened, and we're no closer to the truth. We could find nothing except for the three crewmen who swear she sank, and they each tell different stories. How do I ken the boat even sank? It could be in the Mediterranean for all I ken. I'm still puzzling it out."

"Someone knows."

"Aye. Someone does. I'll discover it eventually."

"That's why you have to leave?"

"Not just that." He sighed and looked above my head. "There was a problem at home. It's trouble in the clan, Mary."

"First your boat and now this. You've had a difficult month."

"Aye," he sighed. "Not a few weeks I'd like to repeat. But"—he straightened his shoulders—"I have no choice. I must be there. I should have left a week ago."

"What is it, Alex? Surely it cannot be as bad as you think. Tell me and I will judge for myself."

He shook his head and looked at me, his eyes very blue. "I am a fool for telling ye this, Mary Lowell. I'm verra afraid it will cost me ye. I want ye to ken I love ye, lass, and despite what Robert Campbell says, I dinna have a clan full of savages."

"What is it, Alex?"

"One of the clansmen was murdered in his house."

"No! How horrible! Who—"

"I dinna ken, lass, and that is why I have to go home at once. I will find the murderers."

I stared at him in horror. "Dear God! This is terrible."

"Aye." He watched my reaction.

"What will you do?"

"I must go home and sort it out, lass. It's no' something I'm looking forward to doing, but only I can do it. So I canna stay. I will discover the truth of it, and I will punish whoever did it."

"How will you punish them?"

"We'll try them, and if they're guilty we'll hang them."

I stared at him. "You'd put them to death?"

"Perhaps." He met my look unflinchingly.

"You can do this? You have that power?"

"The power and the responsibility, Mary. When a clansman is killed I have to act. I canna allow such lawlessness. We would be savages if such a thing were unpunished." I shook my head to clear it. If I were to marry him, what kind of life would I be going to? Was Robert right? Alex's life was far more violent than any I'd known, I thought, remembering him killing the men in the coach. He moved toward me now, his hands extended. I took them and looked up at him as he spoke. "Mary, it's no' always like this. But with all of this happening in just the last few months, I . . . Mary, it is no' always like this," he added, his tone miserable.

"I see." I paused, looking at the haunted look in his eyes. "Our lives have been very different, Alex."

"They have been."

His expression was guarded as he stood there, watching me. He seemed to be calm, but I knew he was as aware as I that the next few moments could change our relationship forever. I watched a vein throb at his throat as I reflected. Was I simply full of brave talk, or was I willing to take all of his life, and not just those portions I understood? Was I willing to trust his judgment? Was I sure he was the man I thought he was? I knew he was a good man, and if I told him to, he would leave me now and I would never see him again. I would marry Robert and have a very safe life, a life with few surprises. A life of comfort and wealth, among my friends and family. A life without Alex. I raised my chin.

"I love you, Alex," I said, and watched his expression lighten. "Can't you send Angus to see what he can discover?"

Alex shrugged and almost smiled. "Angus willna leave me alone. He thinks he needs to be at my side."

"Is he always this protective?"

Alex shook his head. "He thinks I was poisoned in France."

I stared at him. "When you were so sick?"

"Aye." He frowned down at our hands.

"So do I." His head snapped up as he looked at me. "No one is that sick for four days after a bad meal. Your skin was gray, Alex. You were very ill and no one else was."

"Aye, but bad food can do that."

"Angus is right."

"I am not convinced."

"Who would do such a thing?"

He looked at me without expression. "Hatred runs deep in the Highlands, lass. The MacGannons have enemies, as does any clan."

"How many of them are in France, Alex? Only the Stewarts."

"I canna believe anyone was trying to harm me," he said, lifting his chin as he met my eyes. "I willna believe it."

"Could it have been the Stewarts?"

He laughed. "Why would they? I'm not so important, lass. They dinna even ken I exist. No, the Stewarts dinna try to kill me."

"Then who?"

"I dinna ken. But be assured I will find out. Mary, it's no' always like this. And I ken that saying that doesna make ye understand. Yer right to be wary of me just now, I'm thinking." He sighed. "Shall I come back and see ye again, Mary, or shall I say farewell now?"

I stared at him. "Alex, I don't want you to leave this room, let alone the country! I'm afraid to let you go; I'm afraid I'll never see you again. I love you, Alex Mac-Gannon," I said. "We'll sort it out together."

He smiled tenderly. "I was hoping ye'd say that."

"I love you." I reached a hand out to stroke his cheek. "And, Alex, if I am to be your wife, I must know what is troubling you. You were right to tell me. Let me be your ally."

"I dinna want to worry ye, lass. I'm sure it will all pass. It just came all at once and has been verra strange. It is probably nothing." He tried to smile as he pulled me close. "Mary, I promise it willna be like this if ye wed me. Trust me, lass, I'm not bringing ye to a wilderness full of barbarians." He kissed my hand. "Ye have my heart now, lass, and I'll give ye my name if you'd have it." I started to speak, but he put a finger to my lips, shaking his head. "Dinna answer now, lass. Think on it. There's a lot to consider. I have sons already, and ye must decide if that's what ye want. I dinna come without them, nor the clan and Kilgannon. And, of course, the religion. I'd not given it much thought, but the Campbell is correct. Ye must know it is a problem to be a Catholic in Scotland now. Scotland's seen a lot of cruelty in the name of God. So think on it, Mary. I don't want ye to wonder later if ye were hastened into something. Think on it while I'm gone, all of it. When I return we'll talk." He kissed me gently, then stepped back from me, smiling wryly. "I must go now before I disgrace us both. Think on it, lass. If ye tell me yes I'll take ye to Kilgannon. Ye'll live in a castle, Mary, not a crofthouse. But I'll not lie to ye: yer Campbell is correct that I'm only a rich man when I'm on my land. Or my ships, and we've just lost one." He touched my cheek. "But I love ye, Mary. If ye'd have me, ye'd make me verra happy and I'd do my best to be a good husband. I dinna ken what else to say. If ye tell me no, I will understand and I will bother ye no more." He was already moving away.

"Alex, I don't need time to answer you," I said.

He whirled back to face me, his kilt swirling around his knees, and he smiled. "Lass, if it's yes I'll be happy soon enough. Ye must have time to think on all I've told ye. There's no going back. Whichever way ye answer, there's no going back." He crossed the space between us, lifting me to him effortlessly. "I love ye, Mary Lowell. It will be as ye wish," he said. "But ken this, lass. Ye'll never find a man who wants ye, body and soul, more than I. Never." He bent me over his arm and kissed me until I was gasping, then righted me and smiled again as he moved away.

And then he was gone.

The air was thick with tension between Robert and me. When he had come to me after Alex left, I told him I was shocked by his deceit. I had never known him to lie before. He apologized, but I kept wondering, what if he'd succeeded? I would never have seen Alex again.

"Did he ask you to marry him?" Robert demanded, and I nodded, watching him change color as he paced in front of the fireplace. "In my house?" he roared. "The man barges in like the barbarian he is and proposes to you in my house? With me here? And you accept?"

"Yes," I said, facing the naked pain in his eyes. I hadn't intended Robert to suffer, but he had, and my heart leapt out to him. He stalked around the room shouting about Alex's lack of breeding. I listened for a few moments and then moved to a chair. "Robert," I said. "You never asked me to marry you. You were waiting to see if I was fit to be your wife. You never asked me."

He stared at me. I met his gaze calmly, and he was the first to shift his gaze. He paced the room quietly now, and after a while he sighed. "You're right, Mary," he said, sitting opposite me. "I did not claim you." *Claim me,* I thought, *like a piece of land or a good horse.* "If I asked you to marry me now, what would you say?"

"I would say no." I watched as his anger flared again.

"So Kilgannon rushes in and steals you."

"Ten months is not rushing in, Robert. You had two years."

"I was waiting for the right moment."

"You were considering. And you wanted to be sure no other man had usurped your place in my bed."

We looked at each other for a long moment before he nodded.

"No man has been in my bed, Robert," I said softly. "But Alex did not need to consider for as long. Nor did he consider as much."

"But I love you, Mary," he said softly. He was in earnest. For two men to tell me this in one day was absurd.

"Then you should have told me much before this, Robert. I was yours for the asking."

He leaned back against the chair, then leaned forward again. "You will not be happy with him. He is a barbarian."

"He is not a barbarian. He is a gentleman. And I love him."

He sneered. "So Kilgannon comes in like a noisy, ill-mannered child and you fall in love with him?"

I smiled as I thought of Alex. "He is noisy, isn't he?"

Robert was not amused. "Damn it, Mary, it's not funny. You have no idea of what you're choosing."

"I'm choosing a man who loves me, Robert, a man who will let the world know he loves me and damn the consequences."

"Then choose me. I stood by you, Mary. Few men would have."

My eyes filled with tears. "Yes," I said. "You did. And I am grateful for that. But I cannot choose you."

"You mean you will not."

"If I were choosing with my head, Robert, I would choose you. But I am not. I am choosing with my heart. It's too late."

We were silent for a long while. At last he sighed and spoke wistfully. "Would you ever have chosen me, Mary?"

"If you'd asked before I met Alex, I would be your wife now."

"And if you'd been my wife and then met him? Would you have been unfaithful to me?"

I took a deep breath and decided not to take offense. "No, of course not. I would have been faithful."

He stared at his hands before looking up at me. "So my caution has lost me you?"

"Yes."

He closed his eyes for a moment, then opened them as he rose to stand before me. "So be it. So be it. Mary . . . if you change your mind, if you ever need help . . . ever, no matter what, as long as you live, call upon me. Even if you marry him, I will be there for you. You have but to ask."

My eyes filled with tears again. "Thank you, Robert."

He left me alone then.

TWELVE

WE RETURNED TO MOUNTGARDEN, AND LOUISA AND Randolph left the next day for London. I didn't go, for London held no charms for me now. Louisa wrote that word had spread before us from Kent, and Alex and I were yet again the favorite topic of London gossip. As we were in Warwickshire. I listened impassively as Alex's visit to Robert's estate was endlessly discussed everywhere Will and Betty and I went. I kept my calm exterior, but I was thrilled that Alex had come to find me. The fact that he'd not considered his actions extraordinary made them even more so. I smiled to myself a lot. Alex loved me. What else could matter?

A week went by, then a second, with no word from Alex. I thought about what he had said and what Robert had said, but I'd made my decision much earlier. I wanted to be with Alex.

Our weather turned cold and then colder. We'd had no rain, but the cold threatened the newly planted crops, and all the talk was of the weather. I heard none of it, lost in my dreams of Alex and my future with him. On a cold, dark morning in late April, I was brought a letter that held the familiar crest. I broke the seal and folded the paper open.

My dearest Mary, he wrote. *How I miss you. I am in London and will be following this letter in a day or so. We have much to discuss. Since your father is gone and your brother is younger than I am, I have asked your uncles for permission to marry you. Your uncle Randolph has readily consented and I went to visit your uncle Grafton yesterday. He's a strange man, as you have said, but he welcomed me and I like him very much. He told me that you were the one to make any decision as to whom you marry, not he, but he suggested I should ask Will. I think I should ask you. Please be ready with your answer. If it is nay then I will leave at once. If you wish not to see me at all*—a large ink blot obliterated the next few words, then he continued in an agitated hand—*Mary, I will be with you shortly. Yours, Alex.* I hugged the letter to me while a glow spread through me. Alex was coming. All was right with the world.

It had started snowing, and I watched the flakes gather as I waited. And waited. It snowed all afternoon and all night. Everyone complained loudly about snow in April, worried about the damage the late storm would do. In the morning the sun shone weakly for an hour or two before disappearing into the fog, and by luncheon it was snowing again. *He will not be able to come through this,* I told myself. *He'll stay in London.* And I began to worry, thinking of the attack in the coach. *He'll stay in London because of the weather,* I thought. *And someone who does not wish him well might discover that.* Or he might try to travel through it. I didn't know which worried me more. I could not settle. The accounts went untouched, the books unread, my sewing undone. Will and Betty retired upstairs in the late afternoon, and I was in my father's office, idly looking through papers, when a maid popped her head in and said Lord Kilgannon was here to see me. I flew past her.

"We left him in the foyer, Miss Mary," she called after me. "He looks very fierce."

I ran to the hall and found him with his back to me, studying the paintings, dressed in a cloak that covered most of him. Melting snow fell from him onto the marble floor, and his wet hair dripped down his back. Several of the staff hovered nervously nearby, but none of them had welcomed him, and I hurried to remedy that.

"Alex," I said, and he turned. His lips were blue, his cheeks windburned, but his eyes lit up when he saw me. He opened his arms. I was in them without a thought for the staff.

"Mary," he whispered into my hair. My face was pressed against his shoulder and I clung to him for a moment before he kissed me. His lips were cold, his hands like ice when I wrapped my arms around him, and I realized his clothes were wet through. I pulled the cloak off his shoulders and I fussed over him, handing his cloak, jacket, hat, and gloves to waiting hands.

"Bring me one of my brother's jackets, Jack," I told one of the houseboys. "And some socks," I added, glancing at Alex's feet. "The boots come off too, sir." He protested, but I persisted, and in short order I led a barefoot Scot into my father's office and had warm food on the way. I closed the door firmly behind me and studied him as he warmed his hands. He wore some kind of close-fitting leggings made of a plaid knitted material, topped by a very long woolen shirt. Underneath was another shirt of oatmeal wool that reached his thighs, and I persuaded him to shed the top shirt so it could dry. I hung the shirt over a chair. He laid his short sword on the hearth and reached for me.

"Mary, I have missed ye sorely," he said, pulling me to him.

"Alex," I gasped between kisses. "You're beautiful."

I could feel his laughter. "Oh, aye, I've always thought so too. Especially now. Yer daft, lass."

"No," I said as he kissed me again. I ran my hands up his back, feeling the muscles of his shoulders. I lost myself in our embraces until a knock at the door made us spring apart. It was the food, and I helped the girl, who was glancing covertly at Alex. His hair was drying and he brushed it back from his face with the gesture I remembered so well. When the girl left he laughed.

"We're scandalizing them here now, Mary. I'm thinking we have quite a talent for doing that."

"It's you, Alex. They've known me all my life. They thought you looked very fierce." I gestured him to the table.

"Oh, aye, fierce. I'm no' fierce. I'm frozen and verra hungry," he said as he sat before his plate. I asked him if he'd like something stronger than tea. "Aye, that I would," he said, beginning to eat. I knew there was a bottle somewhere in the desk and had just found it when the houseboy Jack burst into the room with the clothes. I was grateful that we had not been caught in a lustful embrace by an eight-year-old. Jack looked at Alex as if he were a creature from another world. Which, I suppose, he was.

"Your clothes, sir," Jack said, thrusting them at Alex, who thanked him and put the clothes on a chair. Jack continued to stare. I poured the liquor—brandy, not whisky—and Alex took it gratefully, watching the boy as he drank.

"Out with it, lad," Alex said. "What do ye want to know?"

Jack stammered. "Are you the Scot who's going to marry Miss Mary? Did you climb the Tower wall? Do you have a sword?"

"Aye. No. Aye." Alex laughed. "I'm going to marry your Miss Mary if she'll have me. But I dinna climb the Tower wall. I climbed Lord Campbell's garden wall. Ye would have done the same, no?" Jack nodded. "And, aye, I have a sword. Do ye want to see it?" Jack nodded again, his eyes huge. Alex pointed out the sword's features and ate slowly, patiently answering the boy's questions while I watched. *He must be like this with his own sons,* I thought, and wondered again what they were like. If I were to spend my life with this man, I would be spending it with his sons as well. I would be their stepmother. I'd been thinking only of my life with Alex, but now I felt a quiver of fear. Would they like me? Would I like them? I thought of the two little faces from the sketches he had sent me. Would Sorcha's memory always stand between us? I would do my best to be a good mother, I resolved. But would that be enough? What was I doing? Caught up in my own musings, I was startled when Jack bobbed a bow to me and ran out of the room. At Alex's laugh, I looked up.

"No doubt he'll be spreading tales in the kitchen," he said. "Before he's through I'll have cut someone in two with a claymore." Alex's voice grew tender. "Mary, how have ye been?"

"Fine, Alex," I said, my thoughts having made me suddenly shy. "Any news about your ship?"

"No," he said.

"And what of the murder?"

His expression was grim. "We found the culprits and I hanged them, Mary," he said without expression. I looked away then, and an awkward silence settled on us. After a moment he sighed and took his shirt from the chair next to him. "Mary," he said. "I thank ye for the food and the fire." He did not look at me as he put his still-damp shirt on, and I realized with a start that he was leaving. I said his name, but he did not look at me. He leaned down to pick up the sword.

"Alex—" I said again, but he interrupted before I could go on, raising his chin as he looked at me, his eyes very blue.

"Mary, ye dinna have to say it. I've been a fool."

I rose to stand before him. "Alex, are you leaving?"

"Aye."

I put my hand on his arm. "I thought you loved me."

"I do, lass," he said.

"Then, for God's sake, ask me to marry you."

His eyes were suddenly angry. "Dinna toy with me, Mary."

"I am not toying with you, Alex."

At last he nodded. "Mary, have ye thought on marrying me?"

"I have thought of little else. And, yes, Alex, I'll marry you. But you must ask correctly."

He blinked. "Correctly. I've been asking incorrectly?"

"Yes." I laughed. "Actually, you haven't asked me at all."

"Ah. Well." He studied me for a moment. "Mary, ye ken my wealth is less than it was?" I nodded. "And that the Mac-Gannons are Catholic." I nodded again. "And that we'll be living in Kilgannon?"

"Yes, and I know that your sons are part of the bargain. I know they need their father. I will do my best to be a mother to your sons." I took the sword from him and placed it on the hearth again. "I need their father too. We'll have to share. I love you, Alex. I trust your judgment and believe that you were right to dispense justice as you did. I will marry you and move to Kilgannon. We will share what you have, and what I bring will be yours as well if you'll have me."

"Ah, lass," he said, his eyes shining again. "I'd love to have ye." He laughed as I put my arms around him.

"That's not what I meant."

"It is what I meant," he growled into my neck.

"Then you must ask correctly, sir."

"Correctly?"

"Yes."

"I must ask correctly to have ye?"

"You must ask correctly to marry me."

He nodded and stood in front of me, taking my hands in his. His expression was tender, his voice earnest.

"Mary Lowell, will ye have me for a husband? Will ye marry me and be my wife?"

"Yes, Alex." I looked into his eyes and smiled. "Yes."

He kissed me softly. "Ah, lass, ye've made me verra happy."

"And you me," I whispered into his neck.

He laughed then, the sound warm and rich, as he lifted me into his arms, whirling us both around the room. "Ha!" he shouted. "She said yes!" He kissed me deeply, and we slowly stopped spinning and concentrated on each other. "She said yes," he said quietly, his eyes dark as he traced a finger along my cheek to my lips, then followed his path with his mouth. At last we paused for breath and I shook my head at him.

"How could you doubt I'd say yes, Alex?" I asked. "How could you wonder? I've done nothing but throw myself at you for months."

His expression sobered. "I canna think of why ye'd love me, Mary, enough to leave all this." He waved his hand at the room. "I love ye, lass, but it's a tremendous thing to ask of ye, and I wasna sure ye'd want to once ye'd considered it fully."

"Alex," I said, reaching for him again. "You'll never find a woman who wants you, body and soul, more than I. Never." He laughed that deep laugh again and I smiled triumphantly at him, then put one hand under his shirts and stroked his back. His skin was smooth, and I wanted to peel the shirt off him and see him. I put my other hand under his shirt and he pulled me closer to him. I could feel his body stir. And Will walked into the room. I dropped my hands from Alex's back and buried my face in his shoulder. His arms were still strongly around me, and I heard him speak over my head.

"We're betrothed, Will," Alex said calmly. The pause was so long that I turned my head at last to see Will's reaction. His expression was unreadable, but he was looking at me when he replied, "It took you long enough, Kilgannon."

It snowed for the three days Alex stayed, and we talked constantly, about marriage and children, books and politics, London and Scotland. Jack followed Alex around like a puppy. He thought Alex truly astonishing. In fact, most of the staff thought him astonishing. He won several of them over, especially the cook, when he insisted on going to the kitchen to thank her for a fine meal. Lord Alex could do no wrong after that, and she outdid herself while he was with us.

We were walking through the gallery when I asked him about the comments I'd heard that his family were Jacobites, supporters of the deposed king James Stewart. The Catholic James, or *Jacobus* in Latin, had been forcibly supplanted by the Protestant William of Orange. William was a Dutch prince whose claim to the English throne was twofold: He was the grandson of the beheaded King Charles I, a Stewart, and also the husband of Mary, daughter of the Stewart king James II. William invaded England in 1688 to claim the throne from King James, who fled to France with his son. Left unchallenged, William had taken the thrones of England and Scotland. Some Scots, now called Jacobites, had risen in James's defense in 1688 and were defeated in the Battle of Killiecrankie the next year. Alex's father had been among them. I watched his reaction to my question. He sighed and looked up at the portraits of my ancestors.

"Why is it, lass," he asked, pointing to the pictures, "that their lives seem so simple and uneventful and ours seem so beset with worries?" He walked on, looking at me over his shoulder. "What ye've heard is that my father went out in '88, no? And that I've been in France. Well, it's true."

"What is?" I trailed along behind him.

"That my father went out in '88." He smiled at my confused expression. "I mean that my father joined the Stewart faction that opposed King William taking over the throne of Scotland and England." He smiled wryly. "They lost Killiecrankie and the rebellion was over. My father signed the oath of allegiance to King William, and the MacGannons have kept his word. It's also true that I've been in France and that I've met James Stewart. I also have a cousin who lives in Paris, and throughout the war I have visited him. He married a French girl, and he's no Jacobite." He turned fully to me. "I have no intention of joining a rebellion, Mary, and certainly not for the Stewarts. They turned their backs on

Scotland and I for one have never forgiven them, despite the fact that I do agree that James should still be king. But he's Catholic and England willna accept a Catholic king again, I'm thinking. James Stewart is no threat to us, lass. Put it out of yer mind," he said, and pulled me into his arms.

Alex was very proud of Kilgannon and told me much about it, drawing plans and sketches of the castle and grounds and explaining when the various parts had been built and what each generation had done to improve it. He confessed that he was the artist of the sketches he had sent, and that reminded him that his sons had sent letters and pictures to me. "Matthew helped Ian write his letters," he said as he handed them to me, "but Jamie was unaided, as ye'll see."

Dear Miss Lowell, wrote Ian in mismatched letters. *My da says you may come here and live with us. That would be good. Come soon.* I smiled up at Alex. At least one of Alex's sons would welcome me. Jamie had drawn a picture that I could not identify and someone had signed his name to it. Alex shook his head.

"I could see nothing in it either, Mary, but he wanted to send something to ye and I told him I'd bring it."

"I'll have him explain it to me when I see him. But when will that be, Alex? When will we marry?"

He smiled. "Well, if ye agree, I thought I'd go home and come back for ye in a month. I need to get some things ready and post the banns, and I dinna know what yer wishes were. Do ye wish to wed here and then go to Kilgannon, or do ye wish to wed there? If we wed in Kilgannon it will be a Catholic ceremony. Will yer family object? Will ye object? I dinna ken what ye'd want."

I smiled. "I want you, Alex."

He looked at me, startled, and after a moment gave me a slow smile in return. "Yer very direct, miss."

"Aye, Alex, I told ye. It saves time." He laughed with me. "What do you wish, my love? What are your feelings on this?"

"Well," he said, rubbing his chin. "If we marry in an English church it will make yer family happy and it's sure to annoy some of the clan. If we do the reverse it will please the clan and will annoy yer family. I have no solution." He leaned back dispiritedly. "I dinna consider this fully. I had no idea it would be so complicated. No matter what we do we insult someone."

I smiled again. "It's simple, Alex."

"No, Mary, simple it's not."

"Aye, Alex, simple it is." I kissed his cheek as he frowned.

"How is it simple, lass? I canna see simple in this."

"When you return to England we will marry in an English church so that my family can be with me. And then we go to Kilgannon and have your priest marry us. That way no one is offended. We marry with both families present and both religions represented."

He gave me a startled look. "Yer willing to do this?"

"Yes. Are you?"

"I have no objection. Perhaps the priests will, but I think it's a good plan. Aye." He sat up straight. "Well, another month it will have to be. Unless, ye think—" My protest was lost as he kissed me.

Alex left the next afternoon, and that night I could not sleep. I remembered my beautiful mother singing and my father's tender expression as he watched her, and Mother overseeing the fitting of my first ballgown. It was all gone now, and I was about to begin on my own. I had never missed them so much. Father would have talked to Alex and given his blessing, and Mother would have been everywhere. The tears trickled down my cheeks and I wiped them away with a sigh. Now life with Alex beckoned, and I was going to be his wife and live in another country with another people. Was I up to the task of becoming wife and mother and countess? Part of me wanted to be a little girl again, safe at Mountgarden with my parents and no decisions to make. I sighed again and thought of Alex laughing on the streets of London, in an inn worrying about the future of his country, lying ill in his boat, climbing a wall to find me, coming through a snowstorm to see me, saving my life. Alex standing alone in a ballroom filled with people. I suddenly realized he was as fearful as I and as vulnerable. But he was braver. He had openly and honestly pursued me, representing all of his drawbacks and never mentioning his attractions. He faced the disapproval and disdain of English society squarely and laughed. By becoming his wife I would forever join him in being an outsider in England. True, he was an earl and I would be his countess, but he would always be less, in the eyes of some, simply because he was Scottish. And what would I be? An Englishwoman married to a Scotsman was neither truly English nor Scots. Would the clan accept me? What was I doing? I shook my head. It was too late to be having second thoughts. All I had to do was think of never seeing him again and all my doubts faded. I thought of his blue eyes looking into mine and hugged myself, which was a poor substitute for his embrace. As long as Alex loved me I could face anything.

THIRTEEN

WE HAD PLANNED TO MARRY IN A SIMPLE CEREMONY
at Mountgarden, but Louisa would have none of it, and
though the time was short she planned an elaborate wedding in St. Rosemary's, followed by a lavish celebration at
her home. Randolph, to my surprise, threw himself head-
long into the preparations and beamed at me constantly.
When I tried to thank him for all his generosity, he stopped
my words with a wave, explaining that neither he nor Louisa
had any children, that I'd become like a daughter to him,
and that he'd grown fond of Alex. I kissed his cheek and
hugged him and pretended not to notice that his eyes were
suspiciously damp as I thanked him again. He patted my
back and strode quickly away.

Louisa was in her element, planning every detail with her
effortless skill, while I trailed along behind her. We talked
constantly, and sometimes I caught her misty-eyed and I
realized how much I would miss her. And how much we
both missed my mother. Will was wonderful, doing whatever was needed. Betty was no help, of course, drifting in
and out of rooms, leaving all the work to the rest of us, but I
didn't mind, for we were not without assistance. Becca's
mother came often to aid Louisa and took credit for seeing
the good in Alex before anyone else. The Duchess, who was
also with us constantly, argued that she was the only one in

London who had seen what a fine man the Earl of Kilgannon was. They debated the point constantly.

A week before the wedding Alex and his family arrived. Malcolm, Angus, Matthew, and nine other men accompanied Alex. His Aunt Deirdre had stayed behind to take care of the details of our second wedding but had sent me a letter in which she graciously welcomed me into the MacGannon family. Nor did Alex bring his sons. When I asked him why, he said that this would be the only time we'd really be together, just us, and that he was anxious for our wedding night. My cheeks had flamed at his teasing. "Which willna be long, lass," he'd said, "depending upon which of our weddings ye'll consider to be our real marriage."

"We'll be together as soon as we're married here, won't we?"

He deliberately misunderstood me. "No, that would be rude," he said. "We should wait until after the meal. Yer aunt and uncle have gone to a great expense and effort, ye ken. We must visit with them and the guests a bit." He ignored my exclamation. "We must, Mary. It's only polite." I laughed.

At last we finalized our plans. After the wedding we would leave London. The MacGannons would sail to Bristol and wait for us there, while we spent the five days of our wedding trip in the Dower House of one of the Duchess's properties, this one in Wiltshire. She and the Duke had insisted that we stay there as part of their wedding gift, and we had gratefully accepted. From Wiltshire we would travel to meet my family and *Gannon's Lady* in Bristol before sailing north. The Kilgannon wedding would be held the day after we arrived, on a Wednesday for luck.

Matthew was enthusiastic, joining in the work so often that we all began to rely upon him. He and Will joked as though they'd known each other for years, and he listened to Randolph's stories with a respectful manner that endeared him to Louisa. Malcolm watched us with a patronizing air, looking always slightly bored. He'd not had one pleasant or encouraging thing to say. I ignored him most of the time and kept my thoughts to myself. Angus refused to be drawn into the plans as well, but he was courteous. Occasionally, though, I caught him watching me with a serious expression. He was Alex's shadow, apparently content to while away the hours as he waited, and when he was not with us, Matthew was. The rest of the MacGannons were unfailingly polite but rarely left Alex's side, often hovering near us when we talked. When my family commented on it to Alex, he shrugged and laughed, telling them he was a very important man.

Our wedding day dawned bright and clear. In the morning Louisa and I had one last wonderful conversation and cried as we talked about my mother. She gave me a pin my grandmother had worn on her wedding day, and I thanked her for all of her kindnesses over the years. She hushed me, but I knew she was pleased. I wore my mother's silk-and-lace wedding dress. The dress had had to be lengthened since I was much taller than my mother had been, but it was a beautiful gown and it brought a bit of her with me. I needed to believe she would have blessed this marriage, and I hoped ours would be as happy as my parents'. And as Becca's seemed to be. She and Lawrence had recently returned from the Continent, glowing with contentment. I was grateful to have her with me, for she was cheerful and reassuring, telling me I would love married life and laughing at my fears that I would prove inadequate as a wife.

At the church we were shown to the bride's suite of rooms overlooking the street below. I was much calmer than I would have imagined, or so I thought as I was dressed and my hair arranged with the advice of all in the room. But when Becca, who was sitting by the window, gestured for me to join her and see something, I nearly tripped over the hem of my gown, and my decorum was tilted even more when I saw what she was looking at. Alex, in the midst of the dozen MacGannons, was walking toward the church.

He was the only one in English dress, but he had a Mac-Gannon plaid over his shoulder and his bonnet on his head. We had had much discussion about what he would wear. Alex said it did not matter. I wanted him in Highland dress, but Randolph and Louisa thought he should wear English clothes. In the end it was Matthew who had decided. "When in Rome . . ." he'd said with a shrug, and that settled it. Alex stood below now, about to become my husband, wearing a gray velvet frock coat and breeches and a snow-white shirt. I could hear the bagpipes plainly and stood transfixed as the Scots approached the church, then stopped below us. Alex stood in the midst of the men, laughing. With Rebecca at my side I watched the men, the crowd around them curious but well behaved. Becca sighed.

"He is so handsome, Mary," she whispered, looking over her shoulder at her mother and my aunt. I agreed, thinking of her Lawrence, who was a wonderful man but very ordinary. There was nothing ordinary about Alex. "You do love the man and not just the handsome exterior?" She had asked me this a thousand times, and I answered as I had a thousand times, that I loved everything about him.

The church glowed with candles and I walked up the aisle on Randolph's arm in a dream, seeing only Alex waiting for me and my handsome brother with him. *Dear Will,* I thought. He had been adamant that he would stand with Alex to show all of London my family's support for this marriage. It was a gesture Alex had appreciated, and it made having Malcolm stand next to Alex bearable for me. Alex watched me reach him, his eyes dark and his expression intent, then took my hand with a nod to Randolph, and the ceremony began. Standing next to him at the altar, I was overwhelmed by the step I was taking. I do not remember the details of our marriage, only a church crowded with well-wishers and Alex by my side. I stole a look at him, wondering if he were as nervous as I. *I will spend the rest of my life with this stranger,* I thought, as he answered the priest's questions in a clear voice that carried. His expression was serene when he turned to look at me, and when our eyes met, he smiled and held my hand even tighter. I felt the knot inside me loosen and I smiled at him in return, able now to answer the priest's questions without falter. Alex put the ring that had been his mother's and grandmother's on my finger and kissed me. I was a married woman.

The reception at Louisa's was full of laughter. I was pleased that so many of London's elite had come to wish us well. Even my uncle Harry attended and seemed to enjoy himself very much, mingling with the crowd with ease, his laughter ringing above theirs. He spent much of his time with Alex's family, and I wondered how I had ever thought this amiable man strange. Harry commented that London seemed to approve of our match, and that did seem so. Louisa's invitations were rarely declined, and many came to the wedding because of her popularity. The merely curious came to see the ceremony and my dress and behavior, or to gape at Alex and his family, who did not disappoint. Taller than most of the other men, the twelve Scotsmen drew many glances. Alex was by far the handsomest, but Meg, now married herself, was very taken with Donald, Alex's cousin of some degree, a huge man, even bigger than Angus. So of course they called him wee Donald.

The afternoon was a blur of faces. Even those who came only to be able to gossip later behaved themselves admirably. When at last it was time for us to leave, Alex took a moment with his family and then with mine, as I did the same. Then we smiled into each other's eyes and climbed into Randolph's carriage. We arrived at the Dower House without incident and were greeted by the Duchess's efficient staff. As we were being shown around we stole glances at each other. We would soon be alone. At least in the house. I had brought no maid, at Alex's insistence, and he had no valet or personal servant, but Angus, Matthew, and wee Donald were in the barn. I had protested that we'd be safe, but Alex had been firm.

"There's nothing that ye dinna ken, Mary. I canna believe anyone would try to attack either of us here, but Angus will no' leave me here when my attention is not on my safety. And I've other things to occupy me." When he'd kissed me I had agreed without further argument.

The Duchess's staff was very thorough, but I thought they would never leave. A few moments later, however, at last alone in our bedroom, I felt shy and moved quietly, putting our things away while Alex watched me. I turned from folding my gloves to find him in front of me. He smiled. He had removed his shoes and stockings and the plaid he'd had over his shoulder. Now he took his jacket off, throwing it behind him, and loosened the lace at his neck.

"Mary," he said, wrapping one arm around my waist and drawing me to him. "I have been well behaved long enough." He kissed me and drew back to look at me. "Are ye afraid, lass?"

"Yes. No. I mean . . ." I took a deep breath. "I'm terrified, Alex. But how can I tell you that?"

He laughed softly. "Ye just did. Come," he said, taking my hand and leading me to the fireplace. "I promise I'll not do anything ye don't want me to. I'm willing to wait until yer ready, Mary. We have the rest of our lives." I watched the light from the flames play across his cheek and I nodded. He pulled me to him then, my cheek on his chest as he stroked my back, leaning his head against my hair. He smelled like soap. "Dinna be afraid, lass. We'll go as fast as ye wish and as slow. This is a good thing we're about to do. Listen to yer body. Yer body kens what to do. Dinna think." I listened to the beating of his heart, and my fear receded. This was Alex. My husband. In the eyes of the world we were now one.

"And two shall become one," I said softly, raising my

mouth to his, delighting as I always did in the feel of his lips on mine.

"I love ye, Mary." He kissed me gently, then more insistently, and reached up to pull the pins from my hair. As it fell over my shoulders he groaned and pulled me tighter against him. I could feel his body's readiness and my own response. Without a word he pulled his shirt loose from his pants and put my hand on his side under the material. I ran my fingers across the smooth skin of his side, then his back. Braver now, I brought my hands to his chest and tangled my fingers through the hair there. Blond hair, I knew, and brought my hands to his shirt to undo the fastenings. His breathing grew faster.

"Mary," he said huskily as I opened his shirt and pushed it from his shoulders. He let the shirt fall to the floor behind him and looked at my face as I stroked my hands across his chest, watching the shadows play on his skin as I moved my fingers. I leaned forward and kissed his neck, then his shoulders. He closed his eyes under my touch but opened them when I stepped back to look at him.

"You're magnificent, Alex," I said. "Absolutely magnificent." He shook his head and smiled, then leaned to kiss me as he pulled the lace loose from atop my bodice. I wrapped my arms around him and felt his skin against the tops of my breasts. *Heaven,* I thought. He opened each bodice fastening with slow, determined hands. I didn't stop him as he concentrated on the task, removing the top of the gown from my shoulders. He stood back from me then and leaned his head to one side as he studied me standing before him. My corset seemed restrictive, and I took a shuddery breath. He smiled and reached for the lacing.

"Alex," I said in a quavering voice as he slowly pulled one lace from its bindings.

"Look at ye, Mary," he said. "Look at how yer skin glows in firelight." He traced a finger across the tops of my breasts. "Yer so beautiful, Mary MacGannon. Wife." He kissed me again, then drew back. "I have waited so long for this. Let me look at ye, lass." He pulled the second lace from my corset and it sprang open. I closed my eyes when first his hands, then his lips, touched my breasts. I don't remember my shift leaving me, but it must have, for his hands were on my breasts, my back, my neck, and I was pulling him even closer. The feel of his chest on mine made me gasp and open my eyes. I ran my hands across his back and pulled his hair loose, letting it fall across his shoulders and my hands.

When he reached for the waist of my gown I showed him how to loosen it, then laughed when he looked askance at the number of petticoats I wore. "This may take the whole five days," he growled, and I laughed again, realizing that I was no longer afraid. I stepped out of each petticoat as he pulled it to the floor, then watched without breathing when he slowly undid my garters and rolled the stockings down my legs, his hands lingering on my thighs before caressing my calves. I blushed when he stepped back to look upon me, naked for the first time before any man.

"Lass," he said, holding my arms wide. "Yer the most exquisite woman that has ever lived. I've never seen any woman more lovely. No, Mary, dinna blush and get shy again. Look," he said, running a hand from the side of my breast down to my waist and hip, turning me in the light from the fire. "Look how ye curve in and out. Ye are perfection, Mary Lowell."

I shook my head. "Not Mary Lowell anymore, Alex. I'm Mary MacGannon now. The Countess of Kilgannon. Alex's wife."

"Aye," he said. "Mary. My wife."

I took a deep breath and summoned my courage. "Alex," I said. "I would like to see you."

"And ye shall." He was out of his pants so quickly that I giggled. "This makes ye laugh?" he asked fiercely, standing before me naked. I shook my head. Indeed, all of me was shaking.

"No. You're divine," I said, drawing in my breath. And

he was. Tall and lean, his body was flawless. His shoulders, arms, and chest were well muscled, his waist trim, and his legs long and lean. I marveled at him. Had there ever been such a man? *My husband,* I told myself. His skin, tan on the legs and arms, was smooth and clear. I ran my hands along his sides and down to where his legs met his body, exploring the thighs I had so longed to touch. He was very ready for me and I blushed again, not sure what to do.

He smiled. "Don't think, Mary," he said, and pulled me to him, cupping my breast in his hand as he bent to kiss it. I stroked his shoulders and leaned back as his hands roamed over me, stroking my legs, my stomach, my back, and more. *It feels right,* I thought, *it feels right to have him touch me.* I reached for him and he smiled.

And I didn't protest when he led me to the side of the bed, letting him bend me back onto it. He leaned over me and smiled. "Mary, ye have no idea how wonderful ye look, yer hair tossed across the sheets, so dark against the white, and yer skin like milk. Ye may be the most beautiful woman that has ever lived. And yer mine." He lowered his body slowly next to mine. "My wife," he sighed, and kissed me. "My Mary."

"And two shall become one," I said, and pulled him down to me.

"And two shall become one," he said. We did not speak for a long time.

It was wonderful. He was tender and generous and patient, and after the first few moments I relaxed, giving myself to him fully. His body was magnificently male, and I explored it with delight. Now I knew what all those women meant when they discussed men and why Rowena looked at him as she did. I would never look at him the same. Cradled in his arms as he slept, I decided I was the most fortunate woman in the world. *This is my husband,* I thought, *for the rest of my life. Nothing will ever separate us again.* I smiled to myself. We would face the future together. Two had become one. He had been right. My body, once I stopped guiding it, had known what do. Alex taught me the rest. I ran my fingers across his back and felt him tighten his grip on me. I turned on my side and leaned into his warmth and slept.

I woke in the early morning and slowly realized that I was not alone. All memory flooded back as I opened my eyes and he was there, propped up on one elbow, his hair falling around his face, his expression tender. "Good morning to ye, lass." He kissed my forehead before he scooted himself down to eye level with me. "The first thing I saw when I opened my eyes was yer face, Mary."

"I'm sorry," I said.

He laughed softly and stroked my cheek. "I'm not. I've waited months for this. I wanted to take ye to my bed the night we met, but I thought it would be impolite. How are ye this morning?"

"Alex, it was amazing." I sighed with contentment.

He laughed again and pulled me to him. I could hear his heart beating and I sighed again. I grew sleepy, but after a few moments he whispered my name. "Mary, are ye awake?"

"Yes." I stretched my arm out as I yawned. He reached out and took my hand and, in the fashion of lovers everywhere, compared our hands, his browner and much bigger. "We're the same size."

"Not quite, lass. Ye come to my waist."

"I'm almost as tall as you are." I propped myself up on one elbow and faced him. He laughed at me.

"Aye, that's the first thing I noticed. The top of yer head."

"That's not true."

"No, it is not," he said, his hands busy again. "I noticed other things first."

I smiled, stroking his chest and sliding my hand down to his stomach. "I think I was born to be in bed with you."

"Ah, Mary, I'm glad yer not afraid of this. I was wondering if . . ." He sucked in his breath as I moved my hand lower.

"If?"

"If ye'd like it," he said huskily.

I laughed. "I like it."

FOURTEEN

WHEN I WOKE AGAIN IT WAS MIDDAY, RAINY, AND I
was alone. I found Alex downstairs before the fire, reading,
looking so content that I smiled to myself, enjoying the
scene.

"How are ye, lass?" he said, and looked up with a smile.

"Very well rested," I said, laughing. "And hungry."

He laughed too. "Strange effect marriage has on ye." I
made a face at him and led the way into the kitchen, where
we sat at the table in the kitchen eating a cold meal.

"Alex?" I said. We had been quiet for a few minutes
and I'd watched him as he ate, his expression thoughtful.
"Alex, I want to discuss something."

"Och, here it comes. One day married and it's starting."

"You're making this difficult."

"Aye." He nodded, laughing. *Look at how beautiful he is,*
I thought. *My husband. I have the right to touch him, to talk
with him, to be alone with him. Any time I wish to, day or
night. And no one can lecture me or make me feel common
because I cannot stop looking at him. My husband.*

"Alex . . ." I said, lifting my chin.

"Yer a verra persistent woman, Mary MacGannon."

"Yes." I glared at him. "Very. So listen to me."

"I willna say another word."

"Good. Now, listen. I've been thinking."

"Mmmm," he said, his mouth twitching.

"Alex!" He grinned at me again. "I want you to buy a boat with my dowry. One to replace the one that went down."

He blinked. His arms fell from his chest and he placed his hands on the table. I leaned against the back of my chair, enjoying his amazement. He looked at me for a long moment, then at the floor before meeting my eyes again.

"I dinna ken what to say. That's a verra generous offer."

I smiled smugly. "Speechless. I'm enjoying it very much."

He ignored my remark and continued, speaking softly and slowly. "It's verra generous, lass, but I dinna think I could accept yer offer. That's to be yer money."

"You must accept it, Alex. You cannot say no to this!"

His eyes grew merry. "Aye? Must I?"

"Yes," I snapped, crossing my arms over my chest.

"I see," he said, imitating me perfectly. "And why is that?"

I leaned toward him. "Alex, when you proposed, you asked me to share what you had and I pledged to share what I have. Now we are married, and I want you to use the dowry money. Rebuild your fleet." He looked at me, considering. "I will have my way in this, my love."

"Will ye, lass?" He shook his head, grinning. "I think not, but ye can amuse yourself." I stood abruptly and my chair fell. He did not move, but his expression sobered.

"Then you can amuse yourself as well, sir." I was dangerously close to tears as I moved to the door. He was there before me and blocked my way. When I reached my hands up to push him aside, he clenched my wrists and turned us around so that my back was to the wall. I looked up into his eyes as he held my wrists above me.

"I love ye, Mary MacGannon, and I accept yer offer. Graciously." He kissed my forehead and then my cheek. I turned my head and he chuckled. "Dinna be angry, lass. Ye won," he whispered in my ear, and released my wrists as he gathered me to him. "Ye won. With one condition."

I turned to face him and he kissed my mouth. "Which is?"

"That the ship will always stay in yer name, not mine. It will always be yer property. Ye may do with it as ye wish. Ye have only to speak."

"No. It will be yours."

"Mary, it will be yer property and only yers, or I willna accept it. And I willna argue the point." He kissed me again.

"Alex," I said eventually. His attention was on what his hands were doing to my laces. "You will buy the boat?"

His hands stopped and he laughed ruefully. "Ship, lass, and aye, I'll buy it. Ye ken yer power, Mary. It's as I've told ye from the first—it will be as ye wish. I feel uneasy using yer money this way, but if it is truly what ye wish, I will do it, and thank ye for it." I slipped my arms around his neck and kissed him.

"Our money, Alex. Our money. And it is truly what I wish."

"Then ye'll have yer way. With my condition." He kissed my forehead again, his hands very busy.

"So you will order it built? From London?"

"No. Yer money will be spent in Scotland," he said, leaning down to undo a stubborn fastening.

"And you'll do that as soon as we get there?"

"After the wedding, aye, lass, I'll spend every penny of yer dowry if it's what ye say." His hands stopped and he looked up. "Mary, tell me, lass. Has no one ever denied ye anything?"

"Yes." I stroked his cheek. "I had to wait months for you."

The five days flew by all too quickly and it was time to leave. We had been left alone but had been well cared for. We had enjoyed the privacy and thoughtfulness and wrote to the Duke and Duchess with our thanks the night before we left. Alex was quiet as we piled our luggage in the foyer that evening, in preparation for the morning, and I asked him what he was thinking.

"I'm thinking that Kilgannon will be a shock to ye, lass. This was the quiet before the storm. We've had time together, the two of us, and that will be rare from here on. We'll be surrounded by the clan, and while it never bothered me, I'm thinking it's a life verra different than ye've known. Have ye any misgivings?"

His expression was troubled, and I put my arms around him and kissed him. "We will be fine. If we were to live at Mountgarden it would be the same. I grew up with staff around me."

"They're not yer relatives."

"We'll be fine, Alex. But there is one thing . . ."

"Aye?"

"Ellen. Could I possibly bring Ellen?"

"Ellen?"

"She's one of Louisa's housemaids. I've grown very fond of her. She would be a companion for me."

He shrugged. "Oh, aye, anything. But do ye think the girl would want to go live in such a far place?"

"She says she does." And she had, just before our wedding. In the excitement I had forgotten her request.

"Then it's done. If she hates it, I'll ship her home."

"How do I tell her? We're to meet everyone tomorrow. I should have thought of it before this."

"We'll have time," he said, moving one of my trunks. "One of the lads can leave straightaway. We don't sail until tomorrow night." He frowned at the luggage. "How much more are ye bringing with ye, lass? Perhaps we'll need two ships."

My family met us without incident and we left with the tide into a clear and cold twilight. Wee Donald had volunteered to go to London to get Ellen, and she was delighted to have been remembered. She stood next to me as we waved to my family, bouncing with excitement. I watched her fondly, wondering if her enthusiasm would fade as we traveled north into the unknown. My farewells had been far more difficult than I had imagined. I had never been without Louisa or Will for any length of time, and I was filled with remorse for not treasuring our last few weeks. Randolph was gruff on the surface but teary-eyed as I embraced him. I was in tears myself, and he wiped them away with an unexpectedly tender gesture.

"Take good care of my girl, Kilgannon," Randolph growled.

Alex grinned at him. "I will, sir. And ye will come to visit us in the northern wilds, no?"

He turned abruptly away and Louisa patted his arm before embracing me. We both promised to write. I knew she would return to her busy schedule in London, but I knew as well that she would miss me, as I would her. I'd never been the one to leave. I tried to thank her again for all her kindness, but she waved my words away.

"Mary, if you need us, we'll be here for you always." She cupped my face in her hands and tried a weak smile. "Always, my dear." I could not speak but nodded and embraced her again.

Will did not try to hide his emotions as he held me to him, talking quietly. "Take care, little Mary. Be happy. And if he is not what you think, come home and I'll cut his heart out."

"Oh, Will . . ." I said, fighting my tears and losing.

He smiled. "Be happy, Mary." I nodded and hugged him again. Even Betty was caught up in the moment and clung to me, wishing us well. One last embrace from all and I was ushered on board, to wave at them as we sailed into the evening.

Our trip was uneventful and I was grateful I had once again proved to be a good sailor. When we reached Scotland the seas were huge and threatening, but no rain hampered

us. The last day we sailed through islands, and the waves
calmed somewhat. Alex pointed out sights and named what
we were passing and whose lands they were, and I heard for
the first time many of the names that were to become so
meaningful later. We were standing on deck together when
Gannon's Lady turned its back on the sea at last and sailed
into a loch. Alex wore his best today and had asked me to
wear the cloak he'd given me. It swirled around me like a
sail as we changed course and the wind came from our back.

"Loch Gannon," Alex said, smiling broadly while he
nodded at my expression and brushed the hair back from my
face. "Aye, the man put his name on everathing. When
Agnus and I were boys, we called everathing 'Gannon.' Tree
Gannon, rock Gannon, boat Gannon. We thought we were
verra clever. Of course, so did Gannon." He smiled again.
"Almost home."

The sides of the loch were rocky cliffs, towering gray and
lifeless over us. I stared around me, wondering what kind of
land I had come to. Could anyone really think this beautiful?
How could this support many people? Who could live in
such a desolate place? We turned around a bend, and here
the cliffs tapered off slowly into barren hills on one side, but
still no houses, no people, and I felt my heart sink. This was
no better. How could he have said it was so splendid? And
his sketches. Where had he been drawing?

"Do ye hear the pipes, lass?" Alex's smile was private. "Ye
will shortly. They're giving us a proper homecoming. And if
ye look up on the top of the headland there"—he pointed to
a rocky precipice that towered at the next turn of the loch—
"ye'll see a boy waving. He's the one who spied us and told
the others of our approach." I shielded my eyes and sure
enough, a young boy jumped from one foot to another,
waving furiously at us. Alex waved in return. "Ye dinna
think we'd not look to see who was arriving, did ye? Everaone knows who arrives by sea before they land in Kilgannon." His eyes were shining as he listened intently, and
soon I could hear the pipes as well. As we rounded the final

curve of the loch, the music grew louder and soared over the valley.

And what a valley. Green, lush, full of trees and growth, spreading before us like an Eden. No wonder he thought it was extraordinary. Nothing had prepared me for this. It was even more beautiful than he said. Oh, yes, I thought, I could live here. The valley was full of sunshine this afternoon, but the mist hung over the mountains above, ready to descend. Pipers lined the side of a dock, a crowd of people with them, more arriving as we watched. From the flat land around the dock, the valley stretched to the end of the loch and into a meadow surrounded by the trees that led up to the mountains.

"Kilgannon," Alex said softly next to me, and pointed. I followed his gaze and looked to my right across the water. It was indeed a castle. It seemed to grow out of the very rock, reigning from atop a steep hill that rose sharply in a series of walled terraces, quickly leaving the valley floor below. Above the terraces were ancient walls that had been amended, creating a formidable fortification of gray stone. The castle was yet above that, more walls enclosing the original keep and the later buildings. It was a noble structure, graceful despite its size and its obvious defensive features. Nine generations of MacGannons had lived and died here, I thought, and I now would be its mistress. The gray stones were silhouetted against the mist above. *Welcome me, Kilgannon,* I said silently, *I will do my best to be worthy.*

And then my attention was caught by the people who cheered as we approached the dock. They called to Alex as we landed, and I was astonished at the casual way they greeted him. Many called him "my laird" or "sir," but more often it was simply "Alex." Except for the two small boys who clambered on board before all the lines were secured. "Da! Da!" they cried as they scrambled over the side and flung themselves on Alex. He hugged them ferociously in return and I stood back, studying them as they greeted their father. The older one looked very much like Alex must have at his age, the younger an exact copy except for the much redder blond hair. Both had their father's long limbs, wild hair, and blue eyes. And affectionate nature. After a moment Alex put them both down, laughing.

"Mary, these are my sons," he said, one hand on each boy's head. Three pairs of blue eyes watched me closely.

I curtsied deeply and smiled. "I am Mary," I said. *Dear God,* I prayed, *let them accept me. I will do my best to be a good mother.* "You must be Ian," I said to the older boy, "and you must be Jamie." They both nodded, suddenly silent and shy. "I am very happy to meet you." I looked into their blue, blue eyes, but they said nothing. They fell into step behind us as we walked down the planks to the dock and did not speak as Alex was surrounded by his kinsmen. Angus followed us onto the dock, Matthew by his side, and the boys came alive again, swarming over both of them. Matthew threw Jamie over his shoulder and took off at a run up the hill, Ian in their wake. I felt very alone in the crowd of Scots as I watched them race away.

Alex threw an arm around my shoulders and I was drawn into what seemed endless introductions. Everyone was named Mairi or Morag or Duncan or Donald, it seemed, although there must have been ten Alexes. And they were all related, "Mac this Mac that" for ten minutes until my head was spinning. They were dressed in Highland fashion, the men in plaids or kilts and bonnets, the women in simple dresses, most in cloaks, but many braving the chilly air without appearing to notice it. Some were tall, blond and redheaded, and I saw faces that showed their MacGannon bloodlines, but there were many others as well with dark hair or smaller frames.

We moved with the crowd up the terraces toward the castle, the pipers following us. I turned just before we entered the outer gate and looked behind me. The castle had a view of the loch and valley as it melted into forest and then mountain on the far side. The loch continued for another half mile or so, still and glacial, reflecting the green of the valley below and the mountains looming above. The water was very blue, the mountains dark gray against the lighter gray mist. The sun made everything sparkle.

"What a beautiful place," I said, but did not realize I had spoken aloud until Angus, next to me, nodded his agreement.

"Aye, lass," he said, his voice gruff with emotion. "It's good to be home. And good to have ye here with us."

And then Alex reached for me and led me into my new home.

PART TWO

Had we never loved sae kindly,
Had we never loved sae blindly,
Never met—or never parted,
We'd have ne'er been broken-hearted.

Fare thee weel, thou first and fairest!
Fare thee weel, thou best and dearest!

Ae Fond Kiss: Robert Burns

FIFTEEN

I FELT VERY WELCOMED. I WAS INTRODUCED TO MAC-Donalds, Macleans, MacKinnons, MacLeods, MacNeills, Frasers, and more MacGannons, until my head ached. It was not enough to know someone's name, apparently; one must also know his patrimony back ten generations. For the first time I completely understood I'd married a clan chieftain and not just an earl. Despite their easy manner with him, it was obvious that the clansmen respected Alex, and by association I was accepted.

Everyone was merry and courteous. Except Malcolm, who stood alone, watching the festivities with a sour look. His eyes followed Alex everywhere, and once, just before our gazes met and he raised his glass to me sardonically, I swear I saw him scowling. That he disliked Alex being the center of attention was obvious. *He will have to deal with it,* I thought, for Alex *was* the center of attention, especially when he jumped atop a table at one end of the huge room, raised his hands for silence, then reached down to assist me in climbing to join him. We faced the crowd together and he spoke in Gaelic, gesturing to me, then taking my hand and kissing it. A cheer unlike anything I'd ever heard rose from the room, and Alex grinned at me.

"I've just introduced ye, lass. Do ye have anything to say?"

"Tell them I'm delighted to be here and thank them for their warm welcome," I said more bravely than I felt.

He nodded, pleased. "Why don't ye tell them?" I did, and was greeted with another cheer that rose in volume as Alex translated. He spoke again and the people roared, and he smiled at me before jumping down and helping me to follow him. "I've just invited them to eat and drink everything in the house, and they've accepted." He laughed, but before I could answer he was approached by a huge man who embraced him roughly and smacked him on the shoulder several times, grinning widely. "My cousin Dougall," Alex explained over his shoulder as Dougall talked fast and furiously to him in Gaelic. I took the moment to look around. The room, typical of the old great halls, was massively paneled and carved, decorated with an amazing number of antlers and shields, tapestries filling some of the taller panels. Over the enormous fireplace were crossed swords and lances and the MacGannon lion crest and motto, HONOR AND COURAGE. I was turning slowly to see it all when I met the very blue eyes of the tall, blond, buxom woman before me.

"Welcome to Kilgannon," she said. "I am Alex's Aunt Deirdre."

"Madam," I said, then embraced her. "Mistress MacGannon, thank you for your letter. It was very kind of you."

Angus's mother smiled. "Call me Deirdre. Ye've already won the hearts of my son and grandson and my nephew, Mary. Ye are very welcome at Kilgannon."

"Thank you. Angus has been very kind, and I adore Matthew."

Her pleasure was obvious. "Aye, he's a good lad. I'm verra proud of both. Now, ye'll be wanting yer room, I'm thinking." I glanced at Alex, deep in conversation with Dougall. "They'll keep him busy," she said, following my gaze. "Once Dougall starts talking he goes on forever. Come with me for a bit."

I followed her through the crowds and up a flight of stairs I'd not even noticed at the side of the hall. When we reached the top she turned to look at the cheerful crowd below and smiled at me. "Noisy, aren't they? It's lovely to have a celebration here for a change. It's been a long while since we've had this much laughter in the house of Mac-Gannon." She took a last look at the gathering below, then led me to a corridor that linked the hall with the newer wing. Alex had explained that the hall had been attached to one end of the original keep, and the newer wing added to the other. A hallway linked the two as it skirted the older building. We were in the Gothic portion of Kilgannon, complete with pointed arches and stone walls and floors. Candles burned in holders designed for torches. I could have been transported back two hundred years. "Angus and Alex's grandmother Diana designed 'the house,' as we call it," Deirdre said. "That's where we're going."

"Alex told me about Kilgannon, but he didn't say his grandmother was named Diana," I said, trotting in her wake.

She laughed. "Aye, his great-grandmother named all of her children with classical names. Her sisters were Juno and Minerva. Count yer blessings! This is the house now." She gestured as she turned into another corridor, this one much more modern, with paneled and plastered walls and wooden floors covered with runners of carpet. We climbed stairs of gleaming dark wood lit by chandeliers and walked along a wide hallway flanked by tall doors, and she stopped at one. "I've put ye in Margaret's room," she said over her shoulder, opening the door. "Margaret was Alex's mother. I know ye were married in England, but ye'll not share a room with Alex until yer married here."

"That will be fine," I said, smiling to myself. On *Gannon's Lady* Alex had slept elsewhere, and Ellen and I had been given the big cabin. He had explained that some of the clan would not acknowledge the Anglican ceremony we'd had and would consider that we were living in sin, and he'd said that it would be the same once we'd landed. I had not argued.

"After yer married again," said Deirdre, leading the way into Margaret's room, "ye'll move next door into Alex's father's room." Within, Ellen was supervising the unpacking of my trunks with two very young girls, who curtsied awkwardly as they were introduced. Ellen gave me a smile of pleasure.

"Alex tells me he's not explained what will happen to ye in the next few days, Mary," Deirdre said. "So I will." I nodded, pleased, and sat on the edge of the ample bed while Deirdre talked. The wedding ceremony would be held in the hall, since the chapel was too small to accommodate everyone. Before the wedding a blessing for the family and close friends would be given in the chapel. After the ceremony the celebrating would begin and was expected to last the night. The next two days there would be games outside, weather permitting, or inside if not.

"Then they will all leave, or most of them, and we'll get on with life," Deirdre continued. "Ye'll not see yer husband much in the next two days. As chief he'll be expected to oversee all the games and to attend all the celebrating, and the others who have traveled for this will want to talk to him as long as they are here, so dinna be alarmed. It will not always be so." I nodded. "Now, as far as yer duties," she said. "Ye must look beautiful and smile all the time. Try to remember names, but no one will expect ye to know everyone yet. Can ye do that?"

"I will try," I said, laughing.

"Good." She rubbed her hands and rose from the chair. "Are ye tired from yer journey, or are ye ready to brave them again?"

"I'd like to wash my face and then I'll brave them again."

She nodded, pleased with my answer, shooed the two girls out, and told Ellen she'd show her to her room. At last I was alone. I took a deep breath and enjoyed the quiet for a few minutes, then washed my face and combed my hair. And turned to the room. This was not what I'd expected in Kilgannon. Margaret's bed was a four-poster with hangings of white lace and a featherbed. If Robert could see this room he might change his opinion of Alex's home, I thought giddily. *Robert.* I'd not thought of him in ages and had not seen him since our departure from his estate. Neither he nor his mother had come to our wedding, but both had sent very proper notes of best wishes and congratulations. Janice said he had not returned to London nor had he been seen at any parties. I felt guilty, but guilt tinged with anger. Still, I hoped he would marry eventually and be happy. I returned to examining the room.

There were two doors in the side walls and I opened one. It was a private garderobe, and I laughed aloud at its luxury. The other door led into another bedroom, much larger and currently filled with the remainder of my luggage. This must be Alex's father's room. The bed was huge, the bedcovers a muted green velvet, and the bed hangings the same white lace as Margaret's. The room appeared ready for its occupant, the fire laid and the bedding fresh. I took a deep breath, very pleased. Tomorrow night I'd be here with Alex. I hurried back into Margaret's room when there was a knock and opened the door to find Deirdre.

Moments later I was in the hall again. People still crowded around Alex, but his smile greeted me when I reached the top of the stairs and I realized he'd been looking for me. I moved to meet him with a smile of my own. *My husband,* I thought as I reached his side. He was in the center of a group of men, most of them his age, and he welcomed me with a smile and an arm that slipped around my waist. His other hand held a glass of whisky, and he gestured with it as he finished his story in Gaelic. He said something else to the group, put down the glass, and took my hand. They laughed good-naturedly as we left them.

"I thought ye'd run away, lass." He led me behind the

table we'd stood on and through a low door in the wall paneling beyond.

"Deirdre showed me my room," I said. "She's very kind."

"Aye," he said absently as he entered a short paneled passage. "I'd hoped ye'd like each other. She's like Angus, a good one to have at yer back." He stood to one side and I followed him out into the bottom floor of the old keep. The room was full of barrels. A narrow flight of stairs led above from one corner.

I gestured to the barrels. "What is all this?"

"Stores. In case of siege." He laughed at my expression as he lit a candle waiting on the floor. "Unlikely, but it's best to be prepared, no?" He pointed to a wooden door in the corner opposite us. "And an emergency tunnel to the sea, of course."

"Alex, is it really so dangerous here?"

"Not unless the English attack." He laughed and raised his eyebrows dramatically. "Do ye wish to attack me?"

"Yes, actually," I said, laughing as well. "I do."

"Well, ye must wait. Come now." He led the way up the stairs, holding the candle high. It was a typical keep, the stairs spiral and built to be easy to defend, not easy to climb. Off each floor there were rooms that had been used to house the family. Alex climbed the stairs effortlessly. "We've not lived in the keep for generations," he said, his voice echoing off the stone. "And ye can see why. It's no' comfortable." I followed, breathless. At last we reached the top, where Alex stepped into a small square room and put the candle on the floor. He crossed the room and opened the door at the other side, gesturing me through. The door led outside to a stone parapet circling the keep, originally intended to be manned by defenders, buttressed by tall pillars that reached to the stone roof above us. The view was wonderful, and I looked at the castle below us, then the inner wall, the courtyard and outer wall, and finally across the valley at the loch and mountains, lit from the side by the last of the sun.

I gasped in surprise. "It's beautiful, Alex."

"Aye, but come over here." He walked to the other side of the keep and pointed. "Here's what I wanted ye to see." The tower was high enough to peer over the headland, and before me was the sea, dotted by islands, the sun about to set behind them. The scene was breathtaking, the sky turning shades of pink, rose, and red, wild and splendid, fitting for the man who stood so still next to me. I stole a glance at him and he smiled. "I wanted ye to see this yer first night."

I clasped his arm. "How magnificent this is," I said as the sun disappeared behind the blue island and the sky roared with the blazing colors. "It's amazing. Truly amazing."

"Almost as amazing as having ye here with me to see it." His tone was gentle. "Mary, thank ye for marrying me. Ye have no idea how many times I've stood here and thought of ye. I still canna believe yer mine." He wrapped an arm around me, pulling me close.

"I love you, Alex," I said, and kissed him.

"And I ye, lass." He lifted his head and listened. "We have company," he said, moving around the parapet to the door.

"Da! Da! Are ye here?" Ian shouted as he and two other little boys stumbled out in front of us, grinning triumphantly. "We found ye!"

"That ye have," said Alex, lifting the boy into his arms. "But yer not to be in the keep alone, lads, are ye, now?"

"We're not alone, Da, we're with you," Ian laughed.

Alex raised an eyebrow but smiled. "Aye, well, come now. We're going down," he said, and kissed me one more time before he led the way inside. We trailed down the stairs in the gloom, the five of us, Ian and the other boys talking without pause to Alex. They moved from English to Gaelic and back within the same sentence without appearing to notice. *I'll have to learn the language,* I thought, *impossible as it seems to be to master.*

The evening seemed endless. As soon as we were back in the hall Alex was surrounded again. I was offered best wishes and welcomes and did my best to put names to faces. During the boisterous meal Jamie was in Alex's lap and Ian between us, while Deirdre pointed out who was who. She had identified almost everyone when I asked who the dark beauty was who watched Alex so closely.

Deirdre laughed. "Ye'd have to be no' wise not to notice her, aye? She's no' happy yer here. She thought she'd have Alex herself. Of course, Alex hasna looked her way for years, which sets well with me. I dinna need another Sorcha in this house. Och, there I go again," she laughed with raised eyebrows. "I swore I'd no' speak ill of Sorcha, and here I am again. Well, no matter." She glanced across the room. "She's Morag, niece of MacLeod of MacLeod."

Morag MacLeod, I thought. The girl Alex had fallen in love with at sixteen, the girl responsible for his year in France. The woman, these years later, with whom Alex's friend Murdoch was still in love. Morag, with her dark hair shining in the candlelight and her eyes bright, was very beautiful. She watched Alex's every move, sometimes shifting her gaze to me as she did now. Our eyes met across the room and I remembered Angus, in Louisa's house, telling Alex that if he wanted a woman's company Morag would marry him in a minute. She nodded to me and smiled, and I did the same, then straightened my shoulders and lifted my chin. I was the one Alex had chosen, I told myself. Still, this one would bear watching. I turned to Deirdre again. "Alex and Morag were once . . . they . . ." I fumbled for words, but Deirdre laughed.

"Oh, aye, they were indeed. She was fifteen, he was sixteen, and we almost went to war because Alex decided he wouldna marry Sorcha MacDonald. They sent Alex to France to get her out of his system." She laughed again, then looked at me shrewdly. "I dinna think ye have to worry, lassie. Alex doesna think on Morag the now. It's ye he's been courting, and ye he married, Mary." We both looked at Morag, her dark beauty luminous. "But I would still ken where he was when she's about. A word to the wise."

I was still musing on her words when Malcolm interrupted my thoughts, leaning across the table. "So Alex showed ye his sunset?"

"Yes," I said. "It was beautiful."

Malcolm nodded. "It is. All of Kilgannon is beautiful. And now it is yers as well." His voice was without inflection.

I was not sure how to react. "Yes, I am most fortunate."

"Fortunate. Aye, fortunate." He sat back clumsily and looked at me with bleary eyes, and I realized he was drunk.

"Time to put the young ones to bed," said Alex with a laugh that I tried to echo. The women were doing just that, I realized, looking out across the hall. Deirdre moved to lift a sleepy Jamie from Alex, and Ian reached for my hand with a smile.

"I always tend the boys myself, Mary," said Deirdre. "Come with us, why don't ye?" I did, glad to be leaving Malcolm.

The boys behaved as though we had done this a thousand times. Upstairs we talked of the day and of tomorrow, and Ian looked up at me as we walked and smiled a smile that was pure Alex. When we reached the room the boys shared, Deirdre tended to Jamie while Ian shrugged out of his kilt and flipped his shoes over his head with a grin at me, watching for my reaction. *He is certainly Alex's son,* I thought, and laughed as expected.

"I knew who ye were," Ian said. "When ye got here, I knew."

"How?" I asked. Without answering, Ian led me to a chest in the corner of the room and opened it, pulling out three sketches. They were all of me and they were very good.

"Da sent us yer picture so we could see ye." He looked

up into my face as if comparing Alex's sketches to the original.

"Your father showed me pictures of you too," I said.

He nodded and pulled his socks off. "He told us."

"Thank you for your letter," I said. "I enjoyed it." Ian nodded again and turned to the waiting Deirdre, who tucked him in and kissed him while I stood next to the bed feeling awkward. But Ian reached his arms out to me, and as I hugged him I realized I'd lost my heart for the second time to a MacGannon.

He snuggled under the cover. "I'm glad yer here at last."

"So am I," I said, kissing his forehead.

Jamie was already asleep, and I smoothed his hair back and kissed his cheek and followed Deirdre into the hall.

"They're good boys," she said, "but they need a mother."

I smiled at Alex's aunt. "They'll have one now," I said.

I remember no more of the second ceremony than I did of the first. It was a blur of candlelight and Scots, except for Alex's smiling face. I had expected to be calmer during this second wedding, but when I stood at the top of the stairs and faced the hall packed with upturned faces, I lost some of my composure. I remember Alex's family smiling as we filed past them into the chapel for the blessing, and I remember walking with Alex through the crowd back into the hall. When we were married again, Alex kissed me boldly as the onlookers cheered and all formality ended. Music started and there was dancing, followed much later by a meal. We danced and talked and laughed for hours, and as the evening wore on, the accents got thicker and the English less frequent.

A few moments into the meal a lean man with tousled dark hair raised his glass as he proposed a toast in English, first to the bride, then to the groom, and the hall cheered. Bolstered by his success, he turned to face us, saying something in Gaelic and raising his glass defiantly as he glared at

Alex. The room hushed and all eyes turned to us. Beside me, Alex stiffened and exchanged a glance with Angus, then rose and raised his own glass. Alex spoke boldly into the silence, and after a momentary pause many guests laughed or nodded and drank. Alex spoke again and the room exploded into cheers. I felt everyone at the table relax as conversation began again. Confused, I turned to Alex as he sat down, but before I could speak he smiled and said, "I'll explain later, Mary. Just smile at me now." There was anger in his eyes and I smiled stiffly, then sipped my wine as I scanned the crowd before us. The tension had retreated. Angus said something in Gaelic and Alex nodded curtly, then Malcolm made a remark and Alex smiled again, this time a real smile. The three of them looked at each other and grinned, and the moment passed.

Hours later, well into the evening's dancing, Alex leaned over to me. "Have ye had enough celebrating, lass?"

"Yes," I said. "I'd like to celebrate with just you."

"Good." He led me through the crowds toward the stairs, calls and hoots following us. Alex bantered with many as we passed, and I could feel my cheeks burning. At the top of the stairs he swung me up into his arms and spoke to the hall below. His remarks were answered with roars of laughter. "I told them they could celebrate until we returned in the morning," he said, carrying me around the corner. "Some of them will."

"And? What else did you say?"

He grinned at me. "I said I had my own celebrating to do."

I nodded, glad I had not understood. He kissed me then and I wrapped my arms around his neck and kissed him fully. Still holding his lips to mine, he whirled us through the hall, then lifted his head and ran up the next flight of stairs, whooping loudly, and dropped me to my feet at the top. When I responded by undoing the lace at his collar, he took me by the waist and lifted me against him, backing against the wall and kissing me until I gasped for breath.

Panting and laughing, I began unfastening his plaid and shirt lacings. He laughed deeply and carried me, still fumbling with his clothes, down the hall and into our room, slamming the door behind us.

Once behind the closed door we threw ourselves at each other with abandon. I peeled his clothes off and tossed them away, running my hands the full length of him, from his shoulders to his feet. He watched, his eyes growing darker, and told me where to put my hands and then my lips. I followed his direction without hesitation. And when he groaned and stopped me to undo the fastenings of my gown, I helped him without a thought, throwing the pieces of my wedding gown aside in my haste to have him. We found the floor and later the bedcover and still later the mattress.

Sated at last, we lay in each others arms, spent and quiet. Alex kissed my forehead and sighed. "Welcome to Scotland, Mary," he said. "I think we're truly married, lass."

"Twice," I said, and laughed.

"Twice," he agreed, and lifted his head to survey the room. His shirt lay across the hearth, his plaid was caught halfway on the trunk, my stockings and petticoats littered the floor, and the sleeve of my bodice hung from the footboard. "It looks like a storm came through. I knew ye'd be an apt student, but, lass, ye have a gift for it." He laughed and kissed me. I felt my cheeks flush. "Mary," he said tenderly, "dinna feel embarrassed. What we did was good, lass. What we did was right."

"What we did was wonderful, Alex," I said, and watched him smile. *It was amazing,* I told myself, and sighed with satisfaction.

"Aye," he said. "What we did was wonderful. And gratifying, wife. I think we'll do." He swung his legs over the edge of the bed. "Somewhere there's whisky and wine," he said over his shoulder as he stood, grabbing his plaid and wrapping it around him. "Let's celebrate that we don't have to marry a third time."

"That would be terrible," I said, sitting up and watching him move around the room. He found the liquor and poured himself a whisky and me a glass of wine, then sat on the edge of the bed.

He touched his glass to mine. "To us." I echoed him.

"Alex," I said, gesturing to the room. "Have you done this before?"

He sipped his whisky and looked at me over the glass. "Drink whisky? Aye, many times. Or do ye mean making wild love with the woman I love? Or do ye mean am I a virgin?"

I laughed. "You have two sons. I know you've made love before. No, what I mean—"

"What ye mean is do ye have to be jealous of what went before, and the answer is no, ye dinna have anyone to be jealous of. And to answer yer next question, no, it was never like this with Sorcha. It wasna like this with anyone, Mary."

"Did you make love with Morag?"

He sipped his whisky and looked at me, and my heart froze. "We were verra young, Mary," he said. I opened my mouth to speak and found I couldn't. Alex had made love to Morag. "It was a long time ago," he said quietly.

"I see," I said, trying to be calm. He stroked my cheek.

"Mary, it's ye I chose. It's ye I married."

"But you still remember her."

He grimaced, obviously unhappy at the topic. "It's no' unusual for a man to remember the first—" I gasped, and he frowned. "Damn, lass, this is no fit conversation for us to be having."

"I want to know. Tell me."

He shook his head. "Mary," he said firmly, "I will no' discuss Morag nor any other woman I ever—"

I stared at him, horrified. "There were others?"

He flushed, then sat up straight and put his glass on the table. "Mary," he said. "I will no' discuss this. I've told ye, lass, I wasna unfaithful to Sorcha, nor will I ever be to ye. Ever. Morag doesna tempt me, or she'd be here the now instead of ye. It's ye I married. Twice now. Come here, lass," he said, pulling me to him and kissing me. "Ye, Mary, it's ye I wanted, no other woman alive. Being with ye is like finding heaven. The others were a pleasant experience is all, and soon forgotten. It's ye I married, in two countries."

I let him lull me into tranquility with his caresses, but I never forgot that Morag had been his first. But he'd married me. Twice. I searched for another topic. "Do the people downstairs know we were married in England?" I asked. He shrugged.

"Some of them, no doubt. I took no trouble to hide it. Some of them are Anglicans, some are Presbyterians, some are Catholic. To most of them this was no more than a formality." He glanced at me. "As it was to me."

"I thought getting married here was important to you."

"It is," he said. "Marrying ye for all the world to see that yer mine is important. That's why I did it. In years to come they'll talk of being at our wedding." He took a sip. "No one can ever say we were not truly married. I'd not bring ye here without them acknowledging ye as my wife."

"I see."

"No." He shook his head. "Ye don't. What ye don't understand is that many of them downstairs despise the English, all English, warranted or no. But the Countess of Kilgannon is a protected person. Don't let them treat ye with anything but courtesy."

"I know how to behave." I could hear the asperity in my tone.

He nodded, untroubled by my reaction. "Aye, but some of them will test ye. Insist they are courteous."

"And how do I do that? Insist that they are courteous?"

He smiled, his eyes gleaming. "Mary, ye look like a goddess. This moment ye look like an aggravated goddess. If they are rude, give them a goddess look and walk away."

"A goddess look?"

"Aye," he said. "Like the one ye gave Morag. Ye fair froze her with yer look." I considered. His mouth quirked as he watched me, and he laughed. I began to ask a question, then shook my head. "What now?" he asked curtly, and I glared at him through narrowed eyes. "Very good," he said. "The goddess look."

"Alex," I said, "Morag is very beautiful."

He shrugged, his eyes dancing. "Is she?"

"Everyone thinks so. And she watches you. Constantly."

"Everyone watched us tonight, Mary. As they will for three more days." He grinned. "Come here, lass, and I'll set yer mind to rest about Morag. Ye ken Murdoch loves her?"

"Which one is Murdoch?"

"Ye met him tonight. He's big and ugly. He's the one who follows Morag around." He cupped his hand on my cheek. "Mary MacGannon, Countess of Kilgannon, there wasna another woman in that room as beautiful as ye." He traced his finger along my chin, then down my neck and to the top of my breasts. "No one, lass, even comes close. Dinna fret about Morag MacLeod."

"I don't think we'll be friends," I said. He laughed again and waved his hand, dismissing the topic. "Alex, what happened at that toast? Who was that man?"

His expression sobered and he looked through his glass into the fire. "A MacDonald. A laird, but minor. He wanted me to toast to King James of Scotland and England."

"What did you say?"

"I said I'd gladly drink to James Stewart and wished him safe journey and proposed long life to our Stewart sovereign."

"What does that mean?"

He shrugged. "It means nothing. That's why I said it. It could mean King James, it could mean Queen Anne."

"I see. So his toast was a trap."

"Not a trap exactly," he said, but he nodded at me. "He wanted a declaration of position. Which I did not give."

"And that caused all the cheers?"

"No, that was an old toast. 'To the land of bens and glens.' That's mountains and valleys to ye. But enough." He put his glass down, tossed the plaid aside, and climbed under the covers with me, kissing me with surprising appetite. And we lost another hour.

"Mary," he said much later, as we lay entwined in spent contentment, his tone gentle. "Do ye understand what I'm trying to tell ye?"

"About . . .'

"Ye are married to a Gael and yer English. I know yer proud of being English, but just as there are those in England who despise me simply because I'm a Gael, there are those here who will do the same to ye because ye are English." He stroked a line down my shoulder.

I smiled. "Alex, I am very proud of being your wife. But you're right, I am also proud of being who I am. If they dislike me because of my heritage, it is their difficulty. I will give them a goddess look and they will shrink."

"Aye," he laughed. "They will at that."

SIXTEEN

B REAKFAST WAS FRENZIED BUT AMUSING, AND THE GAMES began shortly afterward. I was entertained all day watching the competitions. Alex participated in several and won two. He refused to accept a prize, strutting over to me and saying thunderously, "I already have my prize," which drew laughter and many retorts. He kissed me lustily and the people cheered. I watched Morag watch us with a polite smile. The day was short, the evening long; the meal was full of laughter. And no political toasts. When I could keep my eyes open no longer, I rose to go to bed and Alex joined me. Our guests' teasing followed us up the stairs, but Alex was not abashed. At the top of the stairs he lifted me into his arms and kissed me loudly. "Dinna expect me at breakfast," he said, and their laughter sounded behind us.

The second day of the games was just as clear, but a stiff breeze had risen and many stayed within. Ian and Jamie were with me most of the day, and by nightfall Jamie was in my lap. I became better acquainted with most of our neighbors, all of whom, even Morag, treated me with the utmost courtesy. To my face. But I was well aware of the whispers and glances that followed me. I knew they were wondering why Alex had married me, why he had gone all the way to England to find a very ordinary woman. I raised my chin and used the skills I'd learned in London. This would not be the first time I'd been discussed and appraised.

Many of the guests left that afternoon, including the MacLeods, to my relief, and our evening meal was quieter than any before. Outside, the weather had grown stormy, but no one paid it any attention. Tonight the remaining guests were talking Scottish politics loudly, debating the Union and damning the Campbells. Murdoch Maclean and his brother Duncan were among the most vocal, but sprinkled their views with laughter and wit, and I watched Alex laugh with them, the big men easy with each other as they imaginatively decided the best way to deal with those who had made the agreement with England. When I could not stand another minute I left Alex still talking and went to bed alone. And listened to the wind howl. It was too much to have expected three days of good weather in the spring. I was exhausted but could not sleep and looked at the shadows cast by the firelight.

I'd had three days at Kilgannon now. I was a wife and a stepmother, and I wondered for the first time that evening how the boys were. I had not said good night to them, nor had I seen them after the evening meal. Deirdre had told me one of the younger girls was looking after them tonight, but she herself was downstairs with the others. As the minutes dragged on I decided I would rest better knowing that they were snugly asleep in their little room upstairs.

Throwing on a nightdress for the first time in my marriage, I wrapped a cloak around me and stole from the room. There was no one to see me slip down the hall or up the stairs. I paused outside their room, wondering if I should knock. A loud clap of thunder made me jump, and at a cry from within I opened the door. The boys sat huddled on Jamie's bed, their eyes huge. Anger—directed at myself for my thoughtlessness, and at the girl who was to be caring for these little ones—drove me as I moved to them. I would deal with her in the morning. "What a horrible noise," I said in a cheery tone. "I came to say good night to you."

"Jamie doesna like thunder," Ian said, his arm around his brother.

"Who does?" I asked, taking the blanket from Ian's bed and wrapping it around him. "It's all right on a summer afternoon when you can look out the window and see the rain, but on a night like this its horrible." I pulled Ian to his feet and tucked the blanket up so that he could walk without falling. Then I picked Jamie up, blanket and all. He wrapped his arms around my neck with a sigh and I lost my heart again. *That's three times to a MacGannon,* I thought, and held him to me.

"When there's a storm Jamie thinks the monster man will come and set us on fire," Ian said, looking around him.

I met his worried eyes. "What monster man?"

"There's a monster man who comes at night," Jamie said excitedly. "He comes into your house and sets people on fire."

"Well, he can't get in here," I said lightly. "The castle is very well guarded, and no one could get past your father. Come on."

"Where are we going?" asked Ian, looking very little.

"To my room. Can you walk like that or should I help you?"

"I can walk," he said, and demonstrated.

"Good. Now blow out that candle and come with me." Moments later the three of us were in Alex's and my room, and both boys stood with me as I stirred the fire. I pulled them to me and wrapped their blankets around all three of us, hugging them. They snuggled close to me and I looked down at their blond heads. If ever two boys needed a mother, these were they. And I needed them as well. "When I was a little girl I used to love thunderstorms," I said.

"When I was little I liked them too," Ian said, and I smiled above his head. All of five and very old.

"I don't like them," Jamie grumbled.

"Well, I don't like them much now either," I said. "Especially at night. So I thought we'd all keep each other company. Are you sleepy?"

"No," said Ian, stifling a yawn. "Where's Da?"

"He's still downstairs. Talking."

Jamie nodded and yawned. "He talks a lot."

"Yes, he does." I laughed. "Would you like to hear a story?"

"Aye," they said, so I told a long, rambling story that I made up as I went along. My audience was not critical, and before very long they were asleep. I tucked them into our bed and climbed in with them. When Alex came to bed in the early hours, he moved Ian so he could climb in next to me. I murmured a greeting.

"I see they found ye," he said, fingering the nightgown.

"I found them. They were afraid of the storm."

"Oh, aye," he said, his tone chagrined. "I shoulda realized that. Jamie hates thunder. I'm sorry I was not with ye."

"I'm sure you were having a grand time talking politics." I yawned. "I hope you settled everything." I pulled him close.

"I'd rather have been here with ye," he said, and kissed me.

Finally the last of the wedding guests were gone and we were alone, or as alone as we'd be here. All of Kilgannon breathed a sigh of relief. I was very busy learning about my new home. I was now confident of my way within its walls, although I occasionally still retraced my steps. Alex was my guide as we toured the rest of the castle, the boys and Matthew trailing along, enlarging on Alex's explanations. The kitchens were large, clean, and well stocked, managed by a woman whose name I never learned to pronounce correctly. I called her Mrs. M. The young girls on her staff curtsied and giggled as we entered, watching Matthew covertly. He, like Alex, never seemed to notice the attention he drew from women. Alex joked with the girls, making them laugh as he helped himself to food. They called out their goodbyes when we accompanied Mrs. M. to the kitchen gardens. It was too cold and windy to stay there long, but we had a brief tour and she beamed at us as we complimented her on her abilities. She was a very good cook, serving delicious if unimaginative meals, and I was glad that this was another area I'd not have to worry about. Next we toured the cellars and the storerooms, all well kept and orderly.

What surprised me the most about Kilgannon was the armory. A huge room, sunk into the rock of the hill, it extended well below ground, like the cellars, but had a gallery two stories above for watching the exercises. Windows rimmed the top of the walls and it smelled of stale sweat. *This will not be a room where I will spend much time,* I thought, wrinkling my nose. I had always assumed an armory to be a place only where arms were stored, but this one was a gymnasium as well. As we stood on the gallery watching men practice their swordsmanship, Alex explained that the men of Kilgannon kept well-trained. I asked him why, surprised that he should think such a thing necessary in these times. He shrugged.

"We are at peace with most of our neighbors now and I expect to keep it that way, but it's best to be prepared. Besides, men who are fit warriors are better workers, and tired men dinna argue with their neighbors or their wives as much as bored ones."

"And James Stewart tried to land in Scotland just five years ago. If you have no intention of fighting, why are you preparing?"

He fought a smile as he looked at the men below. Angus was in the thick of it, and I realized for the first time that Angus was the war chieftain, the trainer and teacher of the arts of war. Alex answered my question in a mild tone. "Think on it, Mary. If yer a man intent on taking something from another, who do ye attack? The strongest, most prepared, and smartest, or the weakest and least wary? It doesna take a verra bright man to figure that one out. We have always been few here at Kilgannon, but we have a reputation for being very fierce, and I willna let it be said that Alex MacGannon let the MacGannons grow slack on his watch. So we train."

I nodded and watched the men. Next to us Ian and Jamie held on to the railing and bent to look through the slats at the scene below. Angus and Malcolm were showing two younger men how to parry and thrust, and I watched idly, noting how Angus oversaw every movement, every pause. How very different this was than watching Will and his fencing teacher. These men were not using dress swords and they were not practicing their form for its appearance. They were learning how to kill and not be killed.

Below us the men had paired differently now, Malcolm and a partner fending off Angus and a much younger man. Angus pushed his opponent back to the wall and stepped back, lowering his sword and talking earnestly. He stepped back again, then fell heavily over the leg that Malcolm had thrust in his path. Malcolm laughed as he watched Angus land on his back with a thud and a curse. With a curse of his own, Alex leaned over the railing and shouted. Angus picked himself up and reached for Malcolm, grabbing Malcolm's shirt and throwing him against the wall, then leaning into his face and speaking quietly. Malcolm was not laughing when Angus shoved him again and strode away. The younger men turned away, some following Angus out of sight. Alex spoke angrily to Malcolm, who spat a reply. Whatever he said enraged Alex, who shouted at his brother. I could not understand a word, but Alex's anger and disgust was obvious and Malcolm's disdain withered under his brother's attack. When Alex barked an order to the remaining men, Malcolm looked up at his brother and saw the boys and I standing at the rail. He met my eyes, paused, then bowed with contempt. I turned away. No, I was not wrong, he was as disagreeable a man as I had first believed. Alex reached for me then and I grasped his hand. As we left I turned to look below one last time and saw Malcolm standing alone in the big room, caught by a ray of light, dust motes swirling in the beam around him, staring at us malignantly. I never forgot the moment. We never discussed it.

But I didn't dwell on Malcolm, for I was too busy. And

too happy. Alex showed me the grounds, including the gardens and walled orchard that his grandparents had built. And Alex used the time to start my Gaelic instruction. I would say something and he would translate it into Gaelic. Angus watched us benignly, shaking his head at our efforts, but Matthew and the boys joined the game readily and soon I had four teachers, all correcting me constantly. *I will learn the fool language,* I told myself, *if only to stop them from teaching me.*

I learned my way around the valley as well. The glen, as I'd been told to call it, was unusually fertile for the Highlands and had led to much of the MacGannon wealth. I now understood what Robert had meant. When Alex was at home he was a wealthy man, but one cannot readily spend a stone castle or fertile fields that can feed only its owners well. Life at Kilgannon was comfortable, that was obvious, but there was little surplus. When the weather was clear we rode every day, until I had visited every tacksman and crofthouse and every member of Clan MacGannon. Kilgannon's lands were flung over glens and mountains and along the shore, and we had many miles to cover. Alex explained that there were two levels of tenants on his lands: the tacksmen, who often owned their lands and rented them to others, and the crofters, who were at the bottom of the social scale. The tacksmen might be minor lairds as well, depending on their family connections and situation. I believe we visited each one.

Alex showed me everything about his land, even grimly pointing out the two bodies that still swung in the wind from a tree not far from the castle. "Murderers," he spat, and gave me sharp look. "Killed a good man for cattle." His voice quieted. "And did more. So we hanged them. And that, lass, is also part of this land." I stared at the bodies and nodded, trying to absorb all of it.

I was beginning to remember many of the names and remarked to Alex that it was amazing that all of these people were related to him. He shook his head and turned in his saddle to look at me. "They may have the MacGannon name, but not all have the blood."

"They are not all MacGannons?"

"Aye, they are that. But families move and many change their names when they change their allegiance. They become MacGannons and forsake whatever name they used before they came here. They can take the name but not the bloodline. Like the scum that murdered the crofter. They werena MacGannons two generations ago. Many, of course, keep their own names." He gestured to Thomas riding behind us. "Thomas is Thomas MacNeill, and the pipers are led by Seamus MacCrimmon, both names too proud to change. Like MacGannon. Do ye think if I moved to yer lands in England I'd become Alex Lowell?"

"I see. But it's acceptable for me to become Mary MacGannon?"

"Oh, aye." He grinned. "Mary MacGannon. It's a fine name. Ye've improved yerself, lass." I laughed at him. He waved to a woman approaching us as we entered her yard. "Ah, look," he said. "Here's the latest of Duncan of the Glen's bairns. Don't they all look alike? This one is Alexander." He grinned. "Named after me. Aren't ye impressed?" He leaned down and took the small boy from his smiling mother. We were in the remotest northern part of Kilgannon property, near a village called Glendevin. The yard was mud, the crofthouse a long two-story stone building, tidy and well kept. Both the yard and the house seemed full of blond children who all looked the same as the youngest, only taller. Duncan MacGannon, known as Duncan of the Glen, was the proud father who stood in front of his huge family, grinning. He took his son from Alex as we stopped before him.

"We welcome ye to our home, Laird Alex," Duncan said. "And yer new wife as well. Will ye come and have bite or a glass?"

"Whisky would be perfect, Duncan. I thank ye," said

Alex, dismounting and then reaching up to help me. I slipped down into his arms and then into the mud, feeling it ooze into my velvet shoes. Obviously I would have to find something more suitable to wear on these visits. Or stay on the horse.

"My wife doesna have the English, Lady Mary, but she welcomes ye as well," Duncan said, bowing to me.

"Tell her thank you for me, Duncan," I said. "No, let me try." I attempted a simple greeting and could tell by their faces that I had been successful. The woman replied and I realized she had invited me to either eat or drink. I was at a loss how to accept at first and then remembered the words. I wanted to say that I would be delighted to eat her oatcakes, and I thought that I had. Obviously I hadn't. Duncan's wife put her hands to her mouth, her eyes dancing, and behind her the children were giggling. Turning, I saw everyone in the yard trying to suppress laughter and Alex grinning widely. "What did I say?" I whispered to him.

"Ye said ye were delighted to eat her foot." He laughed aloud and kissed my hair as the others guffawed.

"How did I say that?"

"Verra clearly."

I looked at her feet, clad in rough leather shoes that were covered with mud, and I turned back to Alex. "Tell her I've changed my mind," I said. "I'll just have something to drink." He roared then and told them, and the moment passed. Thank heavens I had said something funny and not something insulting, I thought. Otherwise, these smiling faces might now be reaching for their weapons. With a suppressed sigh, I longed heartily for Louisa's drawing room in London.

No doubt they'll remember me as an idiot, I thought later as we rode away. I turned to wave again and a little boy ran forward, grinning widely and thrusting his foot out at me. I laughed and he handed me a flower, limp and bedraggled from being held in the grubby hand. We smiled at each other and he waved as we turned up the glen to go higher. I looked after him and then at the flower in my hand. It was a rose, small and pale, a kind I'd never seen.

"What kind of rose is this?" I asked Alex when at last we paused beside a burn to let the horses drink.

He looked at it through narrowed eyes. "White?"

"No, seriously, Alex," I said. "One of Duncan's boys gave it to me, so it must grow near his home. What is it called?"

"I have no idea, lass."

"Beg pardon, madam," said Thomas, leaning forward on his horse. "It is a wild rose."

"Wild? And so delicate?"

Thomas nodded. "Aye, madam. It is small and easily bruised, but it will grow back again and again. Once it has taken root ye cannot budge it for all the effort ye'd give."

We looked at the diminutive flower and I held it to my nose. "It's beautiful. And very fragrant," I said, pleased.

"Aye." Thomas nodded. "That disguises how hardy it is."

"We should give the rose a verra special name, Thomas," said Alex with a smile, his eyes full of mischief.

"Do ye have one in mind?" Thomas asked in a mild tone.

"Aye, I do at that. And it's only the one name that will do."

"Ah, do tell us, Alex," laughed Thomas.

Alex turned to include all the men. "Who do we know who is small and verra beautiful and easily bruised?" Eyes turned toward me. "And," he continued, "is as pale as those petals? And has numerous thorns?" He laughed heartily at his own joke. "And is the hardiest flower in Scotland?" They all looked for my reaction. I shook my head and raised my hands as if mystified.

"I can think of no one, Alex. Do you mean yourself?"

"Oh, aye, lass. I'm verra small and verra beautiful."

I looked at the faces watching me. *All right, Alex,* I said to myself, and smiled wickedly. "You're not small, Alex," I said demurely, "but you are very beautiful." I ignored the snorts of laughter and waited. Alex laughed.

"Aye, well, that's the truth of it," he said as he restrained his dancing horse and met my eyes. "We'll call it the Mary Rose."

"Aye," said Thomas next to him. "Verra good, Alex."

"Naturally," said my husband as he led us from the stream.

That night as we prepared for bed I found the rose again—Ellen had put it in a cup of water and placed it in our room. Alex took it from me and held the tiny flower in his hand. "Mary Rose," he said, smiling tenderly. "It suits ye, lass."

"Silly man," I said as I turned back the bedcovers.

"Not silly, Mary Rose," he said, and put the rose back in the water. "Smart enough to see beyond yer beauty to yer strength."

I turned to face him. "Which you are constantly testing."

"Aye, but I suspect yer tougher than all of us, my Mary Rose." He wrapped an arm around my waist and kissed my neck, then slipped my robe from me as his lips traced down my neck to my shoulder and my arm. "The toughest rose in Scotland."

"I am not tough," I protested.

"Oh, aye, lass. Yer mind is." He paused as he moved his mouth to mine. "But yer body is verra tender, Mary Rose."

SEVENTEEN

LATE SPRING WAS A BLAZE OF BLOSSOMS, THE HEATHER alive with blues and purples that I could not have imagined. The glen was overflowing with flowers, the trees in light-green leaves that darkened with every day. I was beginning to feel more at home. My Gaelic was stronger now and I was able to talk with many of the clansmen. I still missed London and my family, but Louisa wrote often, her letters full of news and gossip. She promised a visit in the fall. And Will wrote as well, telling me of Betty and our friends and Mountgarden. I wrote to them of my life here and tried to make it all sound wonderful. It was wonderful. But there were days, when Alex was gone, when I wondered what I was doing here at the end of the earth with these strange people. Ellen was a breath of home each day, but she was changing as well as I, and she spent more and more time with the boys or the other young women. Or with wee Donald, who had been enraptured with her since he'd escorted her to Bristol.

The boys helped as well. We had a tradition now—the story at bedtime. I would sit in their room making up silly and fantastic tales, their father often with us, or they would join us in the library. How I loved that room, my favorite in the castle. Alex's grandmother Diana had designed the library as well as the rest of the house, and this room was her most successful. Tall shuttered windows that looked out to the orchard stretched from deep window seats to the ceiling, enclosed by shelf after shelf of books. The wood of the walls and shelves glowed with a deep red gleam. The huge fireplace dominated one wall, chairs pulled up to it in comfortable disarray. Alex's grandfather's desk filled the other end of the room, and it was here that I would sit after the boys went to bed, or on a cold afternoon or quiet morning, and work on the Kilgannon accounts. I was surprised at how quickly that had come about, but I was very pleased. The factor, Thomas MacNeill, was efficient at managing all the details and the people who ran Kilgannon smoothly, but Thomas liked the tallying no more than Alex, and it had been neglected. When I complained to Alex that he would be gone all day and then spend the evening at the desk, he showed me what he was doing. He explained and I asked questions.

"Ye could do it better, couldn't ye, lass? Will told me ye managed the accounts at yer parents' estate for years." He sighed and looked at the papers strewn across the desk. "Would ye consider doing it, Mary? I ken ye've done it before, and ye can ask me or Thomas for any help ye need. Mary, truly, if I never had to do this again I'd be grateful." I considered. Deirdre managed the house beautifully, and although they spent more and more time with me, the boys still had many to look after them. I was going slowly there, trying to avoid a misstep. But the accounts I could do without displacing anyone. As I debated what to say, Alex leaned back and tossed a piece of paper onto the pile with a sigh.

"Do you think you should discuss this with Thomas? Or Angus?"

Alex shook his head. "No, I think I should discuss this with ye. Thomas and I have talked on it, to tell ye the truth. He hates it as much as I do. He'd rather be outside directing the work. And it was Angus who reminded me that ye did the Mountgarden accounts. Tell me the truth of it, lass. If ye dinna want the job, say the word and I'll not ask again." He crossed his arms on his chest as he studied me. *I can do this,* I thought. *I will do this.* I nodded. "Good," Alex said, pleased. "Then the job's yers. And I thank ye, Mary, for I have no love for it."

But I did. The order that I could bring pleased me, and though the task was daunting because it had been so neglected, I soon made headway. Most evenings we would sit in the library after the boys had gone to bed, Alex buried in a book or in a chess game with Angus or Matthew, Deirdre at her needlework, and me at the desk. Malcolm joined us often, and he would play chess with one of the others or just talk. He rarely spoke to me. One night, while Alex and the boys sat in one of the big chairs poring over an atlas and talking about sea monsters, Malcolm restlessly roamed the room. Deirdre looked up from her sewing but said nothing. Angus and Matthew were engrossed in their game, oblivious to the rest of us. I watched Malcolm surreptitiously as I worked and he prowled the shelves. When I put my pen down and watched him openly, he turned to me with a smile, gesturing to my stilled pen. "Yer in no mood to work anymore, Mary. Come and see what I've found."

"What?" I tried to keep my voice light. He smiled, a charming smile that made him look very young, and laughed, beckoning me with a finger. Deirdre looked up with a slight smile as I stood. He drew a wooden box from a shelf and carried it with much ceremony to the desk, placing it in front of me with a flourish. The top of the box was carved with a border of intertwining branches enclosing a regal lion in profile, his front right leg raised and his tail in a flourish behind him. I recognized the MacGannon crest, but below it, instead of the clan motto, ALEXANDER MACGANNON had been carved in bold letters. Malcolm grinned at me.

"Open it," Malcolm said, and glanced at his brother, who was still explaining that no matter what stories Thomas told, there were no water horses or sea monsters in Loch Gannon. Jamie was unpersuaded. Ian was watching to see who was the most convincing.

"Alex," Malcolm called, "look what I found." He gestured to the box and Alex looked up, vaguely at first, then sharply, and smiled.

"I've not seen that in years," Alex said, coming to stand in front of the desk, the boys following him. The brothers smiled at each other while Deirdre watched us from her chair. "I don't even remember what's in it," said Alex as he turned the box to face him. "See, laddies," he showed his sons, "this box was made for me by the MacDonald as a christening gift."

"Did you like it?" asked Jamie, looking up at his father.

Alex laughed. "I dinna think I cared. I was a wee infant, ye ken." Jamie watched his father with a doubtful expression. "It's true, Jamie," Alex said, ruffling his son's hair. "I was a bairn once. And this was a gift to that bairn."

"What's in it, Da?" Ian leaned over the box and traced the lettering. "Baby things?"

"No, yer da's drawings," said Malcolm, as Alex opened the box. "As long as I can remember," he continued, "yer da was drawing, and he used to put all of the best ones in here." The box was full of yellowed paper, some of it very brittle, and Alex picked the pages up with care. Each was a drawing, some of Kilgannon or Loch Gannon, but most of the sketches were of people. Alex spread them out before us one by one. "Look, here's Da, Alex," Malcolm said as Angus and Matthew at last rose from their game and joined us. Malcolm held up a picture of a man who looked remarkably like him, with the same thick neck and chest, but the face was so like both of the brothers that I gasped and met Alex's eyes.

"Aye, it's my father." Alex spoke without inflection. "I was twelve when I drew that. It's who yer named after," he said to Ian.

"It looks just like him," said Angus, picking up another. "And here's ye, Mother." He showed Deirdre the sketch.

She smiled and came to stand next to her son. "I remember the day ye drew this, Alex," she said, taking the sketch from Angus. "Ye labored so hard over it I was afraid to look at the result."

"It looks just like ye did then," said Angus. And it looked like her now. Alex had captured her bone structure, which had not changed, but the softness around the cheeks had faded, and the eyes looked wearier now as she looked at the picture with a fond smile.

Alex took another sketch from the box. "Here's my grandmother, lass," he said, handing me the page. The drawing showed a woman no longer young. Her face was Alex's in feminine form, the same straight nose and well-defined mouth, long eyelashes, and balanced features. Her jawline was softer, and despite the fearless gaze, the face was very womanly. Alex smiled as he watched me look from the sketch to him. "Aye," he said. "We do look like her." He was right; they all did. Angus, Malcolm, Matthew, even Ian and Jamie, looked like Diana—Alex and Matthew most of all.

"She always said she'd leave her mark on the MacGannons," laughed Deirdre, and I realized with a start that Diana had been her mother-in-law. A formidable one, no doubt. I passed the sketch to her. "This was drawn shortly before she died," Deirdre said, "but Diana was not about to admit that she was ill." I looked more closely at the picture, the lines around her mouth and the strain around her eyes now evident. Diana had been older, and ill, when she sat for this picture, but she was one of the most beautiful women I'd ever seen. Alex's smile was bittersweet.

"She made me draw it several times before she was satisfied."

Malcolm found a sketch of his grandfather, and with lips tightened he handed the sketch wordlessly to Angus. "Ah, Grandfather," laughed Angus, and held the drawing for us all to see. "It's Himself." Alex and Angus laughed.

"Alexander was a good man," said Deirdre, and looked down at the boys. "My father-in-law. Yer great-grandfather.

He was dead before ye were born, but this is what he looked like." The boys looked with little interest at the sketch of a man who appeared very much alive. Alexander had Angus and Malcolm's build and a face that I'd seen all over the glen. The same fair hair and strong chin was apparent in his grandsons, and Alexander's expression as he gazed out of the sketch made me smile. I'd seen that look many times. Alex looked at his grandfather's image with affection and then glanced up as Malcolm cried out.

"It's Jamie," Malcolm said, handing a sketch to Alex.

"I'd forgotten all about this," Alex said softly as he showed me the drawing of a young boy with gentle eyes and a sweet smile. "My brother Jamie." Alex looked at the sketch with a tender expression before showing it to his son. "And this is who yer named after. He was eight when I drew this. My bonnie brother."

"Aye," said Malcolm, his tone for once affectionate. "He was that, Alex." The brothers exchanged a sad smile.

Some evenings were noisy and filled with music, when Alex would call for a ceilidh, an impromptu musical gathering. We would sing and dance, and if we had traveling musicians the hall would be filled with smiling faces ready for the entertainment. But we had so much talent here at Kilgannon that we rarely needed them. Thomas's wife, Murreal, loved to sing and often entertained us alone or with Thomas. Their voices blended beautifully, and I loved those nights when their songs rose to the ceiling and I sat with my husband and let the sound move me.

But at other times I was uneasy, and I grew more so the more time I spent with the accounts. The rents and expenditures for Kilgannon were in order with a few minor exceptions. Thomas had been lax recently, but his earlier records were correct and precise, and his accounts were easy to bring current. The revenue and expenses for each of Alex's brigs had been recorded separately, which made them easy to trace. *Gannon's Lady,* captained by Calum MacGannon, showed a profit on each trip, as did the *Katrine.* The *Margaret* was usually reserved for Kilgannon travel and errands, so she showed little revenue. But the *Diana* had lost money, and it was the *Diana* that had gone down off Cornwall. Repairs to her were twice what they were with the other ships, and her income had started dipping two years ago. Not steeply, but steadily. I wondered if there were factors that I did not know, which would make my suspicions unfounded. Alex had neglected the accounts; perhaps there were records I had not received yet. I needed more information, but Alex had gone on his first trading trip of our marriage. He would be gone three weeks and Angus with him. We had talked at great length about him leaving and I had assured him that I would be fine, but now I found myself at Kilgannon with Malcolm and my suspicions. I compiled my notes and waited for his return.

Thomas often asked if I needed any assistance, and one lovely night shortly before Alex was due back, I asked him to walk with the boys and me along the shore of the loch. The boys ran ahead and Thomas and I followed. At first we talked about things of little consequence, but then Thomas turned to me with a smile. "Madam, if ye'll forgive the question, why is it ye asked for my company?" His brown eyes were troubled but his tone was polite, and I was reminded again of my newness to Kilgannon.

"Thomas," I said, unsure of how to begin. "You know that I am helping Alex with the Kilgannon accounts. As his factor you know everything that happens here. I need you to explain what is usual and what is not." He considered, looking off over the loch, while I wondered what was in his mind. I had no reason to doubt his loyalty to Alex or his honesty. All of the accounts for which he had been responsible were in order, and the boats' records were Alex's. It was obvious that he was deciding what to say to me, and after a moment I sat down on a rock, looking ahead to where the boys were poking the water with a stick they'd found. The loch was still and silent tonight, the usual waves so small as to make no noise at all, and I savored the quiet and the beauty. The mountains were mirrored in the water, tall and purple, the tips of them lit by the last of the evening's light. Behind me a bird called mournfully. At last Thomas broke his reverie. Whatever his internal debate had been, there was no sign of it.

"Madam, I will be happy to review all the accounts with ye. At least, all that I ken of. I ken everything about the *Margaret,* but if ye have questions on the other ships, ye'll have to ask the captains, or ye can ask Angus and Malcolm. Or Alex, of course."

I looked at him in surprise. "What do Angus and Malcolm have to do with the ships?"

"Well, ye ken Alex turned the ships over to them, don't ye? Ye don't. I can see it by yer face." He sighed, shifting his weight. "About three years ago Alex was verra busy with Sorcha, since she wasna so good. His mother and Angus's Mairi had just died. So he told Angus to deal with the *Katrine* and Malcolm the *Diana,* and Alex took *Gannon's Lady* himself and I took the *Margaret,* since she was really part of my work. So that's who ye'd talk to." He kicked a stone at his feet. "What questions do ye have so far?"

I tried to sound calm. "None really, thank you, Thomas. I am just beginning to find my way."

"Ah. Well, it's unfortunate that ye'll have to wait for Alex and Angus to return, but Malcolm's here and he'll no doubt be happy to help ye if ye need him."

"No doubt," I said.

I tried to ignore my misgivings and spent more time with Deirdre learning about the management of the house and the housekeeper, Berta. "She's a braw worker," Deirdre said, leading me up a flight of stairs. "Ye can rely on her."

"I won't need to. You'll be here to take care of everything."

She gave me a sideways glance. "I willna always be here.

Ah, here's Alex's room, I'll warrant that he dinna show ye
this. Come and look. He moved in here after his brother
died." She led me into a small box of a room, bare except
for a chest by the door and a squat bedstead in one corner. I
looked around with interest at the room in which Alex had
spent so many years. There was nothing of the boy he
had been in this empty space, nothing of his dreams left here
in these stones. I crossed over to the window and opened
it, leaning out. The view was of the glen, the loch far below
rippled with the afternoon breezes. I took a deep breath.
How many times had that little boy looked at this view and
dreamed of what was beyond the mountains?

"Ye'll need to take over the management of the house
soon," Deirdre said. "I've a mind to see how my daughters
are doing, and my Angus doesna need me as much anymore.
I've been here long enough to see Alex marry ye, and I feel
comfortable leaving him. No, lass, I'm off soon enough, so
ye'll have to learn all this."

I turned, startled, and saw her framed in the doorway.
"Deirdre, you can't mean that. You're not leaving us?"

She nodded with a slight smile. "Aye, lassie, it is time
for ye to be mistress here. My work at Kilgannon is done for
the now."

I closed the window and turned back to her. "Deirdre,
this is your home. I will let you care for the house and I will
never interfere. Do not let me drive you away!"

"Ah, Mary, yer a good girl," she said, her tone gentle
now. "Life goes on, my dear. Ye are not driving me away,
truly."

"Then don't leave." I sounded all of ten.

She smiled. "It's time, Mary. Ye are capable of running
this house and having time for yer husband and his sons and
yer accounts. It's time for me to see my own girls. They
need their mother too, not just Angus, ye ken." I tried to
smile. "Lassie, it's time for me to rest a bit, no? I've taken
care of the boys and the house for Alex and made sure my
Angus and Matthew were all right after Mairi died. Now my

girls need their mother. My Catriona is with child again and has no' had it easy the last few times, and Edanna's husband is traveling a bit the now. It's no' that I'm being driven out. If ye need me here, I'll come back. Ye have but to call me." I nodded and she answered my unspoken question. "I'd like to be with them before autumn, so I'll be off soon. I'll stay for the games and then I'll go home with Edanna. Alex did tell you about the games?"

I shook my head and she sighed. "Men! Aye, well, you'll find out in August. It's Highland Games, Mary, which means the men play and the women feed them!" She looked around the little room. "We have a lot to do before then, no?"

"Have you told Alex?"

She shook her head. "No, not yet. I thought I'd talk to ye first, ye being the mistress now, ye ken." She smiled. "Don't look so fearful, lass. Alex will no' mind as long as we're both happy. And Angus knows. Truth of it is, now that I think on it, Angus probably told Alex. The two of them are like that." She looked around the room. "Some things belong to the past, Mary, and I'm leaving before I'm one of them."

No matter how busy I kept myself, every night found me at the desk going over the figures again and again. Malcolm spent more time with me in the evenings before Alex returned, surprising me by being charming and affable company. I wondered if Thomas had mentioned our conversation, but I would not question Malcolm while Alex was gone. It could wait.

EIGHTEEN

ALEX CAME HOME AT LAST, SAILING INTO LOCH GANNON early in the afternoon on a brilliant day. I shielded my eyes from the sun, which danced on the water, turning the tiny peaks into diamonds, and waved to him as the brig approached, my heart considerably lighter. It was hours before all the work involved in a trading trip was done and the crew dismissed. Then Alex and Angus and Calum sat over whisky in the hall, going over the last of the details. There was an underlying tension in them that I could not understand. I sat next to Alex, waiting, the boys with us as well, and when the conversation dwindled he suggested that the four of us climb the headland behind the castle.

We climbed silently, the boys running before us and then behind us. My hand was in his, but his mind was elsewhere. We reached the top of the ridge and stood looking out over the outer loch and toward the sea, the wind pulling at our clothing and hair. I was not the only one who had noticed his mood. Even the boys were quiet for once, glancing nervously at their father. Alex sighed and dropped my hand to reach out and pull Jamie back from the edge. "Dinna go so close, Jamie," he said in a calm tone.

"Was it a bad trip, Da?" Ian looked up at his father. Alex smiled down at him and ruffled his hair.

"No, lad, it was a good trip. I would have ye tell me what ye did in my absence." He hoisted Jamie onto his shoulder

nd lifted Ian sideways with his other arm. Both boys giggled as he brought them back from the edge and sat on an
outcropping of rocks. I joined him and listened while the
boys talked about what they'd done for three weeks, mostly
little-boy adventures concerning insects and caves and ani-
mals. "I see ye've been as busy as I've been," he said. "And
ye deserve a reward. I've a grand surprise for each of ye
waiting below." He grinned at their excitement. "Murdoch
helped me choose them."

"What, Da?" They stood in front of him now, all attention.

He grinned and poked their stomachs. "Puppies. Go and
see them if ye wish." They whooped in delight and raced
away. Alex looked after them, then glanced at me. "Wolfhounds," he said. "I asked Murdoch for two of his pups.
The boys will be happy."

"No doubt," I said, wondering how we could manage
two more dogs, and wolfhounds at that. We sat in silence
then, watching the sea. He wrapped an arm around me and
looked out over the water. I watched his profile. *He'll tell
me soon enough,* I thought, and then turned to the view.
Blue water, blue sky, blue islands, blue mountains; there had
to be twenty shades of blue visible. I turned to meet his
eyes. *Twenty-one,* I corrected myself, and lifted my mouth to
meet his kiss. Three weeks without touching this man. We
started to make up for the time we had lost.

"Mary," he said after a bit. "I'm sorry I was gone so
long."

"Me too," I said, and watched the wind lift his hair and
the plaid at his shoulder. Behind him the sky was clear
except for a few skittering clouds that only emphasized the
blue of the sky and the water. He sighed and leaned back
against the rock, stretching his legs out in front of him.
"What is it?" I asked. He glanced at me in surprise.

"I should ken ye better, lass. Ye miss nothing."

"I know something's bothering you, Alex, but I don't
know what it is."

He nodded, then looked out over the water. "I stopped

at the Macleans' on my way home," he said flatly. "Murdoch says that for months Malcolm's been telling anyone who will listen that I'm very hotheaded nowadays and am in financial difficulties and that despite his best efforts, I'm ruining Kilgannon." He turned to look at me.

"Where is he saying this?"

"In Edinburgh, in Glasgow. In Clonmor when he goes there. That's his land, in the eastern Highlands. It was our mother's."

"I remember. What will you do?"

"I'll have a talk with him. I'll tell him to stop making himself out to be the grand brother saving the stupid one. I'll tell him to tell the truth of it."

"Why not mention how disloyal he is?"

"Aye, well, ye ken he would not see it like that. I dinna think he means to demean me so much as to make himself look grander. It's difficult to be the one that did not inherit."

"My father was happy even though he was a younger son."

"Yer father wasna a Scot."

"Yours is not the only race with pride," I said sharply.

He laughed. "Yer right, lass, and I'm sorry for the slur." He pulled me to him. "Do ye ken how good for me ye are?"

I relented. "Yes, Alex, I do. You're a very fortunate man."

"I am that." He grinned and kissed my neck. "Ah, lass, I am that." I thought we would leave then and go back to the castle, but he made no move and I sat with him, wondering what was next.

"Alex," I said when he sighed to himself again. "What else?"

"Ah, well, I'm just being melancholy, no doubt, but I keep thinking of what yer Robert Campbell said. He was correct. I am the last of a dying breed, lass, and I ken it. I just dinna know how to stop it." I could not think of an answer but took his hands in mine and watched him as the afternoon sun glowed above us, his eyes narrowed against the glare, his hair a golden halo around his head. Most of the clan would never know the depth of his acceptance of responsibility for their future. Most would never doubt that life as they knew it would stay the same. And it was his duty to see that it did. But I knew, as he did, that Robert was right and that the world would come to our door and bring with it the things that would change Kilgannon. I just didn't want Malcolm to be the bearer of the changes. Or the beneficiary. I sighed, catching his somber mood, but a moment later he smiled.

"Well, we'll just do the best we can, no? I dinna have a better solution and there is not a better man to do it." He laughed then, his grin infectious. "I am a fortunate man, Mary Rose."

"Oh, yes, my lord," I said, and stroked my hand up his thigh under his kilt. "Very fortunate," I said. "Very, very fortunate."

"I am that," he said, and kissed me, laughing. And then moved my hand where he wanted it. "But I'm willing to share my fortune."

When the afternoon cooled we left our perch and started back to the castle. At the top of the hill he stopped and turned to me.

"I'm going to have an interesting discussion with Malcolm."

"Oh?" I said, hearing the worry in my voice.

He laughed. "Dinna fret, lass. I can manage Malcolm."

That night there was music and dancing. Alex did not speak to Malcolm, but he watched him. For his part Malcolm stayed in his corner with his friends, which suited me. But I didn't think about Malcolm long. We were too busy with the puppies. Entranced, the boys debated long and hard over their names and finally decided. Alex raised his eyebrows at their choices and teased them, "What, named after Lowlanders?" But the boys were pleased with their decision and as stubborn as their father, so Robert the Bruce and William Wallace came to live with us.

Later, alone in our room, Alex kissed me and went to bathe. I fell asleep while he was gone, but when he climbed between the covers, trying to be quiet, I raised my head and greeted him.

"Ah," he said. "Yer awake. I was wondering if it would be rude to wake ye just so I could attack ye. Three weeks, lass. I dinna think I'll be going on many of these trading trips, Mary Rose. I missed ye too much this time," he said into my hair.

"I missed you terribly," I said, stifling a yawn.

"Am I boring ye?" He chuckled in the dark.

"No, but I did have to share you this evening with the entire clan. Apparently I do not have the same attractions as they."

"Aye, well, that's the truth of it," he said, kissing me. "And glad I am that ye do not." He kissed my neck and shoulder and slid his hand down my side and then up again. "I am here now, and, Mary Rose, since I can never tell around here when there'll be another opportunity to be alone with ye, let's not miss this one, aye?"

We didn't.

Alex was downstairs before me the next morning. The hall was full, but Malcolm was nowhere to be seen. I sighed contentedly. I'd had a wonderful night's sleep. Alex sat on a bench, quiet and contemplative, leaning against the table, one long leg crossed over the other, the boys playing at his feet. He watched the rain through the open hall door and greeted me with a quiet smile. "Good morning, lass. How are ye?"

"I slept very well," I said with a smile. He nodded.

"I'm sure ye did, Mary Rose. Ye snored considerably." I laughed as I sat next to him. He gestured to his sons. "I'm thinking it's time to get a tutor, lass. I know ye've been teaching them their letters and numbers, and I have as well, but Ian's almost six and he'll be needing more schooling. Have ye any objection?" I shook my head, surprised at his topic, and followed his gaze to the boys where they sprawled on the floor with the puppies.

"Where will you get a tutor?" I asked, watching Ian pet his dog with loving strokes.

"I'll write to St. Andrew's and see if they have a recommendation. I dinna finish, because my father died and I had to come home, but I still write to some of my teachers. One of them will know someone. And Angus and I think it's time Matthew went to university."

"You're sending him away?" I asked, startled.

He shot a blue glance at me. "Not sending him away, Mary, letting him go and learn. He'll go to St. Andrew's like me and his da, and he'll have some learning of his own. But he'll finish, like his da, and both of them will be better educated than their chief. Lass, the boy's ready to go. It's time." When he spoke again, his tone was pensive and his topic different. "Mary, ye and I, we both know a bit about loss. More than most, less than some, but both of us have lost our parents and grandparents, and I've lost a brother and a sister." His eyes met mine. "I would keep the one I have left." I nodded, swallowing my nasty thoughts about Malcolm. This was obviously not the time to mention the *Diana*'s losses. I wondered if I ever would.

The afternoon brought sunshine and half the clan, each man with a grievance or story to share with Alex. By evening he was finished talking, but they stayed, and the hall was full of music and dancing. I had despaired of ever having a moment alone with him again and sat watching the others dance when a hand on my shoulder roused me. I looked up into Alex's eyes, his head bent close to mine. "I was thinking we'd steal a moment, Mary Rose," he said, and smiled as he led me from the hall. In the library he stirred the fire and then crossed the room and poured a glass of whisky. "I've spoken to Malcolm," he said, settling into the chair.

"Oh?" I watched the light play across the planes of his face.
He sipped his whisky. "Aye. It willna happen again."

"Good," I said, afraid to say more.

We sat in silence until he raised his glass and looked
through it at the flames. "Mary, what is bothering ye
about the accounts?" I stared at him. How could he know?
I answered my own question. Thomas, of course. I took a
deep breath and plunged in, explaining about the *Diana*'s
costs and revenues. He listened, then laughed. "Dinna look
so wary, lass, I'm not a fool. I ken we were losing money, I
just dinna ken how much. That's why I took the *Diana*
away from Malcolm and hired that captain to sail her for us.
And ye ken what happened then. We went from having a
ship that lost money to having no ship. From now on we'll
do our own sailing."

"But the repairs—" I started.

"Aye," he said, interrupting me. "I ken about the
repairs." He frowned into his glass and then looked up to
meet my eyes. "They were extraordinary, aye, even for an
old ship, and she is the oldest of the bunch of them. I asked
Malcolm about them. She lost more money faster than any
ship I've seen. It still doesna add up correctly, but he is
young and inexperienced. No one learns these things except
by doing, ye see. When it got to be too much I removed the
Diana from him and then we lost her entirely. So I'm much
better off now, no?" He grinned lopsidedly and finished
his whisky. "Ye ken I'm not a great businessman, Mary," he
said, "but we're doing all right."

"Why do you trade at all?"

He looked at me blankly, then sat up straight, looking at
me. "Have we no' talked of this before?"

I shook my head. "No."

"Aye, well, there's no mystery here. The rents from the
clan dinna pay the taxes on this old castle nor do they even
come close to paying to keep it repaired. Some of the work,
of course, comes from rent paid in kind, but I need cash to

pay the taxes." He sighed. "I canna raise the rents further, and I willna let the tacksmen do it either. And the taxes canna wait. The English need my money to subjugate the Scots. The money for the taxes and everything else has to come from somewhere, so we went and got it. I pay the English with money they give me for selling them French wine. Seems only fair. And then," he shrugged, "there is the fun of seeing other parts of the world. It works out well." His eyes roamed my face and grew darker. "But now I think I'm going to want to stay much closer to home." I smiled and leaned to kiss him.

A knock interrupted us, and Alex raised his eyebrows at me as he called out. Thomas opened the door. "Sorry, Alex, but yer wanted in the hall. Duncan of the Glens has just arrived, and he needs to talk with ye."

"At this hour?" Alex growled. "Can he not just have a glass or two and we'll talk in the morning?"

Thomas shook his head. "He says it's important and he must talk with ye as soon as possible and he'll wait until yer free."

Alex sighed and looked at me, shrugging his shoulders. "What now?" he asked as he stood.

"What now" turned out to be an outraged Duncan. He complained that a MacDonald had gotten a MacGannon girl with child, and he pushed the girl forward. The girl was no more than sixteen, a tall, pretty blonde with bright blue eyes that were huge now with terror. Duncan stood behind her, his outrage making her seem small. Alex sat on the table, leaning forward with his elbows on his knees, and listened to Duncan's tirade about the indignities suffered by MacGannons at the hands of MacDonalds for three hundred years, and I realized that Alex had heard this all before, probably many times. The girl stood in the center of the circle of men, staring at the floor, her tears falling unheeded on the stones. When at last Duncan sputtered to an end,

Alex straightened and asked mildly, "This is yer niece, Duncan? This is little Lorna? An' ye want me to punish her?"

Duncan shook his head furiously. "No, no, not at all. I want ye to force the bastard to marry her."

It was soon settled. Lorna and the man she loved, Seamus MacDonald of Skye, both wanted to marry, despite their parents' objections. Alex calmed the weeping girl and told her he'd write to the MacDonald. Duncan nodded, satisfied.

Later, alone in our room, I was quiet and Alex thoughtful as we sat before the fire. "What will you do if the Mac-Donald doesn't approve the marriage?" I asked at last. "Will you go to Skye?" Morag, I knew, lived at the other end of the island, and I tried to remember how big the island was.

But Alex shook his head. "If the MacDonald says no, lass, I willna go to Skye." He looked at me with a tired smile and reached for my hand. "No, Mary, we'll go to Skye."

But we did not go to Skye. The MacDonalds came to us.

A week after Alex wrote to the MacDonald, the man himself arrived. He came on a cloudy and breezy day, with an entourage of clansmen. And two women. Alex and I welcomed them at the dock. The chief of the MacDonalds, known as Sir Donald MacDonald of that Ilk, was a big man, and fleet, both of thought and word. The striking man next to Donald must be Seamus himself, I thought. This young man was buoyant, his gray eyes gleaming, his dark hair neatly tied back, and his clothes well groomed. The two women stood behind the MacDonald, one in middle age, her hair graying around her pretty face, the other much younger, with brown hair and eyes that were now fixed on Malcolm. Deirdre, who knew both, welcomed them with warmth, and the older woman smiled gratefully at her.

"Kilgannon," roared the MacDonald in Gaelic, "I've come to eat yer food again and to invite ye to a wedding."

Alex grinned at him. "Ye've saved me a trip then, Sir Donald, for which I thank ye. Going from paradise to Skye is always difficult, but returning home makes it worth the trouble."

The MacDonald laughed heartily, smacking Alex's shoulder. He turned to me then and spoke cordially in English. "Mistress Mary, how are ye? The most beautiful bride I've seen in a long while. How are ye adjusting to life among the heathens?"

I laughed. "Quite well, sir, thank you."

"Good," he said loudly, "because ye have no choice now, ye ken. 'Tis done, yer marriage, and from what I hear ye'll no' be able to have it annulled." He laughed and I blushed. "Not that ye'd want to, though." He looked at Alex fondly. "He's no' a bad man, for all that he's so ugly." Both men laughed and I smiled. "Alex, I've brought my cousin's girl, Sibeal," the MacDonald said, pulling the girl forward to stand in front of us. "Thought ye'd like to meet yer new sister-in-law." Alex looked at the older man in surprise. Behind me Malcolm moved uneasily and someone started laughing. Next to the MacDonald, Deirdre's expression was guarded.

"Aye. Yer surprised," said the MacDonald, nodding. "Imagine what I felt when I received yer outraged letter, Alex. We can work a trade, no? I'll take yer Lorna Mac-Gannon and ye take our Sibeal MacDonald, though ye are getting the better of the deal. I had to do a bit of talking to get her parents to adjust to the idea. Still, I do think children are best brought up in their father's house." He turned that fierce gaze behind us. "Don't ye agree, Malcolm?"

Alex and the MacDonald disappeared into the library with Malcolm, Angus, Thomas, and several of the MacDonalds, leaving the rest of us to our own devices. I talked to the women, quickly discovering that the older woman was Sibeal's mother. Sibeal said little, alternately radiant and worried. She was a lovely girl, and I was not surprised that she had caught Malcolm's eye.

Sibeal's mother Edina was quite frank about their visit here today. "We were not sure of our reception," she said as we sipped wine before the fire. "Kilgannon's letter was most displeased, I heard, and then Sibeal came to me and told me she was"—she glanced at her daughter—"in the same condition, and that the child was Malcolm's. Sir Donald thought that verra amusing, and he told her we'd just pay ye a little visit and fix it all up." Edina met my eyes. "I want my daughter to be happy. And she says Malcolm makes her happy."

"I would want my daughter happy as well," I said softly, although I seriously doubted that Malcolm could make anyone happy. I wondered how Alex was faring, and as if in answer, the men catapulted from the library.

Alex came to me at once and whispered in my ear, "Dinna fret, Mary. All is well. I may have gray hair before the year is out, but all is well." I patted his hand and smiled up at him. He straightened then and called for music and whisky.

They stayed for three days. It had been decided that Malcolm and Sibeal would marry in two months in Skye, and Lorna and Seamus before that in Glendevin. Word was sent to Lorna, and I suspected when I did not see him that the messenger was Seamus himself, delivering the letter that Alex had written to her mother. Sibeal, clearly delighted, clung to her proposed bridegroom. Malcolm was his usual self, shrugging when anyone mentioned the marriage. What he thought I never discovered, nor did I care, but he was not attentive to Sibeal and he did not seem the least bit embarrassed.

Alex's manner was reserved, but he held my hand under the table as he listened to the MacDonald's opinions. The man had a lot of opinions. Alex rose the moment I yawned behind my hand, and we said our good nights, inviting everyone to continue celebrating. He took my hand openly then and the MacDonald called out remarks as we left the hall, but Alex did not banter as he usually would have. Upstairs, the staff was bustling under Berta's direction, preparing rooms for the unexpected guests, and I was grateful she was here to oversee the situation, for tonight I wanted to be with my husband.

When he closed the door to our room Alex sighed and leaned against it. I stood in the middle of the room, waiting, having decided not to say anything against Malcolm until I could better judge his mood, despite the many comments running through my mind. Alex moved at last from the door and began undressing, then paused in front of the chest where he kept his clothes, his gaze somewhere beyond the wall he was staring at. I waited for what felt like an age, then went to stand next to him.

"Alex," I said at last, and he turned slowly to me. "Are you all right? What happened that I haven't been told? What did they say? What did you say? What did Malcolm say?"

He shrugged. "Nothing much, lass," he said, but smiled.

"Alex," I began in a low voice meant to be threatening, but he had pulled me to him and my voice came out in a squeak. He kissed me, a thorough, lingering kiss, and then looked smugly down at me.

"Speechless. I can still do it." He grinned.

"I am not speechless," I snapped. "And you will be sleeping on the floor tonight if you don't tell me."

"I dinna think so. If I want to be in yer bed I will be there. Dinna show yer teeth if ye canna bite." At my puzzled expression he threw his head back and laughed. "I do love ye, Mary."

"Alex," I said, leading him to the chairs in front of the fire. "Tell me before I burst. What happened? What's the matter?"

He sat in a chair and pulled me onto his lap. "I'm just tired, lass. I'm verra tired of Malcolm and the energy it takes to sort out the messes he creates. This one went well and we've not made an enemy of the MacDonald, but not without an effort."

'What happened in the library?'

He sighed and ran a hand along my thigh, then down my

skirt and up my leg beneath the material. "The tale's not worth the trouble, lass. We established that both Lorna and Sibeal are with child. No one disputes that Seamus and Malcolm are responsible, and neither lass cries foul. Both want to marry. Seamus is eager to marry Lorna, so that one was easy, but the MacDonald was quite displeased about Sibeal and he cornered Malcolm. I'm not sure Malcolm wanted to marry, but marry he will."

"What do you mean?"

"What I mean is that Malcolm dinna come forward and declare his true love like Seamus, so by comparison he looked reluctant. Sir Donald wasna pleased with a reluctant bridegroom and a pregnant bride, and being Sir Donald, he was . . . persuasive."

"Did you leap to Malcolm's defense?"

Alex shook his head. "No. He got in the predicament without my help, and I let him get himself out of it without my help. Besides, lass, I couldna very well look Sir Donald in the eye and say, aye, my brother's gotten this girl with child, but he's no' of a mind to marry just the now, so will ye go on home and we'll think on this later? Can ye see Donald's face had I said that?"

"No." I laughed softly and brushed his hair back from his face. "Alex, would you have married me?"

"I did. Wait, let me think." He looked at the ceiling and then met my eyes. "Aye, I did. Twice." He kissed me and stroked my leg. "I would have married ye fifty times, Mary Rose."

Lorna and Seamus were married in a quiet ceremony in Glendevin. Alex had invited them to marry at Kilgannon, but Lorna wanted to be married in the little chapel near her home. A buoyant Duncan gave the bride away, and I was warmly welcomed by his family. This time I did not offer to eat anyone's foot, although they teased me and offered me several. I laughed with them, delighted that they felt comfortable enough to banter with me. Still, by nightfall, I was glad to return home. It was almost dark by the time we came through the small pass and entered the glen at the far side of Loch Gannon. I caught my breath at the sight of Kilgannon ablaze with lights, its reflection shining in the water before it. The keep loomed above the yard and was topped by torches. Torches were at each corner of the outer wall as well, and I realized I'd never seen Kilgannon from outside the walls at night.

"How beautiful," I said in awe. Alex, a sleepy Jamie on his shoulder, turned to me with a tender smile.

"Aye, lass," he said. "Paradise. I wasna exaggerating to the MacDonald. The most beautiful spot on earth. Ye see why I couldna marry just any woman. I had to find one who would do my home proud." I smiled, then saw Malcolm's glance at his companion behind Alex's back. The two looked at each other with raised eyebrows, and I knew they would mock Alex later. Alex followed my gaze and gave them an appraising stare. "Of course," Alex said, more to them than to me, "I made my decision with my mind rather than just my body." He added something in Gaelic that caused Malcolm to frown and Malcolm's companion to laugh. The phrase was not one I'd been taught, but I didn't ask for a translation.

What a wonderful day it had been, I thought. Lorna's wedding had been perfect, the bride and groom blissful. And soon Malcolm would marry and leave for Clonmor. It looked like a lovely summer.

The peace lasted for one day. It was Thomas's Liam who came running to us the next afternoon, his arms flailing and his eyes wide. "Sir," he gasped, skidding to a stop before Alex. "Please come. My da—" He glanced behind him as though pursued. "My da says to tell you they found the bloody bastard stealing cattle."

At my gasp, Liam blushed. "That's what he said to tell Laird Alex, ma'am. I'm sorry." I nodded, trying to hide my smile, and glanced at Alex, expecting him to be amused. But

Alex, with narrowed eyes and raised chin, was angry as he looked down at Liam.

"He said 'the bloody bastard'?"

Liam nodded. "Aye, sir, and he told me to use those very words. Da says Dougall's gone to fetch him here."

"Mo Dia," Alex said to himself as he looked over the boy's head. "I dinna expect this. Where is he, lad?"

"At Glengannon, sir, but they're coming here."

"Aye, well, tell yer da I'll be right in." Liam nodded and started away. "Liam," Alex called, and the boy turned. "Find my sons. Have them wait for me in the hall."

We both watched as the boy darted away and then I turned to Alex. "Who is 'the bloody bastard'?" I got a glacial look in return. Alex pressed his lips together. "Alex?"

"Allen MacGannon, though God kens he's no' really a MacGannon. His parents came twenty years ago from Mac-Donnell lands, and my father let them stay. That was a mistake. Allen's father was a drunken lout and his sons no better." His eyes met mine. "It was Allen's brothers that I was coming home to deal with, lass, when I went to Robert Campbell's estate. Do ye remember me telling ye?"

"The men who attacked your clansman?" I asked, remembering Alex showing me their bodies hanging from the tree.

"Aye. And I should have finished it then." He sighed heavily and gave me a sideways glance. "Aye, well, I will now," he said, and strode away, leaving me to stare after him.

NINETEEN

IN THE HALL PEOPLE WERE RESTLESS, AND MORE ARRIVED every minute. I stood at the side and watched as Alex, shadowed by Angus, paced in front of the fireplace. When Liam arrived with Ian and Jamie, the three boys stood uncertainly in front of Alex while he talked to them with sharp gestures. I was about to go to him and ask what was happening, when a commotion in the courtyard drew all of our attention. I followed the others outside and stood with Ellen and the boys as the rumblings increased around us.

Dougall rode in first, his face flushed and angry. Behind him, his wrists bound, was a young man with an anxious expression. Alex and Angus ran down the steps and talked with Dougall as their cousin dismounted. Dougall gestured to Allen angrily, and then Malcolm appeared at Alex's side and Dougall apparently began explaining again. All four men turned as Thomas erupted from the stables, catapulting himself at Allen with a rough cry.

I stared in shock as Thomas, usually the calmest of men, pulled Allen off the horse and half-dragged, half-carried him to the side of the courtyard, shouting harshly in Gaelic, words I could not understand. No one interfered as he slammed Allen against the stone wall of the keep over and over. Alex and Angus exchanged a glance, and Alex at last gestured to Malcolm and Dougall to stop it. They peeled Thomas away with difficulty and he stood between them, still shouting, panting now, as Allen slumped to the ground. Alex watched with a somber expression, then took the stairs two at a time to where I stood. When he met my eyes I saw the rage in them. He took the boys' hands from mine and brought them with him into the hall. The people followed, and Ellen and I were the only ones left who saw Angus yank Allen from the ground and snarl at him, dragging him past us into the hall. Allen, his young face terrified and bloody, tried to stay standing. Malcolm and Dougall followed without a glance at us, then Thomas, still breathing heavily, and at last Ellen and I went in as well.

We found a corner with Matthew, and I turned to him as the crowd settled, taking their positions as though they knew what to do. *A hearing,* I thought. "What did Allen do?" I asked.

Matthew gave me a sharp glance. "Stole cattle, Mary."

"Why is Thomas so angry? Were they his cattle?" Matthew shook his head and moved abruptly away from me, leaving me staring after him. Alex was seated at the table on the dais, the same one we'd climbed on the night I'd arrived at Kilgannon. Ian and Jamie sat on each side of him, their eyes huge and their legs dangling in midair. I pushed my way forward to stand before Alex, who met my look with a fierce one of his own.

"What is this, Alex?" I asked. "Are you having a hearing now?"

He met my eyes for the briefest of moments. "It's a trial, Mary Rose," he said coldly. "Go and sit in the back. Or"— he paused and looked out over the now-quiet clan—"or dinna watch at all. It'll not be something ye need to see."

"What about the boys? If I don't need to see it, neither do they." He turned to look at each of his sons, his expression not softening as it usually did when he looked at them. He turned back to me. "They need to be here," he said curtly.

"Alex, if this is going to be ugly, let me take them away."

"They'll stay with me, Mary. Go and sit yerself now."

"Alex—"

"Mary, go now. I'll talk with ye later. Go."

I blinked and stared at him, unable to believe he'd treat me that way. But he did not look at me again, only watched the hall over my head, and at last, gathering what dignity I had left, I went to the back of the hall and stood with Ellen, feeling very much a stranger. The mood in the hall was dangerous, and I watched as Dougall led the way up the aisle with an expression I'd never seen. Usually blunt and cheerful, Dougall looked murderous, and I looked from him to Alex with a sinking heart. Whatever was happening was serious and causing a change in these people that was alarming. I looked over the sea of faces and felt a thrill of fear, then turned to watch Allen's slow progress as Angus led him toward Alex. Allen, young enough to be called a boy, walked slowly, his expression now remote and somehow insolent, as though this amused him. Looking from Allen to Alex, I felt another chill. This Alex was not a man I recognized. Tall and imposing even at his most relaxed, he stood now, seeming huge and threatening.

And then all eyes turned to the door again as a shriek of rage filled the room. Murreal flew up the aisle to stand before Alex, Thomas in her wake. Thomas, pale now rather than the crimson he'd been in the courtyard, stood behind his wife but didn't touch her. I had known Murreal in only the most surface manner. I knew how lovely her voice was and how beautifully it blended with Thomas's when they sang in the evenings and how natural it seemed to see her surrounded by her cheerful brood. I had thought of Murreal as a sweet and tidy woman and could never have imagined her as she now appeared. She seemed possessed, her garments disarrayed, her hair spiky about her head, her face twisted in her agony. I could not understand what she was shrieking in Gaelic and I was grateful, for the words were filled with hate. Ian and Jamie exchanged a frightened look, and I had to force myself to stay where I was and not go to them. Murreal pointed at Allen and shouted, spit at him, and then crumpled to the floor as her sobs stopped her tirade. Alex's eyes flickered from Allen to Thomas to Murreal, then briefly to me with no change of expression, and I felt another chill. I was invisible, it seemed, and Kilgannon was peopled by strangers.

Assorted clansmen came forward and pointed to Allen, then spoke heatedly to Alex. Alex spoke little, asking questions in a terse and cold manner. And then Alex asked Allen something, and the hall quieted to hear his answer. Allen glared at Alex.

"Swine," Allen shouted in Gaelic. "Ye are a swine and a murderer. Ye killed my brothers and I would kill ye for it."

The people surged forward, but Alex stopped them with a gesture, then raised his hands high. "Yer verdict," he said.

The roar in return was deafening and unmistakable. Allen was doomed. I lost sight of Alex then as the clan pressed forward, then toward the door, bearing Allen like a trophy. I watched in horror as Alex, his hands firmly holding each of his sons, followed them outside. At the top of the stairs I paused and took a deep shuddery breath, then turned as a man stopped at my side. I looked up into Angus's eyes and shook my head. "I don't understand what's happening here," I said.

Angus nodded. "Justice, Mary. Brutal, but justice."

"He's going to die for stealing cattle, Angus."

He met my eyes without expression. "He'll no' be the first to die for stealing cattle, Mary. Cattle are currency here, lass."

"Angus, this is insane."

He shook his head, and we looked together at the crowd forcing its way through the gate. "No, Mary, this is justice," he said, and left me to follow the others.

I joined them as well and regretted it always. We went to the far end of the loch, where the forest met the trees, where the two bodies of Allen's brothers still swayed in the wind. I watched from the side of the crowd as Dougall and Thomas threw a rope over a tall branch. Allen, pushed onto the back of a horse, whimpered as they put the noose over his head, but no one paid any attention to him. Nor to me as I pushed my way to the front, to a spot next to Alex. My husband, his back stiff and his eyes cold, still held his sons' hands and watched silently as Dougall said something to Allen. Allen, sobbing now, shook his head, and the priest stepped forward to give him the last rites. I had been repelled before, but watching as the church gave its sanction to this was too much. I turned to say something in protest to Alex but was met by a look from him that brooked no arguments. The wind freshened over our heads and I looked from the leaves above to Ian and Jamie, who watched Allen, their fear visible. And then we all looked as Murreal, dry-eyed and composed now, spoke briefly to Allen, then turned with stiff movements and met her husband's eyes. Thomas gave Alex a glance and at his nod moved to the rear of the horse. And gave its rump a vicious slap. The horse bolted, riderless, through the crowd and to the meadow beyond. I closed my eyes as Allen screamed, then opened them to see him dangling at the end of the rope. I moved without conscious thought. Breaking Alex's grip on them, I tore his sons from his side and dragged them with me through the people. I held them to me, and they clung to me in a mass of tears. Sobbing myself now, I made the mistake of looking back as we left and saw Allen, still alive, jerk in spastic movements and then grow still. And Alex nodded.

It took a long time to quiet the boys. I could not answer their questions and settled for soothing them with caresses and soft words while my anger grew. By the time the people returned and Alex came to us, I was furious and turned my head away when he spoke. He ignored me then and lifted his sons, bearing them away from me while I watched. I sought refuge in our bedroom, but my anger only grew when I was alone. I had married a stranger. And now, unbidden, Robert's words came to me: *He lives a life you cannot imagine, full of violence and ancient ways. He's not an Englishman and not your sort.*

Robert, I thought, *you did not tell me the half of it.* What was I doing here among such people? I closed my eyes and let my longing for London grow.

After an hour I realized I could not stay in our room, could not sleep in the same bed with Alex, could not bear to have him touch me. I took my nightrobe and a candle into Margaret's room, closing the door that led to our room firmly behind me. And bolted it along with the door that led to the hallway. I had meant to have the poster bed that filled half the room removed, for no one slept here, but I was glad of it as I slid between the sheets with a sob. *How can I stay here?* I wondered. *My marriage is a sham.* All the things that I'd heard of the barbaric Scots came to me now, and I hugged my misery to myself. I wanted to go home.

I drifted off to sleep and woke with a start when I heard Alex in our room. At first he moved quietly, as though I'd been asleep in there, and then he called for me. And again. And tried the door to Margaret's room. There was silence, then he tried the latch again and called my name, shaking the door. I turned on my side and hunched the covers to my ears, telling myself he'd go away. I was wrong.

With a splintering crash the door flew open, and I sat up. The bed-curtains blocked my view but only for a moment. With a swift movement Alex pushed the curtain aside at the foot of the bed and glared at me. "Mary, what are ye doing here?"

"I'm going to sleep here tonight, Alex," I said coldly.

"The hell ye are," he growled, and moved to the side of the bed. I had no time to react or even to think as he thrust the curtains aside and reached for me, half-dragging me to my feet in front of him. "I've had all I can take today, Mary. Come on."

I wrenched my arm from his grasp and backed away from

him. "I'm not going there," I said, raising my chin. "Not tonight."

He watched me with narrowed eyes and tightened jaw. "Fine," he said at last. "Then we'll sleep here."

"No," I said. "I need time to think. I need time alone."

"Lass, it was no' pleasant for any of us."

I shook my head. "No, Alex. I'll stay here. Alone."

"Ye dinna want to sleep with me?"

"No."

"Why not?" he asked quietly, then louder. "Why not, Mary?"

"I don't know who you are!"

"That's stupid, Mary. Of course ye ken who I am." I shook my head. "Mary, ye ken who I am."

"No. I don't know who you are and I don't know why I'm here."

With a curse and grunt he reached for me and lifted me into his arms. "Yer coming with me, lass. Yer my wife, and we'll sleep now and sort it out tomorrow. Yer just upset, is all."

I writhed in his grasp but could not free myself as he carried me through the door and set me gently on our bed. I scrambled to my knees and glared at him, then watched in amazement as he ignored me and calmly began to undress. When he stood only in his shirt I climbed off the other side of the bed and stormed toward Margaret's room. He was at the door before me, no longer calm.

"Ye'll sleep with me, Mary," he said. I shook my head. "Enough!" he shouted, towering over me. "Enough, Mary. Get into bed. I canna deal with any more tonight."

"Oh, yes, Alex, you must be exhausted. It's so tiring to kill a man." He watched me with a cold expression. "Could you not have spared him? He was only a boy. Surely you could have found another way to punish him. How could you do that and not have it affect you? What are you made of?"

"We held a trial."

I made an angry gesture. "A trial, Alex? That was hardly a trial. It was a mockery."

"It was justice," he said, his voice rising now in anger.

"It was like no justice that I've ever seen."

"Then what was it, Mary? What would ye call it?"

"A mockery."

"Ye ken not what yer talking about."

"Then explain it, Alex. Explain it so it makes sense to me. What I saw was a clan lusting for a boy's death."

"A boy—" he spluttered. "A boy. Jesus, Mary, and Joseph, lass, ye ken naught of it. Dinna preach to me."

"Anyone who questions you is preaching to you?"

"Ye ken naught of it."

"Then explain it, Alex. Tell me." He shook his head. "I don't understand your ways. They seem very foreign to me."

"Foreign," he said quietly. "Barbaric, ye mean."

I met his eyes. "Yes. Foreign. Barbaric. Savage. What I saw was bloodlust, Alex. For stealing cattle. Cows."

"Cattle are—"

"Oh, yes," I interrupted. "Angus told me. Cattle are currency. Surely you don't equate cattle and a boy's life."

"In this case I do."

"Then I don't know who you are. Or what you are. And you had your sons watch. A glorious lesson for them, Alex. At their tender ages they saw their father condemn a man and then they got to watch at close range while he died. What a wonderful lesson. I don't know who you are."

"Ye dinna ken who I am," he said flatly. "I'll tell ye then. A barbarian, Mary. The leader of a bloodthirsty tribe. I'm a savage Gael. Or is that redundant? Do ye want to go back to yer own people, is that it? Do ye wish ye'd not come here?"

"I don't understand, Alex. You all seem so—"

"Aye. Barbaric. Savage. Perhaps not quite human."

"Don't mock me, Alex."

"Ye call me a barbarian and a savage, and I'm mocking ye?" We glared at each other, then he turned away. He went to his side of the bed and pulled his shirt over his head, then climbed naked between the sheets while I watched. "Come to bed, Mary," he said quietly as he arranged the covers.

"No."

He sat up and met my look. "Mary Rose," he said. "Get into this bed. If ye go into the other room I'll just come and get ye again. Get into bed."

"Alex," I began, but his voice cut across mine.

"No more tonight, lass." He turned slowly and blew out the bedside candle. "Come, Mary. Get into bed," he said to the dark.

I did. But I refused his touch when he reached for me and ignored his gentle caress as he traced his fingers down my neck and across my shoulder, then down my side, pausing at my waist before withdrawing. I lay stiffly next to him, making speeches in my head that only increased when at last I heard his rhythmic breathing and realized he was asleep. How could he sleep after having hanged a man today? I stared into the dark and thought about London. I was still awake when the window lightened and the first of the morning slowly lit the room. Stretching my legs from their cramped position, I crept silently from bed and into Margaret's room, where I dressed hastily. I stood in the doorway, watching him sleep, before I left. How could anyone who looked so angelic be so callous, I wondered. Who had I married? I was still asking myself the same questions when I woke the stableboy and asked him to saddle my mare and later when I turned her head to the south and away from Kilgannon.

The abandoned crofthouse I'd noted on our rounds was just where I'd remembered, its roofless walls gray against the blue sea beyond it. I tethered the horse, then stood on the edge of the cliff and tried to let the sea breeze heal me. And later, when the rain came and the wind lashed at us, I moved the mare into the only remaining outbuilding while we took shelter from the storm. When the sky cleared in the late afternoon, I brought her out into the weak sunshine and let her forage while I sat on a large boulder and stared out at the sea. Did I want to end this marriage, to return to London and rebuild my life there? To slink back into the company of the Mayfair Bartletts and Rowena with a failed marriage behind me? To take the charity of my brother and aunt for the rest of my life? No, but I did not have to do that. I could withdraw to a small cottage somewhere in the country and live on the meager income I received from the Mountgarden rents. I could start another life. It was possible. I took a deep breath. But none of that was the real issue, the real reason to stay or go. If I left I'd never see Alex again. Is that what I wanted?

I turned at the noise, not realizing what it was at first, and saw a horse and rider silhouetted against the horizon. As the big man thundered toward me I rose from the boulder and turned to meet him. Alex drew up sharply in the yard and looked me up and down.

"Mary," he said.

"Alex," I said, matching his wintry tone.

With a graceful swing of his leg that bared his thigh and more, he slid off the horse and stood in front of me. "Yer a'right."

"Yes."

"Then let's go home." He reached for me, but I backed away, watching as his eyes flickered with anger. Obviously his fury with me was damped, not gone. Nor mine with him.

"No," I said.

"No?"

"No, Alex, I will not go with you. Not now."

"Yer my wife, Mary. Let's go home." I shook my head. He walked away from me, then turned with an angry gesture. "How could ye do that, Mary? How could ye steal away from our bed and leave me? I've half the clan looking for ye. I thought ye were in the castle and avoiding me."

"Then how did you know I was gone?"

"The stableboy told me when I went looking for ye

there. I felt a right fool when he told me my wife had left before dawn. I thought ye'd headed for London on yer own."

"Obviously not."

"No, ye came here!" he shouted. "Of all places, ye came here! Are ye trying to make me go mad, Mary? What are ye doing?"

I felt my anger rise to meet his. "What am I doing? I'm trying to keep my own sanity, Alex. I'm trying to sort out the fact that I married a man I thought I knew and discovered I've married a stranger with values I don't share."

"And what values are they that we dinna share? Ye think it fine that a murdering bastard go free so it doesna disturb anyone's day? That crimes go unpunished so that my sons dinna see the natural effect of filthy behavior?"

"No, but I think a man who holds the power over life and death has a moral responsibility to be better than vindictive."

"Vindictive! Vindictive! *Mo Dia*, Mary, ye've not seen me vindictive yet." He swirled around in a circle and drew his sword as he turned back to me. Brandishing it above his head, he threw me a glare and I closed my eyes. I was too paralyzed to think, too numb to consciously consider that he was going to hit me, but I must have thought that at some level, for when I heard the sounds of his rage and the blows striking the wood, I opened my eyes in surprise. Alex stormed through the crofthouse, knocking everything still intact apart with his blows, then attacked the crude animal shelter where I had waited out the rain, knocking the supports out from the roof and leaping aside as it clattered to the ground in a fog of dust and splinters. When there was nothing left to destroy, he slowly returned his sword to his scabbard.

"Feel better now?" I asked coldly.

He shook his head, still panting. "No. No, I dinna feel better. I feel like hell. I dinna want to argue with ye. I just want ye to come home. I'm tired, Mary."

"As I am, Alex. I didn't sleep last night. You did. You hanged a man, then slept through the night."

He blinked, then turned his head to look past me, staring at the sea for so long that I wondered what he could be thinking. His breath soon quieted and he became very still. When at last he glanced at me, I saw the unshed tears in his eyes and my heart gave a wrench. I stretched my hand to him. He looked at my hand and then away. "Alex," I said, but he looked out over the water, and the echo of my voice hung between us. I withdrew my hand.

"I'll take ye home," he said, meeting my eyes with an icy look. His jaw tightened and he raised his chin.

I shook my head. "I'm not ready to go back. I'll stay here for a while longer."

"I mean I'll take ye to London."

It was my turn to stare and blink. He met my look without flinching. "You'd take me to London?" I asked in a little voice.

He nodded. "Aye. I told ye before, Mary. I dinna beg. If ye say this marriage is over, then so be it. It's over."

"Just like that."

"Just like that."

"I see."

"I thought ye might. Come, let's get it done. That way I can be home for the winter readying."

"One more chore to be done. Take me home, then get ready for the winter."

"Aye."

"A winter that you will spend without your English wife."

"Aye."

"You can send for Morag."

"And ye can be with Robert."

"I will never be with Robert."

"And I will never send for Morag."

"But you'd end this marriage without a qualm."

"I'm not ending it."

"Yes, you are."

"No, Mary. Yer ending the marriage. I'm just taking ye back to yer people."

"I never said the marriage is over."

He gave me a long look, then gestured sharply. "Then what is this, lass? What are we doing? What is this if not ye leaving me?"

"I'm upset, Alex. And I don't understand."

"I ken that. But ye left me, Mary. How could ye leave?"

"I'm troubled because the man I love can condemn a man to death for stealing a few cows and hang him. And insists our small sons watch. And then sleeps through the night. I can't understand how you can be the man I thought I knew and do these things. I don't understand you or your people or this strange land. How could they lust for his death? How could they cheer it? How can you do this and not be touched by it? How, Alex?"

He shook his head and looked around him, then sat heavily on the boulder I'd used before, his hands falling at his sides. He looked at the ground, then up at me. "Do ye ken where we are, Mary?"

"At an empty crofthouse."

He nodded. "The only empty crofthouse on Kilgannon lands."

"So?"

"So, do ye not think it a wee bit strange that no one lives in this spot, that no one would want this grand view every day?"

We both turned to look at the view, the waves crashing below us and the sea stretching before us in undulating shades of blue.

"It's beautiful here," I said.

Alex nodded. "Aye. And horrible here. This was Murreal's sister's house. Fiona's house. She lived here with her husband, Tavis, and her daughter, Nola. Here in the yard"— he waved his hand at the packed dirt—"here is where it happened. Allen came one night, in the wee hours, with his brothers, planning to steal Tavis's cattle. But Tavis heard them and came after them. It wasna a fair fight, three against one, and it dinna last long. Allen and his brothers tied Tavis up and made him watch while they dragged Fiona and Nola out and set the house on fire." Alex's voice was savage now. "And then, while Allen made sure Tavis couldna escape, the two older brothers bound Fiona and the girl and took turns raping them. Nola was twelve, Mary." He glanced at me, then looked out over the water again, his voice lowering to a monotone. "And when they were finished they took Tavis and set him afire. While Fiona and Nola watched. And then they left."

He was silent for a long time while I waited, listening to the sound of my heart's pounding. "Fiona freed herself," he continued at last, "and walked to her neighbors' and they spread the alarm. Dougall caught the brothers that night herding Tavis's cattle east. He brought them to Kilgannon. And then he waited for me." Alex met my eyes with a long, measuring look.

"I was in England, Mary, looking for ye. I was roaming about, going from London to Mountgarden to Grafton, when Tavis died. If I'd been here, or Angus, they'd never have done it. But I'd been gone so much—after the loss of the *Diana,* and courting ye—that they thought I wasna a threat. And they were right." He sighed heavily and looked at his hands. "I was focusing on the loss of the ship. And the possible loss of ye. And I dinna protect my people." When I started to protest he waved my words away. "I have faced it, Mary Rose. I tell myself it couldna be avoided, that they were cruel and greedy men who struck when my back was turned, and sometimes it makes sense to me and I can live with myself. But every time I see Murreal, I think of her sister limping off for help and me hundreds of miles away worrying about money."

"Or me."

He nodded and met my glance. "Aye. My own selfish desires."

"Alex, why didn't you tell me this before?"

"Lass, ye've gotten over yer nightmares. Ye ken, the ones about the men in the coach. I remembered ye telling me

about dreaming of that swine's hand on yer leg." He shook
his head. "And I dinna think ye needed to hear this tale. It's
ugly enough to have kent it as a man, and I dinna think ye'd
want reminding of having escaped the same fate."

"You were protecting me."

"I was trying to."

"I see."

"And, Mary, I was verra willing to forget it myself. I
canna think of this spot without guilt."

"I didn't know—"

He waved his hand. "I ken," he said heavily. "And even
just before the trial I thought I'd better explain it to ye, but
I dinna want to revisit it. And then . . ." He shrugged.
"Well, lass, I dinna think on yer reaction during the trial. I
was thinking on my boys. And yer right, I was thinking on
vengeance."

"Why did you insist they watch it?"

He sighed. "That's an ugly tale in itself. Ye ken how close
Thomas's son Liam and my boys are?" I nodded. "Well,
when I was gone the boys were sleeping over at Thomas and
Murreal's. And when the runner came to get Murreal and
tell her the news, my boys heard it. And when Thomas and
the men went to come here, the boys followed. So they
saw Tavis's body, and they saw Murreal, beaten and bloody,
and Nola the same. And despite anyone's best efforts they
heard the tale." He rubbed his forehead. "So when Allen
was caught, I thought they should see the monster dealt
with. It's a kind of circle for them, Mary. It closes the nightmare. The bad man canna come back and get them. Both
my boys had nightmares, and many's a night they crawled
into my bed telling me that they dreamed someone was
chasing them to set them on fire."

I thought of Jamie's nightmare, of the monster man who
set people on fire.

Alex raised his chin. "But yer right. I was vindictive. I
wasna impartial. I made a mistake when I let Allen go
before, and I couldna risk him repeating his brother's acts."

"Why did you let him go earlier?"

"He was seventeen, Mary. His brothers were older than I am, and they kent what they were doing. I kent it was a stupid thing to do, to let someone who'd been part of something like that go free, but I couldna do it. He'd not raped them nor set Tavis on fire. He'd only watched. I couldna hang the boy."

"Oh, Alex."

"Aye."

We stood in silence then while I thought of all he'd told me. And what a difference it made. "Why didn't you tell me, Alex? Before the trial, after the trial, even last night, why didn't you tell me?"

Alex shook his head. "I dinna ken, Mary. I dinna want to go through it again, and then, when ye were so angry, I was even more angry that ye could consider me a barbarian when I was trying to stop men like Allen and his brothers." He shrugged. "I guess I thought that ye should ken I would behave properly. I guess I thought ye'd believe that of me no matter what. I thought ye'd trust me to—" His words, spoken so calmly and quietly, undid me. I went to him, full of guilt, and knelt at his side.

"Oh, Alex. I should have known there was more. I'm sorry."

He pulled me up and onto his lap, holding me against him. "It's no' yer fault, Mary Rose. I dinna mean to withhold the story. I just thought . . . och, lass, I dinna ken what I thought. I just acted. When Murreal asked me to avenge her sister and her niece and Tavis, I dinna think on it further." He raised his eyes to mine. "I'm sorry for not telling ye the truth of it, Mary, but I'll never be sorry for ridding the world of the likes of Allen. That part was rightly done, even if for the wrong reasons."

"But having the boys watch . . ."

"Aye. I dinna ken anymore if that was good. I've talked to them, and I fear I may have replaced the old nightmare with a new one. But at least they kent their da dinna let the monster man come to set them afire. And that's what I was thinking, Mary, to protect my boys. And the clan. And, aye, to let Thomas and Murreal have their revenge. And me mine. And that's why, when I found ye here and ye called me vindictive, I . . ." He shook his head.

"Alex, you should have told me."

He nodded. "Probably." And met my eyes. "But I dinna, lass, and it's done the now."

"Yes," I said, and slowly rose from his lap. "You're right. There's no changing what has happened." He nodded, watching me, his expression growing colder as he stood. I looked out over the water, trying to sort out my thoughts.

"Let's go then," he said over his shoulder as he strode away.

"Alex," I said heatedly. He turned with a wary expression and faced me. "Where are we going?"

"Where do ye wish to go, Mary?"

"Home."

He nodded. "Aye, well, then there's much to do."

"What? What is there to do?"

"Readying the ship—"

"Alex, you damned fool! Let's go to Kilgannon, not London." He didn't move but looked at me for a long moment, then over my head at the sea beyond. "Alex," I said in a softer tone. "Let's sort this out together. Trust works both ways, you know."

His eyes met mine. "What do ye mean?"

"You assumed that I was ending this marriage because I left your bed for a while to sort things out in my head, that I despised you and wanted to go back to London. Right?"

He slowly nodded. "Aye, that's what I thought."

"I was confused, Alex, and I was angry. I thought I knew you and Thomas and Murreal and Angus, but suddenly none of you were acting like the people I knew, and it made no sense to me. I needed time to think it through." I took a deep breath. "Alex, I love you, and I fear that even if you were a bloodthirsty savage I would still love you. I wouldn't stay with you, but I'd love you."

"Ye thought I was a bloodthirsty savage."

"No. But I didn't know who you were. And I came here to think. Alex, look at you." He gave me a puzzled look. "You're huge. You're beautiful. You're a very intense man. You dominate every room, every group, every moment when you're with me. And when you pulled me out of your mother's bed and back to ours, I was furious that you could do that. I could not think straight when I was lying in bed next to you. I left so that I could sort things out in my mind without you—just by being there—dominating me again." I waved my hand at the yard around us. "As for trusting you, I have already proven myself. Do you not understand how foreign all this is to me? I trusted you enough to give up everything I knew, everyone I loved, to come here to this unknown place just to be with you. With you, Alex. Not your money, not your looks, nor your title nor anything else. You. I don't know how I could demonstrate my love or my trust better than that. So don't assume that I'm ending this marriage. If it's over, it's because you choose it to be. I love you, Alex, and I want to be your wife. But I want you to talk to me. Even about unpleasant things. Talk to me. Explain it to me. If I still don't understand, I'll tell you. But trust me enough to tell me."

His expression had changed from puzzled to guarded to thoughtful as I spoke. Now he watched me silently and then nodded. "I love ye, Mary Rose," he said. "And I'm sorry."

"You're sorry you love me?"

He smiled then and extended his hand to me. "No, lass, I'm sorry I dinna tell ye the story. It caused all this, my silence, and I'm sorry for that."

"So am I, my love," I said, taking his hand. He drew me to him and wrapped his arms around me with a sigh. "Take me home, Alex," I said.

"Aye, Mary Rose," he said. "I will." And he kissed me.

* * *

Later that afternoon, after we'd ridden back to the castle in harmony and been greeted without comment by Angus and Thomas, I stood alone on the top terrace and stared across the meadow to where the three brothers still hung, hidden now by the trees. I wondered how a man could rationalize actions such as theirs, how they could have been so brutal. I was still pondering when I felt a hand on my shoulder and turned to meet Murreal's eyes.

"Mary," she said.

"Oh, Murreal," I cried. "I didn't know. Alex told me today what happened to your sister and niece. I didn't know."

She nodded. "He told me. I thought ye kent, Mary, or I would have told ye myself. Dinna fret, lassie." She gestured to the meadow. "I'm more at peace with it since I ken he'll no' come back again." I nodded. "My sister is avenged. My niece is avenged. And my brother-in-law's shade can rest now. I ken it's passing strange to ye, coming as ye do from England, but I feel as though it's finally over." I nodded again and tried to put myself in her place. If Betty had been killed and Will and their child injured, would I want the life of their attacker? Part of me shouted yes, and I turned to Murreal and met her eyes again, humbler now.

"It's not as strange as you might think," I said, and Murreal gave me a sad smile.

TWENTY

ALEX AND I WERE VERY CONSIDERATE OF EACH OTHER FOR weeks, as though we could shatter the fragile peace between us with the wrong word or deed. But there was, though we continued to share a bed, little passion. After our explosion we both had retreated into courtesy, and while part of me was relieved, part of me missed the intensity of our former relationship. He was careful to tell me most of what happened each day, and I did the same, although there was little of consequence to tell.

The weather continued fair and warm, and the second planting was done with little delay. Everyone in the glen helped with the planting, and I carried food to the workers as they sowed the entire length of Loch Gannon. Arable land was scarce and the MacGannons made use of every bit of it. Alex let the tacksmen and crofters tend their own fields as they would, but the land that belonged to him he oversaw himself. This was, he'd explained, not his favorite duty, but an important one, and he spent hours on the far side of the loch where the land rose in gentle waves before sharply rising to meet the mountains. It was there that the oats and barley were sown and there that I would go and find my husband. And Angus, Matthew, and Malcolm as well. And there that I first saw the ruins of the house where Angus had lived with his Mairi, the house he'd pulled down with Alex's help after Mairi died and Angus swore he'd never live in it again. And it was there, on a breezy, beautiful day when the air was so clear it almost hurt to look across the water, that Malcolm made his first overture to me.

The evenings we spent in the library had grown more comfortable and we laughed more than before, which pleased us all. Knowing Malcolm was leaving made all of us more tolerant of him. On this day, while I stood with Ellen and watched the men, stripped to their kilts, their backs growing brown as they worked in the welcome sunshine, Malcolm came to stand next to me.

"I have a favor to ask of ye, Mary," he said.

"Oh?" I was polite but could hear the wary note in my voice.

"Aye." His gaze followed mine to where Alex stood up the hill with a tight knot of men, wiping his brow with the back of his hand and gesturing to the field as they talked. "Ye ken I'm to marry and go to Clonmor with Sibeal," Malcolm said, shifting his gaze to me.

"Yes," I said, still watching Alex.

"Aye, well . . ." He paused, and for a moment he sounded so like his brother that I glanced sharply at him. But there was no smirk this time, no conscious imitating of Alex, and I relaxed. *They are brothers,* I reminded myself, *and if he can look like Alex, then he can sound like him as well. I must be more receptive.*

"My favor is this," said Malcolm as his blue eyes found mine, his tone charming. "Alex tells me yer a wonder with the accounts. Would ye show me what I need to learn before I go to Clonmor so that I can manage better this time? Ye ken I did not do so well the last time I was handling business affairs?" His grin was infectious and I felt my reserve thawing. "I will be handling my own money this time, ye see, and I'd like not to make such a muddle of it." I nodded, careful not to speak. The comments that had sprung to mind would all sound bitter, and I had only suspicions, no proof. I watched him watch Alex. *This is your brother-in-law, Mary,* I told myself, *and if there is a rift in this family, you will not cause it.* So I nodded and smiled and told Malcolm that of course I would teach him what little I knew.

And I did. Some of our evenings and many afternoons were spent poring over Kilgannon's accounts while I showed him what were the easiest and clearest ways to record all the earnings and expenses. He was an apt student. Sometimes I even forgot that I did not like him, and we would spend hours in amiable conversation, Alex watching us. The days flew by, and while I could not bring myself to say I was fond of Malcolm, I was pleased to have peace between us. And then one afternoon, when the two of us were alone in the library, Malcolm made his second overture. I was showing him how the expenses were recorded for each ship and each voyage, but he was not looking at the page.

"Here, Malcolm," I said, pointing.

"How can I pay attention when ye look so beautiful, Mary?" He brushed a fallen lock of hair off my shoulder and leaned toward me. I was caught off guard and stared at him. He leaned closer and nuzzled my neck, and I jumped up, knocking over the chair.

"No," I said as I backed away, but he was unfazed. He shrugged and smiled at me as he leaned back in the chair, crossing his arms over his chest. It was an Alex gesture and I stared at him, wondering what to do next.

"It's yer fault, Mary," Malcolm drawled. "Ye are exquisite. No wonder Alex pursued ye."

I looked at him through narrowed eyes. "The lessons are over," I snapped, moving to the desk and slamming the ledger. Malcolm stood with slow, deliberate movements, stretched, and left with a backward glance that included a sly smile. It was hours before I realized that he'd made his overture when we were looking at the *Diana*'s ledger and days before I realized the ledger was now missing. I never told Alex, though I wrestled with it, recognizing that by keeping my silence I was now doing what I had chastised him for.

But I could see no useful purpose for the telling. Malcolm would be leaving soon and that would solve the problem. I had no illusions that Malcolm had found me so attractive that he could not control himself. It was quite simple. He had not wanted to discuss the *Diana*. This must have been how he had ensnared Sibeal, I thought, outrageous lies and a smooth manner.

Malcolm and Sibeal were married in a festive celebration on Skye, the MacDonald playing host and every MacDonald within a fifty-mile radius attending. MacDonnells and the Maclean brothers were there as well. Never let it be said, Sir Donald had told me during the wedding feast, that Mac-Donald of Sleat was not a generous man. I told him it could never be said, and he roared with laughter. But I had spoken the truth. The food was lavish and the entertainment lively. All that was missing was a loving bridegroom. I was not the only one to notice that Malcolm seemed more concerned with his own comforts than his bride's and that he left her alone for long periods while he drank or danced with other guests.

Alex and I ignored Malcolm's behavior and danced until we could not take another step, then headed to a quiet spot to catch our breath. On our way we were cornered by a man who talked loudly of James Stewart. Alex listened for a moment before excusing us and moving on. "Kilgannon," the man shouted. "Ye should be listening. Ye ken that Queen Anne has designated Sophia as the Electorate and that if peace is signed and the French agree, then James Stewart will not sit on the throne? A German will."

"I know that well, MacDonald," said Alex, turning back to him. "This is not new, ye ken, man."

The man nodded. "Aye, but it's closer than before, lad. Will ye no' drink with me to the king over the water?" He raised his glass high, the Jacobite toast hanging in the air.

"I have no glass, MacDonald. Ye can drink for me." Alex nodded and pulled me away. "Welcome to Jacobite territory, lass," he said in a low tone as we threaded our way through the crowd then stood for a moment watching the celebration. Even Angus danced with abandon, his face flushed with laughter. Malcolm and Sibeal were leading the couples, and Seamus was right behind them, Lorna on his arm. Alex smiled and led me to a quiet corner on the far side of the room, where he sank into a chair next to me. "Just like yer aunt's drawing room in London, aye, lass?"

"Not entirely." I smiled and then turned back to the room. Men in plaids and velvet spun women in silk around, the bright colors of their clothing lit by hundreds of candles in the chandeliers overhead. MacDonald of Sleat's home had been, like so many of these structures, originally a fortress and it still retained many of those features, but this hall was alive tonight with music and light, and the dancers in their finery enjoyed the huge room with not a thought of its history. I turned to find Alex watching me. He looked wonderful tonight, his blond hair tied simply back, the dark blue of the jacket emphasizing his eyes.

"Ye look like a goddess tonight, Mary Rose," he said tenderly, and brushed my hair back from my bare shoulder, his fingers lingering on my skin. I tried not to remember Malcolm using the same gesture, but when I saw the desire in Alex's eyes I forgot his brother. This was the man I'd met in Louisa's ballroom, the man who had so entranced me then. And now, more than a year later, I was still captivated. I felt the desire flair between us.

"I am happy," I said quietly, and took his hand in mine behind my skirts. He lifted my hand and held it to his mouth.

"As I am, lass, as we always will be. I kent from the start."

"I was thinking of the night we met."

He met my eyes. "So was I."

"You're even more handsome now."

He laughed and put our joined hands between us. "I knew with the proper guidance ye'd be worth my efforts."

"Worth your efforts?" I stared at him.

"Aye." He grinned at me. "Speechless. It's so easy."

I watched him, so well pleased with himself, and I laughed, then leaned to kiss him. And that night, by the light of a full moon, we made love on the secluded balcony outside our room, finding our way slowly back to the intensity that had been ours in the early days. He stood with his arms about me, his hair glowing in the dim light, and kissed me, letting his lips linger on mine, then grazing them across my jawline. I arched my neck to receive his touch and shivered as he pushed my bodice from my shoulders. And I kissed him in return, reaching my hands under his shirt and then undoing his belt and loosening his kilt until it fell from him. He didn't seem to notice the cold as he bent over me and lowered me to a pile of our clothing, our breathing becoming faster as our caresses intensified. I pulled him to me and sighed.

"Alex," I whispered. "I love you."

"Mary Rose," he breathed. "I love ye, lass. I need ye to live. And I've missed ye so, my bonnie wife." He kissed my lips softly. "My wife. Mary, tell me ye love me again."

I ran my hand from his shoulder to his thigh. "Alex," I said, though it was becoming difficult to think. "I love you. You'll never find a woman who wants you, body and soul, more than I. Never. Now hush and come to me." He did.

It was a tranquil summer. The Treaty of Utrecht had been signed and England and France were at peace. All of Europe recognized that Queen Anne's heir would be the Electorate Sophia of Hanover. An intelligent woman, Sophia was nonetheless unsuited, most believed, to be queen of England, let alone Scotland, and her son George was held in contempt on both sides of the border. While there had been murmurings of rebellion throughout the Highlands, few openly declared themselves, and it was difficult for me to take the Jacobite grumbling seriously. More than one man had asked Alex to drink to the king over the water, as he waved his hand over a glass in the supposedly secret signal, but Alex dismissed it as romantic nonsense. The Jacobus Rex engraved on crystal glasses we'd received as a wedding gift raised eyebrows but not arms. Alex said it was a storm in a teacup and I chose to agree, though we both knew it could be much more. For now Anne's health was fine, and we pretended that the Pretender did not exist. The weather was glorious—warm and sunny, not typical West Highlands weather—and we enjoyed it to the fullest, spending as much time as possible outside. Alex, Angus, and Matthew would disappear for the day, taking the boys and half the children in Kilgannon with them, teaching them to fish or hunt. They would arrive home in time for the evening meal, tired and filthy, but immensely pleased with themselves. I was pleased as well. Malcolm and Sibeal were at Clonmor, and Kilgannon had been peaceful.

That was the summer that I learned what had happened to Alex's brother Jamie. He had drowned in the loch in front of the castle while dozens of people watched. Some of the men had tried to save him, but it was too late when they got there. If Jamie had been able to keep himself afloat even for a few minutes, he'd be alive today, which was something Alex never forgot. Since Alex had become laird, I was told, every child at Kilgannon learned how to swim. Their cries of delight filled the warm days as they learned.

And that was the summer that I saw my first Kilgannon Games. It was customary for the western clans to descend on Kilgannon for a week of games and contests, held in mid-August, in honor of Alex's birthday and his grandfather's as well, for it was that Alexander who began the games years ago. The visitors were more familiar to me now and I even remembered many names. The MacDonald and his family I knew, of course, and they were well represented. Donald's teasing of Alex was constant but good-natured. He seemed genuinely fond of Alex, and I liked him for it. The Macleans were here with their huge men-at-arms, determined to win every game.

I watched Morag being courted by Murdoch, and I

watched her talk with Alex at every opportunity, laughing up into his face and occasionally touching him with lingering fingers. I watched her touch my husband and then look to see where I was. There were no words between Morag and me, though she whispered behind hands often enough about me, but we both knew what the struggle was that we were engaged in. And who was the prize. And I luxuriated in my triumph when Alex would come to me and boldly kiss or caress me for all to see. *This one is mine, Morag,* I said to myself, with the arrogance of a young woman who feels very loved.

And I did feel very loved. My marriage to Alex had been all that I had imagined. I loved the physical part of being married. Oh, making love, yes, that was amazing and not at all the duty I'd been told it would be by well-meaning women who had terrified me with their tales of endurance. But there was more. The details of marriage delighted me. I loved to wake and see a cloud of golden hair on the pillow next to me, to be able to reach out and touch a naked shoulder or see a long leg wrapped around a blanket, to have the freedom to savor the sight of him, to know he was mine to touch and explore when I chose. For the first time in my life I was asked to raise my eyes instead of lower them, to touch instead of wonder, and I loved it. The freedom was what most surprised me about marriage. I'd been raised as all proper young ladies were, with propriety and respectable behavior as standards by which we were always measured, and I found it wonderful to be a married woman at Kilgannon. The ring I wore and the name I bore freed me to touch my husband without fear of comment or censure. They allowed me to talk with the clansmen as equals without the worry of reprisal, to go anywhere I chose, to choose the small details of my life. I loved the liberties I was permitted simply because I was no longer a maiden. Most of all I loved being Alex's wife now that we were in harmony again.

He was as I had dreamed he would be, an attentive and

affectionate husband, and if I could have changed anything, it would have been to have more time with him. Wherever we went someone was at him for a decision or complaint, and I often grew weary of waiting for him at night when some of the crofters or tacksmen from the outlying areas would arrive with a problem. He never told them no, he always listened, and there were times I resented that. He listened to my complaints as patiently as he had listened to theirs, and I grew ashamed of adding another burden to his duties. If he thought me silly or annoying he never said it. I vowed to be more independent.

And then there was the baby. Or the lack of one. I had conceived, then miscarried. I'd known very early that I was pregnant and had told Alex at once. He had been delighted with the news, and when I had to tell him later that there would be no child, he had been as despondent as I. I resolved to wait longer the next time to be sure. The depth of my sorrow at the miscarriage had startled me. I had not even particularly wanted a child, but the loss of it had struck something very deep inside me and I mourned silently. I told myself that it was not unusual to miscarry and then have a healthy baby.

I had pondered it often that summer and had realized, which I never had before, that my mother's mother had only two children, my mother only two, and Louisa none. Perhaps there was something wrong with the women in my family. I had never questioned that I could have children, but now the doubts crept in at night and at odd moments like this one, when I was surrounded by women with babies on their hips or with little hands grasped in theirs. Now, standing in the middle of the boisterous clansmen at the games, I smugly smoothed my skirt over my stomach. Perhaps I would have some news for him soon. Perhaps this time I would be more successful. I fought against my fear, then reminded myself that I already had two sons. Ian and Jamie had been wonderful, and after the first tentative weeks we had all relaxed and become the family I had hoped we would. The thunderstorm and the stories had sped that process, I believed, as well as the fact that they were so in need of a mother. I smiled to myself as I recalled the morning I knew I had been accepted by them.

The boys had been sitting on a bench in the courtyard arguing as I walked by, and I had stopped to ask them what was wrong. Ian held Jamie's hand out to me. "Look at his hand," Ian demanded. "He has a great splinter in it and he won't let me take it out."

"Not with that." Jamie gestured to the dirk on the bench next to Ian, his eyes dark with fear. He looked very small, sitting on the bench, one hand cradling the other.

"I wouldna take it out with that, idiot," Ian said in disgust, and stalked away. We looked after Ian and then I smiled at Jamie.

"Let me look at it," I said, sitting next to him and examining the grubby hand. His dog, Robert the Bruce, now huge and perpetually curious, stuck his large nose in my lap and I pushed him away as I concentrated on Jamie. "Ian's right, you know," I said, looking up from his hand. "It needs to come out or it will grow infected. How did you get such a large splinter?"

He shrugged but did not pull his hand back. "Will it hurt?"

"For a moment. If you do not take it out it will get infected and hurt much worse later. What do want to do?" I looked into his eyes, so like his father's, and so fearful now.

"I want it not to hurt at all."

I laughed and nodded. "I understand that, silly, but look at your hand. Do you want it to hurt more later?" He shook his head, his eyes huge as he studied his hand. "Then let's take it out," I said, and he nodded. "I'll get my sewing basket, and you go and wash your hand. With soap." He was waiting on the bench when I returned, though I'd half-expected him to have disappeared, and he gave me his hand, watching my actions with rapt attention. "I will be as gentle as possible," I said, watching his eyes and the way the sun caught the copper in his hair. He nodded. I cleaned the area and then showed him the needle. "Let's pretend it's a great war wound," I said, and he grinned.

"Aye," he said, warming to the idea. "And I'm verra brave."

"You are." We smiled at each other, but just a few moments later I frowned at him in defeat. "Jamie, you must sit still. I cannot get this out if your hand is moving."

"It hurts."

"It will hurt for a longer time if you keep moving your hand."

His blue eyes were defiant, and I was considering what to do next when Alex's voice came from behind me.

"Sit still, Jamie," he said as he climbed over the bench. "Here, I'll sit with ye." He pulled the boy onto his lap. "This is what ye do," he said, grimacing and turning his head away. "Ye give her yer hand and ye bellow." He let out a terrible noise. "She'll like that." Jamie looked at his father and then at me, his eyes twinkling. He thrust his hand at me again, and when I started at it with the needle, he did exactly as Alex had said. I ignored the noise and extracted the splinter. And looked up from the small hand and into my husband's eyes.

"Thank you, Alex," I said dryly. "I'm so glad you were here to assist me." I handed Jamie the tiny piece of wood.

Alex laughed. "Yer welcome. Jamie, say thank ye to Mary."

"Thank ye, Mama," Jamie said, and bounced off, examining his wound. I felt my eyes fill and turned to Alex.

"He called me Mama."

Alex nodded as he watched his son leave, and then turned to me. "Aye, that's what he calls ye to me. Ian does the same. He told Angus he couldn't remember what Sorcha looked like."

"Oh, Alex, that's terrible!"

Alex shook his head. "Lass, we canna change that their mother is gone. They have her portrait and the sketches I've done to look at. They ken yer not their real mother, but they want you to mother them. Sorcha can't, and it's lovely that ye will, Mary Rose." He kissed my forehead as I wiped my tears away. We sat for a moment in silence and then Alex stood. "And now . . ." He reached out a hand to me and I met it with mine. "Now, Mary Rose, I want to show ye something. Come."

I put my basket on the bench and let him lead me across the courtyard and through the outer gate. He stood at the threshold and pointed to the loch and I followed his gaze, thinking he wanted me to admire the view on this glorious day. The mountains on the far shore were purple, the trees on their sides green with new growth, the light breeze rippling through the branches like water. The summer sun was shimmering on the loch, sapphire in the way only deep water can be, and in the loch were the four MacGannon brigs. I blinked and looked again, shielding my eyes. Four brigs. The *Katrine, Gannon's Lady,* and the *Margaret* were moored offshore. And a fourth was tied to the dock, with a crowd milling from the dock to her decks. I felt Alex watching me.

"Alex? Is it the new ship?" I asked, turning to him with pleasure. "Already? She's here?"

He nodded, his excitement visible as he led me down the terraces. "Aye, lass, here she is. Calum just brought her in. She's beautiful, no?" He kissed my fingers.

"What will we name her?"

He gave me a sidelong look. "She has a name already, and one very fitting. Look at her: black sides and snow-white sails and a touch of brass visible now and then. She's a beauty!"

"Alex," I said. "You said I could name her."

He stopped and turned toward me, his voice quiet. "That I did, I know, but, Mary, when I saw her I thought only one name fitting." Annoyed, I pulled my hand from his and slanted a glance at him. He ignored my look and, placing his hand at the small of my back, propelled me forward. We stood at the end of the dock, looking into the excited faces of the crew and the crowd of MacGannons admiring her. Alex turned to me with a lopsided grin.

"Mary Rose, meet the *Mary Rose*."

I looked at the beautiful ship in front of me, every surface gleaming. "You named the boat after me," I whispered.

"Aye, lass. When I saw her I thought of ye with yer dark hair and light skin."

"And a touch of brass visible now and then," I said, remembering his words.

He grinned at me and nodded. "Aye. But look at her, Mary. Isn't she a beauty? And I ken she'll bring us luck."

"You named her after me," I said, warming to the idea.

"It's only fitting, Mary. It's yer money that built her. She's yers."

"Ours, Alex. Our money and our ship." I looked at the *Mary Rose*'s sleek lines and shining fittings while Alex watched me.

"Mine only in that I was wise enough to marry ye, Mary Rose, and I want the world to ken it. Now, come aboard yer ship." He showed me every board and detail of the ship, and I was properly impressed. The crew was giddy with excitement and joined in, explaining the sails and the wonderful new anchor. Calum, who was to be her captain, was visibly delighted. By the time I was on land again, I felt as though I'd spent a week on board, but as we walked away along the dock, I turned to look back at her. The *Mary Rose*. I turned the name over and over in my mind. The *Mary Rose*. I was thrilled.

TWENTY-ONE

Autumn was upon us before I realized summer was over, and as the days grew shorter the tasks grew more hurried. Alex rode far afield as the shielings were closed for the winter and the cattle gathered to be herded off to market. At one time the MacGannons had sold timber and linens to England, but British markets were closed now to those Scottish products and Alex had turned to other commodities. Cattle were a large and lucrative part of what Kilgannon sold over the border. If they could arrive at the selling place. In order to get the cattle to market they had to be driven through MacDonnell and MacGregor lands and dangerously close to the Campbells, so Alex went on the drive, grumbling about cows and reivers. Angus placidly watched his cousin complain, while he made sure all the men were well armed. Matthew was thrilled to be included, and Ian, six now, had tried to convince his father that he would be an asset as well, but Alex only shook his head, pointing to the newly arrived tutor.

Gilbey Macintyre had come to live with us just after the Games, fresh from Edinburgh. He was as tall as Alex, thin and bony, his hair lank, his features craggy and mismatched, but he was young and curious. He asked endless questions, following Alex and Angus around while Ian and Jamie followed him, and he absorbed everything. His tall gawkiness hid a quick mind and a ready wit, both always welcome at

Kilgannon, and I suspected that he regarded his assignment with us as a great adventure. In just a few short weeks we had grown used to his company, and now he was a fixture here, assisting wherever needed.

Deirdre had left two weeks after the Games, staying longer than planned to show me how to prepare for winter. She'd instructed me as she moved at high speed from kitchen to garden to bedrooms. Nothing missed her notice, and though I wrote it all down I had doubts I'd manage it without her. I sighed as I tried to remember it all, but Berta—stolid, solid Berta—was unfazed and smiled at me encouragingly. "We'll do fine, Lady Mary" was all she'd say, and after a while I believed her.

Ellen was, as always, a welcome companion. She had grown to love it here, she told me, and I watched with amusement as she studied the men, knowing she was considering which would be the best husband. She was very popular with men and women alike, wee Donald most of all. Calum brought a letter from Louisa saying they would have to postpone their visit and hoped to come at Christmas, which was a terrible disappointment to me, for I still missed them very much. I was forlorn then and roamed the halls, the boys and their infernal dogs at my heels, and now Gilbey trailing in my wake as well. But sometimes I was alone.

One evening after a particularly long day I climbed the stairs of the keep to watch the sunset and came upon Gilbey sitting cross-legged on the floor of one of the rooms, a boy on each side of him, the three engrossed in a map as Gilbey traced the battles of William Wallace and Robert the Bruce. They neither saw nor heard me, and I stood in the doorway as the boys asked question after question. From listening to Gilbey one would think Wallace and the Bruce to be the greatest heroes ever born and theirs the only noble cause. Feeling very English and very much in a foreign land, I crept down the stairs and walked instead along the loch, pausing beside the indigo water and wondering what I was doing here. But as the sun set and I watched the workers leave for their cottages and the lights begin to appear in Kilgannon's windows, a calm peace came over me. *I am happy to be here,* I told myself, *and it is only because Alex is gone that I feel so lonely.* If I were in London I would be preparing for another social evening, where, no doubt, Robert would be in attendance, or Rowena, or Edmund Bartlett with his waspish remarks. If Alex had never come to London I would be there as well. But I doubted that I would have been happy much longer in that world. I took a deep breath and smelled the pine resin from the stand of trees behind me. *I am glad to be here,* I told myself, and turned to see two little figures bounding along the shore toward me, waving and yelling, the dogs barking as they ran alongside. *I am needed here,* I thought. Jamie threw himself into my arms, and William Wallace jumped on my skirts while Ian circled me with whoops and Robert the Bruce barked furiously.

"You're captured, Sassenach!" they yelled, and Jamie planted a wet kiss on my cheek triumphantly.

"That's your forfeit," he shouted, and Ian pulled him down.

"No, no, ye did it wrong, Jamie," Ian laughed. "Ye must get a kiss from her, not give her a kiss!"

"Oh," said Jamie, and I laughed at them as I paid my forfeit over and over. At last I led the four of them back into the house, swinging a boy's hand in each of mine. *Home,* I thought. *I'm home.*

When Alex returned he was filthy and hungry, but they had sold the cattle for a good price and were pleased. That night, when all were clean and fed again, I followed Alex upstairs and watched as he knelt before the fire and stirred the ashes to life. *That's just what he does to Kilgannon when he returns,* I thought. *And to me.* "You're very quiet, my love," I said.

He smiled. "I hate cows, Mary Rose," he said. "I dinna

want to be there." He unpinned the brooch and pulled off the top of his plaid, handing me the brooch. "Did I tell ye about this, lass?"

"No," I said, looking at the hammered gold brooch, the marks of the tool readily apparent. It did not look very valuable.

"It was my grandfather's. He gave it to me when I was ten. On my tenth birthday, when I had been punished."

"Why?" I smiled at the thought of a ten-year-old Alex being disciplined. "Were you naughty?"

His gaze grew distant. "I had been rude to my father. Or so I was told. I thought I was just telling the truth." He shrugged.

"What happened?"

"It was afternoon and we were preparing for everyone to arrive for the Games. We'd all been clearing the meadow, and I teased my brother Jamie about not doing his share of the work. My father heard me and he hit me. He used to do that a lot, ye ken, when he was in the drink. Which he usually was." He sighed and unbuckled his belt. "I tried not to cry, and when my father asked what I was doing now, I told him I was thinking that whisky made him mean. Ye should have seen his face. Jamie came to stand next to me, and I never forgot that. Jamie was always afraid of our father in a drunken mood—well, he was afraid of him all the time, drunken or no'—but as fearful as he was, Jamie came to stand with me."

"That was very brave of him. How old was he?"

Alex nodded. "Eight, almost. Aye. He was braver than I was. I was not brave; I was stupid. I dinna consider my actions in those days." He smiled a sad smile. "Do ye ken, I still miss Jamie? After all these years, I still miss him." Alex removed his kilt, continuing in a flat tone. "My father beat me until I couldna stand and then he left me there on the ground, crying. I lay there, looking at the dirt beneath me, and then my grandfather was there and he lifted me up. He wasna a young man anymore, but he lifted me up and he carried me to my room. And he took this brooch off his own plaid and gave it to me." Alex cupped his hand around mine and looked at the brooch I held there. "He said that this brooch had been Gannon's, the first Gannon, and that it had been handed down from laird to laird for all that time and that his father gave it to him on his eighteenth birthday and that he was giving it to me." Alex glanced at me, but he was seeing a young boy and his grandfather. "I asked him why he hadna given it to my father, but he said it was his to give and he was giving it to the next laird of Kilgannon. And that I was to remember my duties to the clan every time I looked at it. I do." He smiled. "And someday, when I'm no longer able to lead, I'll give it to Ian." He studied the brooch and I looked at his downcast face, his lashes dark against his skin. I kissed his cheek and he smiled, glancing up.

"So that's why you went on the cattle drive," I said.

"Aye. Not because I like to ride behind cows, lass. I'd always pick a boat before a horse." He wrapped his arms around me.

"Oh, Alex," I said into his chest. "I missed you terribly."

"And I ye, lass," he said. "I may never travel again." He leaned down to his sporran on the chest and withdrew a tiny packet, handing it to me with a smile. "It's vastly overdue, Mary, but I found what I wanted to give ye at last."

"What—" He interrupted me with a wave of his hand.

"Open it, lass. It's no' a white nightgown to scandalize ye."

I opened the package slowly. Inside the deepest fold was a golden ring, fashioned in an intricate and open pattern. At the front was a small circle banded by roped gold. Within the circle was a tiny rose in profile, the stem leading to the right. Alex watched me open it, his eyes dark.

"It's a rose, ye see," he said as he pointed it out to me. "And the stem is to be leading to yer heart."

"It's beautiful, Alex," I said in wonder, turning it in my hand. "I've never seen such a pattern."

"It's a Celtic love-knot pattern," he said, pleased. "If ye look closely ye can see that the weave of it is constant, one piece woven onto itself. It represents a love that never breaks."

"Oh, Alex," I said, my voice faltering as I fought the tears. "It is so . . ." I wrapped my arms around him.

His voice was tender. "Do ye like it, Mary Rose?"

"Do I like it? Alex, it's so beautiful! Thank you, my love."

"I love ye, Mary Rose, and now ye can see it every time ye look at the ring."

"Alex, thank you. But, my love, I have nothing to give you."

His mouth twisted as he gave in to the grin and leaned back. "I'll think of something," he said, reaching for me.

Winter began early with a fierce storm, but we were ready for it, and though restless within walls, we were safe and well fed. The men trained daily in the armory. I hated to think they would ever need their training, but I understood now why they did. At night we'd gather in the hall, where Murreal would sing or Thomas would tell another of his fantastic stories to an enraptured audience. His favorite was about the fairies stealing a horse and changing it into a water horse who lived in a loch in the Western Highlands. So much for Alex's explanations, I thought, and the swimming. From the look on Jamie's face he'd probably not even drink water again, let alone swim in it. Even Matthew and Gilbey sat listening, and I hid my smile. Gilbey Macintyre was, I suspected, a bit younger than I had at first believed.

The boys settled into daily lessons with Gilbey, and Gilbey into daily lessons with Angus. As the months went on he added weight and muscle, filling out that lanky frame, and soon could not be recognized as the same young man who had arrived in August. When I asked him about his family he gave me a sad smile. "My family are dead, Lady Mary," he'd said, lifting his chin. "And I've made my own way. I'm not afraid to work hard. I am glad to be here and I'll stay as long as you'll have me. I am very happy to be with the MacGannons."

"We're very glad you're here too, Gilbey," I said, and we smiled at each other.

I thought of that conversation just a few weeks later as I sat in the crowded hall while the MacGannon men lined up to pledge their loyalty to Alex and the clan. Gilbey was on one side of me, Ellen on the other, we three outsiders watching the pageant. Gilbey was entranced. The oath-taking was held every year just before All Hallows' Eve, when clansmen filled the hall and every room of the castle, arriving with their families for the ceremony. I had been told that the oath-taking in other clans could be dangerous, for the men pledged by drinking with the laird and the drinking continued for most of the night. But at Kilgannon it was a festive evening, the men pledging in the hall before the whole clan, their individual families cheering as each man promised his loyalty. It was not dangerous, but it was loud and raucous, and my head ached with the noise. How Alex could drink so much and still be vertical I did not know. He stood firmly on the dais at the end of the hall, dressed in his finest, his hair shining as it fell to his shoulders. He was armed—for show, he had told me—and looked very fierce and regal. *Every inch a leader,* I thought with pride as I watched him. *This is my husband,* I said to myself. *Let the world know, this one is mine.* Angus and Matthew were on one side of him, Ian and Jamie on the other, and he turned often to them, making them laugh. As the line lengthened and at last dwindled, he spoke warmly to each man who approached him, drawing smiles and comments from them. The room echoed with laughter, and then the pledging was finished and the dancing began. Benches were cleared and the musicians struck a lively tune as the center of the room filled with eager dancers. Alex walked through the crowd and reached for my hand. As I stretched my hand out to take his, wee Donald reached for Ellen's.

Alex slapped Donald on the shoulder. "Behave yerself, man," he laughed. "That's a fine lass."

"Aye," Donald said. "That she is." And taking Ellen's hand, he led her onto the floor as we watched.

"You're enjoying yourself tonight, my love," I said, looking up into Alex's face. He squeezed me to him and nodded.

"Aye, lass, for the whole of it, it was verra good." He looked across the hall and then back to me. "But did ye notice who's not here?" His mouth was smiling, but now I saw the sadness in his eyes. *Malcolm,* I thought with a pang. I had not even thought of Malcolm. And Alex had written to him to remind him to attend tonight. I had put it out of my mind, preferring to ignore that Malcolm would soon be among us again. But he had not come, nor had he sent word that he would not be here. And the whole clan had seen that he had not attended.

"Oh," I said, watching his face. "What now?"

"Well, now, Mary Rose, now I dance and let my anger fade," Alex said, raising his eyebrows and looking at me. "And then tomorrow, when I have not had too much whisky, I'll think on it. And I'll come up with the perfect remedy. As I always do."

I laughed, and he grinned at me. But he had no time to think of a remedy, for the letter from his cousin in France arrived three days later.

I never got to read the letter from his cousin in Paris. Angus did, of course, for the letter was to him. I was in the laundry with Berta, trying to find even more hanging space for the washing that took so very long to dry, when the letter arrived. We were considering whether lines could be strung above the armory and what the men would say about that when I heard Angus bellowing for Alex. Angus never shouted, he never lost his temper, he never even showed much emotion, so for Angus to be raving through the castle yelling at the top of his lungs was enough for everyone within hearing distance to stop and stare. Berta and I stood like ninnies with the other women and watched Angus race through the corridors.

"Where's Alex?" he shouted. "Where is he?"

"I don't know, Angus," I said, and watched as he stormed past, going up the stairs three at a time. Matthew stood at the foot of the stairs with his mouth open. "What is going on?" I asked him.

Matthew stared at me blankly for a moment. "I dinna ken, Mary," he said at last. "My da opened a letter from his cousin Ewan—the one who's in Paris, ye ken—and he started shouting."

"Does he usually do this when Ewan writes?"

He shook his head. "No."

Jamie skidded to a stop next to us, his expression anxious. "Da is with Thomas in the orchard. Shall I get him?"

"Yes, love," I said, brushing his untidy hair back from his face. "Tell him Angus is very upset." We could hear Angus roaring Alex's name through the upstairs hall and I decided I should tell him where Alex was, but as I put my foot on the first step, Angus barreled down past me. "He's in the orchard," I said to his back. Angus made an indistinguishable noise and disappeared into the corridor. I followed. Whatever had enraged Angus had to do with France. And that's where the Stewarts were.

I found them together, framed in the garden gate, the opening arched over their heads with the last drooping leaves. Alex was reading the letter while next to him Angus boiled, talking in a low voice and hitting one clenched hand against the palm of the other. He waved a finger in Alex's pale face, and I stood where I was. Whatever the news was, it was not good and I didn't want to know it. I watched as Alex read and then reread the letter, turning it in his hand to look at the address and then handing it to Angus, and I watched his anger grow. *Dear God,* I wondered, *what is it?* Alex raked his hands through his hair, but he paid no attention to it as it fell about his face. He listened and nodded, then looked over at me, his expression changing as he saw me. He said something to Angus and walked toward me with slow steps, his face bleak. The rain, which had been threatening all day, started falling in a light drizzle, but Alex did not seem to notice. I did not speak as he took my hand, leading me through the corridors, past the curious men in the hall. He gave his sons only a cursory glance as they pounced on him. The dogs had better sense, keeping their distance, for once motionless as we crossed the hall.

Ian stopped in front of his father. "Da, what is it?"

Alex's tone was grim. "Ian, go back to yer lessons." He did not look back to see the boys staring after their father.

He led me through the courtyard and the outer gate. The rain was falling harder now, but I did not complain as he walked to the loch and stared over the water at the three brigs moored offshore. I do not think he saw them. The *Mary Rose* had arrived today from London, bringing letters from Louisa and Will and, apparently, from his cousin. The ships rocked in the surge as the tide moved in and we stood there, getting wetter by the minute. He dropped my hand and crossed his arms across his chest and I watched him, wondering if I should speak. At last I did.

"It's getting very damp, my love," I said. He turned to me as if from a great distance, his eyes hard and his jaw tight, but he nodded, wrapping an arm around me. I turned back to the castle.

"No," he said hoarsely, "come this way." He led me down the shore of the loch, past the rocks at the base of the castle, climbing without pause over them and turning to help me across. On the other side of the building the land was flatter and then rose steeply to join the headland that separated Kilgannon from the sea. We skirted the walls of the castle, and Alex walked up to a vine-covered wall that stemmed from the building. He pulled the vines aside and stepped through the hole he'd made. I followed him and discovered that the vines covered a tunnel, carved or formed out of stone, and split here by a failure of the rock.

It led in two directions. He gestured to the left. "If ye go that way ye come to the door in the base of the keep," he said, and turned in the opposite direction. The tunnel was dark and very damp. I could feel the water seeping into my shoes as I followed him along the steeply declining path and moisture splashed down on us from above. Alex walked through the dark rapidly, reaching back for my hand. I took his, glad of the contact. Soon I could see light ahead. He turned one last corner and stopped.

We were in a large sea cave. The water churned with the storm and the tide, rushing into the cave not thirty feet in front of us where the mouth of the cave dropped to meet it. "At high tide the whole cave is full of water," Alex said without expression, his eyes a frosty blue. "If ye ever need to leave Kilgannon secretly, ye can from here. A shore boat can pick ye up and ferry ye to a waiting ship, and ye'd be off before anyone was the wiser." He was apparently satisfied with what he saw and turned to go back into the tunnel, but I pulled my hand from his, putting both hands on his chest and saying his name. He interrupted before I could continue, his expression thawing. "I'm sorry, lass, I dinna mean to frighten ye." He looked around the cave and gestured. "I realized I'd never shown ye this and ye should ken that it's here."

"Why?" It was a whisper, and he covered my hands with his.

"Ye should know these things, Mary, because ye are my wife."

"Alex, what is happening? Are you leaving me?"

He started and pulled me to him. I could feel the tension and the warmth of his body through my damp clothing. "Leaving ye? Why would I leave ye?" he asked, surprised. *That's better*, I thought. *Come back to me, Alex.* I took a deep breath.

"For the Stewarts. Are you going to France?"

"The Stewarts? Lass, this has nothing to do with the Stewarts. Do ye think everything from France concerns James Stewart?"

"No, but—"

He kissed my forehead. "No, Mary Rose," he said, his voice gentler. "I'm not leaving ye for James Stewart. No. It has nothing to do with politics." His frown was troubled. "It has to do with . . . I dinna ken what it has to do with." He was silent then, and I stood with my head on his chest until a large drop of water landed on my head and I jumped back. He looked over his shoulder at the water level. "Come, lass, we'd better go unless ye wish to be swimming, and swimming at this time of year is no fun." He took my hand and turned to leave. I was in no hurry to go back through that tunnel, although I was beginning to shiver from the cold. I stood as if rooted there, our hands suspended between us.

"Alex, tell me what is happening. Why is Angus so angry? Why are you so upset?" He dropped my hand and stared at me, lost in thought, before at last speaking, his tone weary.

"The letter is from our cousin Ewan in Paris, Mary. Ewan writes that some of the crew of the *Diana* have been seen in Paris and that he found the captain's partner and talked with the man." He sighed and brushed his hair back from his forehead. "And that this partner says that it was Malcolm who poisoned me that time I was so sick. And Ewan believes him."

My mouth hung open, but I was not surprised. *Be careful,* I cautioned myself, *he still will not see Malcolm as you do.* "Why?"

Alex grimaced. "Oh, that's the best part. The story is that Malcolm told this man that he dinna want me to go to a card game I was going to the night before we left."

"He poisoned you to keep you from a card game?"

"Well, the story is, it was accidental, a mistake. Supposedly Malcolm thought he was giving me a sleeping draught that would keep me from the game."

"But why?"

"Aye, that's the question. Why? Ewan writes that the captain's partner says Malcolm told him he was worried because I gambled much and we could not afford to lose a lot of money," he said, irritated. "That's not true. I never gamble overmuch. Money's too hard to come by to waste it in a card game. It was just a friendly evening to discuss trading with the colonies."

"Then why would he stop you from going? Why would he not want you to go to the game? Who would be there?"

"I was playing with three others. Dennis MacGannon— ye ken him, he captains *Gannon's Lady*. The second was the captain of the *Diana*, the man I'd chartered with. The third man is a shipping agent in France. I've kent him for years."

I shook my head. "But why would—"

"Aye," he interrupted. "I keep asking myself that. If Malcolm dinna want me at the game, he dinna have to poison me or give me a sleeping potion. All he had to do was ask me not to go and I wouldna have gone, if there was a good enough reason. He never asked."

"Why would Malcolm do this? Didn't he know it was dangerous?"

He shrugged. "I dinna ken, but it does make yer mind wonder."

"Alex," I said slowly, "do you think Malcolm poisoned you?"

He didn't answer but stared into the distance. Then he sighed and ran his hand across his forehead. "I dinna ken, Mary," he said. "I dinna ken. But it's possible. We'd argued for the most part of the trip, and we were barely speaking to each other the night of the card game."

I studied him. Perhaps Malcolm did not want Alex to be with the captain who would shortly take the *Diana* to the bottom of the sea. Was it simply to stop Alex from talking with the captain? Or, although I didn't believe it for a moment, was it someone other than Malcolm? "How often had you met the captain of the *Diana*?"

"I hadn't," he said tonelessly. "Malcolm handled the details. I met the captain for the first time when I went to the game."

"You went? To the game?"

"Aye," he said. "I felt strange but went anyway. I thought I was just verra tired. And Angus came along at the last minute. It's a good thing too, because he and Dennis had to carry me back to the ship. I fell over in the middle of the game, just stood up and fainted and fell across the table." His smiled wryly. "I'm told I ruined the game. And the table. I dinna remember."

"And where was Malcolm?"

"Waiting on board *Gannon's Lady*. With Matthew."

"Did anyone find poison on the boat?"

"I dinna think anyone looked."

"He could have killed you!"

He looked away, toward the sea. "Aye," he said. "But I prefer to believe it was a mistake. Or a joke."

"A joke." I exploded. "A joke. Oh, yes, Alex, that is very funny." He closed his eyes as I spoke, his expression closed. "Giving your brother something that might kill him or at the least make him very sick, so sick that he cannot leave his ship for a week, that's very funny. Maybe if he ran at you with a Lochaber ax you'd think that was humorous as well." Alex was silent, but he was listening. "This was no mistake. Malcolm is many things, but he's not stupid. If you got this sick from a mistake or a joke, imagine what you'd feel like if he were angry with you. Imagine what he'd do if you were to talk to that captain and discover that the *Diana* was going to 'sink.' " He opened his eyes and stared at me.

"No." His tone was quiet but bleak and I stopped, trying not to say all that was in my mind. I remembered him saying, "I've lost a brother and a sister. I would keep the one I have." *But, Alex,* I said silently, *at any cost?*

I took a deep breath. "You're not stupid either, Alex," I said as mildly as I could. "At best it was a perilous joke. At best it put you in danger. And it might have killed you."

"But it dinna." Blue eyes met mine.

"By the grace of God," I whispered.

"Aye." I was silent then, watching him stare at the wall of

the cave. Behind him the water rushed toward us, but for me there was only the memory of a sick man lying in a berth. And his brother had put him there. A mistake. If it was a mistake I was Joan of Arc. And I wondered, not for the first time, if it had been Malcolm who had arranged the attack on us outside Alex's agent's house. Malcolm would not have known I'd be there, but he certainly would have known Alex would be. Alex rubbed his chin.

"I canna think of it otherwise," he said wearily. "I willna think of it otherwise. It was a stupid mistake, that's all." His eyes met mine. "It mightna even have been Malcolm. Perhaps the partner is lying. I willna believe my brother meant to hurt me."

I could think of nothing to say that he would listen to and eventually nodded. He nodded once in return and led me through the clammy tunnel again. I was not warm the whole evening. I could not shake my conviction that it was Malcolm who had poisoned him and that it had been no mistake. There was no opportunity to discuss it with Angus. He did not come to dinner nor to the evening, and Matthew said he had not seen his father since that afternoon. I resolved to talk to him as soon as possible. But Malcolm arrived the next morning and everything changed.

TWENTY-TWO

ALCOLM AND SIBEAL ARRIVED ON A MACDONALD ship bound for Skye. The MacDonald crew stayed for a meal, joking and laughing with the MacGannons, and if any of them noticed that Alex was ashen and quiet they did not comment. Nor did Matthew, who watched Malcolm, his face shuttered and his eyes wintry. He seemed to have matured overnight. That there was no affection between Malcolm and Matthew had been apparent for quite a while, but Matthew had never said a word to me about Malcolm, as though we had silently agreed that Malcolm was a topic best left untouched. As for the newlyweds, their relationship was a mystery to me. Accustomed as I was to the passion that a look from Alex evoked from me, I could not understand how Sibeal could look with such indifference at the husband she supposedly loved, nor why Malcolm treated her with none of the intensity or affection that one would expect of a recent groom. Why then, I wondered, had she insisted on marrying him? There was no sign of a pregnancy on her slim body, nor did she mention it.

Angus was with us again that morning, having arrived with the news of the ship in the loch. He was silent but watchful. He would not speak of this to Malcolm in front of all of us, I was sure, but what would happen later I could not begin to guess. Malcolm behaved as if nothing were wrong, as if his brother did not look ghostly pale and his cousins were not throwing looks of enmity in his direction. He laughed with his usual superior air as he told stories of how backward his tenants at Clonmor were and how inept Sibeal was as a housekeeper. She smiled without rancor and tried to draw me into a conversation about clothing. I refused to join her and spent my time watching the men. Alex spoke little. I knew how tired he was. During the night I had woken to see him wrapped in a plaid, sitting in front of the fire, staring into the flames. He had crawled into bed in the early hours but had slept restlessly and had been up before me. We had not discussed it, but he had reached for my hand when the news of Malcolm's arrival had come. "Dinna fret, lass" was all he had said.

Malcolm had said nothing of missing the oath-taking, but as Thomas led Malcolm into the hall he had turned to Alex.

"Here's yer brother, Alex," Thomas had said without inflection, while all in the hall had stopped and stared. "Late. Do ye suppose that now that he's married a Mac-Donald he'll be late for oath-taking often? Of course," he had said, turning to look at Malcolm, "ye ken what happens to MacDonalds who show up late for an oath-taking." The hall's occupants had stirred, but no one said anything. I knew what he meant. We all did, and I knew Malcolm understood it, for the flash of anger in his eyes was quickly suppressed but had been obvious. Thomas had meant Glencoe. I had heard the story often enough since my arrival in Kilgannon. The way Thomas told it, after a failed but glorious rebellion against the usurping of King James's throne by William of Orange, the chiefs of all the Highland clans had been given an ultimatum to take the oath of allegiance to King William by the first of January, 1692. MacDonald of Glencoe had missed the deadline. Just why and by how much was still hotly debated these twenty years later. The Earl of Stair, with the knowledge and approval of King William, had instructed Captain Robert Campbell of Glenlyon to accept the MacDonalds' hospitality and then murder the clan in their beds. The plot had been discovered, but the chief and his wife and many others had died. Sibeal's family was of Skye, not Glencoe, but the name, if not the pedigree, was the same. No one had risen to the bait that Thomas offered, and he shrugged as he turned away. But Malcolm looked after him.

The rest of the meal was strained, but uneventful, and soon we were bidding the MacDonalds farewell. The men walked outside with them while I waited with Sibeal. And stared at her when she asked if she could go to her room now. Since we'd had no warning of their arrival, there had been no preparations made, and I was caught off guard by her presumption. Fortunately, Ellen was not.

"Miss Mary," she said at my side. "Berta says she has put Malcolm and Sibeal in Sorcha's room." She smiled mischievously at me. "It only seemed fitting," she said, and my mood lightened the tiniest bit.

I smiled back at her and asked her to thank Berta. "I'll take Sibeal myself," I said, calm again. Upstairs we passed the boys on their way to their lesson with Gilbey, both of them unnaturally subdued. I stopped to hug them and to tease about some silly thing and was pleased to see their spirits rise in response. Within moments they were teasing me in return and went off with Gilbey, acting like themselves again.

"They are wonderful," gushed Sibeal. "Have you thought of having children of your own?"

I glanced at her, thinking of the child I had lost. "Yes, of course," I said cautiously. "And you? How are you feeling?"

"I feel marvelous. Why would I not?" she trilled as I opened the door and she followed me inside the room that had been Sorcha's. It was my least favorite in the castle. The room itself had no grave drawback or unpleasant feature. It was a large and comfortable room, furnished with taste. But Sorcha had lived here, and it was in this room that Alex had slept with her and here where their sons had been conceived and where she had told him horrible things and bade him never to return. It was not a room I spent time in or enjoyed. It was a private joke, shared by Berta and Ellen and me, that those we disliked were always put into this room, and the message Ellen had brought had been intended to cheer me, which it had. I smiled to myself as I showed Sibeal the room and she cooed over its comforts. Berta had been here before me, for everything was clean and a fire had been laid.

"So very lovely!" Sibeal said as she fingered the bed hangings and turned to look at herself in the long mirror. Her slender self.

"And how is the child?" I asked as I went to the window and opened it slightly. The rain that had been threatening all morning had begun falling. In the center of the courtyard Alex, Angus, and Matthew talked. I turned back to Sibeal.

"The child?" Her surprise was evident, but she recovered quickly. "Oh, I lost it." She turned back to her image.

"How terrible for you," I said, wondering if it were true.

"Yes, it was. But you know, I simply lay myself down for a nap one afternoon and woke to find the child next to me." She turned to me with ingenuous eyes. "It was dreadful."

I stared at her, openmouthed, as I thought of my own miscarriage. That such a thing had happened I did not believe for a moment. Such things did not happen. No woman who had miscarried could talk of it in such a manner. Then I saw the irony of it. She had done me a wonderful favor by removing Malcolm from my everyday life, and she had deceived him in the process. Malcolm, the deceiver, had been snared very effectively. I shook my head in wonder but never replied, for we heard shouting through the open window and I leaned through it with a heavy heart to see that what I had feared was real. Alex and Malcolm were below, in the center of the courtyard, arguing. Alex stood, arms crossed over his chest, as Malcolm circled him, talking angrily. Angus came into view then, shouting at Malcolm, who shouted back. Alex watched the two of them and his arms fell to his sides. He looked defeated.

By the time I reached the courtyard it was empty, and I

ran to the outer gate. They were on the top terrace, unmindful of the rain that had turned into a downpour or of the handful of men who clustered around them uneasily. Matthew stood grimly to one side, Angus, his mouth in a tight line, next to him. Alex and Malcolm faced each other.

"The truth," Alex roared, his face red and the cords in his neck standing out. His hands were clenched at his sides. "The truth, Malcolm. Just tell the truth. Or say nothing!"

"I am telling the truth, Alex," Malcolm shouted back. "Ye don't listen. Ye never listen." He waved a hand in the air as he sneered. "Of course, ye don't need to. Yer the earl, yer the chief of the clan. Ye don't need to listen to me. Ye listen to Angus and Thomas and all the others, but ye dinna do what I say!"

"The truth, Malcolm," Alex roared again. "Tell me the truth!"

"Ye want the truth? The truth is ye have everything! Everything! I have nothing. Nothing! Ye have no idea of what a hell my life has been. No idea. Sibeal lied to me. To me! There was no child. It was a trick! My whole life has been a hell!"

Alex's voice was taut. "And so that's why ye poisoned me."

"No! Yer not listening. Ye never listen!"

"And so that's why ye poisoned me."

"Ye wouldn't give me the ship back! How was I to make money?"

"And so that's why ye poisoned me."

"I have told ye this, Alex," Malcolm said, emphasizing each word. "I will not tell ye again. It was an accident."

"Aye, so ye say. An accident."

"Aye," Malcolm said. "Yer making much more of this than it needs to be. Ye were fine. Just a day or so—" He turned as Angus moved toward him. Alex stopped Angus with a gesture.

"I am confused," Alex said coldly. "Why would my own brother try to kill me?"

Malcolm threw his hands up in the air. "For Christ's sake, Alex, I dinna try to kill ye." He leaned into Alex's face and tilted his head. "If I had tried to kill ye, dear brother, ye would be dead now." Alex did not flinch. Matthew started forward and Angus put a hand on his arm.

Alex's tone was the same one he had used with Robert in Kent, the effort it cost him to keep control visible. "Be verra careful, Malcolm. Whether ye like it or not, yer actions almost killed me, and for a year I've been trying to blame it on everyone else, including the Stewarts. And all along it was ye." His voice dropped even lower. "It was ye."

"Ye dinna understand, Alex!" Malcolm shouted. "Ye never think of anyone but yerself! Do ye have any idea of what it was like to grow up with ye?" His voice grew shrill, mimicking a woman's voice. "Alex, Alex, oh, Alex, yer going to be an earl. Alex, yer so wonderful!" Alex watched his brother, his eyes narrowing. Malcolm wiped the rain out of his eyes and continued. "And Grandfather and Grandmother doting on ye. All of them, doting on ye. And all the time there I was. With nothing."

"I gave ye Clonmor."

"Oh, aye." Malcolm nodded. "Yer castoffs. Yer generous with yer castoffs. In fact, I wanted to ask ye if Sibeal's child was yers. It would be just like ye to get there first."

Alex reached a hand out and grabbed Malcolm's shirt at the neck. The speed of it caught Malcolm by surprise, and Alex pulled Malcolm to him, speaking into his face, his words clipped. "Ye have a disgusting mind, Malcolm. I never touched her. If there is no child that isna my concern. Ye slept with her. And now yer married to her." He released his brother and shoved him away as his voice rose. "Is that what this is all about? That I am the older? That I inherit? Ye risked my life because ye don't like the order of our births?" He was advancing now and Malcolm was retreating. "Is that what this is, Malcolm? Jealousy?"

"No," Malcolm shouted back as he continued to retreat. "It is about fairness. It is about justice. Look at yerself, Alex,

bullying yer brother in the rain. Wouldna Grandfather be
proud of ye now?" Alex grabbed Malcolm's shirt again and
held him there for a long moment, the two of them staring
into each other's eyes. I held my breath. And then Alex
released Malcolm and shoved him away. His tone was controlled but wintry.

"Poison is a woman's weapon, Malcolm. Ye may stay
the night. But in the morning ye and Sibeal must be gone.
Calum will take ye to Skye. Do not return until I send
for ye."

They glared at each other for a long moment, then Alex
turned to leave and saw me standing there. As he passed me
I put a hand out, but he shook his head tightly and walked
on. Malcolm turned the other way and left, and the men
faded away.

I stood in the rain with Angus and Matthew.

TWENTY-THREE

THE WINTER CONTINUED, COLD AND WET. WE WERE indoors more than we liked, the men restless. Angus had them practicing constantly, the ringing of their swords sounding throughout that wing. I grew to hate the sound of a sword being unsheathed. The children were underfoot, and we found ourselves scolding them for acting like children. But we also had evenings full of music and dancing.

And no Malcolm. He and Sibeal had gone as quickly as they had come and we'd had no word from them, which pleased me. Malcolm disgusted me. But Alex was not disgusted; he was distraught, and my arguments did nothing to dissuade him of the conviction that he had done something wrong. He searched for a reason that made sense, or something that he could have done differently. To me it was very simple. Perhaps hard to accept, but simple. Jealousy. Self-interest. Malcolm and the captain of the *Diana* had feigned that she was lost, and Malcolm had spent weeks with Alex supposedly searching for the truth while the money from her sale was in his pocket. How anyone could live that duplicity was beyond me, and I said so often, but Alex would not damn his brother and we argued about it many times. I could understand his not wanting to face that Malcolm had behaved so, but in the face of what seemed obvious to everyone else, Alex's behavior seemed only obstinate. We argued often about Malcolm, never more heatedly than when I suggested that the men who had attacked me in London had been paid by Malcolm. Alex had roared at me then, but I had met his anger with my own.

"Ye just want to blame everything on him, Mary," he'd said.

"No, Alex," I'd answered. "Just that for which he's responsible. Look at it, for God's sake. You were about to go to Cornwall and search for the wreck. The poison hadn't stopped you, and you might find something damaging in Cornwall. Don't you think it just too convenient that those men knew exactly when and where to find you? The only thing Malcolm didn't know was that I'd be with you. And that may have saved your life, Alex. If they'd gotten into the empty coach and waited, they would have attacked you as you entered. You'd have been an easy target. Why can't you see this?"

"No," he'd bellowed. "No, Mary, it's not that simple."

"It is. Ask Angus. Ask Matthew. It's simple to everyone but you. Everyone else can see it. Why can't you?"

"Or is it just convenient to blame Malcolm when we both ken the men who attacked ye wore Campbell colors?"

I'd glared at him. "Robert told you he did not send those men to attack you."

"And Malcolm told me he dinna either."

"Alex, you are not a stupid man. Why are you being so blessed stubborn on this? You know what Malcolm is. You know he did this. Face it! Stop excusing him."

"When ye stop defending Robert Campbell."

"He didn't do anything. Malcolm did!"

Alex threw his hands up. "Ye have an idea in yer head and ye willna see anything else. Do ye not see that it's no' that simple?"

"Yes, actually it is. Alex, I get no joy in being right."

"Anyone but Robert," he said, and walked out of the room.

We did not speak for two days and then agreed only that we loved each other. We did not discuss the argument again, but I could think of little else. I told myself I would be objective about Will's behavior if I were in Alex's position, but when Will's letter came saying he and Betty and Louisa and Randolph would be arriving for Christmas, my confidence evaporated. *What if it were Will?* I wondered. Could I face with dispassion that Will had done such a thing? I decided I could not. I watched Alex's agony and relented. My husband needed my support, not my criticism. In his heart he knew what had happened. It was not important that he admit it to me. Things gradually got better between us, and I was relieved to have him return to acting like himself, the signs of his continued preoccupation with Malcolm visible only to those of us who knew him well. With me Alex was always tender and loving. Well, not always. Whenever I mentioned Malcolm he withdrew from me, and I would grow angry and we'd quarrel. Eventually I learned not to mention Malcolm and to my surprise began to forget him altogether. Life was better without him, and we slipped into a routine as if he did not exist.

My family arrived on the *Mary Rose* on a sunny December day, and my mood lightened considerably. Alex stood beside me, and Jamie held my hand, jumping up and down with excitement, while Ian stood on tiptoe to see if Will carried the packages he had written about. Our greetings were noisy and joyous, and the boys danced around us all as we walked up the hill, the precious packages in their hands already. I kissed my brother and Betty, thanked Will for his thoughtfulness, and smiled at Louisa and Randolph's expressions of astonishment as they looked around.

"I had no idea," said Louisa, her eyes wide. "I knew Kilgannon was a castle, but I pictured one of those dreadful brown towers one sees by the border, all square and blunt. This is beautiful."

Alex grinned behind her and raised his eyebrows. "Ye dinna think I'd bring yer precious niece to a crofthouse, did ye, Louisa? I told ye I'd take care of her." He turned to wave a hand at the buildings. "It's no' much now, ye ken, but we have plans to enlarge." He laughed at their expressions.

"Well," Randolph said. "It looks as though you already did. And quite a bit. Tell me about the construction."

"I was no' here for most of it, Randolph," laughed Alex as they left us. Will hurried to join them, and Angus and Matthew appeared at the outer gate. The men exchanged loud and silly greetings, and I smiled to see them laughing together.

"Well, my darling, tell me," said Louisa, linking her arm in mine. "How are you?"

"Happy," I said, smiling. "Very happy."

Christmas was upon us and we were merry. Every night the hall was full of MacGannons and music, and I saw it through my family's eyes. Will loved the fiddlers who stomped their feet as they played faster and faster, and I saw Louisa wiping tears from her eyes as Thomas or Murreal would sing a stirring ballad. On Christmas Eve we gathered in the chapel with most of the household, and the ceremony was one I would always remember. Candles burning in ever-greens lit the room with a soft glow. I stood with Alex and the boys, flanked by my family and his, and surrounded by clansmen, the priest in a joyous mood. The bright colors of our clothing and the white candles and greenery were framed by the gray stones, the air somehow silky tonight and full of magic. And next to me, his hair a golden halo around his head, Alex looked like a very large angel.

After the ceremony we ate in the hall and brought in Christmas Day with toasts and laughter while I looked at these well-loved faces around my table. What a difference from the year before. I gave a prayer of thanks and resolved to be the best wife and mother in the world. I had only one regret. I had miscarried again shortly before my family's arrival. I had told Alex at last of my pregnancy and then had to tell him of the miscarriage. I recovered at once and did not mention it except to Louisa and Ellen and Berta, but I knew the whole household, probably the whole clan, knew we had lost another child.

One rite of the season was a great success with Will, for he was its center. The custom of first-footing was a firm tradition at Kilgannon, and we did it with delight. Shortly after midnight of the new year we all paid a visit to every nearby household. Tradition dictated that the first person across the threshold in the new year should be dark-haired and preferably male, to bring luck to the house. Alex had been the first-footer for years, but because he was fair he'd had to follow the practice of throwing a lump of coal in first before entering. To have a dark-haired man who could be considered one of the laird's family be the first-footer caused great excitement, and Will was a very willing participant. At each house he was handed a glass of whisky, which he drained as more was handed round. Before long we were all singing the old songs with the clansmen, Will leading the group as though he had done this for years. We finished in the hall, where a meal had been prepared, and I smiled as I watched everyone. Next to me Alex beamed as he looked over the happy faces, his face flushed with the warmth and the whisky. He kissed my hand as it lay clasped in his.

Later, alone in our room, he kissed me thoroughly, then leaned back to look at me. "Hard to believe it's the new year, lass. I've kent ye a year and a half now. The happiest of my life."

I smiled at him, but his face blurred with the tears that sprang to my eyes. "And mine," I said.

"Then why do ye cry, Mary Rose?" he asked tenderly.

"A child, Alex. I cannot give you a child." He shook his head slowly and pulled me to him, stroking my back as he spoke softly over my head. "Ye've given me my life, lass, and my future. My life was not worth living when I met ye, and it is the now. It is enough, Mary, that I have ye. I need nothing else. If we are meant to have children, we will. If not, then so be it. I am a verra happy man." He released me and sighed. "Can ye be happy with me, lass? Even if we never have children together? Does it help a wee bit to have Ian and Jamie, or does that make it worse?"

"No. Yes. They are wonderful." I smiled up at him. "And I am happy, Alex, more happy than I have a right to be. But I am greedy too. All I want in my life is to live here and have children with you. I'd like to give you another son. Or a daughter."

He smiled and stroked my hair. "A daughter, lass, would be just like ye, far too much trouble. Better that we have sons. When yer well we'll try again. But we'll have sons, Mary. They'll be as simple to live with as their father." I smiled and kissed him, this splendid man who was mine. And 1714 began.

My family stayed for two more weeks. Will, Louisa, and Randolph had been as delightful as always, and even Betty was well behaved. Louisa had taken a keen interest in the details of managing such a large household and had given me several suggestions that I intended to follow. We had talked for days, and I think we left no topic untouched. The most surprising development had been the mutual affection that had sprung up between Randolph and the boys. He astonished me, and possibly himself, by spending a great deal of his time with them, playing chess or other games, and they begged him constantly for more stories of his youth and more of his adventure tales. More than once Louisa and I had found him closeted with both boys and Matthew and Gilbey, holding them entranced with some far-fetched story of his escapades. When the morning of their departure at last arrived, we stood in the hall before braving the icy wind and rain outside. Captain Calum was to escort them home on the *Mary Rose* and he was anxious to get underway, muttering about tides and winds. And then they were gone. I stood on the dock, watching the *Mary Rose* pull around the first bend, wondering when I would see them again. Alex had promised a trip to London in the summer, but who knew if that would ever happen? I tried to suppress my sadness as we hurried back to the hall, Alex's hand warm in mine.

Matthew left a few days later for the University at St. Andrew's, Angus going with him to help him settle into his new world as the new term began, and Gilbey went along as well, paving the way with those he knew. Gilbey and Matthew had become fast friends, and I knew he would miss Matthew as much as we all would. Angus and Gilbey arrived home two weeks later with the news that Matthew was well settled. It was much quieter with him gone. The boys counted the days until summer. As did I.

In the late morning of a stormy February day, I stood in the chapel with Alex while he looked around the chapel and smiled. "This room is Kilgannon, Mary. Have I ever told ye?" I shook my head. "Well, *kil* means church, or chapel, so it's really Gannon's church. This is the heart of our land. I always wonder how many marriages and funerals have been held here. Nine earls buried from this chapel. Ten generations married and, God willing, eleven someday." He led me to the side of the chapel, where he knelt and ran his hands along the wall. "Can ye see here, in the stone? Down low, here? A small *A*? My grandfather carved it when he was a boy and was punished for defacing the house of God. And when I was nine I carved this one next to it." He pointed at the second letter. "It was never discovered and I laugh every time I see it. I think it's the only mischief I ever got away with. And someday perhaps my grandson will carve another." His eyes met mine. "Let's try again, lass," he said.

The winter continued uneventfully until one dark afternoon when the *Margaret* brought news and an unwelcome letter, which I found Alex and Angus angrily discussing in the library. Alex waved the letter at me as I entered. "This came from our cousin Lachlan, lass," he said. "Queen Anne has agreed that her heir will be Sophia. Not James Stewart, not her own brother."

I struggled to understand his outraged tone. "So if Anne dies, the English throne goes to the Hanovers?"

"Aye," Angus said, "despite the fact that she is a Stewart."

"Why are you surprised?" Both men looked at me, startled. "Well?" I continued. "What else was going to happen? After the Treaty of Utrecht last summer France recognized Sophia's heirship. After the Act of Settlement, which barred a Catholic king—and which, I might add, was thirteen years ago—what did you think was next? Did you think that James Stewart would suddenly convert to being Protestant and that would clear the way for his succession?"

"Do ye understand what this means?" Alex asked.

"It means," I answered, "that the same thing that has happened for centuries is happening again. Someone not English will be on the throne of England. It's been happening for seven hundred years. More if you go back to the Romans."

"It means, Mary," said Alex, his tone angry, "that someone not Scottish will be on the throne that rules Scotland."

"Yes," I said, "but we knew that was going to happen." The men exchanged another glance. "Robert the Bruce was a Norman. Mary Stuart spoke French, not Gaelic, and changed the spelling of her name because she could not pronounce it correctly. James the First was quick to go to London and turn his back on Scotland. Alexander the Third left his throne to the Maid of Norway, and Charles lost the throne altogether. Now Anne gives the throne to a cousin rather than her half brother." Angus laughed, but Alex didn't.

"We got a letter as well from the MacDonald," he said sullenly. "There's a letter being circulated by the English for all the Highland chiefs to sign that we will accept the situation."

"I see," I said.

"I dinna think ye do," Alex snapped. "It's no' a light thing, Mary." His eyes were still indignant. "It means that no Stewart will sit on the throne of Scotland again."

"Unless there is a rebellion." I let my words hang in the air between us. Angus, not smiling now, looked from Alex to me. "Are you two planning an uprising? Or do Lachlan and the MacDonald invite you to join one? Surely everyone in the Highlands has been talking of it for months now." And they had been. I had long ago become accustomed to both the constant complaining about the English government and the half-baked plots to overthrow it. But never from Alex. He turned and looked out the window. Angus stretched his legs in front of him and studied them. My heart stopped. *Dear God*, I prayed, *tell me this is not true*. I watched Alex's back. "Alex?" My voice wavered. He turned then.

"No rebellion, lass. We're not plotting. But it doesna sit well. Surely ye can see that, Mary." I looked up at him. How could I tell him how little the rest of the world mattered to me?

"I can see that, Alex," I said in a soothing manner. "But surely this is not a surprise? It's been years in the making, and Anne's health is excellent. She'll live for ages."

He shook his head. "That's not what I hear, lass. I'm hearing she's failing. But even if she does live, then what? Then Queen Sophia, then King George? God help us. It was bad enough with Anne. What will happen to us with a German on the throne?"

"Surely nothing will change."

"Anne's already surrounding herself with Whigs."

"Oh," I said, realizing Randolph's influence would be considerably less; even the Duke's would be diminished, and Uncle Harry's. All Tories, they would pay the price for a shift of power.

"Aye," Alex said grimly. "I can see yer beginning to understand. It's no' a light thing. Just a few years ago Scotland had ten times the representation we have now, and that was with a Stewart on the throne and Tories in control. I'm telling ye, Mary, we're headed for trouble." I looked from Alex to Angus and back.

"What are our choices?" I asked. "If you sign, perhaps we will be left in peace. What happens if you do not?"

"I dinna ken," Alex said.

I looked at his cousin. "Angus?"

Angus shrugged. "Nor I, Mary. But the MacDonald's signing, and the Camerons and MacDonnell of Glengarry. Lachlan says all the clans are."

"Then that's what we do," I said.

"Aye," Alex growled, turning to look out the window. "But I dinna have to enjoy the experience." The boys and Gilbey burst in then, and I left Alex to his sons and their lessons while Angus walked out into the hall with me.

"We have no choice, Angus," I said, and he nodded curtly. "Do you have another solution?"

He shook his head. "I see no other choice. Our own leaders have sold us to England, and we must obey."

"It will not affect us. We are isolated here."

"Not enough." He looked at me from under his bushy eyebrows. "We see an ugly chain, lass. First Argyll and the others sold Scotland and put us in this godforsaken Union; now we'll have a German ruling us and the Whigs, who have no love for us. What's next? Are we to be beaten into the ground like the Welsh? I never thought to see this. Begging yer pardon, lass, but England and its monarchs have rarely done well by Scotland. And I can see no remedy. As ye say, we have no choice, but as we say, we dinna have to enjoy the experience." He stalked off and I looked after him.

I forgot Angus's words and Alex's worries as spring arrived and we were at last able to be outdoors again. The tasks filled the days, but I was joyous as I worked, for I was with child again. If I carried this baby full term it would be born at the end of September. I wondered if I could hostess the Games and then calmly give birth a month later but decided not to think that far ahead. We celebrated our first anniversary with music and a hall full of people but no dancing and the tamest lovemaking we'd had, for Alex was determined to give this child every chance of surviving.

The letter that Lachlan had warned of never arrived in Kilgannon, and I was not sure if Alex was relieved at the reprieve or annoyed at being overlooked. In any case, Alexander MacGannon's signature was not requested and he never agreed to accept Sophia as Anne's heir. I suspected that Anne had never intended that her half brother James inherit. The fact that James Stewart was male and the true heir, if one believed in primogeniture, was discussed at length. I watched as Alex listened to the talk about whether the first son should always inherit, and I knew he was thinking of his brother.

We had heard nothing from Malcolm, and Alex had not written to him. He was rarely mentioned and I forgot about him, but I knew Alex never forgot. In early June Alex got a letter from his agent in London that hinted at information to be passed, and Alex grew steadily more tense. He and Angus conferred about it for hours, reaching no conclusions but unable to drop the topic. We had canceled our proposed trip to London because of my pregnancy, but I suggested to Alex that he go without me to visit his agent since William Burton seemed incapable of simply writing whatever it was he had to tell. Alex refused, and I wondered sometimes whether he would have been just as happy to have never received the letter. As for me, I had no doubt what the information was. I was certain that it was confirmation that Malcolm and the captain of the *Diana* had plotted to have her appear to sink while the two of them split the profits of the trip. Or that the attack on us had been traced to Malcolm. I never discussed my theories with anyone, for fear of starting a trail of arguments with Alex again, but I knew both Alex and Angus suspected the same.

And then in the middle of June, a week before the

summer solstice, I lost this child as well. I had stood in May
with Alex on Beltane morning and watched the bonfires
burn on the hills surrounding us as he explained the custom and the ancient beliefs. I had marveled then that these
people could harbor such primal fears and superstitions. But
at dawn six weeks later, on the summer solstice, I admitted
to myself that if I had thought the ceremonies taking place
in quiet glens and meadows would help me keep a child, I
would have joined the celebrants without a qualm. Last
year, I knew, these same dates had been celebrated, but I
had been too new to Scotland and too enraptured with my
new life to notice that half the staff and most of the clansmen were nowhere to be found. And that they returned,
exhausted, to stumble through the day. Alex turned a blind
eye to these celebrations, although, he explained to me, he
did not believe in the old superstitions or customs.

"But, lass," he'd said. "I've been educated and I ken that
there's a world beyond Kilgannon. Some of these people
have never been off MacGannon land and will never see anywhere else. I willna take away their customs. As long as they
dinna harm anyone it's best to let them follow the old ways
as well. Now, if they decide to start sacrificing humans again,
we'll have to discuss it." He had laughed at my expression,
then shrugged. "I have two choices. Leave them as they are
and try to change the little things, or get their backs up and
nothing will ever change and we'll always be doing things as
our great-great-grandfathers did. I decided years ago to
change the small things and let them have their beliefs. It's a
compromise, lass, and one I can live with. They'll listen to
my ideas for new crops or something else to try, but I'd
better not tell them what to think." He grinned at me. "Of
course, I am open to all new ideas and suggestions myself,
so I dinna understand their resistance." I had shaken my
head and decided not to think about how very different this
was than London.

London. I had wanted so much to visit. And on the day
that I lost this latest child, as I stared at the bed hangings

and waited for Alex to come to me, I decided that the best thing for me was to go home. No, not home anymore, I corrected myself, for Kilgannon was home now. But I wanted to go to London, to hear only English, to eat food I relished, to visit with friends, to see a play or an opera. But most of all I wanted to see Louisa. And a doctor.

Alex exploded into the room, his expression alarmed, and I burst into tears at the sight of him. I didn't have to tell him what had happened. He gathered me to him, his tears mingling with mine at this new loss. Later I asked him to take me to London as we had originally planned. After his worried comments about whether it was wise for me to travel, I told him I wanted to see a doctor and my aunt. We left three days later.

TWENTY-FOUR

LONDON. AFTER THE QUIET AND ISOLATION OF KIL-gannon, it seemed even more boisterous and chaotic than I had remembered, and I felt out of place. No, not out of place, I felt remote from London. My clothes were out of fashion and I didn't care. The gossip swirled around me and I didn't know the names. The politics bored me for the most part, and I thought of the many hours I had spent listening to the discussions and then dining with those who had been discussed so thoroughly. Those days were gone. Randolph's power was seriously diminished and, I was discovering, so was that of most of the men I had known as influential. The Whigs had won the war of persuasion for Queen Anne's ear. Although it was difficult for my friends and family, I could feel no resentment toward her. Any woman who had lost her husband and seventeen children was a woman I could sympathize with. Her health was failing, and London dissected every symptom.

Feeling ran high about the succession, although no one had any doubts what would happen. Sophia, the Electorate, had died, and it was assumed that her son George of Hanover would be king when Anne died. Those in England who felt that the first son should inherit were outraged, since by that notion only James Stewart could be the next king. Others were just as outraged at the idea of a Catholic king. Given England's history with Protestants succeeding

Catholics and the reverse, it was not surprising that emotions were elevated. I longed for a country in which religion was not such a divisive factor. But I realized, listening to my uncles and their friends, that the struggle really was not about religion. It was about power. And money. *What else?* I thought.

I paid little attention to politics and basked in Louisa's welcome and attentions. She grieved with me, and although Randolph never mentioned my losses, he would often seek me out and hold my hand without speaking. I was grateful to both of them and told them so, but as always, they waved my words away. We saw Will and Betty, of course, and Will confided that he understood our grief, for Betty had never conceived. We wondered together if Will and I were the last of the Lowells. Uncle Harry would not listen to one word of sorrow or regret and kept telling me to smile and to count my blessings. While I enjoyed his cheerful company, I often wondered if he had any understanding of our pain. No, I thought, as I watched him laugh with Alex, he does not know what we've suffered. I saw the underlying sadness in my husband's eyes as he glanced at me with a smile, but Harry never seemed to notice.

We were busy, our visit full of social engagements. Alex and I dined with the Duke and Duchess, who were as welcoming as ever, and listened to Duke John bemoan his loss of political power. And we accompanied them to other evenings, including one hosted by Lady Wilmington. At her request Alex wore Highland dress that night, his accent noticeably stronger. When I teased him about becoming a parody of himself he grinned at me. "I couldna refuse her, lass, and the others have to be polite," he said. "If they think to ignore the Scots, I willna make it easy for them."

I shook my head at him and went to join Louisa. *She never changes,* I thought with affection as I listened to her skillful evasion of Madeline Shearson's questions. I watched Katherine watch Alex and turned with a start when Madeline said my name.

"Pardon me?" I said.

She simpered. "I said, Lord Robert Campbell is most visible in London now and very influential these days. What a shame that your husband is not a Member of Parliament as Lord Campbell is."

"I'm delighted that he's not, madam, for he is home with me."

"Yes, of course." She nodded. "Have you seen Lord Campbell?"

"Not yet." I tried not to let the note of annoyance creep into my tone. How very like her to play this game. "But I'm sure our paths will cross during our visit."

"Of course." She smiled and turned the topic to some unfortunate young girl who had been whisked off to a relative's home. While Madeline speculated who the father was, I thought of Robert. I did not expect to see him in London, for Robert was with his cousin Argyll, and Argyll had switched his allegiance again. A year ago he had opposed the Union, daring the Crown's displeasure, but now he was currying favor with the Whigs and finding it. No, our paths would not cross. Robert did not move in the same circles as we did these days. Which was as well.

The rest of the evening passed pleasantly enough, I thought, but later at Louisa's, as we sat discussing the evening, Randolph complained about a snub to Alex. Alex laughed and told Randolph to pay it no mind. "It was rude, Kilgannon," my uncle said. "I would not have thought it possible that someone would behave so abominably. It was very surprising."

"What happened?" I looked from Randolph to Alex, who shrugged and sipped his whisky. Alex had sent several cases of whisky home with Randolph and Will after they had praised it at Christmas, and one of the benefits was that he had a ready supply when he visited. Alex held the glass before him now and studied it.

"Some rude Whig refused to shake Kilgannon's hand,"

said Randolph, shaking his head in disgust. "It was an awkward moment."

"Why would he do that?" I asked, and Louisa sighed this time.

"I told you that feelings were running very high, Mary," she said. "There are many in London who believe that the Jacobites are waiting for Anne to die and planning an attack on London."

"That's ridiculous," I exclaimed, and Alex met my eyes.

"Of course it is," Louisa said in a soothing tone, "but ignorant people who are frightened are dangerous." She looked at Alex. "I suggest that you wear English clothing while you're here."

He shifted in his chair and met her look. "I will not. Even if I did, I have only to open my mouth and they all ken who I am. I have Angus and Matthew with me at all times. And a ship full of men a short distance away."

"It makes no difference, Louisa," said Randolph. "Look at him. He looks like a Scot."

"I look like a Gael," said Alex flatly.

"I am thinking of my niece's welfare as well as yours," Louisa said icily. "And I think it a small request, Alex." After a moment Alex laughed and agreed to wear the English clothing.

"And Angus and Matthew when they're with you," Louisa said.

"And Angus and Matthew," Alex echoed. Louisa nodded.

Later, alone in our room, I asked Alex if his feelings had been hurt by the snub, and he smiled at me. "I dinna let other people's view of me influence me, lass. What does it matter what they think? I think their venom is due to jealousy that the most beautiful woman in the room was on the arm of a barbarian."

"I love you, Alex," I said, and he grinned and reached for me.

"I ken ye do, Mary," he said. "And I encourage it."

* * *

The next afternoon was cold and cloudy, and I went to visit Janice and Meg. I marveled again at Janice's constant biting remarks and at Meg's sweet disposition. The visit was amiable enough for the most part, but I realized how much I missed Becca. The four of us who had once been inseparable were now all married, Rebecca and I far from home, and Meg was drifting away from Janice's incessantly disagreeable behavior. *I will not miss Janice,* I thought, *and Meg is, well, Meg is sweet. But boring.* I was delighted to have Alex announced, and I departed with him feeling that I had little in London in the way of friends to hold me.

That night we dined at the Mayfair Bartletts. I had hoped to avoid them this visit, but it was too much to expect. The evening was, as theirs always were, well attended, a very mixed company. Rowena was there—without her marquis—on the arm of Edmund Bartlett, and she smiled distantly when we joined them. Across the room the Duke and Duchess talked with Becca's parents, and Louisa and Randolph had just drifted down the hall when Rowena gave a mew of pleasure and a surprisingly throaty laugh.

"Well, well," she said to Edmund, "look who's here," and pointed at the group that had just arrived and stood in the doorway chatting with Edmund's parents. "Isn't that Lord Campbell?"

Alex and I turned together to look just as Robert and the woman on his arm walked away from the Bartletts. Rowena waved to attract their attention. Next to me Alex stiffened as Robert, with a word to his companion, headed in our direction. I made a silent prayer and cursed Rowena. Robert looked the same and I realized, with the clarity that a year's absence brings, how very handsome he was. He seemed taller and more imposing than I'd remembered and was dressed as exquisitely as ever, this time in a chocolate-colored jacket and brilliant white shirt that set his coloring off well. I was suddenly aware that my rose dress, so fashionable two years ago, might seemed dated now. I nodded when he bowed to me and met his eyes hesitantly. I need not have feared his rancor. I'd expected reproach or bitterness, but to my dismay his gaze was warmer than I'd ever seen. Some things, it seemed, had not changed with a year's separation. I felt Alex watching us and my cheeks flush as Robert greeted Edmund and Rowena politely, then turned to us.

"Kilgannon, Lady Kilgannon, may I present Miss Buchanan?" he asked smoothly, and I breathed again. How could I have forgotten Robert's impeccable manners? He gave his companion a quiet smile. The young woman—a girl, really—looked confused.

"Lady Kilgannon was formerly Miss Mary Lowell," Rowena said, and I saw the recognition register in Miss Buchanan's eyes. Slim and dark, she was lovely and obviously very taken with Robert, for she looked to him for guidance with each remark. She glanced at him now before making a pretty curtsy to us.

Alex bowed in return and I nodded my head. "Miss Buchanan, it is a pleasure to meet ye," Alex said with a smile, his voice so calm that I gave him a sharp glance, but his expression gave nothing away. I smiled at her the best I could, but I'm sure it was only a hideous caricature of a welcome. Next to her Robert stood immobile, watching me. I did not look at him.

"Robert," Alex said quietly, extending his hand. "How are ye?" As Robert clasped Alex's hand their eyes met for a long moment, then Alex laughed and released Robert's hand. "We were rivals for my wife's attentions, Miss Buchanan," he said cheerfully. "It seems a long time ago."

Edmund Bartlett snickered and Rowena watched attentively, but Robert smiled placidly and nodded. "Yes, it does," he said, and turned to me. "Mary," he said. "How are you?"

"I am well, thank you, Robert," I said, my voice sounding strained. "And your mother?"

To my surprise Robert laughed. "My mother sends her best." He looked from me to Alex. "What brings you to London?"

Alex nodded at me. "Mary wanted a visit with her aunt and uncle. Ye ken how fond she is of them and they of her. And it's been a bit since we've been here."

"It's a different place than it was, Alex," Robert said.

"Lord Campbell has done quite well with the new regime," Edmund said, and smiled, looking to see both men's reaction. Robert had the grace to look embarrassed. Alex laughed.

"Are ye hoping for a sword fight in the middle of yer parents' party, Bartlett?" Alex asked lightly. "If so, ye'll be disappointed. I only wish Robert Campbell well, and there's naught to report in that, is there?" Edmund tilted his head to study Alex, then chuckled and batted Alex's shoulder.

"Kilgannon," Edmund began, but Alex interrupted him.

"Good for ye," he said to Robert. "I'm glad some Scots are prospering in these times. And I canna say I'm surprised." Robert flushed but smiled.

"Doesn't Lady Kilgannon look well?" Rowena asked Robert.

Robert met my eyes briefly. "Lady Kilgannon," he said to Rowena, "looks beautiful. Lady Kilgannon has always looked beautiful. Some things don't change." He smiled at Rowena and turned to Alex. "And how are you, Alex?"

Alex pulled me to him. "Grand," he said. "It's been a fine year and we're looking forward to a hundred more together."

"Glad to hear it," Robert said smoothly. "But, Alex, be careful while you're here. No doubt you've heard of the problems down at the docks. I assume you came on one of your ships?"

Alex nodded. "Yer talking about the effigy burnings? I've heard some of it." Robert nodded and Alex turned to me. "There have been burnings of figures meant to represent

James Stewart, Mary," he said, unruffled. I had heard nothing of the burnings.

Edmund Bartlett nodded. "Several," he said.

"And some Scots have been attacked," Robert said. "Mind your back while you're here. Will you stay long?"

Alex's eyes narrowed slightly. "As long as my wife wishes. I thank ye for the warning." Robert nodded and Edmund's mother joined us then, mercifully interrupting the conversation.

That night as we prepared for bed I asked Alex if it bothered him seeing Robert again. He shook his head. "No, lass, I thought we might see him. Ye seemed taken aback, though."

"It was awkward. I thought he might be angry."

"Why should he be? He had his chance, Mary Rose. It's his own fault yer not with him now." He climbed into bed and blew out the candle. "His Miss Buchanan looks a bit like ye."

"Did you think so?" I asked as I joined him, feeling his naked warmth. I nestled close to him.

He put a hand on my waist and pulled me closer. "Aye. A poor man's Mary Lowell," he said, and kissed my shoulder as his hands roamed over me. I turned to meet his caresses and forgot all about Robert. His lovemaking that night was impassioned and fierce, and I met him in kind. Afterward, when we lay in quiet satiation, he kissed my shoulder again.

"Yer mine, Mary Rose," he said. "Robert Campbell was a fool and he kens it. Tell me ye love me, lass."

"I love you, Alex," I said as he pulled me to him.

"Mine," he said to the dark.

We had come to London for three reasons: to see my family, a doctor, and Alex's shipping agent. The doctor, one of Dr. Sutter's colleagues, had examined me and pronounced me fit, saying he'd found nothing to prevent me from carrying a child. He had tried to be very tactful, suggesting that we refrain from activity, as he expressed it, for three months. Alex had been delighted at the lack of long-range problems but sighed over the timing. Three months was a long time, I'd thought as I watched my husband. I wondered if I could endure it. I would have to be inventive.

Alex's news was not so pleasing. William Burton had confirmed what I suspected and had given Alex letters from Malcolm and the captain of the *Diana* that clearly showed their plot. Alex read them over and over, as though they would say something different if he studied them often enough. Both the captain and the *Diana* were in the Caribbean now but were expected to return sometime in the autumn. Alex and Angus discussed it at length, while Matthew and I avoided the subject and talked mostly about his first term at university. I knew Angus's views, which mirrored mine, but Alex would not talk about it to me. All he would say was that he was going to see Malcolm after the Games. But he brooded.

I had come to terms with what I suspected Malcolm of doing long ago, and my contempt for him could grow no larger, but I felt no satisfaction at having been right all along. What Alex felt about having the written proof of his brother's perfidious behavior he never said, and I did not press him, content to have the mysteries that had haunted us for two years solved. But I was saddened, for the flashes of what Malcolm could have been haunted me. I remembered happy evenings at Kilgannon when we were all together, and I sighed. The night we had pored over Alex's sketches had been one of my favorite memories, now tainted by what came after. What must Alex be feeling, I wondered, if I, who had known Malcolm for such a short time, was saddened and bereft? How sad to lose your brother and have him still be alive.

Queen Anne's condition worsened and London seethed with apprehension. When I suggested that I needed to shop for gifts for the boys and Ellen and to bring back goods for Kilgannon, I was met with cries of protest from Louisa and

Randolph. Angus agreed with them, but I was firm that I could not return home empty-handed. I argued that they'd exaggerated the dangers, that an Englishwoman with a reasonable escort could be safe on the streets of London. Louisa reluctantly admitted that she'd not curtailed her activities, and after much discussion, during which Alex sat quietly watching us, it was at last agreed that we would go shopping—Alex, Angus, Matthew, me, and two of Randolph's footmen. I thought it ridiculous.

The day was bright and we did well, buying the sweets and tea and other foods that Mrs. M. had requested from London and gifts for the boys. I bought Ellen perfume. Pleased with my purchases, I told the five men who had trailed behind me through the shops that their ordeal was over. Before returning to Louisa's we stopped at the *Mary Rose* to drop off my bundles and to check on the ship. All was well on board, but the men were nervous and told of remarks that been thrown at them. The Scots were too visible, it was decided, and with the agitation in London it seemed wiser to move her across the river. Calum, Angus, and Alex talked of where we'd find the *Mary Rose* berthed, then Calum, with a lighter expression, told us that a runner had come just before we did, looking for Alex. The MacDonald, it seemed, was in London and had just discovered we were. He asked Alex to go to a nearby inn.

"The runner said Donald asks ye to come immediately when ye get the message, for he's leaving in a few hours. Apparently they tried to find ye at Lord Randolph's and were told ye were coming here. The inn is no' far, Alex," Calum said. "The lad said ye could walk it. Do ye ken where it is?"

Alex nodded. "Have ye seen MacDonald's men or his ships?" Calum shook his head and Alex looked over the river behind us. "Wonder what he's doing here?" He exchanged a look with Angus, and I knew he was thinking of the rumors of an uprising. Then he looked at me. "Mary Rose," he began, and I laughed.

"Yes, I'll go home, Alex," I said, but Alex frowned.

"I'm thinking ye should come with us, lass. Calum and the men need to be off to get a berth across the river before dark, and I dinna think ye should go home with just the footmen."

"And he kens we'd no' let him go alone," Angus laughed.

"The inn's no' a bad sort of place, Mary," Alex said. "We'll only stay long enough to ask Donald to join us elsewhere." He frowned again and gave Angus a glance.

"What's wrong?" I asked.

Alex shrugged and frowned to himself. "I dinna ken. Just a . . . it's nothing. We'll see ye home and then return," he said.

I shook my head. "You'll miss Donald if you do. Either I'll go home with the footmen or I'll come with you. This is silly."

"Matthew could take Mary home," Angus said, his mood darkening with Alex's obvious uneasiness. Matthew nodded his willingness.

"Alex, what is wrong?" I asked. "Is the inn a dangerous place for me?"

Alex shook his head again. "No, it's actually a decent place, even if it's close to the docks. Lots of travelers stay there."

"Then let's go. Just don't plan to stay long," I said. "The Duchess expects us for dinner."

Alex told the driver to stay with the coach, and we set off on foot through a labyrinth of shops and stalls. Alex led the way, then Matthew, then Angus and me, and finally the footmen. We had no difficulty wending through the crowds. At first.

We'd gone two blocks when I saw two men come from the side alleys and walk next to Alex. They did not look at him but matched him step for step. He turned to look at first one, then the other, and his hand moved to his sword hilt as he glanced back at us. Behind me Angus cursed and pushed forward, the footmen with him. He grabbed Matthew's arm and mine and, with a nod at the intruders, whispered hoarsely to us to wait in the butcher shop we were passing. Matthew pulled me into the stall, ducking between the sides of beef, ignoring the sharp looks of the shopkeeper. We stood next to the hanging meat and watched as Angus reached Alex. And then, as if from nowhere, the street was full of armed men, shouting and raising weapons. I saw Alex draw his sword and Angus do the same. We lost them as the street became a battleground.

Matthew pushed me into the back of the stall while the shopkeeper called his helpers and then shoved us toward his back door, shouting at us to get out. Matthew took my hand and we ran through the alley, away from the noise behind us. At the corner I dragged him to a stop. "Matthew, we have to go back," I panted. "We cannot leave Alex and your father there."

His eyes widened. "Mary, ye canna mean it. I have to get ye away from here," he shouted, and yanked my arm as he ran forward again. I had no chance to argue. We ran the two blocks back to the ship, where, shouting and cursing, Matthew got the attention of the crew. Throwing me at Calum, he called for the men to help him, and within moments Calum and I stood alone on the dock, watching the men disappear around the corner, Matthew in their lead.

Fifteen minutes later some of the crew returned. The battle was over. I stood with my hand to my throat as they explained that they did not know where Alex was. Angus and Matthew and the footmen were searching with the rest of the Kilgannon men. Four of the attackers were dead and more had limped off bleeding, but there was no sign of Alex. The shopkeepers had cursed them and thrown things, shouting foul words about Scots and Jacobites. Angus had questioned one of the wounded attackers, discovering only that they'd been paid to wait for Alex and Angus and waylay them. By an Englishman who had paid them well and who was not concerned whether Alex and Angus lived through the attack.

Calum returned me to Louisa's house, riding with me and four armed men in Louisa's coach. Bronson received us with a horrified expression and hurried us into the house, where I explained what had happened. Calum and more of Randolph's men returned to the ship with the coach, and I waited with my aunt and uncle. By seven I was frantic. At almost nine, still light on this summer's evening, Bronson came to us and said my husband was in the yard. We raced to the back of the house.

Alex stood just outside the kitchen door, his clothes and hair covered with filth, his face grim. But he was alive. The two footmen, in better condition, stood behind him. Alex's shirt and jacket were torn and bloodstained, his face and arms covered with dried muck. Louisa and I exclaimed and Randolph muttered a curse.

I threw myself at Alex. "What happened? Are you hurt?"

Alex stepped out of my reach. "Dinna touch me, Mary, I am foul, but I'm not hurt, lass. And neither are Angus and Matthew." He looked over my head at Randolph. "I thank ye for yer good men here, sir," he said, gesturing to the footmen. "They were in the thick of it and dinna flinch. But for them and Angus I wouldna be here." He turned to the two men. "I thank ye again, sirs. I'm in yer debt. I'll send ye the whisky I told ye of." The footmen nodded, pleased and apparently uninjured. Alex turned back to us. "Louisa, I'm afraid yer coach will need a bit of cleaning."

We all exclaimed and asked for the story. It was, Alex said, simple. Someone had planned the assault on us, but it had not gone as devised. He and Angus and the footmen might have fended off the attackers if the crowd the fray had attracted had not gotten involved. Alex had seen Matthew pull me into the butcher shop, and when he found himself at the edge of the fracas, he'd battled his way to the shop to find us. Once there he'd been accosted by the shopkeeper and had fought his way out the back door. And then faced the mob of townspeople that had gathered.

"Yer right, sir," he told Randolph. "London does not welcome Scots these days. They thought I was leading an invasion." When we all asked him what had happened, he shrugged. "They pelted me with things and dumped chamber pots on me. But Angus and the crew and yer men here found me, else I would have been dead in the gutter tonight. Calum told me he'd brought ye home, Mary Rose." He gestured to himself. "I need to get out of these clothes and I need a bath. But not in yer house in this condition."

In the end two tubs of water were brought to the stables, where Alex stripped off his clothes in silence and stood in his bare feet while the men set up the tubs. He wrapped the filthy clothing inside out and handed them to one of the men. "Burn them," he said, his accent thick, and the man nodded as he left, holding the reeking clothes away from him. Alex would not let me near him until his body and hair had been washed twice. At last he stood in the tub, the water reaching mid-calf and foul now, and he stepped into the second tub of water with a sigh as I stepped forward to wash his back and hair again.

"Alex," I said. "Talk to me."

"There's no' to say."

I rubbed my hand along his shoulders and down his back as he leaned into my strokes. "Alex, my love, what happened when you were alone?"

He sighed. "They pelted me with that filth and they spit on me and tore at my clothes. It was unpleasant, but they dinna harm me."

"Of course. That's why you have this bruise on your side and a cut along your cheekbone."

"They meant to torment me, is all." He leaned his head back and reached for me. As I bent to kiss him I saw that his lips were swollen and cut.

"And this, my love?" I ran a finger along his lips.

"A token of an Englishman's esteem, lass," he said, and pulled me to him again. "They canna resist me either." I stepped back and studied him. He had cuts and scratches and would have several new bruises by morning, but nothing that would not heal.

"Alex, who was it?"

He didn't pretend to misunderstand me. "I dinna ken, lass," he said heavily. "I dinna ken."

"You must have some idea."

"I have lots of ideas, Mary Rose," he said. "But I'm too tired to be sorting it out tonight."

Malcolm, I thought. *Damn him.* I would talk with Angus in the morning. He'd tell me more. "Alex," I said quietly. "I know you're very tired and sore, but we have to talk."

"No, lass," he said, rubbing his forehead. "Not tonight."

"Alex, someone planned that attack. Someone tried to kill you, someone who knew where you'd be, who knew you'd respond to a summons from the MacDonald. Someone who knew what you looked like." He watched me without expression. "What would you say if I suggested we go home?"

He shook his head. "I'd say no, lass. Ye wanted a visit, ye'll have a visit. We will not be frightened off by a mob of unruly vermin." He gave me a crooked smile. "I'll heal. Now, come here, Mary Rose, and I'll direct where ye should wash next."

"Alex, we're going home."

"Aye, lass. But not just the now. I need whisky and a clean bed. We'll talk on it in the morning. Please, Mary. I'm too tired to sort it all out tonight. Will ye not let it go for now?"

I nodded.

Hours later I woke alone. The door to our bedroom was open, and a glimmer of light came from somewhere. I wondered where Alex was and then heard male voices, at least two, talking in hushed tones. I listened for a few moments and rose. One of the voices was Alex's, and he sounded very serious. In the hallway I found him and Randolph, Alex dressed only in his kilt, Randolph with a night-robe pulled loosely around him. Alex's naked back was to me and he blocked Randolph's view of my approach. Another of the promised bruises had appeared at his ribs.

"What is it?" I asked, and both men turned, startled. Alex's expression was somber, Randolph's face flushed.

"Mary . . ." they said in unison.

"Ah, lass." Alex pulled me to him, and I could smell the soap on his warm skin. "Yer aunt and uncle are verra worried. Queen Anne is close to death. Randolph wants us to leave as soon as it is light."

"Some hothead may start something," Randolph said. He nodded at Alex. "Look at him. Look at what happened today. It could be worse the next time." We both looked at Alex's bruised face.

"Mary," Alex said, his distress evident. "Ye wanted a visit here. We'll be extra careful if ye wish to stay."

"My love," I said tenderly, well aware of Randolph listening. "I am ready to leave London. I came to see Randolph and Louisa and the doctor, and I have done that. There is nothing else here for me. Take me home." Alex nodded and met my eyes, but before he could answer, Louisa came around the corner, wrapping a robe around her, her face very pale.

"Did you convince him?" she asked Randolph.

Randolph shrugged. "I'm not sure."

"Aye, ye did." Alex nodded. "We'll do what ye think is best, and what Mary wishes. We can leave as soon as it's light."

"Good." Louisa hugged me. "Now, get your husband dressed. If the maids see him like that they'll never stop talking."

My farewells to Louisa were rushed and worried. Randolph insisted on accompanying us to the ship and had armed three of his men to join us. It was a strange group: a

Scotsman, four Englishmen, and a woman crammed into and atop a carriage barreling full speed through the dawn-lit streets of London. We arrived at the *Mary Rose* without incident, and as Randolph ushered us aboard I turned for one last embrace.

"Thank you for everything," I said, hugging him to me fiercely. "Take care of yourself, Randolph. Be very careful now that the Whigs have taken over."

He chuckled. "I'll be fine, my dear. I promise not to wear a kilt in London." He kissed my forehead. "Write to us."

"I will," I said, and Alex extended a hand to Randolph, thanking him warmly. As the *Mary Rose* pulled into the river I turned to wave to the lone figure on the dock and felt a sharp pang of loss. When would I see Louisa and Randolph again? I suspected I would not be in London for a long while. Despite everything, I still loved the city. And I knew London did not harbor Alex's enemy.

TWENTY-FIVE

OW STRANGE, I THOUGHT AS WE SAILED PAST THE Isle of Mull, that in such a short period of time I had become very accustomed to sailing on my husband's brigs and especially on one named for me. The voyage had been blessedly uneventful and I was anxious to be home. I glanced at Alex, lost in his own thoughts. Twenty-five months since we'd met and I'd been his wife for most of them. The period between our meeting and marriage had seemed so very long at the time. That young girl, so uncertain of Alex's feelings and so overwhelmed by her own, was no longer me, and I thought of her with a fond smile. The woman I was now had other worries—having children not one of them.

What had happened in London, however, was. Angus and I had discussed it at great length. He was furious, sure it had been meant to be a fatal attack, and sure as well that it had been arranged by the same person who had planned the attack in the coach last year. *Malcolm,* I'd said, and when Angus had met my eyes I saw his agreement. But we had no proof. Angus had left men behind to see what else they could discover in London. What he'd found out so far was of little value. Malcolm, we'd been told, was still in Clonmor. It was difficult to see how he could have arranged the attack from there, but I still considered him our best answer. The attackers said an Englishman had paid them, but Malcolm could have allies. Angus and I agreed that it could well be the captain of the

Diana or one of his cronies, but Alex and I did not discuss it, despite my many attempts.

I was biding my time. Mindful of the months Alex and I had spent arguing over Malcolm, I was hesitant to bring up my theory to him. Alex had not commented on the incident except to say that he thought it particularly interesting that Robert had warned us to be careful and soon thereafter we were attacked. That made no sense to me. In both attacks I could have been a casualty, not just Alex, although in both cases Alex was obviously the target. Would Robert risk my life to have me be available to marry him? Or would he take such a revenge for my refusal of him? Robert would not have used the ruse of the MacDonald to lure Alex to a trap, but Malcolm would have known Alex would respond to a message asking him to meet Donald. And I could not believe, whatever Alex thought, that the Robert Campbell I knew so well would ever stoop to that level. Malcolm, yes, I thought, remembering the day in the armory when he'd tripped Angus. But Robert look me in the eye and plan my husband's death? I would never believe it.

We arrived at Kilgannon in the afternoon to find preparations for the Games well under way, the meadow dotted with men cutting the grass for the races and children bouncing from one group to another. Ian and Jamie and Gilbey met us looking like heathens, barefoot, wearing stained kilts and expressions of exhausted delight. Alex hoisted a boy over each shoulder and ignored their giddy protests while he quizzed Gilbey on their activities. I gave each boy the bag of sweets that Louisa had sent to them. They kissed me with grimy lips and hugged me with grubby arms, and I held them tightly as I laughed at their enthusiastic welcome. *Home,* I thought. *Safe and sound.* Four days later the news of Queen Anne's death arrived with Murdoch Maclean, on his way to Skye. That night Alex and I had one of the worst arguments of our marriage.

I started it. Murdoch had said that London was uneasy and there had been riots after Anne's death. Any Scot or

Jacobite was suspect now, and many had been burned out or driven out by unruly mobs. Later in our room, Alex shook his head, remembering his own experience. I meant to be sympathetic, but that soon changed.

"At least none of those people in London had to face that his brother started the fracas. You had to survive Malcolm's attack before the Londoners'," I'd said, forgetting for a moment that we didn't discuss Malcolm. Alex faced me with a cold stare.

"And what is that supposed to mean, Mary?"

I met his look, instantly growing as angry as he was. I was very tired of the game we'd been playing. "It means Malcolm tried to kill you, Alex. Three times. Once with the poison, once at your agent's when they got me instead, and the third just this July."

"How can ye say this to me?"

"Because I don't fool myself, Alex, like you do."

His voice was deceptively calm. "I fool myself?"

I took a moment and watched him. How could he be so intelligent and so perceptive in so many things and so blind in this? "Alex," I said, intending to soothe. "You don't want to admit it, but you know it's true."

"I'm fooling myself, am I? Truly an idiot, I suppose."

"Not an idiot. But we all know the truth, Alex. You do as well. You're just not admitting it."

"It's ye who is fooling herself, Mary," he said scornfully. "It's plain who planned the attacks. Yer sainted Robert Campbell. And ye'll protect him at all costs, which is verra interesting."

"Alex, that is absurd! Why would Robert try to kill you?"

"To have ye, Mary. If I'm dead, yer his, and we all ken it."

"That's ridiculous! Robert would never do that."

Alex continued as though I hadn't spoken. "I ask myself often why my wife defends another man so strongly. A man who courted her and after her marriage still tells her she's beautiful in front of her husband. While he's trying to have me killed."

"Alex, that's unfair! You know Robert didn't do this!"

"I ken Robert Campbell still wants ye, Mary, that's what I ken. And we all ken that if I were dead ye'd go to him."

I slapped him. I don't want to remember the rest, an ugly battle, with hateful words and accusations on both sides. We didn't speak for days and resolved nothing. I felt defenseless facing his jealousy, for he was correct. I would defend Robert against his accusations forever. And, apparently, he would defend Malcolm. It was a repulsive impasse.

The Kilgannon Games the next week were dominated by endless discussions of what Anne's death would mean. Many of the chiefs had signed the letter accepting George as her heir, but there were several who were surprised that the very thing they'd agreed to had come to pass. Still, all the talk amounted to no more than talk. Sir Donald told us that he'd not been in London. Angus's runners reported that Malcolm had been at Clonmor all summer.

Malcolm and Sibeal appeared unannounced and uninvited, just before the Games began. I could not believe that Malcolm would have the audacity to come here when Alex had told him not to, and when, I suspected, he'd just launched yet another unsuccessful attack against his brother. The Clonmor men who accompanied him confirmed that Malcolm had not left his property except to come to Kilgannon. I no longer knew what to think.

Alex welcomed Malcolm in a brusque manner. To the rest of the world the brothers' greeting probably seemed subdued but unremarkable. It was only to Clan MacGannon that the strained expressions and sidelong glances were obvious. They arrived just before a meal and we sat together, talking about trivial matters. I could hardly be civil. To my astonishment, Malcolm leaned over to me midway through the meal and whispered into my ear.

"I have been a fool, Mary," he said, in a contrite tone, "and I beg yer forgiveness." I looked at him, my surprise no doubt visible. I saw Alex look from his brother to me and

back again. Angus watched from the end of the table, his
hand clenched on the wood next to his glass. I could not
think of what to answer and stared like a simpleton at Malcolm. "I've learned a lot the last few months, Mary," Malcolm continued, "and I ken now what it is I've done and
how wrong I've been. My behavior was regrettable. Will ye
forgive me?"

I took a deep breath, trying to think. *I will never like this
man,* I told myself. *I will never forgive him for hurting his
brother.* But apparently I could not put the blame for the
attack in London on him, and in the face of that I had to
find a compromise.

"Tell me ye'll try to forgive me, Mary. Just say ye'll consider it. It would mean so much," he pleaded.

At last I nodded, and he smiled a smile so like his
brother's that I caught my breath. *Peace,* I thought. *Peace
between the brothers.*

"Thank ye for that, Mary." Malcolm glanced at Alex. "I
can only pray that he will be as generous. Of course, he has
much more to forgive." Malcolm sighed before turning to
me again. "Help me to repair what I have almost destroyed.
Please." I nodded again and felt a tightness I had not even
recognized release from my chest as I followed Malcolm's
look. *Alex will welcome this,* I thought. *Thank God, Malcolm
has come to his senses. The attacks in London must not have
been his doing. No one could lie so smoothly.*

After the meal I watched Malcolm lean over to Alex and
speak to him in a quiet tone. Alex looked at his brother
without expression, but I knew him well enough now to see
his resistance. He watched Malcolm with his lips in a firm
line, his fingers white on the cup in his hand. And then, after
staring into the distance, he nodded. Angus and Murdoch
exchanged a look.

The brothers closeted themselves in the library. At first
Angus was with them and the shouting of all three could be
heard in the corridor. When it at last quieted I relaxed, but
still Alex did not come out. Angus said nothing to me when

he emerged, simply nodded as he took the stairs three at a time. Hours later I went to bed alone, comforted only by the thought that had they not reached some sort of accord Alex would have been out of there much earlier. When he crept into bed in the wee hours, I woke and reached out to him, surprised to find his cheeks wet. "What happened, my love?" I asked as he pulled me to his chest.

He gave a shaky sigh. "I dinna want to go through it all, lass, but my family is whole again. For the now, at least, and I willna think more on it." He stroked my shoulder and kissed my hair. "Malcolm wearies me more than anyone on earth. He does vile things and then begs me to forgive him. I dinna ken what to believe anymore, so I've decided to believe what I wish to be the truth. And I'll leave it at that."

I wrapped my arms around him and stroked his back. "If you are content, Alex, then I am. Perhaps we can have peace now."

"Aye. Perhaps," he said, and sighed again. But I knew in my heart that despite my best intentions I would never forget, nor forgive, what Malcolm had done, and while I was pleased for Alex that the brothers were again in harmony, I doubted that it would hold long. *The leopard does not change its spots,* I told myself.

But the leopard behaved himself admirably during his visit. Matthew refused to be anything but icily polite, as did Angus. Most guests seemed not to notice anything amiss, but Murdoch and Duncan and Sir Donald did. All three watched Alex and Malcolm. I saw Malcolm talking earnestly to Murdoch but could tell from Murdoch's stance that Malcolm had much more to do to convince Murdoch of his sincerity. Duncan took his brother's cues and stayed distant from Malcolm. The MacDonald watched from under his bushy eyebrows, missing nothing, not even me watching him watching them. He winked at me once, and I knew he saw much more than he'd ever let on.

But there was more going on in the Highlands that summer of 1714 than the disagreements between the MacGannon brothers. The mood among the guests was rebellious and resentment toward the English high. No one said anything impolite to me, for which I was grateful and which I believed was due to the clan's unabashed acceptance of me. The MacGannons gathered around me protectively when the conversations centered on the sins of the English. None of them overtly guarded me, but the message was clear, and for the first time I understood what Alex had been trying tell me when he'd said that the Countess of Kilgannon was a protected person.

And then the Games were over and we bade farewell to all of the guests, even Malcolm and Sibeal. Kilgannon seemed at once both peaceful and isolated. Matthew had already returned to university and I knew we would miss him every day again, but we were busy, for it was time for us to prepare for the winter.

The men went on the cattle drive again this year, but Alex stayed behind. Thomas and Angus were joined instead by several of the younger men who were anxious to take part. Angus had laughed at Alex's delighted expression when told that the party was well filled. To my surprise Gilbey's request to join the group was readily welcomed. He was thrilled. When I told Alex of my amazement, he shrugged and said Gilbey needed the experience. He stood at my side and grinned as we watched the herders ride off.

The next two days it rained but we were merry, for Alex had determined that the women were much too melancholy about the men being gone. He was loud and silly as he roamed the castle, and I could stand still and listen to his laughter ring from wherever he was. Soon we all were laughing. The third morning dawned clear and bright, if cool, and Alex woke me with a kiss. He wore ancient trews and a warm shirt and told me to wear an old gown and walking shoes and my warm cloak. He left with a smile but without an explanation. When I came downstairs he was strapping a bundle to his back and told me with a grin that we were going for a walk, but refused to say where. He told

Ellen that the boys were hers for the day and warned them to behave. Ellen laughed as we left.

We walked around the edge of the loch, the mountains reflected clearly this morning in the still water, and went into the trees at the far end, walking on the thick layer of fallen leaves. The path was steeper here, but we walked quickly, hand in hand. Alex would not tell me where we were going and laughed when I asked. His expression, free of the worry that had been his for months, was merry. *I would go anywhere he wished just to hear him laugh like this,* I thought. It had been far too long since my husband had been carefree.

At the entrance to the pass he turned away from it and followed a trail I would have missed on my own. It led sharply upward, following a stream that plummeted to the loch below. We climbed for what seemed like a very long time, Alex helping me up the largest boulders and holding back the branches where they overhung the track. When at last we reached the top of the hill, I gasped with delight. From here the view seemed never-ending. Kilgannon spread out before us, the loch flowing into the sea and the sea swirling around the near islands and then rushing to the far islands in the distance. To the north the hills and lochs of the western coat were shimmery in the pale autumn light, the hills lit with the last of the summer's bright heather and the lochs glowing silver between them. To the south we could see the coast fall away from our peninsula. The blue mountains wrapped around us to the east and north and southeast. It felt like we stood on the edge of the sky. Alex gestured to the glen below us. "This is why Gannon stayed here, lass," he said softly.

"It's so beautiful, Alex."

"Aye," he said, and we stood in silence for a few moments on the top of the ridge, watching the light play across the landscape. He kissed me as the cool autumn wind whirled around us and then urged me on once again, ignoring my questions, his eyes merry. He followed the path and I followed him, turning often to drink in the blues and grays spread out below me. A few moments later he paused.

"I suspect that ye soon will refuse to go on," he said, and I nodded. "All right, then, we'll go no farther." He grinned at me. I looked at him and then around us. We were in a small clearing, flat here, trees sheltering us from the worst of the wind. Behind him rose a large mound of rock and dirt. To my left was a lovely view of the mountains north of Loch Gannon and Skye beyond that, the ocean surrounding it a deep slate blue. Alex spun on his heel as my eyes returned to him and marched off around the mound of rock with a glance over his shoulder. When I pursued him I found a small clearing on the other side. A ledge, to be precise. A large ledge, to be sure, but still a ledge, which overlooked the pass below, the path clearly visible as I peered down at it and then turned. The mound that had seemed to be rock and dirt proved to be a cave about twenty feet deep, the opening wide and tall, the floor carpeted with pine needles and showing signs of past fires.

"Alasdair's cave," he said, and looked triumphant as he swung the bundle from his back. "My great-great-grandfather, the first Alasdair, or Alexander, MacGannon, used to post men here to watch the pass so no one would approach Kilgannon unnoticed. Now, of course, it's easier to watch from the houses of Glengannon." He waved across the pass at the village that was not far but out of sight from here, then untied the bundle, pulling packets of food and a bottle of wine from the folds of three plaids. Grinning at me, he spread one plaid on the ledge before the cave and placed the food on it, then spread the other two in the cave on top of a pile of pine needles. He lit a fire while I watched. "I thought ye might want a bit of food, lass, after our walk. Come and join me."

"This is wonderful," I sighed. The wind rustled in the trees above us, but we were sheltered here from its chill. "Why didn't you tell me?"

He tried not to laugh. "I wanted it to be a surprise. After

we eat I'm going to seduce ye." He leaned back on one arm and watched my reaction.

"Seduce me." I was trying to remember the date of my visit to the doctor in London. I decided it had been long enough.

"Aye," he said. "Do ye ken what today is?"

"No."

He lifted his cup in salute to the sky. "The ninetieth day!"

We laughed together, but I felt suddenly shy. It had been months since we'd made love thoroughly. We'd been affectionate and often inventive, but not more. He had obviously planned this well and wanted me to be enthusiastic. I wondered if I'd have to feign ardor. But as we talked and ate I relaxed, and a short while later it seemed the most natural thing in the world to be undressed outdoors with the trees as witnesses, to savor each other's body in a long, slow reawakening. It was natural to give him pleasure as I took mine and then to be wrapped in plaids on a bed of pine needles, Alex's arms around me as he murmured words of love. I kissed him one more time, and we closed our eyes for just a moment.

He woke me when the wind was rising and the shadows were long. The fire had burned itself out while we slept and he kicked the embers apart, then helped me dress. I helped him bundle the cups and empty bottle, and he kissed me softly as he wrapped my cloak around me. "I'll long remember this day, Mary Rose. Thank ye for coming with me without an explanation, and for being my dear lady."

I wrapped my arms around him, looking into the tops of the trees that guarded the pass. "I'll remember this day too, my love. Thank you for it." I kissed him once more before we left.

The return trip seemed much shorter. We stopped only once, at the spot where we'd paused to admire the view. Alex surprised me by jumping off the path and onto a ledge some four feet below, to stand in an empty eagle's nest.

Rummaging through it and at last picking something up, he climbed back to me and opened his hand, showing me a small brown stone.

"What is it?" I asked as I picked it up and turned it over. It looked like an ordinary stone, speckled with amber swirls and worn smooth by water. I looked up at him, puzzled.

"It's an eagle stone, lass, a stone from an eagle's nest. It's believed to be a talisman, to protect against miscarriage."

"I thought you didn't believe in the old ways."

He smiled. "I am a Gael, Mary Rose. If it works I'll be most remorseful for my past skepticism. But if we've created a child this day, I would use everything I know to protect it." I kissed him, put the stone in my pocket, and took his hand. We arrived at Kilgannon just as the sun was setting and a cold evening wind rising and were greeted warmly by everyone. No one except the boys asked where we'd been, but Berta pulled broken pine needles from my hair and wordlessly handed them to me, her eyes twinkling.

The men returned from the cattle drive without incident, with stories and news as well. The east was full of talk of an uprising to come. Some rumors had James Stewart already in Scotland, walking the moors and raising his own troops, but Alex snorted in derision at that. The stories he and Angus credited the most were the ones that told of French aid—men and gold—being shipped to the eastern clans for an uprising in the spring. They exchanged looks and said little in front of me, though I was certain that they talked about it at length when they were alone. But nothing came of the rumors, and we settled into the final preparations for winter.

The oath-taking was held as usual just before All Hallows' Eve, and this year Malcolm came, after writing first to ask permission. His behavior was too perfect and I wondered what he wanted, but I said nothing to Alex, willing to let him enjoy his repaired family. Malcolm was the first to swear, and he lifted the pewter cup high for all to see as he knelt before his brother and swore his loyalty in loud, clear tones. Ian and Jamie followed, then Angus, and I relaxed and enjoyed the spectacle, glad to have discord behind us.

Gilbey was among those swearing fealty for the first time. "I have no one else, Lady Mary," he had said, peering at me through the lank hair that always fell into his eyes. "I am very happy here. I'd like this to be my home." I had kissed his cheek, bringing him scarlet, and thanked him.

"You will always have a home here, Gilbey," I said, knowing that Alex would echo my words, for he had said the same to me many times. Gilbey waved aside my thanks, but I could tell he was as moved as I. I remembered our conversation now as Gilbey turned from swearing his oath and found me with his eyes, his smile triumphant, his step stronger. What a difference a year had made in this man.

But not in Alex. He looked the same as the night I'd met him, as handsome and as sure of himself. Tonight he was aglow, from the whisky, no doubt, but I knew it was more. He was happy. As I was. Next to me Ellen smiled as wee Donald swore his oath and roared something in Gaelic that set the room echoing his words. Alex grinned and pushed him playfully, and wee Donald turned to find Ellen. I thought of Louisa's phrase for Robert's behavior: *eternal courtship,* she had called it. It was fitting for these two. A year ago wee Donald had begun courting my Ellen, and still there was no sign of any movement in their relationship. I shook my head. Alex and I were more impetuous than they, but it suited me. I could not imagine life any different.

Winter set in just as the clansmen left for home, and we settled in to endure it. My family came for Christmas again this year and they arrived on the eighteenth, bearing gifts. And news. Nothing surprising or interesting, we determined, and decided to ignore the world for a few weeks and enjoy one another's company. Matthew had returned home for the holidays, full of news of the discontent in the east, but without news of an uprising. He was enjoying the university greatly, and he looked older and more sophisticated. When I told him as much he laughed. "I'm still me, Mary," he said.

Angus pushed him playfully. "As if we'd tolerate ye becoming someone else," he said, and Matthew laughed again with him.

"Je suis content," Matthew said, flaunting his impeccable French accent. I smiled as the others hooted at him.

That's just how I feel, I thought. *I am content.*

TWENTY-SIX

THE YEAR 1715 BEGAN WITH THE FIRST-FOOTING, WILL anxious to enjoy the tradition again and the clan delighted to have him join them. He was so silly and such a willing participant that I laughed all night and forgot Malcolm watching us from the side, as always with that superior air. To my dismay Malcolm and Sibeal had surprised us by joining us for New Year's, and at times I had wondered if they were ever going to leave. Theirs was quite a different marriage than mine. And than Seamus and Lorna's. Lorna's baby, a big healthy boy, had been born without incident and had been named, to everyone's amusement, Gannon Mac-Donald. Seamus was not a foolish man.

Nor was my husband. He visited with his brother in a polite manner, but it was not the same. There were no shared looks or laughter, although Malcolm did try to create the mood several times. I wondered if Malcolm actually thought we'd all forget what had happened. Did he mistake his brother's endurance for approval? I kept my thoughts to myself, or actually on other things, for I was with child again. Louisa and Berta spent hours concocting special teas and herbal drinks for me. I knew I worried them, but I felt fine, and although I told myself it was foolish, I kept the eagle stone with me at all times.

Matthew left just after the new year to return to school. We would not see him again until summer. We'd all miss him, but he was obviously anxious to return. Gilbey sent him off with greetings to their now mutual friends, and I wondered if Gilbey was not wishing he could go along. Life for him here, I thought, must often be boring. I was relieved when Malcolm and Sibeal left us as well, off to Skye to visit her family. With luck they'd not return for a long while. And then the month was over and my family was gone as well. I was alone often then, for Ellen spent much of her time with wee Donald, and Alex and Angus rode to all the clan lands, making sure all was well. I worked on the accounts, but there was not much to do, and I roamed the halls with Berta, finding that she was, as always, efficient and thorough. The boys spent most of their time with Gilbey, and the winter days were very long. I dreamed of summer and a babe in my arms.

But it was not to be. On Easter morning I miscarried again and could not face the Easter celebration. The news from the other clans was not cheering either, for everyone spoke of rebellion and the troops that James Stewart was sending with French gold to the eastern seaboard. I spent the day in my bed, crying. Alex was torn between his duty to attend the Easter festivities and being with me, but I sent him from me with tears and the assurance that I would be well soon. He left me at last, his expression bleak. I mourned for this child and for the others we had lost and cried until I slept. I think I slept for a month, for I remember little of that spring except for the day I found the eagle stone in a pocket and realized I'd not worn that skirt since February. I held the small stone in my hand and wondered if it had any power or if I was being ridiculous. But I could not help feeling that if I'd had the stone with me I'd have the child as well.

I told Alex my thoughts one afternoon as we stood on the dock watching the brigs being moored, the wind pulling at our hair. He turned to me, gently holding my chin in his hand. "It's no' yer fault, Mary," he said, and I felt my eyes fill with tears again.

"I know, Alex, but—"

"But nothing, lass. It's no' yer fault. We will accept what we are given, and no stone in yer pocket will change that." And then he laughed as he released my chin and stroked my cheek. "It's supposed to be the opposite, Mary Rose. I'm the Gael and yer the Englishmen. Yer supposed to be scoffing at my superstitions, lass, not me convincing ye." I laughed then as well, pulling him to me.

"Perhaps I've lived here too long."

"Aye." He kissed me tenderly and sighed. "Or not long enough, aye? We've no' had our lifetime together yet, lass."

"No," I said, and put my head on his shoulder, looking past him to the loch and the blue mountains beyond. *Blue water, blue mountains, blue eyes,* I thought. *No, I've not lived here long enough. Forever will not be enough.*

Alex left soon after that for a trip to the Low Countries and France, and Angus went with him. They'd be gone at least two weeks, perhaps three. I didn't want them to go. I stood on the dock in the rain with the boys and Gilbey and waved farewell with a heavy heart. We trudged into the house together, and the boys went off for their lessons while I wandered the halls and at last settled in the library. The rain had steadily increased and Kilgannon was very quiet today. I had no wish to find Berta or Thomas and interrupt their work, and I settled down to check over the accounts, but that was disturbing, for the first entry I saw was the one that noted the money Alex had given Malcolm. As if it were not enough that he'd almost killed Alex and that he'd stolen from him, Malcolm had had the audacity to beg a loan. And Alex, as Malcolm had known he would, had given him the money. Every time I saw the notation it irritated me, and today it was too much to deal with. I closed the ledger with a slam, trying to put Malcolm out of my mind. I pulled down Alex's box of sketches and opened it, expecting to see the drawings we'd looked at so often, but on the very top was one of me, standing in the mouth of Alasdair's cave, the wind tossing my hair around me and tugging my skirt hem up. *He'll be home soon,* I told myself as my eyes filled with tears. I put the sketches away. It was time to go and do something useful.

The next two days were uneventful, but the third brought Malcolm and Sibeal. They arrived unannounced yet again after visiting Skye, and I was less than pleased. Sibeal was warmer than she'd ever been, and she and Malcolm seemed to be at peace with each other. *Alex will be home soon*, I told myself again.

At midafternoon on the third day of their visit, a gloomy April day when the mist hung low over the water, the *Katrine* returned from her trip to London and Ireland loaded with goods and news. I went to meet the ship as she landed. The crew was tired but cheerful and waved as they approached. Their families stood with me on the dock, and the greetings surrounded me like a wave. The captain, usually a calm and measured man, was visibly agitated as he jumped onto the dock and brushed his wife's welcome aside. She and I exchanged a look of surprise.

"Has the laird returned, madam?" the captain asked anxiously.

"No," I said. "I expect him any day. Malcolm is here, though."

He met my eyes. "Malcolm is here?" I nodded, feeling the all-too-familiar tightness in my chest. The captain seemed lost for a moment, then squared his shoulders. "I give ye this letter, Lady Mary, from Laird Alex. I'd hoped he'd beaten me home, though I dinna see the *Mary Rose*. Read it when yer alone, will ye not?" He handed me the sealed letter as if it might explode in my hand. I looked at him in confusion and began opening the letter. "No, lady," the captain said, putting a hand on mine. "Dinna open it here. And dinna let anyone ken ye've received word from Alex."

"Why?" I whispered, his agitation contagious.

"Read the letter, madam."

"You know what it contains."

His troubled eyes met mine, and he shook his head. "Not

for certain, but I ken what I was told. It's best ye tell no
one."

"I see." I put the letter in my pocket.

As soon as I could I went to the library. The captain had
brought other letters as well—one from Louisa, another
from Rebecca—and I put those aside now as I tore Alex's
open. There were two letters, not one. Alex's agent had
written to Alex, and Alex had written to me enclosing the
agent's letter with his. William Burton wrote that the *Diana*
had been in London recently and was now in the Mediterranean but was due to return to London very soon. She had
been renamed and repainted, but he felt there was no mistake. It was the same ship and the same captain, and he
awaited Alex's instructions. Alex's letter said they were going to find the *Diana* and would be home when they had.

It was a very long evening. I went to bed as soon as I
could, pleading exhaustion. I had not lied. The strain of the
evening had enervated me. But in my own room I could not
sleep and rose again to pace before the fire. *I must find a
way to get Malcolm and Sibeal to leave at once,* I decided. I
stirred the fire, wondering how I could do that and how
warm it was in London this evening, then settled into one of
the chairs to read my letters.

Becca wrote that she'd had her baby, a healthy girl she
had named Sarah Anne after the child's grandmothers. *I
pray, my dear Mary, that she finds a friend as dear to her as
you are to me, though a great ocean separates us.* I sipped my
wine and watched the fire. *How I miss you, Becca,* I thought,
and how I envy you your sweet daughter. I sighed and read on.
She wrote of how happy she was, although she confessed
that sometimes she was overwhelmed with loneliness and
the feeling of being very far from home. *This is my home now,*
she wrote, *but sometimes, when the rain falls and the roses
smell a certain damp way, I remember us being girls and I
miss who I was then. Do you ever feel this way?*

"My dear Becca," I whispered to the letter, "I do know
how you feel." I sighed again and reached for Louisa's

letter. My aunt wrote of the affairs in London, both political and love. The names were often unfamiliar to me now, and I realized as I had last July how very distant all that seemed. No one but the Whigs was pleased to have George as king, but while London complained and bickered, no one was interested in changing it.

I woke early, to bright sunlight for a change, and was busy at once with the boys and the household. Berta was thrilled to have a chance to hang the laundry outside, and Mrs. M. was convinced that the charm she'd made the night before had brought the sun to us. It was midmorning before I got into the library and then I came to an abrupt halt. Malcolm was searching the drawers of the desk.

"What are you doing?" I asked.

"Looking," he said, straightening and smiling boyishly.

"For what, Malcolm?"

"I heard ye got a letter from Alex. I thought to read it."

"Why?" His audacity amazed me, and I felt my anger grow.

He shrugged. "I miss him. Who could not miss Alex? I know I shouldn't read yer private correspondence, but I wanted to hear how he is doing on his trip. Forgive me, Mary?"

Alex, I thought, *I am harboring your enemy.* "No," I said. The word hung in the air, and his eyes narrowed before he lowered them. When he looked up he was in control once more and smiled slowly.

"I'm sure Alex will," he said. "Mary, are ye not making too much of this? What did the letter from the agent say?"

"Why do you want to read it? Are you afraid it's about you?"

He shook his head. "No."

"Liar," I said, watching his smile fade and his eyes flash with anger. He did not answer and I turned to leave, but he was quicker. As I reached the doorway he grabbed my arm and leaned over me, his tone threatening.

"Do not misunderstand our positions, Mary. I am the MacGannon here, not ye. Ye may not speak to me so."

"You are not the MacGannon, Malcolm," I said with contempt. "You are the MacGannon's younger brother."

"I meant," he said, emphasizing each word, "that I am of the bloodline. Ye've only married into it. Dinna equate the two."

"I do not. I would never equate you and Alex."

"Understand this well, sister." His eyes were hostile and his grip painful. "I will not have ye coming between me and my brother again. Take yer dirty suspicions and go among the women."

I lifted my chin and met his look with disdain. "Release me," I said icily, and he loosened his grip but did not let me go. He watched me through narrowed eyes, then smiled and tilted his head.

"Mary," he said, his tone cajoling now. "Can we not be friends? I thought we'd settled the differences between us." I took a deep breath and then laughed shrilly, the sound echoing. Where was everyone? Most times it seemed I could hardly move without climbing over someone, and now, when I needed someone to come by, no one was in sight. "Can we not be friends?"

"Never. I cannot forget what you have done, Malcolm. And I will not forgive you. Perhaps Alex will, but I never will." I moved my arm again. "Let me go."

His grip tightened. "Mary, I only wanted to help ye with the business affairs. That's why I wanted to know what the agent said."

"Of course." I shook my head at his pretense. "How stupid do you think I am, Malcolm? Do you have another plot, perhaps another attempt on your brother's life? The last three failed. What have you done now? What will we discover next?" He twisted my arm cruelly, and our eyes met again. I considered screaming and took a deep breath. A hand reached between us and clasped Malcolm's wrist. We both looked up to see Gilbey standing behind me, his face pale with anger.

"Release her at once," Gilbey said through clenched teeth.

Malcolm laughed harshly, but he let me go. "Dinna mistake this, Gilbey. It was nothing." I rubbed my arm and watched him.

"I do not mistake what I saw, Malcolm," said Gilbey, his tone fierce. "And what I heard. I will tell Alex that you were holding Mary against her will. No doubt he'll find that most interesting."

Malcolm moved next to Gilbey. Gilbey was taller but Malcolm twice as wide. They glared at each other. "Ye saw nothing, Macintyre," Malcolm said.

"I saw you holding my chief's lady against her will."

"Yer chief," spat Malcolm. "Yer chief. Ye saw nothing."

"I know what I saw, and Alex will hear of it," Gilbey said.

"Aye, Gilbey, run to Alex." Malcolm sneered at both of us. "Ye both are scared rabbits. Run to Alex. Bah!" He pushed past Gilbey and disappeared around the corner.

"Thank you, Gilbey," I said at last, turning to him. His face was flushed but when he spoke his tone was even.

"You're welcome, Mary. I hope he did not hurt you."

"No. He only made me angry," I said, though I knew my arm would be bruised. Gilbey nodded.

"And me. He is not to be trusted, Mary."

"No." I looked down the corridor, but Malcolm was gone.

"Mary." Gilbey's voice had a new note, and I turned. "Berta says she must speak with you at once. I was looking for you."

What now, I wondered? "What is it, Gilbey?"

"You should talk to Berta."

I nodded. Whatever it was, the news was not good. Wonderful.

I found Berta in the kitchen with Mrs M. and a hysterical kitchen maid. The girl, Leitis, only fifteen or so, was sobbing into Mrs. M.'s ample bosom as Berta stood over them. The two women looked up as I entered and exchanged a look that did not bode well for my fragile good humor. *No doubt she's with child,* I thought with exasperation, and sighed. I could not imagine what else could be so very distressing. In some households a pregnant unmarried girl would be cast out, and I had no idea what was done at Kilgannon. At Mountgarden I had dealt with the situation for the first time two years ago and had been incapable of turning the girl out. I could not imagine doing so here and not to pretty young Leitis, who had served us so cheerfully for months. My suspicions were quickly confirmed. Berta and Mrs. M. were both troubled by the news but more by my possible reaction to it. I watched them as they fussed over the girl and cast sidelong looks my way. Leitis blew her nose and wiped her eyes and was at last able to stand before me in some sort of order, although she still took deep ragged breaths and wrung her hands. She waited for my response and I sighed again, realizing I was unwilling to add to her misery. I smiled and suddenly the situation changed. Instead of Mrs. M. and Berta wondering what the mistress would do, we were three women sorting out the problems of a foolish girl.

"Sit down, Leitis, and talk to me." I motioned to a nearby bench and she joined me. "Tell me who the father is."

"He says he loves me," she sobbed.

"Of course. Let's call him and I shall talk with him," I said, thinking that this would be quickly solved.

"Oh, madam," she shrieked, and I had to wait for her to control herself. "He canna marry me."

"Why?" I asked, but I knew why. The man was married. Leitis didn't answer, she just cried, and the more I pressed the worse it got. Berta stepped in and assured me that she would discover who it was and talk with me later. I nodded and left, grateful to escape.

I made my way to the library, where I sank into one of

the big chairs and looked at the ceiling. *Why do these things always happen when Alex is gone?* I wondered. No doubt Thomas will arrive any moment to tell me the stables are on fire and English soldiers are in the yard. What should I do now? I was still wondering an hour later when Berta knocked on the door. She entered when I called, leading a sobbing Leitis by the hand.

"Madam, ye must hear this for yerself," Berta said, her eyes indignant. "Tell her," she commanded the girl.

"I was to tell ye it was the laird, madam, but it wasna him." Leitis was wailing now, and I closed my eyes for a second. I wished to be anywhere but this room at this moment.

"Why were you to tell me it was Alex?"

Leitis moaned. "He said it would serve him right."

"Who said that?" I asked.

"He told me the laird had been with all the girls and I believed him, but then Berta made them all tell me and he wasna and I've been such a fool, madam, and I hope ye can find it in yer heart to forgive me." She had drifted into Gaelic and sank now to the floor, continuing. Between her sobs and hiccups I could not understand all she said. "And I canna marry him. What will I do?"

"We'll sort it out, Leitis."

"Oh, this one canna be sorted out, madam, and ye'll be turning me out and I'll starve on the hillside. Oh, Lady Mary, can ye ever forgive me? I dinna mean to cause no trouble."

I smiled while a terrible suspicion grew within me. "Leitis, I won't turn you out," I said kindly. *Oh, Alex,* I thought. "Let's start with the story. Tell me. Who is the father?"

She gave me such a wild look that I thought she'd bolt from the room. "Lord Malcolm, Lady Mary," she wailed, and I closed my eyes.

TWENTY-SEVEN

I STARTED LAUGHING. I KNEW IT WASN'T FUNNY, BUT I HAD to force myself to stop. When the story came out it was pathetic. Leitis had conceived at the end of December. Malcolm had told her that he loved her, that Sibeal did not understand him, and that if he were free he would marry her in a moment. But, of course, he was not free. When Leitis had told him she was pregnant, he had told her to say the child was Alex's. He'd said that Alex slept with all the young girls and would not remember whether he'd slept with her or not, that many of the children of the clan were Alex's bastards and that she'd be able to stay if she was bearing the chief's child. How anyone could be so gullible amazed me, but she was very young. Berta, bless her, had been furious and had gathered every maid and helper in the house, all of whom told Leitis that they had never been with Alex. I listened grimly. If my marriage had not been as sound as it was, this could have been a death knell. *Damn him*, I thought savagely.

Before dark everyone in the castle had heard the news. Sibeal and Malcolm did not appear at the next meal or for the evening, and Berta's girls told me that they could be heard loudly arguing. *Poor Sibeal*, I thought, and wished again, for the thousandth time, that Alex were here. And yet, I told myself, who knew what would be happening now if he were? He would not take the slur to his honor lightly, and what he would have said to Malcolm I could only guess. In his absence I would have to talk to Malcolm. After this morning I had no wish to see him again, but it would have to be done. I told myself that tomorrow would be soon enough. Poor Sibeal. How bitter it must be to find this out about her husband. I wondered how I would react to the news that Alex had been unfaithful. When I pictured Alex in another woman's arms I grew enraged at my own creation and I shook my head to clear the image, then went to tend the boys.

They were still awake and I sat with them, talking about inconsequential things before I kissed each of them and received their sleepy hugs in return. "Sleep well," I said, and closed the door, my heart much lighter than before.

But they did not sleep well. None of us did. In the wee hours a knock came at my door and I sat up, struggling against the sleep still holding me. Ian was in the doorway, his eyes huge and his expression frightened. "It's Malcolm and Sibeal," he said. "There are horrible noises coming from their room. It sounds . . ." he faltered and I started past him, then turned back.

"Where's your brother?" I demanded.

"I told him to stay in bed," Ian said, and I nodded.

"Good. Go to him, my love. Stay there until I come to you."

"Don't go, Mama," he said shakily. He paused and swallowed. "It sounds like a monster in their room," he whispered.

I stopped then and squeezed him to me. "There is no monster in their room, Ian," I said calmly while my heart raged. "Just Malcolm and Sibeal. I'll go and find out what is the matter."

He raised his chin bravely. "I'll go with you."

I shook my head. "No. You will go take care of your brother. Stay with him. I will come to you when I can." He nodded.

* * *

The corridors had never seemed so long. My candle flickered with my movements as I ran. I saw no one until I rounded the last corner and saw Gilbey standing in the hall, a knife in his hand. "What are you doing?" I whispered as I moved to his side.

His eyes were wild as they met mine. "If he hits her again, I will stop him," he said grimly, and I turned to look at the door in horror. "It's quiet now. I could hear the noise from my room."

"So could the boys," I said. His expression changed and softened as he looked at me.

"I dinna think on the boys." His accent, so carefully neutral most of the time, slipped back whenever he was unsettled.

"We'll see to them after," I said, and we looked at the door together. It was silent on the other side. I knocked then and called. "Sibeal, Malcolm, it's Mary. Open the door." There was no answer. I knocked again and there was still no answer. I tried the latch. The door was not locked, and I let it swing open.

She was alone, sobbing in a heap on the floor. The room looked like a madman had careened through it. *Perhaps that was exactly what happened,* I thought, and took a deep breath as I walked slowly toward her. She did not at first acknowledge my presence or stop sobbing, but when I knelt next to her she threw herself in my arms and spoke incoherently. When she quieted I pulled back from her and looked at her face. Her cheeks, still red now from the blows, would be bruised by morning, and a nasty red welt was on her neck, handprints there as well. I stared at them in horror. Behind me, Gilbey cursed and, turning, strode out of the room. I gave him only a moment's thought as I turned back to her.

"Mary," she croaked. "Why, Mary? Why would he do that? He says it's my fault. Where did he go?" She sobbed uncontrollably.

Hours later no one still seemed to know where Malcolm

was. He had not been seen leaving. No horse was missing, nor boat, and it seemed unlikely that he would have left on foot. All of his things were here, even his money. Where could he have gone on foot without money? I could only imagine that he was being sheltered by a friend, no doubt the same one who told him of the letter, I thought bitterly. But no one told us anything of him.

Sibeal spoke very little. Most of the time she stared off into the distance, tears trickling down her cheeks. After two days I roused her and made her come downstairs, where she sat in the hall, pale and listless, and let the noise of everyday activity flow around her. The boys tried to talk to her, but she only smiled vacantly, and they did not try again. I must have asked myself a thousand times where Alex was. Malcolm would never have behaved as he had if his brother or Angus, or even Matthew, had been home.

Malcolm walked into the hall a week later, on a rainy morning when Gilbey and Thomas had gone to Glengannon looking for him. I rose, flanked by the boys, and faced him. He bowed and smiled as though he'd come for tea, while he searched the hall.

"Where is my wife?" His tone was light, his expression calm, and I felt my temper rise. Several of the men who had been about the hall gathered now, watching us with wary glances.

"Sibeal is upstairs, Malcolm," I said. "She—"

He interrupted me with a sharp gesture. "We argued, Mary. It was nothing more than that. Dinna exaggerate."

I tried to keep my voice even. "I am not exaggerating, Malcolm. I've said nothing beyond that she is upstairs. But you may not see her." Dougall came to stand at my side.

"Oh?" Malcolm looked at me with scorn. The boys looked from him to me, Jamie drawing nearer to my skirts. The men stiffened and waited. "Really? I'd advise ye to stay out of my marriage There are things ye dinna understand, Countess." He spun on his heel and loped up the stairs. I stood with my mouth open for a moment and then followed him, the boys and Dougall and several of the men at my heels. Berta stood in the hallway outside Sorcha's room, looking at the closed door. I did not even pause but flung it open, and there was Sibeal, crying as she sat up in bed, her arms about Malcolm. Both of them looked up as I entered.

Sibeal gave a shaky laugh, her smile triumphant. "I knew he'd return," she said, and Malcolm smiled his sly smile. I looked from him to Sibeal and closed my mouth.

"Leave us, Mary. Yer not wanted here," said Malcolm.

"Not until Sibeal tells me that's what she wants."

She smiled at her husband. "It is. I knew he'd come."

I nodded then and backed out, pulling the boys with me. In the hallway I exchanged looks with Dougall, who shrugged. The men were already fading away, and I took each boy by the hand as we left. I do not believe I explained it well to them. How could I, when I did not understand it myself? There she was, the bruises he'd caused still vivid on her skin, and she had opened her arms to him. We walked along the loch and I did my best, but none of us was certain what had happened.

Malcolm and Sibeal left that afternoon. Malcolm stood aloof and did not bid me farewell, but Sibeal embraced me, and I peered into her eyes and tried one more time.

"Is this truly what you want?" I asked her. "You do know that you can stay here with us?"

She nodded with a slight smile and a shrug. "I love him, Mary," she said. Defeated, I released her and watched them ride away. Later I discovered that Malcolm had spent the week with a woman he'd often kept company with in Glengannon. Gilbey and Thomas would have found him that morning.

Alex came home the next day. They had been gone a month. I stood on the dock waiting for the *Mary Rose* to come around the last bend of the loch and watched as she sailed home with more than Alex: she was followed by the *Diana*. Alex, Angus, and the crews were triumphant, and the clan clamored for the story before they left the dock. I kissed my husband fervently and then settled in the hall to hear the tale with the others. The audience paid rapt attention as the travelers told the story in turn, each taking a piece and then watching as the other continued. When they were in France they learned that the *Diana* was due any day, so they waited for her, as well as the claret for the *Mary Rose*. She arrived a few days later, called the *Goddess* now, and Alex and Angus approached the captain at an inn onshore. They had argued before witnesses and had parted in anger, but the next morning when the captain awoke on the *Goddess*, his crew had evaporated and Kilgannon men were in possession of her. Asked how that had happened, Alex shrugged and said the crew had been amenable to persuasion. We all laughed. The captain was another matter and he left the ship vowing violence, saying the ship was his. He had, he declared, paid good money for her. Alex and Angus waited another day for *Mary Rose*'s cargo to arrive, and the captain arrived with the authorities in tow. It took some time to sort it all out, but the shipping agent and their cousin Ewan had smoothed things over. Alex left France in possession of their lives and the *Diana*. I did not for a moment believe that it had all been smoothed over so easily, but I was in no mood to quibble and rejoiced at their return.

And then Gilbey and Thomas and I took Alex and Angus to the library and told them what had happened in their absence. Alex and Angus listened with growing anger to the end. When Gilbey added the scene in the library with Malcolm, the change in Alex's mood was immediate.

"Lass, ye should have told me this at once," he said, rising. "Get me a horse, Thomas," he roared. I jumped up and followed him to the hall, but he did not slow his stride.

"Alex, what are you going to do?"

"Bring him back."

"And then what?" I blocked his way and he looked down at me, his rage visible.

"Mary, I have had enough. Malcolm has turned my life upside down for the last time. No man touches my wife. I'm going to bring him back."

"He's been gone since yesterday."

Alex nodded curtly. "Aye, but he has Sibeal with him. They canna travel quickly. We'll find them. And we'll bring him back."

"How?"

"With ease," he said. "Cowards dinna fight armed men."

"And then what?"

"I will tell the clan," Alex said, waving a hand in the air. "I will make his lying schemes public, Mary. No Mac-Gannon has done such things. I willna take his life, but I will shame him."

"If you do that, you will make him an enemy."

His eyes, a frosty blue, met mine. "And what do ye suppose he is the now? No, I have been patient long enough, more than long enough. It's time to tell the truth. I willna shield him again. And I willna discuss it further, lass."

He stepped around me. I watched them leave.

They returned two days later, Alex in the lead, then Gilbey and Angus flanking Malcolm, their expressions grim. Sibeal rode behind them with the others, weeping. At the rear were the assorted clansmen and their families who had been summoned from their homes along the way. When they reached the meadow where the Games were held, Alex called for Thomas to gather the rest of the clan. He stayed on his horse, waiting, as the people collected. The other men dismounted, forming an ever-increasing circle as the clan arrived. Malcolm stood alone and defiant in the center, meeting no one's eyes, his outrage evident in his stance. At the side of the ring Sibeal sobbed, but no one comforted her. I stood in the crowd, watching Alex and his brother, my heart pounding. Alex had not come to me nor had he acknowledged I was there. His color was high, his fury obvious, and he made no attempt to hide it. When the crowd had grown enough to please him, Alex dismounted and circled his brother, pointing at him.

"Behold my brother, Malcolm," Alex shouted, "and ye see the man who poisoned me in France and almost killed me, the man who conspired to steal the *Diana*." He told in full detail the story as the crowd listened with growing dismay, shifting position and meeting one another's eyes in discomfort. "And so we searched," Alex said, his voice hoarse now with emotion, "for a week on the coast of Cornwall for the crew of the *Diana* or for any piece of her. And Malcolm was with us, pretending to search as well, when all the while he knew that she had not gone down, while the money from his sale of her lay in his purse. And Malcolm knew it. He lived among us and kept his silence. And his money." Alex faced the circle again and spread his arms. "I am not asking ye to try him nor to punish him. I ask only that ye see what he is and to acknowledge with me what he has done, so that the entire clan knows Malcolm MacGannon for what he is: a man who betrays his brother, who steals from his family, who canna keep his wedding vows, and who beats his wife when she protests, a man who tries to place the blame for his infidelity on his brother, a man who threatens my wife in her own home in my absence. See him for what he is. And never welcome him here again." He took a deep breath and looked at Malcolm with contempt. "I have no brother." Alex broke through the circle and strode toward the castle, looking at no one. The clan faded away, avoiding one another's eyes, and few spoke at all.

Malcolm stood alone in the meadow until Sibeal ran to him.

Alex did not come to bed that night. I found him in the chapel just before dawn, sitting in a pew, his head bent over his hands. I sat next to him and stroked his back and he turned a ravaged face to me. "Mary," he said, tears on his cheeks. "What have I done?" He looked into the distance. "What have I done?"

I kissed his cheek. "I'd say you lost your temper."

"Lost my temper." He shook his head. "Lost my mind, I fear. What was I thinking?"

"You were angry."

"Aye. I was that." He sat back against the pew with a sigh. "What have I done?"

"You told them what happened."

His eyes met mine, his voice ragged. "I have lost my brother, lass. I have shamed him before the whole clan."

I considered before answering. "All you did was tell the truth, Alex," I said at last.

"Aye, but Mary, ye don't shame yer own family by telling its secrets to the world."

"The clan is your family, Alex. You did not tell the world."

He sighed. "I shouldna have done it."

"Probably. But, my love, remember what he did. He almost killed you, and he feels no remorse for it. He almost killed you so that you wouldn't discover that he was plotting to steal from you. More than once, Alex. More than once. He lied for years. He looked into your eyes and he lied. And then he tried to kill you and he looked into your eyes and denied it." I took a deep breath. "If only for what he did to Sibeal he deserved it. If you had seen her, Alex, you would not be so distraught now."

"I shouldna have done it."

I nodded. "Probably not. But you did. And your sin in shaming him doesn't even begin to compare with his." I looked at my bruised arm, tender still.

"I lost my temper, lass. I was out of control."

"Yes."

He looked at his hands. "As he was when he attacked Sibeal."

I shook my head. "That's not the same. Even when you were in the midst of your rage you still had some control. You did not touch him, nor did you let anyone else."

"I was afraid I'd kill him," he whispered.

"Alex, my love, he has no such reservations about you."
We sat in silence, and I took his hand in mine and looked at
the two of them against my skirt. "Alex," I said slowly,
"Malcolm feels no remorse. He can justify any deed, no
matter what it is. Who knows what was next? Even if you
will not protect yourself, you have others to think about.
Your sons and the clan, Alex, they need your protection.
And me." He did not answer and I looked at him, seeing the
dark circles under his eyes and the golden stubble on his
cheeks gleaming in the dim light. He looked depleted.
Damn Malcolm, I thought viciously. *Damn him.* My voice
held none of my anger as I continued. "My love, you cannot
allow him to seduce the girls of Kilgannon and go unpunished. Even if you choose to forget that he almost killed you
and that he stole from you—from all of us—you cannot let
him prey on innocent girls under your care."

After a very long moment he nodded and stole a quick
glance at me. "Aye, I ken yer right on some of it, lass, but I
canna forgive myself. I lost control. Since I was ten years old
I've been training myself to think, always to think, before
acting. It does no' come natural to me, Mary, but I learned
it, and I've rarely broken my own rule." He took a ragged
breath. "In all those years I've broken it twice. Once at the
crofthouse, remember, when ye'd left. And now I act like an
idiot and go roaring about the meadow, pointing a finger at
my brother." He shook his head. "I dinna just shame Malcolm. I shamed myself." When I took my hand from his he
did not move, just stared into the air, as though expecting
my rejection. I smoothed his hair back and kissed his cheek.

"I love you, Alex," I said, and took his hand again.

He turned to me slowly. "How? How can ye love such a
man?"

"I love the most wonderful man in the world," I said
with a soft laugh. "But he is human. And he should hold
himself up to the same mirror that he uses for everyone
else."

"I canna," he said.

"You mean you will not, Alex."

"As ye will, Mary. I behaved very badly."

"No," I said fiercely, tired of his self-blame. "You told the truth. That's all you did, Alex. You did not lie; you did not embroider the truth. You didn't even tell them all of it. You did not beat him. You didn't punish him. You told the truth and then you let him go. And it was time, my love. You've protected Malcolm long enough. Let him live with the consequences of his actions." We sat in silence for a long time.

At last Alex sighed and turned to me. "Did they go?"

"Yes." I nodded. "Very quickly too." He nodded but did not speak. "And I, for one," I said, "am glad of it." I watched the dim light cast shadows across his face, throwing the lines of his cheeks into relief. "Do you know what Ian said?"

"What?" His voice was very low.

"He said it sounded like a monster was in their room." Alex's eyes met mine, unreadable now. "Your sons heard Malcolm hitting Sibeal and her screaming for him to stop. Alex, if you had heard your sons' stories and done nothing, what would they think of you? What would the clan think of you? They would think that everyone else had to act in a reasonable fashion, but that the rules were different for Malcolm. Just for Malcolm. What kind of message would that be? Is that what you wish your sons to see? Better that they see you angry as you defend Sibeal and yourself—and me, my love—than that you let Malcolm hurt people while you look the other way. It would be a betrayal of all you've taught them." I paused and continued in a calmer tone. "You should not be ashamed, my love. You should be proud. You told the truth and damned the consequences. I'm not glad it happened, but I'm not sorry either."

He was silent for so long that I wondered what he was thinking, but at last he nodded and squeezed my hand. He held it to his lips and kissed my fingers. And then he met my eyes again, his tranquil now. "I love ye, Mary Rose," he said softly.

"I know you do, Alex," I said, looking into his eyes. "And I encourage it." He smiled at me.

TWENTY-EIGHT

I STRETCHED OUT ON THE PLAID WE HAD BROUGHT, PULL-
ing my skirts to my knees and settling down on my back
with a sigh of pure pleasure, then closed my eyes and soaked
in the warmth, listening to the roar of the surf breaking on
the other side of the headland.

"When was the last time we spent a day like this?" I
asked.

"When was the last time the sun was here for more than
an hour?" Alex answered, flinging himself down next to me.

We had stolen away and climbed up to the top of the hill
behind Kilgannon, admiring the view but most of all enjoying the sun. The mountains were grand every day, but the
sun was heavenly this late-summer afternoon. The summer
of 1715 had been wet and cold, and today was the first perfect day in over a month. Even the Kilgannon games had
been rained out. We had held them despite the weather, but
few attended and it was a soggy and less-than-successful
gathering. I felt Alex's shadow over me but did not open my
eyes as I lifted my arms to him.

"Mary," he said. "Mary Rose, I love ye, lass." His lips
were soft on mine and I felt his hair fall onto my cheek.

"And I you, my darlin' man."

"Thank ye for marrying me." He kissed my forehead.

"Thank you for asking."

He played with my hair where it spilled onto the plaid

next to him. "Do ye ever think on Robert and what yer life would have been like had ye married him?" I opened my eyes and looked at him, his eyes the same blue as the loch below us and as unfathomable.

"Yes," I said, and watched his expression close. "And I congratulate myself on my escape." I wrapped my hand around his neck, drew him to me, and kissed him again until he smiled.

"Yer a one." He stretched himself next to me and leaned on one elbow, his other hand on my stomach. My flat stomach. I stroked his face, watching his hair frame his cheekbones.

"I would like to have children with you, my love," I said.

"And I with ye, lass," he said, his eyes finding mine. "Get yerself well and we'll see what time brings." He looked out over the loch and glen and back to me. "I want ye well. I canna live without ye, Mary Rose. And when yer well, then we'll just have to practice. No doubt we're just doing it wrong."

"No doubt," I laughed, and he kissed me again, then sobered.

"Mary, are ye upset with me that I plan to sell the *Diana?*"

I turned onto my side to face him. "Upset? Why would I be upset, Alex? It's your ship."

"Aye, it is for a bit again anyway," he agreed.

"I would be upset if you sold the *Mary Rose* or *Gannon's Lady,*" I said. "But I'd never seen the *Diana* before you brought her home. As far as I'm concerned, anything that reminds us of Malcolm is not welcome here. I think it for the best. Why do you ask?"

"Ah, well, Thomas is no' so pleased. He thinks we could use her to start trading with the colonies."

"But you told me she was the oldest of all the brigs and that she needed repair. That's not a good ship to send on a far voyage."

"Aye, but we could have fixed her up. No, lass, I'm going

to sell her because she reminds me of what is not mine any longer. Do ye ken what I mean? Malcolm and I used to play on her when we were lads, and he took her without a thought of what had been. I canna feel the same. When I look at her all I see is Malcolm."

"And what did Angus think?"

"It was his idea to sell her."

"That doesn't surprise me. What will you do with the money?"

"I havena decided."

"Life is better now without him," I said quietly.

He nodded. "Aye, yer right, it is. And certainly more peaceful, no? But I canna help wondering what he's doing." I stroked his cheek but said nothing, thinking of the baby that Leitis had lost. Or gotten rid of. I had not asked many questions when Berta told me. Alex looked into the distance, lost in his own thoughts, and I watched the clouds, no threat today, pass behind his head. Suddenly he tensed and sat up, looking down the hill, sheltering his eyes with a hand. He swallowed a curse as he stood.

"What is it?" I sat up and rearranged my skirts as I saw the boy, Thomas's Liam, scrambling up the path below us.

"A runner coming for us," he growled, shifting his weight from one foot to the other. "All I wanted was an hour in the sun."

"What do you suppose it is?"

"Either we've received a message or someone's in the loch. Or someone's dead. It had better not be less."

"Sir," Liam said between gulps of air. "I am sorry to disturb ye, but my da said to tell ye a boat is in the loch and it looks like the MacKinnon and to apologize if yer angry."

"The MacKinnon." Alex's expression grew serious. He glanced at me and raised his eyebrows as if to say he knew no more than I. But he did, I was sure. The MacKinnon's visit worried him, not surprised him. And I was certain it had something to do with James Stewart. "Thank ye, lad," he said to Liam. "Tell yer da that he was right to fetch me. I'm on my way. Go and find Angus."

"Aye, sir." The boy nodded and darted back down the path.

I scrambled to my feet. "What does it mean?"

Alex looked out over the glen and then turned, his eyes slowly focusing on me. "I'm not sure, but something's in the wind again." He straightened his shoulders and pulled me to him fiercely. "We'll know soon enough," he said. "We have five minutes and then I must go and find out. Kiss me, lass, and we'll use the time well."

The MacKinnon stayed for two days, the only two perfect days of the summer. The first morning he was with us, Alex hastily arranged a hunting party and went off with most of the men, their work left undone in their hurry. The women stared after them as they left and muttered among themselves. I said nothing, but a feeling of foreboding surrounded me as I stood on the top step at the outer gate, watching Alex ride to the end of the loch and into the trees at the far side, his blond hair brilliant under the green bonnet. I felt an apprehension I had never felt before. And I could not shake the fear all day. It hung over me like a personal cloud though I spent the day in the sun, forsaking my own work. The boys and I rowed out onto the loch, and I watched them fish but catch nothing. They had been annoyed at having been left behind and were irritable at first, but soon their spirits rose, and by the end of the afternoon they were their usual good-natured and silly selves. They sang as we rowed ashore and carried their fishing poles as though they were weighted down.

The men arrived in the evening's gloom and settled in for a night's drinking. Alex had spent last night talking with the MacKinnon as well and he had come to bed in the wee hours, angry and smelling of whisky. When I had questioned him he had said only that, yes, it was James Stewart they were discussing, but, no, he'd not agreed to anything. This morning he'd explained that MacKinnon was here to get him to agree to raise the clan and to help raise the Highlands. He said he had no intention of doing either, but Alex had spent the day and the evening with the MacKinnon and although he was leaving in the morning, I feared that he might yet prove successful. The summer was bringing more than bad weather.

Tonight Alex was thoughtful as he prepared for bed and kissed me absently on the forehead. When he did not finish undressing but sat on the chair in front of the fireplace lost in thought, I climbed from the bed and went to kneel in front of him, asking him to tell me what was happening. His gaze, which had been far away, returned to me and he smiled wryly.

"I am being besieged, lass, and I am resisting. We've held our ground this time, but I fear this willna be the last. MacKinnon wants me to join the Earl of Mar in the east. Bobbing John Erskine. Ye ken why they call him Bobbing John?" I shook my head. "Mar was verra important under Queen Anne, and when King Geordie dinna recognize his worth he was most put out." Alex yawned. "Mar wrote a fawning letter to George, but that dinna work; Geordie dinna give him a place in his government. So now Bobbing John is leading a rebellion against the King. MacKinnon says all the clans are rising, but I've heard differently, and I said I needed more time and more information before I decided." He stroked my hair. "Dinna look at me that way, lass, I've not agreed to anything. Dinna fear that I am off to war. I've told ye I dinna like James Stewart." His smile was tired. "They'll be off in the morning, and no doubt this will pass as all the other rumors have. Put it from yer mind."

But I could not. And neither could Alex. The news spread quickly of the MacKinnon's visit, and within a week Murdoch was in the hall telling Alex of the other clans that were joining the rising. The MacKinnon had gone to visit the Macleans as well.

"And ye, Murdoch? Are the Macleans joining?" Alex asked his friend. His face was calm, but his hand gripped mine behind my skirts. Murdoch nodded and my heart contracted. Alex sounded undisturbed. "Are ye indeed?" he asked. "And what, besides a split head, do ye think of gaining from this exercise, Maclean?"

Murdoch shrugged. "I dinna ken if we'll be successful, Alex, but I canna stay under King Geordie's yoke the more. Ye ken what happened to the letter all the chiefs sent?"

"No, what?" Alex poured more whisky in Murdoch's glass as he listened to the other man's story of outrage. After George's accession to the throne a letter accepting his sovereignty had circulated the Highlands, signed by many but not all. That letter, like the one accepting Sophia as Anne's heir, had never reached Kilgannon. But the Macleans had signed it, hoping for peace.

Murdoch sighed. "He wouldna even open it. Wouldna even open it, Alex. He dinna read it. Well, he canna read English, but it wasna even read to him, he was that disinterested. It's an insult."

"Aye, it is that," said Alex, nodding.

"And ye ken what happened to my cousin?" Murdoch's eyes were bright. I watched him talk, this enormous man who was Alex's closest friend outside the clan, and I thought of Morag. She and Murdoch had married at Dunvegan in Skye in the early summer, on a rainy—what else this year?—day in June. The talk at the wedding had not been of the beautiful bride, though she had been, or of the fortunate groom, but of James Stewart. When the dancing was well under way, Morag had approached and embraced me. I'd murmured something polite in response as she followed my gaze across the room to where Murdoch and Alex stood with a group of men.

"Who knows how long I'll have my husband home. Or ye yers." Her eyes met mine, a deep sadness overlaying the happiness of the day. "James Stewart might have other plans. I've been foolish, Mary," she sighed, "keeping him waiting for so long while I was waiting for Alex. I dinna ken how much he meant to me, and now I may lose him. I have no wish to be a bride and a widow at once." She'd left me staring after her, and I remembered the moment now as I listened to her husband's arguments. *Morag,* I thought, *I would not have wished this for you.*

We had visitors or letters almost daily, and although I tried to believe Alex would not agree to join the rebellion, my hopes dimmed with every discussion. Angus worked the men very hard, drilling them in swordplay and horsemanship until they dropped, and the meadow was filled with the sounds of men shooting their pistols at targets. Only an idiot would not know what it meant, but I pretended to myself until the day Alex marched into the library.

"Mary," he said. "I must talk with ye." I looked up from the accounts I was working on and then glanced at Jamie, sprawled on the floor next to the desk, his nose in a book and his dog at his side. I nodded at Jamie, and Alex looked around the desk. "Jamie, lad," he said calmly, "go and read yer book elsewhere and take Robert the Bruce with ye. I must talk with Mary the now." Jamie looked at his father in surprise.

"Aye, Da," he said, but gave me a puzzled glance as he left. I watched him go through the door and then turned back to Alex.

"Well?" I asked. Alex was pacing in front of the fireplace.

"Mary," he said abruptly. "I've sold the *Diana*."

"Good. Did you get a good price?" I straightened my papers.

"Aye." He stopped in front of me, and I put the papers down and watched him. "And I bought pistols with the money."

"Pistols."

"Aye." Blue eyes met mine. "I'm simply being cautious."

"Cautious," I said. "You bought guns to be cautious?"

"Aye. My men must have the best."

"When did you do this?"

"Last week."

"You did not tell me."

"No."

"I see." I concentrated on the trim waist that I had so many times put my arms around. The waist of a stranger. "You did not tell me."

"Every time I started to, I thought of how angry ye'd be and I dinna want to argue with ye about this as we argued about Malcolm and Robert. Dinna look at me like that, Mary Rose. I dinna mean to not tell ye. I just—"

"Did not tell me."

He looked at me without flinching. "Aye. That's the truth of it, lass." I said nothing. His belt was worn at the buckle. "Mary, lass, look at me. I am simply being cautious. I dinna ken what will happen. But even if we do not join, it may come to us. We must be prepared. I was simply—"

"Preparing to go to war," I said flatly. He was silent, and we looked at each other. "Alex, are you going to join the rebellion?"

"I dinna ken, Mary. At this point, no."

"At this point."

"Aye."

"But that may change."

"I will tell ye if it does."

"Don't tell me, Alex. I won't want to hear it. I'll never forgive you if you leave. Never." He studied me for a moment, then nodded and left me alone with my fears.

That evening Alex and I climbed to the top of the keep to watch the sunset. We stood in silence, Alex preoccupied, as always these days. I sighed heavily as I watched his profile, afraid to ask for his thoughts. At last he reached for me, draping an arm around my shoulders and kissing my hair. "Beautiful, no?" He gestured to the sunset before us, magnificent tonight, the rose fading into the indigo line of the horizon, broken only by the uneven shapes of the islands offshore.

"Yes," I said, and wrapped my arms around his waist. "Alex?"

"Hmmm?"

"Do you remember when we met?" His eyes, focused and amused now, found mine, and he nodded.

"Aye, lass, I'm no' so old that I'm forgetting things yet. I remember it well."

"Do you remember telling me that it would be as I wished?" I could feel him stiffen under my arms and I waited.

"Lass, I promised only to give ye what I can, not what I canna. I am aware of yer wishes, Mary Rose. Dinna mistake me, lass, I love ye more than my life, but I must do what is best for all of Kilgannon, no' just me." He paused and looked at the sunset, then back to me. "Look at me, lass. Look at Angus and Matthew and Thomas. What do ye see? Ye see Gaels, Mary. We're no' bred to sit by the side of the road and watch the others go by. We were bred to be warriors, and that's what we are. Someday the world may have no need of us, but that's what we are. That's what Gannon was, ye ken, and that blood has come down to me." He sighed. "I must listen to what they're saying, the MacKinnon and Murdoch and the others, before I decide, and I must make my decision based on more than my own wishes. If I tell the clan to rise they will, and they will abide if I say no. I must be right and I must decide soon." He kissed my forehead. "Mary, I have always told ye what's in my heart, and I willna change it the now. What I would like more than anything is to let the rest of the world carry on without us, and if I thought I'd be successful, that's just what I'd do."

"But it will not, Alex," I said softly. "It's coming to us every day, demanding that you join them."

"Aye." He nodded. "I have noticed that myself."

"What are you going to do?"

He shook his head and frowned. "I dinna ken. Try to stay out of it if possible. I dinna ken what will happen, Mary."

We stood in silence for a long moment. "Don't go." I had not meant to say it, and it surprised me when I did.

"I ken yer wishes, lass." When he spoke again, his tone was soft. "And I'm weighing all the choices, Mary Rose. I dinna mean to act in haste." He kissed me again, and I had to be satisfied with what little I had.

The next two days were placid. The calm before the storm, I remembered it later, and wished I had enjoyed it more. The days were growing shorter at the end of the summer, and preparations for winter were already under way. After the wettest spring and summer anyone could remember, the fall was lovely, although early. We had warm and clear days followed by cool nights.

On September sixth the Earl of Mar had raised the Stewart banner on the Braes of Mar and declared himself for James Stewart, and the cry, so long in coming, had gone out throughout Scotland for the clans to rise and join him. Three days later the MacDonald arrived in the loch. I turned to Alex in agitation.

"You know why he's here," I said. "What will you do?"

Alex shrugged. "Listen. It canna hurt to listen to the man."

"I didn't expect you to love King George or be his ally, but neither did I expect you to change your mind about James Stewart."

His eyes flashed, but his tone was calm. "I havena changed my mind about James Stewart, Mary," he said. "But this is less about Stewart and more about MacDonald. I am only going to listen. Surely there's no harm in that."

"He is a persuasive man, a man used to having his own way."

"Aye. And so am I, Mary Rose."

"He's very fond of you and thinks you are fond of him."

Blue eyes met mine. "Aye, well, I am, lass, but I'm no' likely to be swept away by friendship. I'm a great deal fonder of Murdoch and he left without my agreement, if ye'll remember." I nodded. *Dear God,* I prayed, *make the Mac-Donald turn now and sail away.*

But he didn't sail away. He landed, determination obvious in his brusque manner when Alex and Angus greeted him as though this were a simple social visit. The MacDonald merely nodded at me, not bothering with his usual greeting. Something serious had brought him here, and it wasn't more wedding plans. Alex led the way into the courtyard and then the hall, calling for food and whisky. Most of the MacDonald men had stayed with their boat, which was odd enough to cause many raised eyebrows among the MacGannons. Those that had accompanied Sir Donald into the hall stayed close to him and watched. I grew uneasier by the minute.

Alex led the way to a seldom-used room on the other side of the keep. The hallway skirted the ancient structure, and at the last corner, instead of turning left to go the armory as we so often did, we turned right and entered a room built of stone, its walls unrelieved by paneling or plaster. The room held one long table, surrounded by chairs, and one chest placed to the left of the tall western-facing window. A few chairs were lined against the walls. Dust motes danced in the beams illuminated by the last of the afternoon sun, setting the worn surface of the oak table shimmering with light, and I felt the same sense of foreboding that I had felt when Alex rode into the wood with the MacKinnon.

This time, I thought, I will be with him.

TWENTY-NINE

ALEX AND THE MACDONALD FACED EACH OTHER ACROSS the table. Angus, Thomas, and the other men each sat on the same side as his chief. No one noticed me, I thought, as I crossed the room behind Alex and sat next to the chest, away from the table. The light from the window behind me lit Alex's hair and cast shadows behind him, while the Mac-Donald's age showed clearly in the brilliant beams. And showed something more in his manner as well. Weariness? Hostility? I could not be sure. I put my hands in my lap.

Alex's tone was unruffled. "Ye are welcome to Kilgannon, Sir Donald, but I fear ye have a message that is not."

"It should be, Kilgannon," the MacDonald said. "I ask no more of ye than ye should be offering freely. To join with us."

"In?"

"Ye ken what in, Alex," Sir Donald snarled.

"Say it," Alex said, his voice as fierce as the older man's.

"In restoring our rightful king to his throne, in putting a Stewart at the head of Scotland again."

Alex leaned back in his seat and put his hands on the edge of the table. "No." Although he spoke softly, the word resonated through the room. The MacDonald looked through narrowed eyes at Alex as he sat back in his chair. The other men exchanged glances and I met Angus's steely blue gaze. Alex watched the MacDonald.

"Say it again, Kilgannon," said the older man.

"No," Alex said. "No, I willna join in a fight that puts my family and my clan in jeopardy for a man I dinna respect."

Sir Donald's tone was flat. "Ye do not respect James Stewart."

"I do not." Alex crossed his arms over his chest and waited.

The girls from the kitchen entered then and served whisky, placing platters of food on the table while we sat in silence. The liquor was gratefully accepted; the food went untouched. Sir Donald sipped his whisky and looked at Alex over the brim of his cup. When he spoke again, the Mac-Donald's tone was mild. "Ye'll have heard about Mar raising the standard at Braemar."

Alex nodded. "Aye, I did."

"And ye'll have heard that many of the clans are rising."

"I've heard that."

"MacKinnon came to see ye."

"He did."

"And me," Sir Donald said.

Alex nodded again. "That I heard as well."

"Murdoch Maclean has come. And told ye he's joining us."

"He did."

"And yer own brother sends ye this," said MacDonald, pulling a letter from his plaid and slapping it on the table between them. Alex did not look at it. "Yer brother is a vassal of Mar's, ye ken."

"Aye," Alex said.

"And Mar has ordered all his vassals to rise with him." Alex was silent. "Will one MacGannon join us in restoring Scotland while the other sits home with his English wife?" One of the MacDonalds snorted with laughter but stopped at a harsh glance from Sir Donald. Alex slammed the table with his fist, and the other MacGannons muttered and started to rise, but Angus gestured for them to sit. Alex sat back in his chair, his expression stern. If I did not know him as well as I did, I would have thought him, despite his pounding the table, very calm. I wondered how well Sir Donald knew him. "Ye'll know I'm leaving my family to join the rising?" asked the MacDonald.

"I have assumed that."

"Ye ken my family means much to me, and I listen to my wife, Kilgannon, as ye do yers, no doubt, but I make the decisions. Do ye ken what they're saying about Alexander MacGannon these days?"

Alex rubbed his chin. "No, Sir Donald," he said. "Tell me."

The older man sipped his whisky and his eyes flickered toward me before returning to Alex. "They're saying that when Kilgannon was married to a MacDonald he was allied with the MacDonalds, and now that he's married to an Englishwoman . . ." He let the words hang in the air. Angus looked at Alex, his anger visible for a second before he carefully blanked his expression again. Alex leaned back, then laughed, shrugging.

"Aye," Alex said lightly. "I've always been known for how easily I am led. That one willna work on me, Donald. Try again."

The MacDonald's mouth twisted as if he would smile, but he sipped his whisky again. "Ye'll ken that Marischal is with us."

"I've heard that."

"And the Emorys. And the Frasers."

"Some."

"They're yer kin. What will they think if ye don't join?"

"I care not what they think, Donald."

"And Drummond and Lindsay, MacKinnon, Mac-Lachlan, MacEwen, Maclean, MacKenzie . . . Do ye not care what any of them think?"

"No."

"Ye'll be a lonely man here in Kilgannon, Alex." Sir

Donald scratched his chin and then sipped his whisky. His tone was light as he continued. "Do ye ken how I got here today?"

"By sea."

"Aye, but, Alex, think of the route." The MacDonald shifted in his chair and traced a route on the table, ignoring the letter. "This is Kilgannon." He pointed to a spot. "And this is yer normal route out of Loch Gannon." He drew a line on the table. "If ye leave Kilgannon and go south, ye go by Mull and the other islands. If ye go north, ye go past Skye. Do ye understand my drift?"

Alex leaned forward, his voice mild but his eyes gleaming. "No, explain it to me further."

MacDonald spoke as though his words were of no consequence. "Well, Alex, ye'll be surrounded in yer sea routes by those who joined the rising. What will they think of ye for not joining?"

"I care not what they think."

"And by land, let's think on it. Clanranald to the north and east, MacDonalds to the north and south and west. And MacDonnells beyond them. It seems to me yer travels would be very restricted."

"At Braemar," said Alex, "the clans were ready to go home when the top of the standard fell. Some think it an omen."

"I ken yer not superstitious, lad." The MacDonald leaned back, then shifted his weight and slapped the arm of his chair, his anger evident as his voice rose. "Why will ye no' join us?" he shouted. "Speak to me, Alex. I'm too old for these games."

"As I am," Alex answered grimly. They stared at each other as if they were alone in the room. Alex sipped his whisky and watched the older man, then leaned forward, his voice for the first time his usual tone. "When the Stewarts gained the throne, the first James turned his back on us. He went to London, and Scotland suffered because of his indifference. He could have ensured us equal treatment in

England, but he dinna, and no Stewart since has lifted a finger to help us. All the Stewarts have meant for Scotland is trouble and more trouble. We'd have been better if Queen Mary had been barren."

The MacDonald narrowed his eyes. "Those are strong words."

"Aye, but think on it, Donald. How have the Stewarts aided their own? From the first James to Anne, they've not made Scotland's lot any better. Why should I risk all I have for a man whose family has never thought of Scotland, or the Highlands, or the MacGannons, except for how we can assist them?" He put his hands on the table. "In '88, my father rose. What was his gain?" He waved his hand sharply. "James Stewart canna manage a rising. Ye remember the battle of Killiecrankie."

"Aye, I remember it," Sir Donald said grimly. "Ye were three, lad. Dinna tell me ye remember it."

"I do not, but I was raised on the stories. We had Scots on both sides of the battle. What has changed?"

"That was then. This is now."

"Do ye remember Glencoe?"

The MacDonald's voice was grim. "Ye use the massacre as yer reason to join the English?"

"No," growled Alex. "I use the massacre to remind ye of what happens if ye do not win."

Sir Donald's voice rose. "Ye think we willna win?"

"Are the Campbells with ye?" Alex asked heatedly. "And the Camerons? And all the Frasers and Munros and MacLeods?"

"No."

"Exactly my point, MacDonald. It's the same as ever. Did James Stewart win in '08? No." Alex spat out the words. "The man got the measles and dinna even land."

"Ye blame the man for getting the measles?"

"No." Alex shook his head in scorn. "I blame the man for his usual lack of planning. I could get my household to China before he could get himself to Scotland. By the time he got here the English were ready. He's no soldier, Donald, and he's no leader. Ye've met him. The man whines about his comforts. He doesna win my respect." Alex paused, and continued in a calmer tone. "He has ignored the Highlands except now when he wishes us to shed our blood for him. He ignored us and it was an insult. And now, when he chooses, we're to leave our homes and families and risk all for a man who, seven years ago, could not even remember that we existed?"

"Yer King Geordie insulted us as well, Alex, when he would not open the chiefs' letter. He wouldna even open it."

"He's no' my Geordie, man, and ye prove my point. Why should I risk me and mine for a king who canna rule? And neither can."

Sir Donald stroked his chin and watched as Alex, his color high, poured them both more whisky. "Buchanan is with us," Sir Donald said mildly. "And Farquharson and Carnegie and Forbes and Maxwell and MacDougall." He paused. "Alex, will ye no' join us?"

Alex put his hands flat on the table. "No."

"It's no' like ye to be afraid of a fight."

Alex smiled. "I'm no' afraid of a fight."

"But ye willna join with us."

"We willna join with ye."

"Ye will join the English."

"No, we will remain aloof."

"That may be difficult to explain to yer neighbors. Some of Clanranald may be difficult to control."

"What do ye mean, MacDonald? Say it."

"They'll burn ye out."

Alex smiled coldly. "They may try."

"They'll attack ye at sea."

"Ye mean ye will. MacDonalds rule the straits here."

"I may not be able to control all of my men, Alex."

Alex laughed harshly. "That will be the day, Donald. If

yer threatening me, man, say it out. Are ye saying that if we do not join with ye, ye will try to burn me out?"

"We will burn ye out."

The MacGannon men reached for their weapons, but Alex stopped them with a gesture and turned back to Sir Donald, speaking very slowly. "I canna believe this from ye, Donald. Yer great-uncle to my sons, and yet ye say ye will burn me out if I do not join ye."

The MacDonald nodded. "Aye."

Alex lifted his chin. "I would like to see ye try." They glared at each other while their men shifted uneasily. Angus scanned the faces of the men opposite him, his hand nearing his knife. Alex poured more whisky with a steady hand. "I think ye should rethink yer position, Donald," he said mildly.

To my surprise, the MacDonald roared with laughter. "Ye've a bit of yer grandfather in ye. I miss the bastard."

"Aye." Alex smiled, but his eyes never left the other man's face as Sir Donald emptied his glass and placed it on the table, turning it slowly between his fingers.

"Alex, do ye remember staying with me before ye wed Sorcha?"

"Aye."

"And do ye remember us talking about history, lad? About Scotland, about the Romans and Robert the Bruce and Kenneth MacAlpin and how victors win?" Alex nodded, and the older man leaned forward again, his tone weary. "Do ye remember how many times ye told me that the tragedy of the Gaels is that they do not unite?"

"Yer using my own arguments, Donald."

"Aye, because they are good arguments," Sir Donald said, and sighed. "Alex," he continued, his voice heavy now, no longer threatening. "If we do no' unite we are doomed. If we band together we may win our independence. Can ye sit idly by and know ye could help yer own but refused? Can ye watch us fail because ye would not lift a hand for Scotland?

Will ye no' join us and try one more time to set yer country free? I thought I knew ye, laddie, but the man I knew would not sit by and watch us struggle without him." He shook his head. "I have no more words, Alex. We need ye. We need yer brain and yer courage and yer men. Help us. And if ye do not . . ." He pushed his chair back and rose. "God help ye." His words echoed against the stone.

Alex stood and extended his hand to the older man. "Good day to ye, Donald MacDonald," he said calmly. "And safe journey home. Ye'll have my answer shortly."

The other men stood as well. The MacDonald nodded, clasped Alex's hand, and left the room without another word. His men followed him. We waited in silence until the clatter of their footsteps faded away.

"When they're gone, Thomas," Alex said evenly, with a glance at Angus, "light the torches. Call the clan." Both Thomas and Angus nodded. Alex turned to the other men. "Leave us now." They were gone at once and Alex, with a sigh, picked up Malcolm's letter. "Ye ken what this will be," he said. Both Angus and I nodded. Alex read the letter, then read it again before handing it to Angus with an abrupt gesture. "Show Mary." He spun away from the table, tossing a chair out of his path. It clattered to the floor with a din. *"Mo Dia,"* he snarled, "the only thing they've left out is my father's ghost." He stalked out of the room.

I stared after Alex, then turned to Angus and watched him read the letter. He handed it to me. "It's as I thought," he said. I read it for myself. Malcolm had written that Mar threatened to destroy his holdings and drive him out if he did not join Mar.

Alex, we have had differences in the past, Malcolm wrote, *but I forgave you long ago and ask you now to come to the aid of your only brother. Let us put the past behind us and begin again. I beg you, for the name we share, come to my assistance. You cannot refuse to help me keep what little I have when you have so much.*

I was instantly furious. How dare Malcolm forgive Alex

when all the wrong was his? How dare he write so to his brother after all he had done? And how well he knew Alex, to write just what would tug at him. How I despised the man. I met Angus's angry eyes. "Is there no way to combat this?" I demanded.

"No," he said. "It is true. Mar is threatening his vassals."

"You are going to join the rebellion."

His voice was weary. "It's Alex's decision."

I shook my head. "No. He'll turn it over to the clan. You know what will happen. Angus," I cried, "help me stop this!"

"Mary, we're damned if we do and damned if we don't. If we dinna join with them and the Jacobites win, then we are enemies and we will pay the price. All of Kilgannon will pay the price. They have thousands, between the Mac-Donalds and Clanranald. Eventually they would win. And if the Jacobites lose, then it will be the English coming to burn us out, surrounded as we are by Jacobites. The English willna take the time to sort out our politics. No, lass, we sink with the others or swim with them." I shook my head. "Mary," he said harshly. "What I think or ye think no longer matters. We've a decision to make that involves the whole of us. What we decide tonight will determine the future of clan MacGannon. And I dinna like either of the choices." He turned on his heel and left me alone. I stared after him, still holding Malcolm's letter.

It took me an hour to find Alex, walking on the rocks at the far end of the loch. He held his arms out as I ran to him, and I looked back at the castle from the shelter of his arms. *Kilgannon,* I thought. "Alex—" I began, but he shook his head.

"Hush, lass," he said softly. "Dinna speak. Let me just hold ye and not face it yet." And so we stood on a rock and let the late-summer sun bathe us in light. Around us the activity increased and the clansmen began arriving. I knew he could see them, but he held me to him as though we had forever. "I'm glad ye were there," he said at last. "It would have been difficult to explain it to ye. And I'm grateful ye were wise enough to remain silent."

"You are going."

"That is yet to be decided."

I shook my head. "You decided in that room."

He dropped his arms from my shoulders. "No."

"Yes." He was silent, watching me. "Alex," I cried, "think of us! Think of all of us! We can defend ourselves. You've told me how safe Kilgannon is, how easy it is to defend. We can sink a boat and prevent any ship from entering the harbor, and we can stay within the walls when there is danger."

His voice was quiet. "Forever? Forever, Mary?"

"For as long as it takes. If the rising fails, they will not have the strength to attack us. They will forget and we'll go on."

"That's where yer wrong. They'll never forget. Glencoe was over twenty years ago and it's as if it were yesterday. If MacDonald declares us enemies, they will never forget. And neither will the English."

"Then we will defend ourselves."

"And what of those in the outlying areas? Am I to wall myself up and let them fend for themselves? And never leave? Let Duncan of the Glen and his family be left without my protection? Let them burn Glengannon without lifting a hand? Tell the fishermen they must stay within the walls? We'll stop all trade and never leave Loch Gannon while we cower within the walls? I dinna think so."

"The MacDonald wouldn't attack you."

"Make no mistake. If he decides we are enemies, he will."

"Do you know that you are contemplating treason?"

"Treason?" He faced me again, his eyes cold.

"If you join them, you will be taking arms against your king."

"Mary," he said, watching my face, "understand me well. I am not fond of the Stewarts, but never have I thought of your Geordie as my king. Scotland is my country, not England."

"They are united now. It is treason."

"Only the English would call it that."

"I am English."

"Aye," he said, his jaw tightening. He looked over the loch.

"It is treason, Alex. Can you not see that?"

"Aye, as the English define it, it is treason."

"If the English win, you will be called a traitor. At best we could lose Kilgannon."

"That willna happen."

"It could. You could die. You could face a traitor's death."

"That willna happen."

"It could."

He shifted his gaze and met my eyes. "And we could win."

"Against the English? Not likely."

He lifted his chin. "Do ye think so little of my abilities?"

"No." I shook my head. "But I think very little of Scotland's abilities to withstand England."

"So we are to submit again and this time learn to like it?" Blue eyes flashed at me. "Is that yer opinion, Mary? Do ye really think so little of my people?"

I waited until I could answer in a reasonable voice. "They are now my people too, Alex. I don't want you to go. I don't want to risk losing you."

"Ye'd not lose me." He looked over the loch.

"You cannot guarantee that. If you loved me you'd stay here."

He looked at me. "I do love ye, lass. Dinna say such things."

"Alex, there is no reason to go. Malcolm is not threatened."

"He is."

"I don't trust him. He's lying again."

"Aye, Mary, he is a liar, but he's also my brother. Would ye have a husband who refuses to help his own?"

"I don't trust him. Think of what he's done! He's lied and stolen from you, and he tried to kill you! He is a monster!"

"Ah, Mary, ye dinna understand him."

"You are defending him? After what he did to Sibeal? After the *Diana*? He's lying again. How can you not see this?"

"I am no' defending him, Mary. Mar has written to all his vassals. I've heard it from several sources. I am not surprised."

"Then perhaps that part is true, but how can you trust him? After he stole from you? After he lied to you?"

"Mary, ye do no' understand. It's no' a matter of me trusting him or no'. I inherited everathing. The title, the lands. It's verra hard on a younger son. He got—"

"He got your mother's lands, for which most men would be grateful. He got a wife who loved him, to whom he could not be faithful and to whom he showed only brutality when she complained of it. He got money and other aid from you even after he stole from you, and still it is not enough for Malcolm MacGannon."

"Malcolm is my brother. I canna ignore his plea."

"Why not, Alex? You seem to be able to ignore mine easily. Do you choose Malcolm over me?"

"No, Mary, I wouldna do that. But I canna ignore him."

"Then you are a fool, Alex, and God help you both."

His eyes grew cold as he looked at me, then nodded curtly. "Aye, Mary, I am a fool. In that at least we agree" was all he said before he left me standing there.

The men of the clan met that evening. I was not invited nor did Alex come to me. I sat in our room and fumed. I knew he would go. Some part of me had known it since the day the MacKinnon came, but it was still difficult to face. I was so angry. At Alex, at Malcolm, at the MacDonald and

James Stewart and all men who wage war without a thought to those whose lives are upturned by it. Or lost. *Dear God*, I thought, *he could die for James Stewart, for Malcolm, for the MacDonald*. And then my fear was lost in the wave of anger that broke over me again. I did not even pretend to sleep but paced and paced until I heard the whole house quiet. *Where is he*, I wondered? And my anger rose again and I paced.

In the early morning I could not stand it another moment and left our room. The hall was littered with men wrapped in their plaids, snoring, and I quietly made my way to the library. Angus sat before the fire, his legs extended to the hearth, his chin on his hand. He looked very tired and he was alone. He looked up as I entered. "He's not here, Mary," he said.

"Where is he?"

"I dinna ken. Walking, no doubt. He's not in the house."

I moved to stand next to him. "Angus, what will we do?"

"Hope we win."

"Then you're going?"

He looked at me gravely. "Had ye any doubt?"

"Did any of you even think of us who will be left behind?"

Angus met my angry look without flinching. "Aye, Mary, ye crossed our minds. Do ye think that we do not know what we do?"

"Angus," I cried, "there is a great excitement in the men. They want to go. I recognize it, but I do not understand it."

He looked at me for a long moment, then sighed. "Aye, yer right, Mary, there is excitement for many, but not for Alex nor for me. We understand what it is we go to. Ye must trust us, lass. We do not go for glory."

"You go for Malcolm."

"No." It was Alex's voice, and I spun around. He filled the doorway, looking exhausted and grim. "We go for honor, Mary, and for loyalty, and if ye dinna understand both, I have misjudged ye."

"There is honor in staying here and protecting your own."

"That is not honor. And in the end it is certain defeat. If the rebellion wins without us, we will be driven out. If it loses without us, we will be hunted and destroyed to calm their anger and then the English will come."

"We can remain neutral," I said. "We can stand aside and let them fight around us."

"No. We canna."

"You mean you will not." We glared at each other.

"As ye will, Mary," he said, and turned away. I let him go and returned to my bed alone.

THIRTY

MORNING WAS NO BETTER. I ROSE LATE, STIFF AND tense and still angry. Downstairs there was no sign of Alex or Angus or Thomas. They did not come home for two days. I soon discovered that they had gone to the outlying areas to talk to clan members who had not come for the meeting. When Alex did return, he was gray-faced with weariness and nodded curtly to me as he passed me in the hall. Hours later I went to our room and found him asleep, still in his clothes. I spread a blanket over him and kissed his forehead. He stirred, reaching for me, and I slipped into his arms without a word. He slept again then and I rested in his arms, trying to persuade myself that it was all a dream, that I would wake and have our life back. I fell asleep still trying to convince myself.

I woke when he moved and opened my eyes to see him sitting on the side of the bed, brushing his hair back from his face and staring into space. He sighed as he stood and straightened his clothing. The room was dim, autumn's gloaming providing little light this evening. Below us the yard was quiet. He turned and we looked at each other for a long moment, then he reached a hand out to caress my cheek. His voice was gentle. "I love ye, Mary. Ye may not credit that, nor understand me, but I do love ye."

"I know, Alex. And I love you."

"Aye, I ken ye do." He looked at the blanket, fingering

the wool, then turned to stare into the shadows as he spoke in a flat voice. "I have sent word to the MacDonald that we'll be joining him. And we've sent Gilbey to get Matthew."

I did not speak. Having him put it into words made it almost tangible. I closed my eyes. *This is not real,* I told myself. When I said nothing he sighed again and quietly left.

I gradually realized that he had known he was going for a long time, but it struck me most intensely the morning that I came upon him supervising the unpacking of the last of the pistols. I had seen the boxes, neatly stacked in the bottom of the keep, but had not known what they were. After our discussion about their purchase we had not mentioned them again, although I had assumed that the pistols being used in the constant practicing were the new ones. The knowledge that it was time to unpack the last of them was unnerving. Angus and Dougall were showing the younger men how to load the pistols, while Alex sat on one of the barrels aiming at the wall opposite him, sighting down the barrel with one eye closed. I stood in the doorway, horrified, unnoticed at first. And then Alex, with that uncanny ability of his, turned and looked into my eyes. I watched him freeze as he saw my expression and slowly rise from the barrel. Angus glanced up and looked from Alex to me. I turned and walked back through the hall, blindly seeking the door. Outside I took a deep breath and walked rapidly toward the water.

He reached me at the foot of the dock and stood before me, a pistol tucked in his belt. I focused on his chest. Abruptly I turned and walked away from him, and he was before me again.

"Mary Rose," he said hoarsely. "Mary, come with me now, lass."

"No." I hardly recognized my strangled voice. "No."

"Aye, lass, come with me." He took my hand in his. "Come with me." I looked at him then, this stranger.

"To war, Alex? Do you want me to be one of those

women who follow soldiers and tend to them?" I snatched
my hand away.

"No, lass," he said sadly, shaking his head. "Just come
with me a bit on the loch. Please."

"No."

"Aye, Mary. We must talk. Come."

He took my hand again, and this time I did not resist. He
rowed us out on the loch while I looked to my left. If I turned
to the right I would see the men preparing on the shore,
preparing for war, preparing to leave us, and my anger
would boil again. So I looked across the still water and I
thought how blue the water was today, how green the last
of the leaves of the trees on the far side, how gray the mountains above. I listened to the rhythmic sounds of Alex's
strokes and I watched the water swirl around the oar as he
dipped it in. In the middle of the loch, with a sigh, he
stopped rowing and we drifted. I looked at the far shore for
a long time. When he still didn't speak, I stole a glance at
him. He was watching me, a guarded expression on his face,
his eyes as blue as the water behind him. The sun had turned
his hair to gold, and the breeze blew little wisps of it into a
halo around his head. Without intending to I leaned over
and brushed a lock of gold back from his cheek. He caught
my wrist as I pulled away. Our eyes met, and his image
blurred and shattered as my tears fell. I tried to blink them
away. He still held my wrist, but he said nothing, and I
glanced at him again. He was looking at my hand, his head
bent, and I watched his shoulders rise and fall under the
linen. He looked up at me, meeting my eyes, and he released
my wrist.

"Mary, can ye forgive me?" He sighed deeply. "I am
sorry that I am making ye so angry."

"Don't go. Don't leave us, Alex. I'm so afraid."

"I'll come back, lass."

"You'll intend to."

"I will come back."

"Why?" I whispered.

"Why am I going or why will I come back?"

"Both."

He shook his head. "Ah, Mary, I have no magic words to explain it. I can only tell ye that I don't want to go and I must."

"Why? For Malcolm? Are you going for him, Alex?"

He took a deep breath and looked at his feet before lifting his blue, blue eyes to mine. "No, lass, not for Malcolm. I am mindful of all he has done. I have no illusions left about my brother. I would never make this sacrifice for him." He shook his head. "No, Mary, I am going because I am a Gael and I canna stay behind when my people go to war. Sensible or no', warranted or no', I canna stay behind, safe, and I canna fight for yer King Geordie. When they drew the line of who is to be enemies, I am on this side, and I canna let those on my side fight without me. I canna stay here with ye and hear them dying. If I go, perhaps I can make a difference. If I stay home I'll only wonder, I'll always wonder."

"And if you don't come home?"

"I'll come home."

I watched the light play in his hair. "How do you know?"

"I know." I looked away, at Kilgannon, feeling his gaze on me. "I'll come back to ye, Mary. And to my sons. This is where I belong. I'll come back."

"I don't understand."

"No, I ken that, lass. What I'm saying is foreign to ye."

"Not just to me, Alex, but to most of the women. What difference does it make who is king? We watch you all preparing as if for the Games, as if for a long hunting trip. Do you not understand what can happen? Does none of you understand?"

"We understand. Some don't, of course. They think this is just a great adventure, something to tell their grandchildren on a winter's night, but most of us understand. We have no choice."

"You do have a choice. You are choosing to go." He watched me for a long moment, then looked at the far shore. I studied his profile, his eyelashes glinting in the sun, and I wanted to scream. Why couldn't I think of something to say that would stop him?

He turned to me again. "Aye, lass. Yer right in that. We are choosing. And I have no words left to explain it to ye." He took my hand from where it lay on my skirt. "I can only say that I love ye more than life, Mary, but if I stay here with ye I will die. My body will continue, but part of me will die." He kissed my palm and I watched his bent head. "I canna stay," he whispered.

"And part of me will die if you leave," I whispered back.

"Aye, but ye'll be born again when I return whole to ye."

"Alex . . ." I wanted to rage and strike out, to scream and pull at my hair. Instead, I looked at my husband and I cried. He drew me to him then and held me as I sobbed, patting my back and making soothing sounds, his tears mingling with mine. We sat huddled in that little boat until the sun set.

But it changed nothing.

I could not sleep, and Alex slept hardly at all. He was everywhere, overseeing the preparations in every detail, the preparations for war and the preparations for leaving us behind. He had carefully chosen men to stay with us, to protect us, and to help us survive their absence. Because they were leaving before the harvest, with the cattle still in their summer shieldings and the grain not all yet reaped, some men who knew such things would stay behind at first and help us, but we would all have to work or we would never last the winter. My anger dipped and arched. At some moments I was resigned and calm, and at others I could hardly speak without bitterness. The men avoided me. Most of the women agreed with me, but I kept my own counsel.

I tried to explain it to the boys but failed. Alex took them with him everywhere and I knew he was talking to them, but how could children of six and eight understand what their father meant when he said he was going to war? I understood the words and the ideas, but when I applied them to my life and realized he was leaving because of those ideas, I balked, and if I could not understand, how could they? But they seemed to accept the idea of Alex leaving, and I marveled at their faith that he would return. All I could think of was what could happen, and the vision of my life stretching out before me without him haunted my every step. Matthew came home and brought the news that most of the Highland clans were gathering to join Mar. The men of Kilgannon cheered.

The morning that he cut his hair was one of the worst. I had been in the kitchen seeing to the packing of food for them when I looked up to see Matthew reaching for a knife, Gilbey behind him.

"What are you doing?" I asked, surprised.

"Alex said to cut my hair," Matthew said, "and I thought I could do it faster with one of the kitchen knives. I dinna want to use my dirk. It might dull the edge." He met my eyes uneasily.

"Cut your hair?" I asked stupidly.

"Aye, so that hair doesna get in yer eyes when yer fighting."

"When you're fighting."

He nodded. "Aye. Mary, are ye a'right? Ye look verra pale."

"Where is Alex, Matthew?"

"In yer rooms." I was out the door before he stopped talking.

Alex stood barefoot in front of my mirror, pulling strands of his hair up and cutting them unevenly. He turned when I entered and looked at me but did not speak then nor when I took the knife from his hand and pushed him down on the chair. We were silent as I cut his hair close to his head. I ignored my tears and how the gold of his hair looked against the red of the rug beneath our feet, trying not to think that the rug was the same shade as blood. When I finished I gathered the long locks from the floor into a bundle and put them in a square of plaid in a chest. I left the room without a word. We never mentioned it. By nightfall every man and boy in Kilgannon had cut his hair, even Ian and Jamie. I kept the hair they'd chopped off and I scolded them as I trimmed what was left, but I never said anything about it to Alex. I put their hair in the same bundle as his, and my tears fell on the wool as I buried it in my clothes chest.

The evenings were the most difficult, for my work was done and his was not. I followed him around at times, but every motion reminded me that he was leaving. The boys were excited by the bustle and preparations and begged to go to war as well. I made it very clear that they would not be leaving. But Gilbey would, and somehow Matthew and Gilbey leaving made me feel even more betrayed. The distinctions between us had never been so underscored. Young as they were, they were men, and men went to war while women stayed home and waited. Gilbey was not sad to leave his tutoring days behind him. Angus had trained him well in the years he had been with us. And Matthew as well. I watched him with new eyes. Full grown now, he had never gotten as wide as his father. Instead, he looked more and more like Alex, with the same grace and ease of movement. I sighed as I thought of his interrupted studies. He had not shown any regret when I'd asked him but had laughed and said that no one would be left to study with.

Alex sought me out one evening as I stood at the top of the keep watching the sunset but seeing only blood in the red of the sky. I had not heard him approach and I gasped when his hand touched my cheek, wiping away the tears. "Don't cry, Mary Rose," he said gently. I shook my head and looked out to sea. He sighed. "We canna part like this."

"Don't go."

He sighed again. "Mary, I have some things I need to tell ye. Will ye talk with me?" I was silent, and he turned me to face him. "Lass," he said, his expression tender. "I'm stubborn as well as ye. Ye ken that. So listen and I'll leave ye alone, or I'll just keep saying it forever until ye respond."

I took a deep breath. "Let me see if I understand this correctly, Alex. If I listen you'll leave, and if I don't you'll stay and keep trying to talk to me? Even if it takes forever? Goodness, Alex, what should I do?"

He looked at me with narrowed eyes and then pulled me to his chest, laughing softly. "Yer a one," he said over my head.

I wrapped my arms around him. "Don't go," I said into his chest. He kissed the top of my head.

"Lass, listen to me. There are things we need to discuss." He leaned back and looked in my face. "Ye must hear them and it must be the now." At last I nodded. "Good. I want ye to go to Ewan in France. Deirdre is on her way there now with her daughters. Angus just heard this morning."

"No."

"Why?"

"This is my home, Alex. I will stay here."

"Mary, I would rest easier knowing ye were safe."

"Imagine thinking that about someone you love."

"Mary—"

I shook my head. "No. No, Alex. I will stay here."

"Why? Why will ye not go?"

Why will you not stay? I thought. "If you need me, Alex, I will be here. I can come to you. Anywhere in Scotland. And I will hear of what is happening. If I am in France I will not hear and I will be too far to come to you."

"Then go to Louisa. Or to Will. Ye ken they'd take ye in."

"No."

"Why not?" He was becoming angry.

"For the same reasons. This is my home." I paused as I tried to find the right way to explain it. "With you gone, the clan will need someone. There's never been a time that you were all gone, but now you and Angus and Thomas and

Dougall and Matthew, you'll all be gone, even wee Donald and Gilbey. All of you. Who will care for the people?" He looked at the sunset and I watched him. At last he nodded.

"Aye. But, lass, I would have ye safe from harm."

"Then stay here and protect us." I watched his lips tighten.

"Mary, promise me that if ye think that Kilgannon will be besieged, ye'll leave at once. Dinna try to defend it. Get the boys and as many of the clan and get out. Let them have it. Promise me, lass, or I'll ship ye off to France, willing or no'."

I met his look and raised my chin. "You won't be here to do that. Dinna show yer teeth if ye canna bite, MacGannon."

He stared blankly at me and then laughed. "Mary Rose," he said, pulling me to him. "Ye do surprise me at times."

"And you me, Alex."

He kissed me and continued. "If ye need to leave, dinna go to Glengannon. That's where troops will arrive. Go to Skye. Morag's family is staying aloof and will shelter ye until ye can get to England."

I stared at him. "The MacLeods are staying aloof?"

"Dinna say it, lass. I ken what yer thinking." I turned from him and stood against the railing, the stone cool under my hands. "If ye canna or willna go to Dunvegan, then go to Sleat. Someone will be there. And if ye are besieged unawares and canna get out, then surrender, Mary, and demand safe passage home as an English citizen. Dinna fight for the land. Tell the clan to take to the heather. Ye can tell the English our marriage was unhappy and that ye were here against yer will. The English army will easily believe ye were unhappy married to a Gael."

I looked up into his eyes. "No one who knows me would believe that my marriage has been unhappy. Until now."

He sighed. "Lass, there's more I must tell ye. If ye leave, there're some things ye must take with ye. In the desk are all the papers ye ken about, but on the shelves there is a box with papers ye may not have seen. Not my drawings but a box very like it, on the right side of the shelves. It has the crest on it, like my box, and inside are all the papers for ownership of Kilgannon and Clonmor and all the ships. I've written to my lawyer Kenneth Ogilvie that I've given Angus *Gannon's Lady* and Matthew the *Margaret*. I only own the *Katrine* now, for the *Mary Rose* is still in yer name. There are copies of my letters in the box. Ye should have those with ye. Ye may have need of them. If I forfeit, we'll only lose the one ship." He sighed again. "There's gold in two bags behind the box, and my mother's jewels are there as well." He raked a hand through his short hair, making the ends of it stick up. I reached up to smooth it and our eyes met. "I ken that yer trying, Mary, and I ken that ye dinna understand."

"Alex, I understand why you're going. I do not agree with you." He nodded and sighed, and we looked over the water together.

Before I was prepared, they were ready. The night before they left I retired alone to our room and took to my bed. Wrapped in the covers, I tried to pretend that none of this was happening, that the commotion I could hear beyond my room had nothing to do with me. I was unsuccessful. When Alex came to find me I refused to answer him and kept my eyes closed as he stood next to the bed. He sighed deeply, kissed my hair, and started to leave. At the door he turned. "Mary Rose," he said, his voice strained. "I ken yer awake and can hear me, lass. I wanted to tell ye that I love ye." I turned over and looked at him. When our eyes met he made a futile gesture. "I love ye, lass."

"Then stay."

"I canna."

"You mean you will not."

"As ye will, Mary," he said wearily, and put his hand on the knob. I threw myself from my bed and stood in the middle of the room. He watched me warily.

"I may not be here when you come back, if you come back."

"Then I'll find ye. Wherever ye are, I'll find ye."

"And then what?"

He shook his head. "I canna guess, Mary Rose. We'll sort it out then. But I will find ye after."

I dropped to my knees and put my hands out to him. "If begging will change your mind, I'll beg, Alex. Is that what you want?" My tears rolled down my cheeks and my voice shook. "Will this change your mind? Please, Alex. Please, don't leave me."

His expression was horrified, then furious, and he rushed to me, pulling me roughly to my feet and shaking me gently. "Dinna beg, Mary Rose! Dinna ever beg! Good God, lass, I dinna mean to have ye come to this. I love ye, Mary, more than my life."

"Then stay—" I began, but he interrupted me.

"Dinna say it, lass. I canna stay. Dinna say it again," he cried. I was sobbing now and so was he as he kissed my cheeks, then my hair and neck, and then peeled my clothes from me, kissing each exposed segment of skin. He tore my shift and threw it from us and continued while I cried and watched him. And then, caught in the emotion, I tore his clothes from him and clutched him to me. We made love on the floor in a frenzy and then moved to the bed to continue. And when at long last we lay quietly in each other's arms, I sighed, for I knew it had changed nothing. He kissed my hair and pulled me closer.

"I love ye, lass," he said hoarsely. "I will love ye forever, Mary Rose. Dinna doubt that. Ever."

"Then stay," I said to his chest.

"I canna." We were silent for a while, then he leaned to kiss me. "Do ye still love me, lass?"

I raised my head to meet his gaze. "I will love you until I die, Alex," I said. "Beyond death." He watched me for a moment, then nodded.

"And I ye, Mary. Dinna forget that."

* * *

The next morning, with the sun bright on the glen, I stood on the step of the outer gate and watched the clansmen, some of them hardly recognizable with their cropped hair and war dress, say farewell to their families. Alex, dressed in doublet and plaid, a bonnet atop his wavy hair, was giving last-minute instructions and joking with the boys who were too young to go. They crowded around Alex and the other men as if it were a celebration, and I wanted to scream. *Don't you understand what is happening here?* I cried silently. *Don't you see that some of these men will die? That some will be maimed? How can you let them go?* But I said nothing. And I said nothing when Alex at last came to us, the boys by my side, too excited to stand still. He bent down and embraced them, speaking softly to each one, and gave them final pats on their shoulders as he faced me.

"Mary Rose, kiss me, lass," he said. "We're going now." I kissed him, my tears salty on my lips. I tried to memorize the feel of him against me and threw my arms around him one last time.

"Alex," I cried, "Alex, please come back to me. Please."

"I will, Mary." He stroked his hand along my cheek. "My beautiful Mary Rose. I'll come back to ye. I love ye, lass, and I'll miss ye every minute. Now, kiss me again and then I must go."

So I kissed him and stood on that step with an arm around each of his sons as we watched their father lead the Kilgannon men away from home. The crowd followed them to the edge of the wood on the far side of the loch, the pipes skirling around us and then fading as Seamus led his pipers off to war with the others. Alex paused before heading into the trees, his sleeve white against his red bonnet as he raised his arm to wave to us, and I remembered my feeling of foreboding when he had done the same during the Mac-Kinnon's visit. The last sound I heard as he disappeared was "MacGannon's Return." And part of me died with each note.

Mary and Alex's love story continues in
THE WILD ROSE OF KILGANNON,
available from Dell in November 1999

As the fires of war engulf Castle Kilgannon, Mary stands fast, protecting her family and home. But when news comes of the capture of her beloved Alex, Mary vows to rescue her brave husband. As a defiant Alex is tried in London as a traitor, Mary unleashes her own campaign on London society, determined to win justice on the most dangerous battlefield of all, risking everything to free the rugged freedom fighter who has claimed her body and soul . . .